They Came to Pick Tomatoes

THE DANCE

Book 2

Jacqueline Hendricks

This book is a work of fiction. The characters, incidents, and dialogue are drawn from the author's imagination and are not to be construed as real. Any resemblance to actual events or persons, living or dead is entirely coincidental.

ISBN 978-0-9914682-5-6(ebk)

ISBN 978-0-9914682-4-9 (pbk)

Cover Design –Rachel Manzo
            Joelle Ahrens
Author Photo – Sarah MacLaughlin

For Janet, Jenn, Jacqui and Vernie

They Came to Pick Tomatoes

THE DANCE

ଓ Book 2 ଚ

Looking back on the memory of
The dance we shared 'neath the stars above
For a moment all the world was right
How could I have known that you'd ever say goodbye?

And now I'm glad I didn't know
The way it all would end, the way it all would go
Our lives are better left to chance
I could have missed the pain, but I'd have had to miss the dance

–Garth Brooks

Chapter 1

The drizzle penetrated through the zip-in lining of her London Fog raincoat. Drizzle? Rain, showers, drenching water, Elliston, State, April. Holding her opened umbrella she walked quickly toward Aloyishes. Oh well, a heavy downpour suited her this morning. April showers reminded her of every April at State. On April 2, 1962, Hector called from the Medical Center to say he had been accepted to Johns Hopkins, a goal achieved, all the years of studying duly rewarded. He had been so happy. Oh, to be able to bottle that happiness and take a sip today in the miserable gray, the wretched, soaked, pond scum…Elliston. No, stop. I am achieving my goal, too. Yes, Dad, in eight weeks it will be all over. Over? No, beginning, no, commencing. Commencement, June 5, 1964, 10A.M.

Jill walked hurriedly dodging the small pools of water on the convoluted walkways through the campus. The Amazon was full, redefining itself, becoming a true creek, the beginning of the water link to the much larger Elliston Creek. With enough rain, Elliston Creek could overflow its banks and close the narrow bridge necessary to leave Elliston. I hope dad won't have a problem coming down to pick up my furniture.

He had assured her in their early morning telephone conversation that Bud had several trucks at the lumberyard. He would be able to use whatever he needed. "Your bases will be covered, Princess. And I'm bringing a couple of gents to load stuff, one for you and one for Bobbie. You worry too much. It must be the Kohlhass like your Grandma Kohlhass. She used to worry me to death."

The cold rainwater splashed on the back of her legs, creating mud speckles on her hose and ruining her effort to impress her supervising professor, Dr. Reader. In a patronizing way he insisted his teachers should leave only "positive imprints" on their host schools and their new pupils. She saw positive imprints in the long mirror before she left home. The dark suit and long-sleeved, buttoned-down white oxford shirt, and black pumps were the "professional teacher" image Dr. Reader alluded to over and over again. The umbrella protected her short haircut, the Bobbie-never-changing-page-boy look. The soupy drizzle now worked to destroy her best intentions.

"In order to get respect," Dr. Reader had boomed, one of the few who could lecture without a microphone, "from these young whipper-snappers who are almost your age, you must dress properly," he began his lecture. He wore what she had dubbed his first teaching suit, navy blue with narrow lapels and a wide red and gray striped tie always slightly askew and permanently stained. His white shirt appeared to be un-ironed. She sat at many monotonous lectures, imagining his dabbing his mouth with the wide end of the silk tie leaving little split–pea soup spots. He nervously yanked French-cuffed sleeves, rubbing the cuff links, then grabbing both sides of the lectern thundered, "The clothes must be conservative, nothing you might find in a fashion magazine. Look in your mother's closet, look on your father's tie rack."

She had parked as close as she could to Aloyishes, but still ahead–two blocks of rain and puddles.

The heavy solid wood door opened to the brightly lit, busy Aloyishes Hall, and a wave of steam heat. But while this first hot rush was a relief, she'd soon be sweltering. Her heels clicked on the marble floor, reminding her of teachers coming to class back at Caylor High School. She walked quickly to the first floor bathroom of Aloyishes. One last make-over before Dr. Reader's final inspection. Bobbie said she looked like all of Bobbie's high school teachers at Gold Oak, boring. They had laughed. Wasn't laughing prescribed therapy for gray rainy days? Answering with a reflexive shake of her head, "No, not now, not going to think unhappy thoughts."

She had chosen a stark black wool pinstripe suit, but Lillian would not have worn something so dull unless she was attending a funeral. No, not a funeral, think happy thoughts, Miss Havlicek. She had added a circle pin of pearls and small pearl earrings.

The pearls were for Miss Horn, freshman English teacher, Caylor High School, 1956-57. Miss Horn with her folds of aged skin that had hung like a turkey's loose neck. Eight years ago, why did it seem like eternity? The students wanted to snicker, but were restricted from making eye contact with anyone, except Miss Horn. And so Jill had memorized each wrinkle, the one with a dark mole and another with a swollen vein. Her hair feathered around her colorless face and piercing gray-blue eyes. The white baby fine hair would not stay in the bun on the back of her head. But the pearls, every day, three strands that flattened the neck wrinkles and the last swell of skin that made an apron on her clavicle, the ridges almost obscured with the pearls. She and Sadie made a pact – never would they wear pearls. She now fingered the tiny circle pin as she stared at her image in the mirror. The pin was appropriate. The Bronze Star would have been better, but the Bronze Star would make a political statement and Dr. Reader's, "Verboten, forbidden, totally unprofessional," warning kept the medal in its velvet case.

Hector's mother Mrs. Martinez, Juanita Martinez, jeezus, she did not even have his name, "Give this to Jill," she told Arturo, "Jill should have it." She shook her head, "No, not now, not Mrs. Martinez or Hector." The pearls were Miss Horn and Dr. Reader, the now. She smiled. The irony, "Here I am, Miss Horn, one of your "thorns" is about to join your team, but not English, Social Studies."

She dampened paper towels and wiped the small mud smudges from the back of her legs. "There, finished, Dr. Reader," she whispered, then took one last look at the reflection. Her eyes looked much darker with the mascara and eyeliner, and her face appeared older. She applied a dab of foundation at the corners and underneath her eyes. Next month – twenty-two, twenty-two, it sounded so old.

Opening Dr. Reader's outer door, she took her place next to eight of her classmates who had also been scheduled for the final interview appointment. She hung her wet coat, rain hat and umbrella on the coat rack by the door. The students looked like eight penguins in black and white, all lined up sitting quietly, legs crossed. Their tie colors were the only variation. Their serious faces looked like a funeral home arrangement room. Jill smirked, staring at Harvey Driscoll; his hair had been shoulder length. Now she wanted to say nice barber, but he was called just as she sat down. He had asked her out their first day in class. She'd said something about Luisa and he said he would give her a call. Saying something about Luisa to any of the fraternity boys got the same reaction. Would anyone...who cares...we are a team, a number one team, Luisa, you and me.

Dr. Reader had told them the interview would not take more than ten minutes. She glanced at her watch; Henry was due to arrive within the hour. Bobbie had cried off and on all week saying goodbye. "These last eight weeks of school," she resolved, "I will bury myself at the library. I won't even miss you. I'll just be Miss Phi Beta Kappa, nose deep in the books. I do that best." And Mo the big sap, why did she have to cry? We're all saying goodbye on June fifth, anyway. Commencing. Commencing what?

"Jill Havlicek," Dr. Reader's demanding voice could be heard all the way to the outer room. She used a tissue to pat the sweat from her upper lip; she did not want to appear nervous. Four years of training and now going into the classroom to see if she had "it," those special talents and communication skills to teach. She took a deep breath and then walked through the door. The bulky man with the uncombed bushy hair, waved toward a hardwood chair. Seating herself, she pulled her skirt straight on her lap. She glanced at the professor and gave him a nervous smile.

"Miss Havlicek," Dr. Reader's heavy jowls like a boxer dog, fell down with each word, "have you figured out how to write your name phonetically, so your students will have no problems with pronunciation?"

"Well, sir..." she paused.

"You have three days, but it is important they know your name and you theirs as quickly as possible. Your appearance is acceptable," he nodded with an inverse smile. "I will be up to Marion in four weeks unless there is an emergency. This university has given you a number for the last four years and expected you to take your place in the herd," he paused, opening a rolled pack of tobacco that sat on his desk. He pushed this moist tobacco into a pipe bowl and continued talking as he prepared his pipe for smoking, a fluted carved ivory bowl. He looked like the eighteenth century sea captain she had seen pictured in the Old Spice commercial.

"For the next eight weeks, I want you to be confident and independent. As far as I'm concerned, you have passed 'Student Teaching,' so experiment. Stretch your wings. This is one of the few times in your teaching career you'll be able to do this. Principals, department heads, other teachers, school boards will have their own ideas about what they want taught and they will be paying you so they'll expect you to follow their agendas. Sometimes student teachers discover they hate the profession, so be honest with yourself. You won't be a failure and your education can be applied to other fields of endeavor. A couple of years ago, one of my student teachers left with his degree and became a banjo player; another went to law school." He stopped to relight his pipe, then chuckled. He flicked the match, searched for the ashtray and then continued "Jill, I am very familiar with your…uh…your delicate situation."

He puffed on his pipe and absently pulled the cuff of his shirt. With the pause and emphasis, Jill stared at the gray-haired professor who seemed to hold her life in his hands. He continued, "I can only judge you on your class work and your interaction with your fellow students. I have nothing but the best recommendation for all of those things, but you are choosing a profession that prides itself on being some sort of progenitor of moral fiber. Your host school knows nothing of your past, but your future employer will ask. You must have thought about this?"

"Many times, sir, many, many times." Jill pulled her skirt over her knees, then traced the thin stripes of the skirt, "I have discussed it with my parents. I have decided to leave Indiana and move to a large city back East, if possible. I had planned to move to Baltimore, but…" and then she bit her lip and the tear that she had held back in the restroom fell down her cheek.

"Miss Havlicek, I did not mean to upset you. I only hoped to assist you in your future planning. We want all of our teachers to be happy in their vocations. The placement office works to help find the places and people you need to talk to," he gushed.

Jill found a Kleenex in her coat pocket, a permanent accessory now, "Dr. Reader, in four years my life took many turns, some to painful destinations. I am ready to teach. Oh god, am I ready to teach, to be independent. I am sorry to bring this up…."

"No, no, my dear, I...I apologize for any discomfort my remarks caused you. My interest comes from my perception that you are very bright and well-suited to this profession. I just don't want this profession to reject you with your talent."

"Thank you, Dr. Reader," she blushed at the unusual compliment.

"I am your professor, but I am also a people person. I, too, am a teacher and one who loves his students. Call me if you ever need to talk."

"The school sent me the notice saying I would be working with Mr. Brown and to arrive at 7:15 my first day. I'm nervous. It seems strange that I have been a student for the last sixteen years and now I will be a teacher."

"Enjoy your students, but keep reminding yourself that you are their teacher. I talked to Mr. Brown; he seems like a very genial chap. He is looking forward to his State student teacher. I want to wish you luck, and I want to advise you, but I can only offer a small bit of encouragement. I have been teaching at State for the last ten years, and the profession has made a progressive shift in those years. Not very quickly I must qualify, but movement none the less. You, no doubt, learned in Education History that many years ago women teachers were forbidden to marry. We have gotten past that arcane practice, but...We'll talk when I get up to Marion next month."

"Thank you for everything, Dr. Reader."

She left the office, put on her raincoat, walked by the six remaining penguins and then into the hall. This is it, the beginning of the end. Four years to come to these last eight weeks. The term papers, blue books, how many books had she read? Lost sleep? Would she ever get those hours back? Now she would teach, a teacher. Could it be this preparation all comes down to the next eight weeks? Henry's investment. She owed so much to him, to Bobbie, to Mo...a long list to make it here today.

"Jill?" Armentria stood in the hallway, dressed in a gray suit. Out of her mother's closet, Jill concluded. She wore an A-line skirt, a slimming look, but Armentria was much thinner than when Jill had seen her as a freshman.

"Gosh, Armie, how have you been? Dr. Reader, too?"

"Yeah, can you believe we're almost finished? Student teaching? I'm going to Crispus Attucks. What about you?"

"Marion High School. I just wasn't ready to teach at Caylor High School," Jill said.

"Have you talked to Mo? I rarely see her since she moved into the sorority house."

"We cried like babies when she stopped by last night to say goodbye. She begged me to move to D.C. with her and Stewart. I told her she needed to live with Stewart first and see how *she* liked it. You're okay?"

"Pretty much. I have to watch what I eat," she paused to pat her tummy under her suit coat, "and exercise."

"You look great."

"Jill, what about that gorgeous Puerto Rican doctor, Mo said ...let's see...how long ago was that? He was going to school in Baltimore?"

"Yeah, he was accepted to Johns Hopkins," Jill rolled her eyes and reached into the raincoat pocket, pulling out the crumpled Kleenex.

"Well, he should be getting close..."

"Armentria Beales?" a student leaned around the edge of Dr. Reader's office door.

"Good luck, Armie," Jill held out her hand, and then they hugged. Jill spoke with her chin on Armentria's shoulder, "Life never seems to turn out the way I plan."

"The baby? She's all right?"

"Oh, she's fine, full of energy. She'll be three next month," Jill spoke, turning from Armentria.

She exited the side door of Aloyishes Hall. The unopened umbrella was her cane and she tapped it on the brick path. The rain from the dirty dishwater gray sky fell on her face. Moving away from the VW, she stepped deliberately now in the puddles. She bit her lip and started retracing the paths that had taken her to the unknown places she had not wanted to go. The bricks with grass grout brought her back to the familiar -from frustration to satisfaction and now completion. She had had three years of love, hope, support, all those disgusting feelings!

She purposely walked the circuitous path to Grimley's Gazebo. The soggy grass squished under her heels. Each past visit had been a new prediction. "If you kiss in April," Hector said, putting the picked cherry blossom behind her ear, "you'll have a long life and many children," then his kiss, lifting and turning her around, squeezing her as if this was the most important kiss she would receive. Each season, the red-leafed maple leaf in her ponytail, "If you kiss a redhead, with a red leaf in her ponytail, your passion will burn forever." She now stepped into the covered open-sided structure. The concrete floor was damp and a small puddle had formed from the roof's run-off.

She took a deep breath, and then swirled around. With her eyes closed, the smell of the moisture on the sodden earth filled her lungs. The "farmer's promise from God," she used Luis's phrase. What promise? What omen? Was it here and I didn't see it? Or hear it? Hector, you promised on this day, I would be leaving State, packing all my, *our* things and shipping them to an apartment in Baltimore. You promised, Hector, but you see me? Right back to Caylor; all the boxes packed to be stored in Lillian's basement, waiting to go somewhere. I know, "Chin up, one day this too, shall pass." And you and Sadie assured me, "Oh, Sarah B., straighten up. It will be all right, one year – 365 days – start to finish and at the end…" How about it Hector? I'll close my eyes and you make a pronouncement. What does it mean Hector, to be in Grimley's Gazebo and the man you love won't ever kiss you again? She spun around and around, the gazebo's sides blurred into a dizzy pattern of wood and concrete. Suddenly she stopped, planting both feet securely on the floor, and then opening her umbrella.

Just singing in the rain…singing in the rain? Crying in the rain is more like it. Crying? No it must be raindrops, it feels like raindrops… I must have a cloud in my head…she hummed the popular song and walked out of the gazebo. Her heels sunk with each footstep in the saturated ground. The rain beat heavily as she cut through the pine trees to her last stop. The soaked bark and gray muck, was this really a dream and she could, she would wake up? …Stop Jill, this is not, this is….She could not finish.

What a life time ago fighting with T.J. on the drive from Georgia and yet this year there was talk, an actual discussion of legislation for a voting rights act. The President, the one she so hoped would make the changes demanded by the Freedom Riders, was assassinated. When would that war end? An undeclared war, but what else could it be called? When would it stop? Baton wielding police beating people, then allowing the dogs to bite them and finally, the fire hoses to wash them away as if cleaning up after a parade. High-powered hoses swept the streets of human bodies. And all they are asking for is their civil rights. Civil rights? White people, we have them, but others do not. Are we special? "A little melanin in our skin, that's all it is Babe, melanin in the skin to protect us from the sun." Special? for a lack of protective melanin? Privileges? for a lack of protective melanin? How could something so natural be used as a reason to unleash dogs and clubs on innocent people? Yes, *my* students will learn American History.

My wedding, small and beautiful in three months. "June. Jill, I'll take my thirty day leave and come to your graduation, then back to Caylor, an intimate wedding at your church...Mrs. Andujar and Luisa Andujar, then we'll be off to Baltimore."

Her feet were cold and wet by the time she pulled open the heavy carved door with its tarnished brass handle. The steam heat warmed her as she smelled the peculiar odor of books and lemon polish. No one was on the stairway to the main reading room. All the times she had come here, she had rushed downstairs, down to....The downstairs handrail was smooth, and the well-worn hardwood had a rich familiar feel. The stairs to the library basement twisted back on themselves, curving in a semi-circle. The patina of the wood and the painted limestone of the basement confronted her with their absolute sameness. The library tables and mismatched chairs, randomly placed and moved. She stood still on the stairway, then closed her eyes, smelling the coffee aroma. Do this, Jill, do this.

April 15, 1963, a year ago. It had been the last time she would hear his voice. "We're leaving in the next two hours. There's a line for the phone, Babe. I love you, always," he had paused, taking a breath before he continued, "Kiss the angel everyday from her daddy. I'll be alright. I'll be there for your graduation and then this will all be over. We'll write, send pictures. Chin up, Babe..." his voice cracked at the end, then the dial tone. He had not finished...this, too, shall pass.

May 26, 1962, Luisa's First Birthday. They celebrated on Saturday. Lillian and Henry came down. Hector now owned Sadie's old blue Dodge. Mo helped bake the cake in a heart shape, chocolate with white frosting. They made a small one for Luisa. Lillian and Jill did the dishes. Chocolate cake had managed to get everywhere. Bobbie swept up the crumbs before heading back to study. Hector changed Luisa out of her frosting covered party dress. He heated her bottle, then carried her with him to watch baseball on TV. Lillian

17

talked of Hector's acceptance to John Hopkins and how that would change his time with Luisa. Jill would not finish for two more years. She suppressed these thoughts until someone asked her about his absence, an absence that would take money and time to bridge, both in short supply. Lillian had brought up the possibility of his joining the service.

"They will help pay his college expenses, Jill."

"No, Mom, we haven't discussed it."

She took her dishtowel to the living room to find Hector stretched out on the couch with Luisa curled up in his arm, the empty bottle lying on the floor. Henry dozed in the large reading chair....

"Kiss the angel from her daddy."

"Jill Havlicek? What brings you here in the rain? Come, come, you look like you need some mud coffee."

Jill opened her eyes, "Professor Tarkington, I'm surprised you remembered me. I haven't been here for so long."

The elderly man, not much taller than Jill, with hunched shoulders and glasses perched at the tip of his pored, veined nose, spoke, "I know my memory is not what it used to be, but you and that young man, Hector, should have paid the rent as much time as you spent in the basement."

Jill followed the professor whose corduroy vest and pocket watch made him look more like a train conductor than a teacher. How many mornings had he sat at their table arguing the validity of the communist scare that had permeated so much of the news? He had joined Hector, then her, complaining about the brink of destruction that the Soviet and American military had created over the missiles in Cuba. He seemed to relish the interaction with the two of them.

They had never enrolled in any of his classes which had a reputation for being tough. Instead they drank "mud" coffee and argued with him in the informality of the lounge. When he had laughed at Hector's clever retorts, he flushed with embarrassment and whispered, "Don't tell my students, it'll ruin my rep."

Now he looked at Jill, "So young lady what brings you to the bowels of State?"

"I love this special place, professor." He eyed her with one eyebrow raised and harrumphed. "I've come to say goodbye, actually," she continued, "I'm getting ready to student teach and will not be back here. Well, except to pick up my degree in June."

"Saying goodbye to a place?"

"A time, sir, a special time…" and she pulled out the soggy Kleenex.

Professor Tarkington pinched his lips in his fingers, then spoke, "That young man of yours, must be close to becoming a doctor. Johns Hopkins, wasn't that the place?"

"Professor Tarkington, Hector was killed last year in Viet Nam."

The old man reflexively reached and patted Jill's hands, the twisted arthritic fingers gentle on her hand, "Oh, my, that saddens me. He was so young, so much life to live. Oh, my, I'm sorry Jill. It's that damned red-mania. Like some virulent disease, it keeps breaking out everywhere. How many men did we lose in Korea? And now Indo-China. You see why I hide down in this cave?"

"Your reputation goes way beyond this cave. My roommate had you for a class and you set her conservative politics on its head. She argued with me every day, about who was right McCarthy or Joseph Welch. You certainly made her rethink some of the local John Birch propaganda that she grew up with in Gold Oak."

The professor grunted like a satisfied hog. He tapped her hand with his index finger as he spoke, "Jill, you know death is a devastating experience for those of us left behind, but it can also be a gift. You must take off the ribbon, unwrap the package and look for what was given to you through the life. We all take each other for granted, not appreciating the gifts we give each other, only when we lose someone do we stop to think what all those things were. I learned that lesson one chapter at a time when Mrs. Tarkington died several years ago." He shook his head, "Great woman." His shoulders seemed more hunched.

Jill kissed the man's wrinkled cheek, then grabbed her umbrella. She hurried up the stairs. The rain changed from drizzle to heavy drops.

The rain, Babe, everything stays wet, does it ever stop? No, it just changes from drizzle to rain to drizzle. And if it stops the humidity rests on your skin, no drying, no breeze to cool off. The only thing I want this close on my skin is you. Dak Pek. June 6, 1963. The Drang River. COSVN. All the words strange and cryptic. William could explain it. He was in Viet Nam, over Viet Nam. But the pen and paper? She had picked them up and put them down. Maybe the explanation needed to be buried under those sixty foot teak trees Hector described.

August 21, 1963, it had been three weeks and no letters. In five months it had never been so long without a letter, the airmail letters. She had called Sadie every day, but every day the mail came and nothing. Michael tried to explain the problems with the service from half-way around the world. It happened often, SOP (Standard Operating Procedure) for the Army, not to worry. The registration notice for her classes had come in the mail; State had finally made the process easier. The phone had rung, she still had the pre-registration schedule in her hand. Luisa sat on the kitchen floor stirring water in a pan, water was all over the floor.

"Jill Havlicek?" a man's voice asked.

"Yes?"

"This is Arturo Calderon, Hector's brother-in-law. Juanita asked that I call you. Her English, she was afraid she could not make you understand. Hector was killed on the sixth of August. We were told almost nothing. They came to Juanita's, two officers," he paused. She heard him take a breath, "They said he will be buried in Arlington National Cemetery; he was given that honor because of heroism..." He paused again, "They will be returning his body, his personal..."

His body? Dak Pek. Then "the feeling" as she came to call it, something in her stomach, an opening like she had been punched through, stomach-to-back, flattened then through, a giant fist smacked into her and forced pain up, up to her throat. She had to swallow and swallow, dry cotton, handfuls, no sound came, just a cough of stuffing, then the feeling started in her stomach again. She had leaned against the kitchen wall and slid down like Luisa's rag doll.

"I'll call you with a date," Arturo kept talking, "we cannot make arrangements until..."

Luisa brought the pot and sat between her legs, handing Jill the wood spoon. She grabbed Luisa against her stomach, squeezing her tightly, trying to fill the hole made by the punch. She held Luisa, crying on her baby soft cheek.

No, she could not go to Washington, D.C. But she "went" in November, three months after Arturo called, with all of America – the soldiers, the horses, the caisson, the American flag stretched out over the wood box of the fallen hero, the cortege, the white tombstones, rows and rows all the same; the family and friends in black and

Jacqueline Kennedy, stoic, kissing the box of her man, her husband the slain hero. John-John stood waving his small American flag. John-John like Luisa, a man died who loved him, loved her, and neither would ever know these men or their love.

Andy Williams sang, "Mine eyes have seen the glory...." She had cried, cried for the president, cried for Hector, cried for the change, the loss. She stared at the television, the sacred ground of Arlington Cemetery and thought of the others who cried for them - Viet Nam. She knew Hector was with the others, and one day she would go to the Arlington chapel when she could talk to him, alone at his resting place, and then she would say goodbye.

The rain now ran down her sleeve as she used her fingers to count the months, August, September, October...Christmas...nine months since he died. It had all made so much sense. He was going to be drafted, he must serve. If he joined the Army now, they would pay for medical school later, actually give him credit for the experience almost like serving his residency. Lillian had said it to her, she should have listened, maybe come up with a convincing argument. His student deferment ended with the awarding of his Bachelor's, he could pick his place if he joined, but he would serve three years instead of two. "This way is best, Babe," he had tried to convince her of the appropriateness of his decision. "I'll have one year left in the Army. They promised a U.S. base, Ft.Detrick in Maryland.

"I can start classes. I'll take my thirty days leave in June. You graduate and we'll be married, like Sadie, you'll be a military wife. You can teach, and I'll go to school, Baltimore is only 45 miles away. The G.I. Bill will take care of everything."

Sure, Hector, it made sense, so much goddamned sense. Special Forces. Why Special Forces? They needed medics in Special Forces? They needed *a* medic in Special Forces. I need a Medic, a doctor, my own Dr. Andujar, not the goddamned Special Forces.

Why did I think I was going to be some new version of Cinderella and live happily ever after with my handsome prince? He sent pictures, no curls, and an American flag in the background. America, she hissed, she could say it just as Luis had. Land of the free? He trained at Walter Reed, she went to see him in Washington, D.C. a few wonderful days, and then they shipped him to Germany, Landstuhl, "An amazing facility, Babe." She wanted to go, but the time was too short and she was in the middle of Final Week when he could get days off.

"Water over the dam, Princess." Princess? A Princess without her Prince. My glass slipper shattered. Goddamned U.S. Army, Dad, like this rain, on and on; it's too hard, so much more than water over the dam. So much more than April showers can wash away. April showers bring May flowers, she repeated the poem. "Unwrap the gift," Professor Tarkington said.

Grieving widows? Mrs. Minnix never stopped speaking of her ongoing nonstop memories of the Mister. She never re-married and grandma… "Jill, I miss Pop every day," Grandma Caitlin assured her.

"But…Grandma."

"Nothing wrong with missing the man you love," Grandma Caitlin said.

April. April showers, the cycle begins. Her soaked hair dripped now as she opened the car door. "Bye Aloyishes, 'You can get all your wishes with coeds in Aloyishes,'" she repeated Hector's phrase from their first walk through the campus. Okay, Hector, I *wish* you were here. Ha! I knew it wouldn't work. The raindrops from her bangs streamed down her face, "Oh it must be raindrops…raindrops falling from eyes…"

ﯨﺦﯨ

Henry had parked the large moving truck in the driveway. The couch was being carried by two young men, brawny, with curly brown hair. Twins? Sweaty or rain drenched t-shirts? The furniture had been wrapped in heavy plastic sheeting. Leave it to Dad, she thought, climbing the front steps.

"Mommy," Luisa rushed up and grabbed her knees, "Grandpa's here. We're going to Grandma's today! Ferlin and Farren let me get in the truck!"

"Where's Bobbie?" Jill asked.

Bobbie had been so happy to move in last September for her last year of school and her first year of eligibility for off-campus housing. Two years living with Mo, then Mo moved in with her Alpha Kappa Alpha sorority sisters, one year of living alone, and now this last one with Bobbie, who adored Luisa and cared for her as a second mom. Sometimes she and Khalil even played "house," and took Luisa to a park or to State's outdoor family music festivals.

The kitchen was all in boxes; she searched for a cup, then opened the cupboard, only two left on the shelf and four glasses. She removed a cup and poured coffee, knowing Henry would make fresh coffee before moving one piece.

"Princess," Henry spoke, walking into the kitchen. She hugged him. He patted her head, "Gee, you're soaking wet. You need a towel?" Crushed against his chest she couldn't answer. "Princess, I think we are almost ready. Stop. I only brought one handkerchief, and Bobbie has been trying to use it. Come, come, let's take a look-see and make sure we've got it all. Bobbie has been directing the fellas. I think she kind of likes Farren."

Jill and Henry left the kitchen. Bobbie tried to smile, but hugged Jill.

"Aunt Bobbie, don't cry. You can come and live with mommy and me at Grandpa's. Grandpa, Aunt Bobbie can go with us?" Luisa pulled on Bobbie's sweatshirt.

Bobbie had lost weight in her four years at State. Jill teased her that living at 1254 Butler was the weight reduction clinic because the cooking was minimal. Bobbie had laughed and said eating the curry rice Khalil made helped her the most. Jill promised to call as often as possible. Henry harrumphed, "Me and Ma Bell, when will it ever end? We got Sadie too far away to call. Now…"

"Stop, Dad…you act like you live at the poor farm."

"I will be moving there soon enough with your propensity to…"

"Okay, let's go. We can talk about your relationship with Ma Bell in the car."

The pieces were wedged, stuffed, jammed into the truck. Farren and Ferlin were ready to pull out. Henry had introduced them as, "the two boys from Arkansas." He said they showed great promise for "child labor." They laughed at his teasing and swore they respected their elders, "Strong on elders."

She hugged Bobbie one last time; the house looked empty. The rent was paid through June. "1254 Butler" she'd written on the card at the post office for former address, "749 S. Catalpa" for new address. They forward for six months. At least if William wrote, no, he had made that clear, "*My taboo girl, as an officer and a gentleman,*

I relinquish. Love." No question mark, the last letter, *24 September 1961.*

The VW was filled. The only open space, the backseat, was now Luisa's bed. She used her large teddy bear for a pillow and Henry had thrown his work coat over her for a blanket. Her cheeks were pudgy and pink. Her long black curls had been combed into two ponytails. Bobbie had begged Jill to let her comb it one last time. Bobbie parted the thick strands and tied ribbons on each section. Luisa's eyebrows were rounded, making her large brown eyes appear bigger.

"Your mama's eyes," people said to her. Luis's everything else, Jill responded to herself. And when Luisa was mad, she frowned and stared, as if she had seen him do that a hundred times. Jill had nicknamed her Lo, for Luis Ochoa, she was his daughter; her "daddy" had died in some goddamned jungle on the other side of the world.

"Poor man's rain," Henry now said.

"I guess you would know, Pops, you are the poorest man, I know. I hope you have enough money to buy gas and lunch."

"Chip off the old block, huh?"

"I've been accused of worse. Well, now that I think about it, maybe not."

Henry shook his head. The tiny windshield wipers could barely keep up with the heavy rain.

"Dad, I think I may need a new car before I move to Boston. What do you think?"

"Jill Caitlin, I don't think you've considered that Boston thing very carefully."

She turned from the road to look at him.

"Okay, okay," he held up his hands in his mock surrender position, "you hard-headed Havlicek, what will it cost me to keep my daughter and granddaughter in Indiana?"

"Dad, stop doing this to me. You know how I feel about these small-minded people…they will never accept Luisa or me. I've committed the cardinal Caylor sin – unwed motherhood."

"It will be all right, Princess. These people learn to accept those who haven't fit into their pattern. They're not so righteous themselves. You know Charlie Edwards came home from Korea with a Korean wife. She could not speak a drop of English, not one word. The church, oh they tizz-tizzed about that for months, then slowly Kathy Edwards, I'm sure that isn't her Korean name learned English.

24

Lillian tutored her many afternoons. Kathy worked in the church kitchen and took care of the nursery babies on Sunday morning. Well, you know, now everyone accepts her and Charlie. At the time Charlie created a scandal, now no one thinks twice about it. The church folks know you. Please think about it."

"No, I'm going to Boston. What school would hire me? Dr. Reader already warned me it could be a problem. Teaching is not the profession for those who make 'mistakes.' I miss Sadie. I wish it didn't cost so much to call her. I would talk about this with her. Maybe I could just move with her. It would be so much simpler."

"Europe? Simpler? That's worse than Boston!"

They rode silently. Luisa slept soundly, her usual when they drove. The rain blocked any view of the limestone bluffs. The tiny wiper blades beat back and forth, the small defroster kept only the windshield in front of her clear. Jill reached for a Kleenex from the box wedged by the gear shift. She wiped her side window and the wind wing. She tried to see if there was anyone behind her. The loaded VW, Imogene, crawled along.

"That's it!" Henry wamped his palm against the glove box.

"What's it Dad?" she turned, looking at his face. He was smiling broadly. "What's *it*, Dad? I don't trust that look."

"I love a bribe as well as the next man, Princess, so think about this. Don't say anything until we get to Indianapolis – twenty miles." She nodded and listened as he explained his bribe. She could go to Germany for two weeks to visit Sadie and he would pay for all her expenses, "maybe three weeks, if you are having an especially nice time. I remember the bribe I had to come up with to keep you at State instead of moving to Baltimore, when *your* doctor was headed that way. I know it's been hard for you.

"Hector was a good man and served his country, damned good. And the Army barber took care of his hair. I am truly sorry it's worked out this way for you, Princess. It is why I think you need to stay close to us. I know you are still missing that young man. It takes time for a heart to heal, but being with those who love you makes it easier."

"But, I promised myself I'd move to Boston, well, someplace away from Caylor. I wanted to leave for so long and now seems like an opportune time. I will be finished with school. I can start a new life someplace where Luisa can grow up…"

"Grow up?! Without her grandparents!?"

"Germany and Sadie, it would be exciting. I'd love to see Sadie pregnant after all the times she laughed at me four years ago. I'll think about it, Dad."

"Thanks. It's all I'm asking. Lil and I can keep the angel. And it has been a long while since you and Sadie have been together to do all those...kicking up your heels, flirting with catastrophe, wasting my money things. Maybe cheer you up a bit."

Chapter 2

When Jill had coffee at home, Henry said the sunny spring day was a positive sign and sang her a few lines of "Oh What a Beautiful Morning," before she forced him to quit. They'd laughed. He toasted her first day in a real profession and said that she looked almost old enough to be a teacher. As she drove to Marion, she knew he was happy to have her living again under *his* roof. She had agreed to think about staying in Caylor, maybe for a year.

Jill now circled the parking lot twice, then pulled into an unnumbered space in the faculty area. Faculty, it sounded different, but satisfying. She slammed her door, and then asked a husky man parked next to her for directions to the office. He wore sweat pants and a golf shirt with a lanyard around his neck. "Follow the sidewalk and go up the front steps. It is on your immediate right. The names are posted. I'd be happy to show you, but I'm headed the other way…" He flipped his thumb toward the grassy football stadium abutting the faculty parking lot. He smiled and waved as she headed to the front of the school.

At the school's entrance, parents unloaded their children wearing letter sweaters and carrying armloads of books. Dr. Reader was right, they did look her age. The front sidewalk led to big double wooden doors. The carved limestone and red bricks reminded her of Caylor High School, a square box structure with symmetrical windows on three floors and grooved marble steps. She had not noticed this building when she and Sadie had driven over to watch Jim play football.

Jim? No. She opened the door to the familiar smell of sweaty bodies and floor wax, Caylor High School all over again? Well, not quite, this time I am the teacher.

The chest-high counter of the administration office was busy. Two teachers dressed in spring flowery-print dresses huddled at one corner. Jill looked down at her plum colored suit, a straight skirt with a short jacket. She decided to try conservative until she saw the other faculty members. When they looked up from scanning an AVON book, she smiled. They held announcement bulletins, books and papers. Behind the counter a mimeograph machine whirred, sending its alcohol-like smell through the room.

A secretary stood up from behind her desk, smiling at her. She also wore a flowered dress, splashes of pink and green with large white rick-rack trim on the sleeves. "Orders are due by Friday," she said. She turned to Jill. She wore no make-up and was chubby, bouncy. A great school secretary, Jill thought, after the miserable 120 year old spinster in dark wool dresses, who squished her thin wrinkled lips together and looked down her nose and over glasses at every student who dared walk in the principal's office at Caylor High. The secretary now gushed, "Good morning. May I help you?"

"Good morning, I'm Jill Havlicek. I was told to meet Mr. Brown…"

"Hi! You're the student teacher. Welcome to Marion High School. I'm Bunnie Dawkins. If you have any questions, please come to me. Dan said he was expecting you."

The secretary paused and looked behind Jill, "Margie?" The secretary called to a slim woman with a page boy of several shades of blonde hair, ashy, gray, white, yellow. Was it natural or a mistake? Margie in a white blouse with a Peter Pan collar, a khaki skirt and khaki leather wedges to match was thirty-five or so. Her Army green cardigan hung around her shoulders fastened with a gold sweater clamp. Her freckled face was devoid of make-up. The khaki brown spots marked her face like splattered ink. She carried a ream of paper and an exasperated look, "Yes, Bunnie? What's on your mind?" Margie had a smoker's hoarse voice. She gave the secretary a half-smile.

"Margie, would you please show Miss Havlicek how to get to Dan's office. She is our new student teacher."

Margie raised one eyebrow, Bunnie continued, "Oh, I'm so sorry, Margie Merriweather, please allow me to introduce Jill Havlicek."

"How do you do, Miss…" Jill started.

"I am *Mrs.* Merriweather…" Margie interrupted, sticking out one hand from under the sheaf of papers, "Welcome to the breeding ground of juvenile delinquency."

"Margie, this is her first…"Bunnie said.

"Don't you think I know that Bunnie. I can see that dazzled, 'gee whiz' look on her face. Come on Miss…"

"Havlicek, Jill Havlicek." Jill smiled.

"Yeah, Jill, too bad you can't use your first name, these idiots will never figure out how to say Havlicek. Come let's go meet the animals and their keepers."

Bunnie apologized with a shrug and half-smile; she waved slightly. Jill followed Margie out the door.

"Where are you from?" Margie said as they climbed the marble stairway.

"State University, but my home is Caylor."

"Well, all these Indiana high schools are the same, so you'll think you're right back at Caylor. We're probably using the books you used four years ago. I think you're going to be teaching my third period U.S. History class. I will be happy to give the sons-a-bitches to you. They might like some young teacher." She tossed her hair and turned up her top lip. Margie opened the office door of the Social Studies Department. Margie snarled when she talked, "Here's your latest victim, Dan." Margie walked toward the inner office door, talking, "I already told her about that bunch of lame-brains I have in third period…"

"Marge, enough," he interrupted. A short man, shiny bald head outlined in trimmed dark brown hair stood behind an oak desk built for someone twice his size. The top was covered in papers, folders, cans of films. Pencils and pens were wedged at all angles between reams of paper, stacks of magazines and several sections of newspapers. He removed his dark framed glasses and held out his pudgy hand. He stood straight and was only slightly taller than Jill. He shook his head at Margie, "Jill, I'm happy you're here. I want you to meet the members of our department, the *other* members," he paused to point to the supply room where Margie had disappeared, smiled, then said, "We try to be one big happy family of professionals."

Standing behind a cabinet door, Margie loudly cleared her throat. Dan continued, "Come, let's get some coffee at the Social Studies Lounge and I'll introduce you to the crew."

"Don't let her near Ross, Dan, his balls are already swollen over Miss Leland…"

"Marge…"

"Oh, yes, I forgot, 'Proper language is to be used at all times' in front of the delinquents."

The faculty lounge was the busiest place she had seen thus far. Mr. Brown stopped by the work table, "Jill Havlicek, meet Ross Hass." Ross, a big football-looking type, wore a suit uncomfortably, the top button of his shirt was unbuttoned; his tie was loosened to accommodate his thick neck. He smiled at Jill, but spoke to Mr. Brown, "Hey, Dan, send her to my room first period. She can see how a pro does it."

"A pro? As usual, you need to zip it up, Ross," Marge said from the coffee pot, "Too bad your brain is not as big as your neck."

Before Jill could speak, Mr. Brown raised his hand, open palmed, "Everybody, may I have your attention?" The room got quiet as the seven people standing looked at Mr. Brown. Two men wore crumpled suits, one using a v-neck sweater as a vest. A woman of retirement age with pearls and black oxford shoes stood next to a platinum blonde woman who seemed to be Jill's age. Another teacher resembled a golfer in plaid pants, lemon yellow sweater with a yellow tie hanging from his shirt pocket. His light brown hair was bleached blonde at the temples. He smiled and winked at Jill.

"This will be brief," Mr. Brown spoke, "but we have two new additions this week. Jill Havlicek comes to us from State for her student teaching. At your own time, please introduce yourselves and provide her with any assistance or helpful hints to make her teaching experience easier. She'll be working with Marge's third period and my sixth period. She'll be observing your classes, asking questions."

"Walk out while you have a chance," Margie quipped.

"Whatever Margie Merriweather has to say, ignore," Ross responded.

Mr. Brown looked sternly from one to the other, "You don't need to show her who the real problems are just yet. She'll learn soon enough. And the second newcomer I want you to cooperate with is Jack Jones from Johnson Electronics. They want to use Marion as a guinea pig for some new fangled idea they have about computers. He will not be here until next Thursday, April 9. We will be making impromptu visits to each of your rooms. Please be courteous and cooperative. His assignment will continue for the next six weeks, he will be in and out observing and taking notes. Please answer his questions in a *professional* manner. Now get back to whatever you were doing…" The words had barely slipped from his tiny mouth and the din in the room increased again. He grabbed Jill by the elbow and escorted her from the lounge.

ﻻﺀﻻ

Jill had her back to the door as the day-ending bell rang. She erased April 10, 1964, from the upper right-hand corner of the chalkboard and the phonetic Have-la-check, she had written. She wrote her name correctly, then erased the acronyms she had written for FDR's New Deal social service programs – WPA, PWA, FHA, CCC, FCC, FDIC, AAA, REA. When the board was clean, she turned back to her empty room.

"Miss Havlicek?" Mr. Brown's voice called to her from the backdoor.

"Yes?" she said, staring at Mr. Brown and the tall man standing next to him. The stranger was thin, not too thin, though. They continued talking as they walked to the front of the classroom. The man cocked his head toward Mr. Brown, listening as if absorbing each word. He wore round wire-framed glasses and combed his dark brown hair away from his face, but a swatch fell across his forehead, a curled wave. As they got closer, she saw the gray at his temples; but when he turned to face her, his blue eyes lit up and the grin was an ornery boyish smile. His narrow nose, added symmetry to his high cheek bones. He wore a navy blue sport coat and a cream turtleneck with khaki trousers. He pulled a small notebook out of this pocket and wrote.

"Jill," Mr. Brown said, "This is Jack Jones."

"How do you do?" Jill said extending her hand across her desk. His palm was soft. He smiled again; his crow's feet reinforced the congenial appearance.

"It's a pleasure to meet you, Jill. I understand that you are student teaching. Where do you go to school?" His voice was low, a heavy voice. Polite like his handshake. He sat on the edge of her desk and wrote in a large stenographer's notebook as she talked. She watched his upside-down left-handed writing. At 3:30 they all said goodbye. Mr. Brown and Mr. Jones left, but Jill stayed to put the papers she needed to grade in her leather case.

Margie charged in the front door of the classroom.

"Jill, here are the *Weekly Readers*; you might want to look through them over the weekend. Oh, I apologize, you're young and salubrious you have other things to do than read *Weekly Readers* over the weekend."

"Thank you, Mrs. Merriweather. As a matter of fact, I plan to be as prepared as possible for my solo sessions next week. *Weekly Readers*? I read these in 7th grade...."

"These little bastards don't read, well actually, can't read much above that level."

"I'll try to find some things for them; we had discussions about reaching all the levels..."

"Enjoy your weekend; don't spend time on that group. Dan's sixth period? Now they'll appreciate your effort."

"Well, Henry Gonzales..." Jill said, thinking of the attentive quiet student in the third period, who had asked to do extra work. He had looked like a grown up version of chubby Carlos at the migrant camp. He asked Jill if he could he draw a Civil War soldier's picture.

"That little wetback..."

"Mrs. Merriweather, you call them by awful names, but I've watched you this week, and you have time for all of them, for everything. You are *very* prepared."

"I've done this too long. I do have a lot of preparation time...." she faded, looking away from Jill to the empty seats. "Isn't this a wonderful sound, Jill? No students?"

Jill removed her sweater from the back of the desk chair. "No, I like the chatter of students. They make these dead boring classrooms live. Come, Mrs. Merriweather, it's Friday. I have to drive to Caylor. I'll take the papers and see if there is something."

"Do you want to stop and get a drink? A few us have a local watering hole we go to on Fridays. It is easy to find. It's on 26, on your way home. I also asked that handsome Mr. Jones. He said, 'Perhaps.' I thought he sounded like an arrogant asshole, but he is cute so.... And, speaking of assholes, Ross definitely won't be there. He went to Indianapolis to pick up trophies for the Awards Banquet next week." When Marge finished, she sighed. Her face appeared sad, resigned.

Faculty or student? Drinking with the teachers? Dr. Reader had not provided for this situation. Maybe for one beer?

ﺭ٤ﺭ

What a strange afternoon, she thought while driving to Caylor. Mrs. Merriweather too obviously wanted to do more than meet Mr. Jones. She was embarrassing in her desperation as she kept trying to get Mr. Jones attention. What was her story, really? Was it like Ross had said, trying to sound confidential? "A married spinster."

He heckled Mrs. Merriweather whenever he could, labeling her, "too mean to love." He told Jill she was married to a weird sculptor who crafted sexually engaged couples, men with men, women with women, men with women. No one had offered any other insights besides the common reference, "Oh, that is just Margie." She drove an old, old Rolls-Royce.

At the Italian Gondola, all red and black, dark and smoky, Mr. Jones engaged in an intense conversation with Mr. Hillagoss, who'd graduated from Purdue last year and now taught math. Kent Hillagoss, tall, dark deep-set eyes, wavy black hair. He was hefty through his chest, a football player, perhaps. Roman nose, yes a gorgeous hunk of man, the "handsome" Margie had used for Mr. Jones.

Miss Leland flirted with him at every possible moment. Leann Leland, her parents had really given her that name? "Yes," Leann whispered in the baby-talk she used when there were no students around. Leann had blonde Marilyn Monroe hair and Marilyn's shape, big breasts and rounded hips. While most of what she said was nonsensical childish gibberish, Jill found, if pressed,

Leann was interesting to talk to. She did know her subject area –art. And told Jill to visit the Louvre in Paris and any place she could manage in Tuscany when she went to Europe. Leann talked of Toulouse-Lautrec and Gauguin.

"Why do you socialize with the Social Studies Department?"Jill asked.

"I guess they parallel my philosophy of teaching more than the "farmer-teachers," in the other departments." Leann had laughed and mocked Ross, "He is like Hoss on 'Bonanza.' Oh, I shouldn't insult Hoss like that."

Jill asked, "As long as we're at the Ponderosa, don't you think Mr. Jones, looks like Little Joe?"

"Maybe," Leann said, "Little Joe is so cute. He'd have to let his hair grow into curls."

Curls. The word and she saw the bandana tied around all of them. Was it a million years ago? Or yesterday? The memory evoked the empty pit in her heart. She shook her head as if a simple shake would make the thought go away. A deep breath, then back to the Italian Gondola. She looked at Mr. Jones who was staring at her.

"Are you okay?" he turned his head slightly.

"Yes. I guess I need another beer."

"Sure. I'll buy you one."

"No, no you don't…" Jill started, then Ross said, "I'll get the lovely red-head a beer. Sit tight Jill. Do you have a preference?" Ross had made it to Indianapolis and back telling everyone he wouldn't miss TGIF.

"Hamm's I guess."

Ross, who had been obnoxious in his descriptions and conversations with Margie, generously walked to the bar. Leann lambasted the big-necked "buffoon" as much as Mrs. Merriweather. Jill had also noticed whenever Ross entered the room, Leann would gush in her baby-talk. Ross under his breath said, "Idiot."

Jill liked watching Leann talk because her dark blue eyes danced and her hands constantly reinforced points she made. Leann had only been teaching two years; she asked Jill to make sure she came back to Marion after she graduated. She told Jill that her father had been superintendent of the Marion Public Schools for many years before taking a job for the State Department of Education. And graciously, Jill thought, Leann told Jill that if she wanted to work in Marion to let her know and she would talk to someone.

Mr. Hillagoss had charm and a smile that opened onto straight paper-white teeth. Jill tried to listen, to the conversation between himself and Mr. Jones, but got lost in the discussion of calculus, the "concept of function, the domain of function, the curve of function, the linear function, the quadratic functions and the poly...." A couple of engineers she concluded.

Mr. Jones stayed attentive to all of the math conversation. They discussed the progress being made on President Kennedy's promise to put a man on the moon. Mr. Jones had glanced at Jill once when Leann giggled inappropriately. She had then asked Leann if she wanted to go to the ladies' room. Kent Hillagoss and Mr. Jones had both looked relieved when she and Leann left.

Jill drank her second beer when they started the poly-whatever discussion. As the jukebox played, Mrs. Merriweather had forced Mr. Jones to get up and dance on the tiny dance floor. Jill watched as they danced a slow swing to the Shirelles, "Soldier Boy." Mr. Jones could probably dance, but Mrs. Merriweather was Hector's epithet to T.J., "White girls can't dance."

Hector, again the punch. She reflexively shook her head, and then asked Leann if student teachers were required to attend the Spring Prom. The question triggered a flow of responses about hairdos, formals, corsages and dancing in long dresses. When her watch said five-thirty, Jill heard herself promising Lillian she would be home for dinner at six, dinner time never changed at the Havlicek's. She excused herself from the table. Mrs. Merriweather grabbed Mr. Jones hand as he rose with Jill. His gentlemanly rise was so proper in the middle of Marion at the Italian Gondola. He even more politely excused himself and followed her from the table to the door. He had reminded her that he enjoyed meeting her and looked forward to talking to her again, "Next week, Wednesday or Thursday."

As she drove to Caylor, she thought of Mr. Jones, such a common name. Jack Jones, and she hummed his song, "for wives should always be lovers, too." I wonder how many times he is asked that question, do you sing? She heard him tell Mr. Hillagoss that science had changed so much in the eighteen years since he had completed his master's. Now she used her fingers tapping the steering wheel, eighteen when he graduated from high school, plus four years of college for his B.S. two more for the M.S., made him twenty-two plus two would have been twenty-four when he received his master's and now eighteen years, twenty-four plus eighteen…he must be forty-two or close. Hey I can do math Mr. Hillagoss and Mr. Jones. Forty-two, he looks much younger, maybe the smile. How old would William be? Thirty-seven when I was a freshman, forty-one, now.

ᴦξᴦ

Jill sat at the back of the room grading her sixth period advanced U.S. History class. Each morning as Mr. Brown opened the room's windows, he chirped, "A spring breath of fresh air." At 2:30P.M., the hot breeze was filled with the sounds of the marching band practicing in the field next to the parking lot. They repeated, "Pomp and Circumstance," bungling it measure after measure. The students took turns giving speeches in front of the class. Darlene Simpson was barely taller than the lectern where she placed her note cards. She made eye contact with the other students. Her red hair came just below her ears and flipped up slightly. She wore a sleeveless pastel plaid cotton dress. Her big green eyes matched the green bow she had placed at the top of her bangs where her hair parted. And she had freckles. Blanketed in spots. Darlene talked clearly, "Peleliu is about 500 miles east of the Philippines…"

Viet Nam. 500 miles west of the Philippines? Maybe 700.

"The Marines," Darlene continued, "were ordered to the small island to protect General MacArthur when he invaded Mindanao…"

Why do the generals do the ordering? The grunts," Hector had said, *"the grunts go into the fire fight, hump the mountain, while some general sits in an air-conditioned hooch…."*

"The island had looked unfortified, but as the Marines landed the Japanese proved once again their incredible discrete defense techniques…"

Jill, these people, I refuse to call them gooks, yet, can defend themselves under air assaults. We are no match for them on the ground even with the M-16's and M-60's. Many guys come in…"

"There were hundreds of Marines killed on the beaches and in the traps set by the Japanese to immobilize and destroy the tanks. These trenches had been placed close to the shore…"

The guys go into the jungle and it looks quiet, but it is booby-trapped. Their legs and arms become separate pieces and they call "medic." I just hold them until they die, "Doc, tell my girl…"

"They gave their lives on that beach. It was impossible to dig into the hard reef; it tore their clothes, cut their skin. The temperature was 115°…"

It never stops, Babe, the heat, the dampness, the mosquitoes. We can't bathe, wounds become infected, well, our hell is bacteria's heaven. The guys are picked up by the medevac, but when I get back to the field hospital, I think death would have been more gracious.

"The slaughter of Peleliu continued for six days and in the end the 1st Marines no longer existed as an assault unit."

As each platoon comes back in body bags, I wonder who will be left. It makes no sense. I sew them up, drain their lungs, perform emergency trachs. Sometimes even before I finish, they are screaming "incoming" and it starts all over again.

"Peleliu was human sacrifice with no satisfactory war goal achieved; almost 1800 Marines killed in those few days. Killed in an action that to this day military experts are trying to understand why Admiral Nimitz ordered it."

One day I'll be out of the incomprehensible and on the big bird to Paradise, as we call our trip out of here, but I hope the destruction and maiming are not a waste. We may have to let Luisa's generation figure it out, then again, maybe no one will.

Jill glanced up from the evaluation sheet. Peleliu, but she had written Pleiku over and over again. She pulled a clean sheet and started checking the grading squares all over again. The back door opened quietly. Mr. Jones let himself in. He took the empty seat next to her, then pulled out the green stenographer's pad. He looked at Jill, smiled and winked. Darlene had ended her speech.

"Thank you, Darlene. Does anyone have any questions about the U.S. Marines landing on Pleiku?"

"Peleliu, Miss Havlicek," Darlene said.

"Yes, Peleliu, I'm sorry. Your graphic description was excellent. I think you have reinforced for all of us the human sacrifice of war."

The room was silent. Mr. Jones stopped jotting and wrote in large letters, "Viet Nam?" Jill tightened her fist, squeezing her pen, and pulling her lips into her mouth. She looked into his questioning eyes, then turned back to the class.

"Okay," Jill spoke, her voice hoarse. "You may sit down. Darlene. Let's see, who's next? Craig Engstrom..." A frail tall dark haired boy, wearing thick black-rimmed glasses ambled to the podium. He walked like a wooden puppet as if someone were pulling each leg and arm to make him walk. He pulled note cards from his gray blazer pocket, then looked at the class and Jill. She smiled reassuringly, as she had tried to do with each student.

Craig began in a loud voice that made them all look to see where it came from, "General Douglas MacArthur was one of the great generals of all times and a prophet in his own time, warning the world of the red menace that..."

Jill checked off five for enunciation. Mr. Jones wrote in his left-handed curve that prevented her from seeing what he wrote. He quietly tore off the sheet of paper and slid it on her desk. "Passing notes?" she imagined Craig loudly announcing in his next sentence, but he kept speaking, "as he left Manila, he promised the Filipino people he would return..."

Jill read the note, "Will you have dinner with me Saturday night?" Jill folded up the paper and slipped it under the stack of grading forms, then looked at him. Mr. Jones asked her again with his eyes. Craig ended his speech. And what would she mark for closing argument? She had not heard it. The bell rang and she reminded the class that they would finish the speeches and have a test next week over the Pacific-Japanese part of WWII. It had been four weeks; Dr. Reader would be arriving soon. May 1, in a month, graduation.

"Jill," Mr. Jones interrupted her thoughts.

"Yes?"

"You did not answer my question."

His voice was low; it sounded all of his forty-two years or maybe more, a heavy voice. "Mr. Jones..." she shoved the grading forms into a manila folder. She closed the bound "Lesson Planner" booklet, then hooked her red grading pen onto the cover.

"Jack, please just Jack."

"Jack, my supervising professor will be here next week and I want the report he receives to be great. I'm reluctant to do anything that might be interpreted as not proper conduct for a student teacher."

"Okay, I'll take a rain-check. When will you go to dinner with me?"

"Let me see what Dr. Reader says. I'll ask. I've spent four years trying to get to this point..."

"You've invested much time," Jack nodded, "I'll wait. My last week is the week of May eighteenth."

"It's just very important to me to maintain an absolutely professional stance. I've…" she stopped.

"Yes?"

"Long story, Jack. My last four years…sometimes it feels like forever, but I see the end and…"

"Whenever," he paused, then lightly touched the back of her hand, "I would like the pleasure of your company over meat and potatoes."

"Thank you." She smiled, then scooped up her papers, putting them in her case.

ᴙξᴙ

The restaurant in Crabapple, Indiana was as out of the way as the village itself, half-way between Marion and Caylor. Jack had come to her parents' house to pick her up. "As long as your meeting is away from the school and will not affect your performance or the perception of your fellow teachers and the students…" Dr Reader had warned, but the stipulations had all been met. Jack would no longer be at the school. No one would know. The restaurant was not in Marion.

Dr. Reader had talked with Mr. Brown and Mrs. Merriweather, then sat in on both of Jill's classes. They spent an hour together in Mr. Brown's office alone. He had told her she was handling the lower competency class faultlessly. Mrs. Merriweather had shown him the lesson plans – geography games; group play – enacting the discussions of some prominent U.S. figures. Mrs. Merriweather had praised Jill's creative plan and when Jill asked, Dr. Reader said, "No, she did not curse."

Dr. Reader had put away his notes, taken off his glasses and prepared his pipe, but did not light it in the school office. He spoke from the side of his mouth, "I reread the file you prepared for the placement office. You spent much time volunteering in your high school summers with migrant children. Are you interested in pursuing this area of teaching?"

"As a volunteer? Or as a regular teacher?" Jill said.

"As a regular teacher."

"Sure…but, just migrant children?"

"Let me explain," Dr. Reader interrupted, "There is a school not far from Caylor, Southeastern County that has had some influx of migrants staying permanently. They are currently looking for, not necessarily fluent Spanish-speaking teachers, but teachers with an understanding…"

"Dr. Reader, I'm really planning on leaving these mid-western environs. You know my daughter…"

"Well, exactly, Jill. I have an old friend who works in the superintendant's office at Southeastern. I kind of felt the situation out, to see…just to see. We want so much to place our teachers where they'll be happy. Well, in that vein, Robert Sartoris and I talked. He would like to interview you for an opening in their high school social studies…"

"Dr. Reader, I appreciate….but you didn't have to go that far on my behalf…"

"No, no, Jill, it's my job, but what is the point to invest all this time? Well, think about it. 'Sarty,' Mr. Sartoris, will be interviewing until July first. He wants his faculty positions filled by then."

She and Jack now pulled into the crowded parking lot. He'd met Luisa, who hid behind Lillian's legs and then bowed her head when Jill picked her up and held her so she could be closer to Jack's height. The cool spring night burst with the smell of lilacs. Jill paused inhaling slowly. Visible in the outside lighting, the reconverted barn was surrounded in lilac bushes.

"Jack, I love lilacs. They are my favorite. Sometimes I think I would like to follow spring and go wherever the lilacs are blooming instead of the two or three weeks they give us in Indiana."

"I made a lucky guess. You look like a lilac kind of girl, sorry, woman. But if you smelled them for months, they wouldn't be so special."

The heavy dark wood tables were covered in red-checked cloths. There were mock candles in holders attached to the rough hewn walls and in the large wagon wheel chandeliers that hung from the high barn ceiling. The ceiling was dark, but the outlines of beams and ropes used to pull bales of hay and straw up to the loft were visible. As Jack held her chair at the small table for two, he spoke, "I grew up hating lilacs, but as my distance from the farm increased, I began to appreciate them. They remind me of hard work, lots of it at the...well, at a place just like this." He stopped and waved his arm at the beams and lofts. "We always had to plant when the lilacs bloomed. My father ruled by the strap, so we were up and at 'em with the crack of dawn, and the crack of his belt against our bedroom door."

"You didn't want to be a farmer?"

"No, not really. I think Hawk, my father, gave me the cure. But I have two brothers who still work the property." Jack told of his father and brothers. He was the oldest of stair-steps, Robert-forty-one, Beau-forty, and Charles-thirty-nine, whom they called "Chick." Hawk left the family when Jack turned twenty-one. The stair-step brothers were mostly grown. They worked with Hawk before school, after school and all vacations. Hawk trained them in all the parts of running the big place.

Early on Hawk recognized Jack's "knack for numbers" as he called it. Hawk made Jack detassel corn and slop hogs, but taught him the accounting aspect of running the farm business. All the boys were forced to do the chores. Hawk watched the Chicago Board of Trade to determine his storage times on the corn, and the Chicago Mercantile Exchange to keep track of the ever-changing pork bellies. Jack said he only now appreciated Hawk's advanced thinking about the business part of farming. Robert had become the chief operating officer. He tracked the fluctuations and tried to make the highest profit for the other brothers. Beau had become the farmer in charge of actual plowing and planting. When Beau talked of plowing, the tractor, the land, the absolute parallel symmetrical rows, he became a boy in love. Spring was the awakening.

"And Jill if you think you love lilacs, wait until you meet Beau." Jack described Beau as the big and brawny type. He birthed the calves and bottle fed the sow's runt. Then he told of Chick, who hated the farm and everything about it. He rebelled as a kid, but when Hawk left, he sulked and dropped out of school. Chick had never participated in the Future Farmers of America or grown a hog for 4-H. He craved women, many women. "Occasionally," Jack said, "he'll still call the house and ask if some woman called and left a message for him."

"You don't see him?"

"He seems to have made the road his home. He'll call and say he has found the right woman and he's living in Des Moines or some place. Then we don't hear anything for a long time. He seems to walk to the same beat as my father, a wandering hobo existence. We are never sure where either of them lives. After Chick and Hawk left, Mom...she just fell apart. Chick was her baby. I realize now that as Hawk pulled away from her, she clung to Chick. The rest of us considered him a mama's boy, totally irresponsible, but when he left shortly after Hawk...it was as if those two were her life and nothing..." Jack shook his head, "Poor May Rose, she didn't know what to do without her Chick and Hawk. Yes, when I say it, it sounds funny, birds leaving the nest, but Mom's heart was broken, so we never mentioned it in that way. Enough of my family."

"Well, not exactly, Jack. What about you?"

Jack sat back in his chair and grinned, then spoke, "Why am I forty-two and single? Have I ever been married? Children? Are those your questions? They are the ones most frequently asked. Even Margie Merriweather wanted to know how I'd escaped the 'institution of *holy* matrimony.'"

Jill laughed at the thought of Margie making the sarcastic remark, then she said, "Okay, Mr. Jones, I give."

"I came close a few times, but I know close only counts in horseshoes, which I can play." He stopped talking and looked down at the table, "I cared for... I tried to consider marriage, but in some ways...I am too easy, too predictable, boring perhaps. And I love my work. I rarely just work forty hours a week, I do research on the weekends and go in early and stay late. Maybe they are related, no wife, no children, so I stay at work." He shrugged his shoulders. "I do like Johnson Electronics, they let me stretch my wings; it is very satisfying." He looked directly at her, "These few weeks have been a highlight. I've started thinking about children again...How old are you?"

"I remind you of a child or child-bearer? Twenty-two as of last Monday."

"Neither, a young pretty woman is what keeps coming to mind as I sit here and watch you speak. Watching you in the classroom, you interacted with the students so effortlessly. I hope your supervising professor noticed."

"Thank you. I have surprised myself, not really knowing if I could go from student to teacher or if I would like changing roles."

"And Happy belated birthday! Next year I will try to do better."

"Next year? Keep your address book open, I may be in Boston."

He smiled and winked, "One never knows what life has in store, does one?"

"No, one does not." Her mouth tightened as she looked down and finger-folded the checkered table cloth.

"Please, Jill, the story. Your expression has taken me someplace, a place with a touch of sadness. I saw it when we were at the Italian Gondola and when the students were giving speeches, the one about Peleliu."

As they ate homemade bean soup and cornbread, she started her story, parts of her story. He did not need to know, or she did not want to tell it. She chose a condensed version, "I made a choice to keep my baby and be the best mother I could be. I accepted the fact that I would never see her father again, but I wanted my baby regardless. My father is always telling me I make decisions with no consideration of the consequences because I have access to the 'mother lode,' his bank account."

Jack laughed, "Your father sounds like an uncommon kind of man." Jack paused, "Is he hard on the men you bring home? I mean that you've dated?"

The men I have dated? Dated? William, not exactly dating, a fling, a response to being dropped? And for the last nine months, no one. Hector's presence, an over-hanging shadow, even a mention of his name, Hector, Dr. Andujar. She shook her head. "My father talks like he will sell me to any available bidder, but your handshake with him tonight was favorable for an initial meeting. With Henry Havlicek, believe me, he sized you up, and I'll get a full report when you take me home."

Jack chuckled, and reached across the small table to touch Jill's hand, "What was the last bid?"

"I'm not sure, he didn't... well, the plan...not completed." She shook her head.

"Your hesitancy...I will not press. It just seems so painful when I watch your face. What about you, though, 'favorable' for a first date?"

Jill pulled her hand away. Jack sat forward watching, smiling. "Candlelight makes your face glow. Told that before once or twice?"

"It's dark. And yes, once or twice. I think I need to walk around holding a candle. It has fooled many a man. I bury them all under a mountain of wax."

"Lesson learned, no candle-lit dinners. However, let me say you also look radiant in the sunlit classroom."

"Thank you. But enough. I'm not competing for Miss America, here. Eat your pork chops."

"I would like to propose a toast. Pick up your iced tea."

Jill picked up her glass. Jack continued, "To many more pork chop dinners with Henry Havlicek's amazing and saucy daughter."

She shook her head, but touched the lip of his glass. "Emphasis on the saucy, please."

Jack asked for details of her future plans upon graduation. When the waitress brought the apple pie and coffee, Jill explained Boston and Henry's promise for a trip to Germany.

"You've mentioned Boston a couple of times," Jack asked, "Why so far from home?"

"You sound like my father. But for exactly that reason. I want to be as far as I can go from Caylor and these damned cornfields. I am more than ready to try life in the city."

"You're determined? Nothing can change your mind?"

"I may not stay, but I'm determined to go. I want to take care of myself without my father 'bailing me out' as he often reminds me."

"When will you leave?"

"Next month if my roommate Bobbie makes the arrangements."

"Arrangements?"

"She has a place for me to stay, a friend of hers, well, the friend's parents."

"This does not sound like a stable arrangement for your daughter; I mean I think your daughter needs a home, a father."

Jill stopped stirring her coffee and stared at him.

"It sounds like," he continued, "you need to be more organized for this move to a big city."

"Thank you for that, Mr. Jones, but organization is not something I do."

"Jack, please, not Mr. Jones. I'm sorry. It is something I do very well and I always think in those terms. However, the sweep of anger across your face is very attractive. May I kiss you?"

44

Jill wiped her mouth with the napkin, threw it on her plate and stood up, "Let's go now."

Jack followed her out of the restaurant and to the car. He leaned in front of her, placing his hand on the handle of the car. Jill turned to face him with her back to the door, preventing him from opening it. She put her arms around his neck and kissed him. "Jack Jones, you may kiss me, but I prefer spontaneous. Spontaneity is something I do very well."

"Jill, will you marry me?"

"You just said that to practice spontaneity?"

"No, I'm serious. I want you to be my wife."

"Jack, pain on my face, you asked…nine months ago my fiancé was killed in Viet Nam. I do not want to talk about Viet Nam or marriage. Not tonight. Not…until…I don't know when. I don't know you and you don't know me which is even more difficult to explain."

"I think you just did. Timing, I understand completely. I'm a simple person, basic, ordinary engineer, and former farm boy from Swayzee, Indiana. And my proposal still stands."

"The answer is no, now take me home."

Chapter 3

The air was thick, thick as the red mud that covered everything, sucking up each footprint. The boots are ready, good for the gook. A steam bath without the Turkish towel, ah, to be in Adana, the massage on the cold ceramic tile steps and the option to leave when it's over. The big bird to Paradise. Rotate in. Into a fucking hell, the goddamned jungles of Southeast Asia. Impossible mission, no asinine, didn't I write that on the first goddamned intelligence report? Intelligence? And now I'll write it again and they keep sending them, troop deployment, in-country.

The letters, finally mail, a million miles from reality, thirty-six hours by air, well thirty-six by Air Force first class, but the mail, pony express – let's see postmark dates, three weeks, two weeks, damn, Uncle Sam. At least it's hand delivered into the officer's hooch, ah, it's great being an officer – personal mail delivery, personal small hooch, personal gook to shine my boots, personal whore at the Hung Dao Hotel. Six months of hell, one day left and let's hope the Soviets go on a tear and keep the sky busy. Yes, sir, six months TDY in the jungles of Indochina, coordinates: 12 degrees, 5 minutes north; 109 degrees, 17 minutes east; 10 degrees, 59 minutes north; 106 degrees, 49 minutes east. 100° Fahrenheit, 56° Celsius with humidity. Sembach here I come. Goodbye greenhouse.

He sorted through the letters, and then smiled as he recognized the handwriting before he saw the return address. Four weeks, goddamned four weeks, Uncle Sam, I am still in your goddamned Air Force. My taboo girl, what a pleasant surprise. Damn. She caught up with me. Her name is still Havlicek, now there is a story. He closed his eyes and smelled the envelope.

"Where can we go? You have no home. I have a baby, she needs to be safe not on some military base."

I asked her in the letters, Love? I asked her, Marriage? She looked with those dark mahogany maroon...intense...questioning innocent...young eyes. What did I mean? I explained the Communist scare showed her the articles in the *New York Times*, yeah we drank coffee in the kitchen, her blue and white checked kitchen, but she asked. I couldn't be honest, well, honest about feelings, no, not Uncle Sam's spy. I was honest about my job.

"I don't want to sit and worry if you're coming back; if we're going to be blown to smithereens."

Yes, goddamned smithereens. She was right. How many gone to where? Smithereens, taboo girl. To be swallowed up in this giant Venus-flytrap.

"And if not the military base, then I'm an Air Force widow, waiting for your twenty-four hour leaves, and hoping you'll call or get a hop that comes close."

She had sounded like all of them, well, some of them, the honest ones, the others didn't speak much English, Pidgin English, "fuckee, fuckee" or some version of that theme. The soldier's life is hell, surely one of those goddamned generals said that somewhere. Hell – a jungle strip 14° latitude, 107° longitude and all variants in between. In the great quadrant book in the sky, this was the intersection they showed to Michael the archangel; these would be his coordinates. Dante emblazoned the marquee, "Abandon all hope all ye who enter here."

I belong up, up in the bird. Give me an A12 and nothing but sky. Grunt work? No, the old man wants everyone to take six months, rotate in and rotate out. "Read the pictures, Colonel Cunningham, listen to the tapes. The young fellas, they need you." Yes, sir. "You're the best we have, Cunningham. You've been looking at the jungle for three years, you know the terrain, you've listened to them speak all that gibberish." Fuck the jungle. Fuck the Chinese. Give them the goddamned place. The jungle will eat them, Venus-flytrap them to death. Leeches, mosquitoes, maggots, red mud – swallowed whole in a flash. Rotted, eaten in the goddamned jungle, the flytrap.

Let's see what she has...all those red curls, wonderful strawberry-blonde curls covering that soft...god, where did she learn it? The Puerto Rican? Goddamned Puerto Rican kid. But the name, Havlicek, still like always, an enigma – keeps the ticker...always one, just that one. Three years ago and it's like yesterday all white and pink, and the incredible softness, like a baby's ass, but lithe, lithesome, supple, writhing, writhe, wrap. Yeah, wrap, she did that, god did she wrap. Around my waist, those legs, gripping muscles in those legs, around...she locked it in. Locked my face, like some bucking bull, too much strength. Damn she needed to be tamed. The sweat, running down that face from the red gold mane. Where did all that rage, wild mustang, wild out of control come from? Was it the big pay back to the kid who dumped her? No, more than that, way more. She had a taste, then a hunger, ah, my taboo girl, like some starving emaciated refugee, then the goddamned Soviets want to send some troops, "troop deployment, Cunningham. They're putting you up, Incirlik." And what did you really want? What were you saying to the flyboy? Icarus? You wanted to melt the wings?

Let's get some Chivas, Chivas to toast the ...the stallion, you were a stallion Jill Havlicek, a goddamned stallion begging to...okay a mare, wet, so wet, waiting, wanting to be taken. Chivas.

He took his dented metal canteen cup and shook it upside down. Using a camouflage handkerchief to wipe it out, he poured the scotch, then swallowed half of the full cup. He refilled it, and rewound the cap on the fifth. Another drink. He put the empty cup on a small metal trunk. Whew! Chivas.

Okay, taboo girl, you hadn't ever done it before, never ridden a man's face, but you knew.

He picked up the envelope.

Let's do this.

April 30, 1964
Dear William,

48

Please read this letter. I know you may want to throw it away, perhaps you've thrown me away – the book of the dead –as you called the women who passed through your life. "No going back." I remember the phrases and they've kept me from writing for the last nine months, but today I said hell with it. I'll be twenty-two in a couple of weeks, free (thanks to you guarding the skies), graduated from college and lost.

Lost! Has she really figured out how to be honest on the page? He reached for the fifth, when a young man in fatigues and shaved head peeked into the untied tent flap, "Sir, excuse me. Colonel Killingbeck needs you at Recon, HDQ. He said he knows you're just off twelve, but wants you to see the photos they just brought. 'Come as you are,' sir, he said."

"Ah, Cunningham. Thanks for coming over. We need the expert's opinion…"

William saluted the older man who was a head shorter, thinner with gray and blonde cropped hair. Killingbeck was tanned and his face lined. He gave a half-smile while returning William's salute. He wore a short-sleeved blue shirt, open at the collar; the three rows of multi-colored grosgrain ribboned-bars decorated his breast. He was humble, an admirable quality, William concluded. He made the last sixty days sufferable.

"Yes, sir," William answered, "The expert will be here exactly twenty-four more hours…"

"I know, that is why it's even more important….Would you like some scotch? I got some JB on the last supply train."

"Sure, scotch is the only thing that makes any sense out here."

William looked over the blurred black and white aerial photos, using his finger to point on the map. He held the metal cup in his other hand. "Sir, what do you want to know? What is going on in this picture? …The bridges? Here, here, here," William pointed to a section that resembled a Rorschach inkblot test, "no one can hit them because the SAM's are right under here, here and here."

"But they will be sending the B-52's in there, where? Where should they start?"

"It doesn't matter, sir. You're fighting a battle with a woman and if you know anything about women you can never win. It is aggravating; many men come out swinging, as if smacking the bitch will solve the problem, sorry sir, I had a drink or two before, before this one..."

"No, go on Cunningham, I'm interested in this battle with a woman."

"Some of us join the service to avoid the fight....Sir, these are ramblings...this Recon man had...some scotch..."

"The woman?"

"Mother Nature. She has chosen this spot to cover in green. The French fought it and fought it, then Dien Bien Phu. In the end she's going to win this one, sir. Does the phrase sweeping back the ocean have any meaning for you? You could clear cut, start at the tip and work your way up, but the Mekong, you can't dam the river, the water, Mother Nature – she controls the goddamn place. The only option – the central supply route – Laos, Cambodia, when you can and if you can. Stripped. No noise. No knowledge, the Special Forces. Otherwise, the people receive the supplies and they have lived here, hidden in her skirt, to continue the analogy, for thousands of years. They are a part of the land, no different than the trees." He pointed at one of the photos, a darkened spot, slightly different from the brushed shades of gray, "Here, sir. The UTM from Mercator projection, then start here."

The colonel shook his head, "Yeah, that's why I called you. You pick fly shit from pepper better than any of them. I'm recommending you for the next step. I appreciate your work. You came highly recommended by the folks at Offutt. They'll be waiting in the basement to hear what you have to say, but are they giving you some R&R first?"

Lite Colonel to Colonel Cunningham. Yeah, it's time, past time, there ought to be a bump up for this goddamned duty assignment. "Yes, sir," William answered, "about eight stops between here and another little black speck on the map - Elliston, Indiana, 39 degrees and 10 minutes north; 86 degrees and 32 minutes west. My daughter will be graduated from college at 1000 hours, 5 June."

"Congratulations to her and you, another job well done. I'm sure it will be worth the next forty-eight hours of Air Force first-class travel."

"Yes sir, every hour," William said.

"I'll miss you, Colonel. I'll try to get the bump up by the time you're back in the saddle, thirty days."

William saluted, "Thank you, sir," then shook the colonel's hand. The airman saluted as William left the Quonset hut.

ɤξɤ

The heavy military tanker plane lumbered onto the taxi runway at Tan Son Nhut. William looked at his watch, forty-minutes; it must be time to take to the air. The plane squeezed in behind a Pan American jet and a "skyrider" laden with napalm. Thank you God. I am leaving this goddamned fucking jungle.

"Sir," a young man with camouflage shirt and pants, bent over addressing William above the loud engine noise in the limited travel compartment, "You're set? We should be airborne in five minutes approximate; the captain wanted me to ask if there was anything you needed before takeoff. Air traffic is unstable."

"Yes, Airman Rodgers. I have flown in and out of Tan Son Nhut too many times."

The young man smiled at the colonel. The young men, always sacrificing the youth. Their whole life...well, we all had a turn, I just stayed....

"If you need anything, sir," the airman spoke.

"Thank you, I know my way around the bird. Air Force first-class has been my choice for many years now."

"Yes, sir. I understand, Colonel Cunningham."

William fastened the belts that criss-crossed his chest and lap and made him a part of the hard fold down seat. The jet engine, thrusters, each reverberated, not the acoustics of Pan Am, but from San Francisco to Indianapolis -TWA. Next stop Guam. He adjusted the ear muffs to fit, placed them over his ears to mute the excessive din of the cargo hold. He leaned back, resisting the forward motion of sitting backwards during the take-off of the C-130. He closed his eyes and pictured the diagonal view of vertical stripes, green jungle, blue ocean, and lavender gray sky. The wheels locked into the belly. The

51

jet leveled off, and the airman returned with a Thermos lid of coffee. "Compliments of the navigator, sir," the airman mouthed the words and pointed toward the cockpit. William nodded. He sipped as he unbuttoned his shirt pocket and removed the folded envelope.

> *I assume Mo tells you of my life. She is a nosey best friend. Since she moved to the AKA House, we don't talk so often. I know where you are and have known, but obviously wasn't ready to make that connection. As you can see, I've read, reread the letter a few times. Mo winked when she told me that you were going to be able to attend graduation. Thank God you can leave Viet Nam. I think of that place and remember looking down a well shaft and seeing nothing, the great abyss. Nothing.*
>
> *I no longer live in Elliston, and have plans for leaving Caylor as soon as I finish student teaching. Bobbie's friend (a friend of a friend) has offered a place to stay in Boston until I get a job. I think it is time to really make the break from Caylor, the one I've been talking about for four years.*
>
> *I want to see you when you come to Elliston. Do you have enough time? Will it be possible with Elke? I'll be waiting to hear from you. CAN DO, Major, or should I say, can do?*
>
>

Always,
Jill

Well, taboo girl, you've been more honest than I was. I apologize for that, but honesty? Sometimes it must be sacrificed at the altar of prudence.

Honest? Can a Recon man be honest? And with whom? How many years have I done the tell-them-only-what-they-have-to-know. FYI? NTK? Eyes Only. The goddamn training, never talk to anyone, not your wife, not anyone. Twenty-four years in the uncle's service and each person only gets to hear one piece. Listen, watch, decide. And no one to talk to, only the vertical stripes – green earth, blue ocean, gray sky. Can't talk to yourself, someone might be listening. Can't talk to the whore, she might be a spy.

Elke, wife, mother of my children, but you were denied the flyboy. What kind of woman were you? Pretty, all I know is pretty. What did you think? At least she left the craziness. We were young, each with our own idea of the way life ought to be, but never honest. Always in some deceptive play. We never used the same UTM coordinates. You had two children. We had two children, made two children. Separate people making children.

Children? Christian starts high school and Madeline is finished, almost married, getting ready to take on the world, no, correction she came out taking on the world. What are you saying flyboy, is it enough? General Smith said it, said it at that graduation in Colorado; eight years ago, to that bunch of Academy grads. I tried to teach them the finer points of Recon, but he told them, "There is a wild blue yonder out there, fellas, but there'll come a time when the sky becomes your prison. It sneaks up on you. You become a contradiction, fighting for freedom, but not free yourselves. When it comes, and as sure as I'm standing here, it will come; get out of the cockpit, put the wings in the hangar. Know when to put the wings in the hangar."

Put the wings in the hangar? What do you do with the love of speed? Mach I? Mach II? Just you and the bird; the jet kicking your ass. Know when. The Greeks said it…Know Thyself.

"Sir," Airman Rodgers tapped his shoulder. He pointed at his watch and spoke with a unique Air Force version of "signing," indicating arrival at Guam in fifteen minutes.

William nodded, then put the letter back into his pocket.

ϫξϫ

Jill stirred the pudding "slowly" as per Lillian, to make sure there were no lumps and it did not stick. Luisa sat at Lillian's kitchen table, eating graham cracker sandwiches, the brown squares filled with powdered sugar frosting.

"Mommy, these are yummy. May I have one more please? Just one?" Luisa opened her eyes wide, sucking on her index finger.

"Who taught you that word, yummy?"

"At Sunday School, Kim said it when they gave us our cookies."

"Okay, but no more even if they are yummy. We're eating dinner soon and Grandma would say 'you'll ruin your appetite.' And she's right, one is enough."

Jill heard footsteps on the porch, then the knock. Luisa jumped off the chair.

"Go see who it is, Lo, and tell them just a minute."

Jill lifted the spoon. Thick. She removed the pan from the burner and wiped her hands on her apron. Four P.M. who would? She walked through the kitchen door, "Mommy," Luisa said, "It's a man for Jill Havlicek."

On the other side of the screen door stood a short young man with chubby cheeks. He wore a brown work shirt with the Western Union emblem on the pocket. He smiled.

"Jill Havlicek?" he asked.

"Yes?"

"I need you to sign for this telegram."

Jill opened the screen door and stepped out onto the front porch.

"Here, ma'am, right here on this line. Is she your daughter?"

"Uh-hmm," Jill answered writing.

"She looks like an angel, sweet little girl," he said, handing Jill the yellow envelope.

"Thank you," Jill said as she walked back into the house. She ripped open the envelope.

GUAM. ANDERSON AIR FORCE BASE
3 JUNE 1964
2200 HOURS

Today. Today at 10P.M. Today at 10P.M.? Oh, yeah the international dateline, two days in a row.

TABOO GIRL – CAN DO. 5 JUNE. WILLIAM.

ᴦξᴦ

Jill cut Luisa's toasted cheese sandwich into quarters. She cut the candied dill pickle strip in half, then poured a glass of milk.

"Mommy, please can I have chocolate?"

"May I have chocolate?"

"Yes, mommy, may I have chocolate?"

Jill opened the cupboard, then removed the square box of Nestlé's Quick. She stirred two spoonfuls of the brown powder in the glass. The phone rang. "Lo, say, 'Hello.'" Luisa excitedly slid from under Jill's arm and ran to the phone on the counter. She picked up the receiver and holding it carefully with both hands said, "Mommy, it's for you."

Jill set the small china sandwich plate on the placemat. Lillian's house had everything. Could she live here again after four years away? Day after tomorrow, graduation, two more days, she needed to decide what she was going to do. And where would William be? At the house for the party? Or at the graduation tents with the degrees? Mo would be at the journalism...oh, god, William. She picked up the phone and motioned for Luisa to sit down and eat her lunch.

She held the phone to her ear, but spoke to Luisa, "You can't go out to play unless you eat all of the sandwich." Luisa scowled as she took her first bite.

"Hello, I'm sorry..."

"Jill?"

"William?! It's you, oh my god, think of the devil. Where are you?"

ϒξϒ

The drive to Indianapolis had gone, where had it gone? She turned west on 100 to the airport. He had arrived from San Francisco and slept fourteen hours, "to make up, to catch up, to forget." His worst TDY. They would talk when she got there, could she get there? How soon could she get to his hotel?

She had explained to Lillian and Henry she was leaving a day early, actually an evening early, to celebrate with the girls before the parents came, one last time. "Sure," Henry had said, "enjoy your friends. We'll see you after it's over, at the Education tent, light blue banner, by the football field." She would get ready at 1254 Butler. Her robe now danced and swished in the plastic garment bag as the wind blew through the car. William. They would have "dinner, a drink, dance, just come ASAP."

She parked, then straightened her robe on the back seat. It seemed unreal that in twenty-four hours, a degree from State University. B.S., Education. "Off the lobby is a small lounge," he had directed her, "I'll be holding up one corner of the bar."

She pulled down the tight skirt of the lavender sleeveless dress, then combed her hair looking in the narrow rearview mirror. The straightened hair made her look older. She had tried for the last eight weeks to look as old as possible. Mrs. Merriweather had hugged her and told her to stay in touch, "You need a reference, I'll give you one. You can add it to the letter I submitted to the University Placement Office."

A little frosty mauve lipstick and ready to meet the major, deep sigh, and…here I go.

Coming from the bright afternoon sun, she was temporarily blinded as she opened the door to the dark bar. The jukebox was playing, "Heart and soul, I fell in love with you…" William stood from his barstool, and then walked to the door. He wore a light blue shirt and dark blue tie and pants and the opened jacket of Air Force day dress. "Always easier to travel in America as a military person," he'd said when he dressed to leave for the airport from 1254 Butler. Three years ago. So much has happened.

His short cropped hair and broad smile, the bow-shaped lips and white teeth, he looked exactly the same.

"Hi, my taboo girl. You look terrific. Come let's sit in the dark corner; I'm not sure how they will react to our version of race mixing. Perhaps after another Chivas, I won't care. Your hair…straight? You've found our secret."

He walked upright, the military stance; she had forgotten the confidence. "William, you didn't toss me out with yesterday's trash. I thought no going back…." He held her chair.

The twenty-something, dark-haired waitress wore a very short skirt, with a black and white checked apron. Setting a basket of popcorn on the table, she asked, "What can I get for you?"

William ordered Chivas on the rocks and Jill a Bloody Mary. William waited until the waitress was away from the table, then leaned forward and stared at her. What did he see? Slowly, he spoke, "Only when you've been. Six steamy days in July was a beginning, the appetizer…" he picked up a piece of popcorn twisting it in his fingers before eating it. He continued, "The appetizer."

He reached into the bowl and she touched his long fingers, rubbing the back of his knuckle, she smiled, "And when we get to dessert, you'll tell me?"

He chuckled, the pleasant low cadence. Once again it gave her a reaffirming sense of approval. They sat at a small round table. Her eyes adjusted, and she saw the pictures of Indy 500 cars that decorated all the walls. The pictures were old race cars and their winning drivers. In the dimness she was unable, to see J.C Agajanian, her favorite. The paper cocktail napkins the waitress put under the drinks were the black and white checkerboard pattern of the race flags.

William reached into his shirt pocket and pulled out a small silk brocade pouch. "Here, your graduation present. Congratulations. I'm proud of you and Madeline. After the first semester, I wasn't sure you two would be able to reconcile your personal fire engines and the rather restrictive confines of the State engine house. Open it." He handed her the 2" x 2" miniature purse. She unsnapped it, then removed a twenty-four karat gold chain, long bar links with a small pear-shaped emerald which hung from a lyre shaped clasp.

"William, it is unusual and elegant, soft gold and an emerald…"

"I know, your birthstone. Put it on." He paused, leaned over and kissed her, "I want to see it on your bare chest," he whispered.

"Here," she handed it to him, "show me how to do this." He carefully unbent the clasp, then put the chain around her neck. "Thank you," she said, fingering the stone and chain.

"I want to hold you. Let's dance," he said, reaching for her hand. Dionne Warwick was singing, "Don't make me over, now that I've done everything for you…." His chest pressed against her and she smelled his aftershave, a clean fresh scent. She inhaled, resting her head against his shoulder. He held her closer, nudging her legs apart to accommodate the slow rub of thigh to groin.

"William, thank you. I needed to see you…needed to talk to you. It's been such a painful year."

"Nam," he whispered, his body gripped her tighter like potent adhesive, "I've been. I've never seen anything like what is going on over there. Thank god for those who make it out of that hell, perhaps death may be an equal option."

Jill stopped on the dance floor. He squeezed her; he kissed the sensitive skin in front of her ear at the hairline. He nuzzled like a horse seeking a sugar cube, then whispered, "If we stay in this public place, I might be court-martialed for conduct unbecoming an officer and a gentleman."

᛭ξ᛭

The heavy hotel curtains were open; the gauzy liner floated back and forth against the screen sliding door. The room's patio faced west and the evening sun cast a peach glow to the beige and brown room.

"There is nothing so ravishing," he spoke, "as an American woman–fleshy, big legs, full breasts. I want to undress you, each piece just to touch your shoulders, back, ass."

He unzipped her back zipper starting at her neck and going down to her butt. The lace collar had one small hook, she had not fastened. He pushed the sleeveless bodice down to her waist, brushing each of her shoulders with his mouth, then tracing her neck and spine with his tongue. She shivered reflexively at his kiss on the nape of her neck. He pulled each of her arms from the dress. She tried to relax. He carefully laid the dress on the back of the creamy overstuffed chair. He unhooked her white lace bra, gingerly touching each of her breasts. Her nipples became erect in his fingertips. He placed the bra on the arm of the chair then sat down, took her sandals off and kissed her toes, sucking on each. He stood and laid her back on the bedspread slowly pulling her lace panties off and tossed them toward the chair.

"William, it's been a long time...."

"How long, taboo girl?" he asked as he unbuckled his web belt, and unzipped his pants.

"A year and a half..."

"Too long. We'll take care of it..." He reached into his pocket as he took his pants off, removing a condom.

"William..."

"Yes?" She grabbed the small package and put it on the end table, then whispered, "I take birth control pills."

"Perfect," he whispered, lying on top of her, kissing her. He pressed his smooth chest against her, wedging his naked body between her legs. She wrapped her legs around his legs. They sweat in the heat of the friction. She saw their bodies reflected in the mirrored

58

doors of the closet. Her legs paled against his dark skin, her bikini lines were white; the small triangle patches that had covered her breasts were now easily seen. She looked at the mirror, then his face with the whiskers shadowing his beard, but not felt. She gently bit his shoulder. Her cheeks and arms were white patches against his black. Could they be their own checkerboard pattern?

He pushed her up to the headboard, making her sit with her legs apart.

"Goddamn, I've missed this. A clean sweet tasting, healthy American woman, built to satisfy my size. I want you to watch…"

His hands squeezed her tummy, smiling at her with each tweak. He grasped and clamped her thighs, holding flesh in big gentle pinches. He massaged her as a sculptor with his own block of clay, gently forming, stimulating with each touch, then kissed her navel and the inside of her thighs. He spread her legs, putting his head between them. She wanted to scissor lock his head, but he gripped her thighs tightly, keeping them open. She grasped both sides of his face. She came, holding her breath, then whispering, "William," as she exhaled. He rolled over on his back, grabbed her hand, pulling her on top of him, "Come on my wild mustang, do your fucking. Make me tired."

ᴙξᴙ

The pre-dawn dew hung in the air. A few birds had begun their sunrise wake-up call. The eastern horizon was barely lighter than the darker expanse of sky. Standing next to the VW, William pointed to the movement of the navigation stars with one arm around her neck and the other pointing to the sea captain's coordinates.

"But William, far easier for them to sleep an hour and know exactly where East is."

He chuckled, then wrapped both arms around her and hugged her tightly, "Are you sure we can't try this…" he paused, kissing her while sliding his hand over her breast and down to her crotch. She mumbled an objection, his thick lips pressed against her mouth.

Last night had melted into this early morning. They had had room service; showered; made love. They had been to clubs, only one she could remember the name, "The 19th Hole," and the last one an after-hours "joint" where they had listened to a local guitarist named Wes Montgomery. They drank Canadian Club from a brown paper sack; the ice and glasses were provided for a couple of dollars. She had been the only white person in all the clubs. At 3:30A.M. they stopped for White Castles, a baker's dozen and French fries, then back to the hotel. She brought in her under-the-graduation-robe-outfit – shorts and sleeveless scooped neck t-shirt. After they made love and showered, she had thumbed through his well-ordered suitcase and "stolen" one of his large camouflage t-shirts.

They now stood by Imogene, trusty Imogene.

"Why don't you buy a new Imogene while you're in Germany and ship it back? People do it all the time. You'll be able to drive all over Europe." He'd drawn a map showing the proximity of Sembach Air Base at Kaiserslautern to Wiesbaden where Sadie and Michael were. He had Sadie's number and address.

Indiana's dawn moisture embraced them as they hugged each other.

"William, we'll see each other, we'll see all of us in…"

"Eight hours–1200 hours, cake sandwiches, ice cream, Mrs. Brenton and the infamous Mr. Havlicek. Ah, Mr. Havlicek, you have a lovely daughter…May I kidnap her and take her away from Indiana in my duffle bag?"

"Okay, okay," Jill said.

"Maybe we could…once more for old time's sake at 1254…"

"No."

"Will you introduce me as Bob Smith?"

She pinched him and jumped in the VW. "Thanks for everything, Colonel; I needed all of it, including the box of Kleenex. Viet Nam… I don't like it, but I must accept it."

"Taboo girl, life is loaded with garbage; we learn to sort through it and take what we can use. Key… use it."

She drove away and played back their conversation, the pieces of his life she had not known well; some were things Mo had talked about sketchily. Of Christian, his only son, starting a private high school, the Blue Ridge School in Dyke, Virginia; of Elke's marriage to a New York attorney who was building them a home in one of the Hamptons on Long Island; of placing his mother into a full-time nursing home. Who he was…."Why," she had asked, "are you telling me?"

"Because of the murderous insanity in the world I left. No one knows how I feel. Life and the finiteness of my own were so clearly reinforced, and my credibility is minimal. You see me as a rogue philanderer; 'whore-monger' was one of Elke's favorites that worked. She was right, but seeing, touching, smelling the war, these last six months; I had no frame of reference, no comparable pain to secure a beginning point. I've spent all my time flying over, or briefing the 'stars' five stories below, reading charts, maps, transcripts. But this time, I was on the ground and living at the gateway for the young boys, eighteen and nineteen, scrubbed, barely shaving, too young to vote, sent into the black mulch of jungle firefights, but coming out in bags. Bags, body bags stacked and waiting to be shipped. Nothing prepared me for the madness of their no longer youthful eyes. Old now, the shock stripped them of their innocence.

"Maybe I am becoming an old man, maybe wiser. Use it. Who I am has no significance if no one knows. You look as if I'm a stranger to you. I sometimes feel like a stranger to myself. Let me meet the taboo girl and fuck her to death, but it's not that. And then what is it?....Yes, I want to try honesty this time. You said 'lost' in your letter, I understand lost. The equation implies that found is demanded, actually, the yin-yang of interaction. Can you and I be lost and found? Can your lost be my found and vice-versa? Can we do this? Do we want to do this? I'm talking to people at the Pentagon, a briefing and…I wanted to talk to you first. What happened between us three years ago, I dismissed it. You made a choice; you acknowledged love for the Puerto Rican kid. I lost. Was I lost? No. The military has me scheduled for all the years I want to be scheduled. But I didn't get to complete what was started, barely begun, and frustrating in this symmetrical way, Karma, the Asian explanation for the effectuation."

She drove and planned the itinerary for the day, the month. She confirmed an interview with Southeastern, a promise to Henry for a paid trip to Germany. Jack, oh god, what? She had told him about the interview and he said, "Exactly what you need. Your roots are in Indiana. You'll see."

Mr. Sartoris, such a nice man and spoke highly of his friend Dr. Reader, "Any student, promising teacher, Vern Reader recommends, I take seriously." He scheduled her for Tuesday June ninth. Her flight to New York left Friday the twelfth. She would be in Bonn early on the thirteenth. Sadie would pick her up. If Mr.Sartoris said yes…she shook her head. Why Luis? Why does it feel like you're manipulating my strings? "Learn Spanish and teach the children."

1254 Butler. It looked dark. The sun shone brightly on the kitchen window. She grabbed the graduation robe and make-up bag. She glanced in the rearview mirror, admiring the emerald and gold chain. The bright green clashed with the camouflage green t-shirt. She walked up the driveway. Bobbie's bicycle was leaning against the porch rail. The side door was open; fans hummed making it cool in the darkened dining room. She opened the door to her bedroom. There were some boxes of books by door; the curtains were open. The early morning stillness, all those mornings with Hector. You died in hell, my love. And I must move on. Yes, William, life is loaded with garbage.

She hung her robe on the closet door then took her make-up bag to the bathroom. In the kitchen, each side of the sink was filled with dishes – clean or dirty? She opened the cupboard where the coffee pot was stored. It seemed unused. She removed the lid. There was a small slip of paper in the strainer, "Wake me up when you get this far. The coffee is fresh. B." Jill chuckled, but finished making the coffee before knocking on Bobbie's door.

They had three hours to clean, set up tables in the back yard, and get ready for the graduation exercise.

"Bobbie, did my parents call?"

"No, why?" Bobbie dried the glasses and set them on the table. They would be packed soon. Elke was bringing paper cups. She had volunteered to furnish the paper products. Mrs. Brenton and Lillian had planned the rest.

"I said I was coming *here* when I left…yesterday."

"Obviously…okay where did you spend the…on the other hand, where did the necklace come from? It's beautiful…"

"I was bad, but it was good…"

"Jill! Who? Where were you?"

"A man I worked with asked me to marry him."

"Jill! Your eyes are lit up, that Hector look of the devil. Tell me."

"I'll let you work on it today. You'll have more clues."

"Khalil and I are getting married and moving to Lebanon. He got a job at American University. My parents….Oh, there will definitely be clues today." Bobbie laughed.

"My Bobbie, always the understated. Congratulations!"

ﻻﻹﻻ

Jill closed the door to her bedroom. She had removed Bobbie's books and set them on the front porch for Mr. Brenton to carry to his truck. The Brenton's brought the cake and sandwiches. Lillian had brewed her thirty cup coffee maker and made fruit punch with oranges and lemons. The party went well, considering all the different parents, hosts and grads. She could hardly wait until the pictures were developed. Mo and Stewart – Mo flashed the diamond engagement ring she had gotten for graduation, "Christmas, Jill, you'll be the maid of honor unless you get married first, then you'll be the matron of honor. And think forest green velvet…"

William had leaned over and whispered, "You'll be a queen, Queen Boudica, the red-headed Celtic Warrior. We'll dance all night, then…" She reflexively slapped his arm.

Stewart had said T.J. had been reclassified to 1A status. He joined the Army, attorneys were exempt from fighting. They were assigned to the Judge Advocate General Corps. Stewart's Foreign Service connection and his father's pull on "certain Congressional Coattails" exempted Stewart.

Luisa wore her white sundress with big bows tied at the shoulders; her dark curls were brushed back and tied with a white satin ribbon. Lillian had laughed telling of Luisa's insistence on a white dress, but Jill knew Luisa demanded and put her hands on her hips, the stance, the narrow brows – Luis, then as quickly the infectious smile, pushing up the rounded cheeks – the cherub. In the white ruffles and ribbon everyone said, "An angel." Luisa helped Lillian stir punch and then fell asleep with her teddy bear in the Buick's back seat.

Mo took a picture of Luisa posed with William; they held Jill's degree held between them. She asked about William's air planes and told William, "Let's go," pulling on his hand to take her. Jill wanted to see the picture of William showing Luisa the mint plants. Then the picture in her mommy's mortar board with the light blue tassel hanging askew. Mrs. Brenton promised to make extra copies to send to Jill. The Brentons seemed sort of pleased when their daughter introduced them to her fiancé. When Bobbie said she was moving to Lebanon, before Mrs. Brenton could react, Henry jumped in, "Oh, yes, my daughter is leaving in two weeks for Germany. It is these kids, today, Mrs. Brenton. They get gypsy blood as soon as they graduate." He smiled and put his arm around her shoulder. She'd let out a sigh, shrugged and took more pictures.

Jill now removed the blue silk tassel with the gold '64 charm attached. She folded the black robe and placed it back in the State University sack. The bedroom door opened.

"Hey, Miss College Graduate," William spoke, walking into the empty room, "I would have given you a degree in carnality three years ago."

"They don't offer that program. But maybe we could work on my masters. You took care of everyone?"

He walked to the windows, then sat down on the windowsill, crossing his ankles and folding his arms. He spoke, shaking his head, "Stewart's U-Haul was loaded, and the trunk of his car, the back seat, the dog shelf. Elke held a box of something on her lap. She's flying to New York, but Madeline and Stewart must drive all the way to Washington loaded down. Stewart should have heeded the warning…"

"Stewart? You should have seen the truck when his parents moved him. Thank god he has money, they'll need a huge house, a couple of pack rats."

He came to where she stood, pulled her to him, hugging her, smashing the robe between them. He kissed her, then said, "Did you find the surprise I left in your purse?"

"The key to your room? I thought you had to catch a flight out this evening…Where are the Brentons?"

"They just pulled away. I decided to extend…Jill, I wanted to stay," he uttered the phrase, in an exhaled breath.

"If you wanted to stay, you wanted to stay. I can meet you, but I will have to leave before the night is over. Is everything in the car?"

"The VW will not hold one more thing. Close your eyes and leave, no keep them open, so you can see how clean the place is. Mr. Brenton said he was stopping to pick up the damage deposit. So that's it. It's over taboo girl. You're leaving your hooch."

"1254 Butler, I've spent…William, have you ever said goodbye to someone and thought this could be the last time I hear their voice, the last time I will ever see them…the *last* time?"

"Yes, too often. In war time…flying. My work defines itself by loss."

Jill shook her head, "I said goodbye to Bobbie…."

He put his index finger to her lips, "One box of Kleenex is enough." He squeezed her tighter in the still room. Silence filled the space, the whirring fans gone. No breeze. No music to remind her of this moment. An empty room, an empty house, the last goodbye to Luisa's first home.

"Who sent the roses?" he said.

She cocked her head, remembering the conversation with Lillian. Right after Jill left, a dozen pink roses had been delivered. Lillian had put them in water, the card said Jack Jones. "You..." she said, pointing an accusatory finger, as she pulled away from him.

He smiled, and then said, "A spy – a listener, an interpreter, a Recon man..."

"A man who wants to marry me, Jack Jones."

"You're taken."

She inched toward the door, slinging her purse over one shoulder, "Taken by whom? As you say, 'I've been.' Are you following me? Or shall I meet you in Indianapolis?"

"Jack Jones? I'll follow you."

She laughed, and then turned back from the door. She walked to where he was, stood on her toes and kissed him. "Colonel Cunningham, it seems with your keen sense you'd notice that Jack Jones was not invited."

He reached around her head, holding her face to his. He kissed her.

"Your father knows I've had my way with you."

She backed away, opening her eyes wide, "That's what you were discussing so intently over coffee?"

"We talked about a lot of things – the war, my children, his daughter," William paused, grinning.

"You told him, 'I had your daughter all night, Mr. Havlicek, the perfect lay?'"

He chuckled. "The perfect lay? Yes, ma'am, those were my exact words."

"So what did he think of you having your way with his princess?"

"He asked a few questions, and then thought about my answers. He likes the money in Virginia, the discipline of the military, believes I am much too old for his princess and the angel, *and* he hates my travel schedule."

"He said that?"

"Ask him, taboo girl. And if I'm right…"

She raised one eyebrow, "And if you're right?"

"You'll spend more days with me in Germany than Sadie."

"You thought the Viet Cong were treacherous? Sadie Fredericks on the warpath? Watch out!"

She tucked the robe and mortar board under her arm and walked into the dining room, nothing and immaculate. Without the curtains the kitchen was bright in the daylight and spotless. She opened the cupboard under the sink. Two empty pickle jars were in the back corner. She removed one, and then rinsed it in the sink. William stood in the doorway watching. Carrying the jar half-filled with water, she walked past him, motioning with her head to follow her down the back stairs.

"Finished?" he asked.

"Yes, let's go." She spoke, heading up the driveway toward the garage. She bent down in the mint patch, yanked three plants with their roots, then stuffed the dirt covered dark green stems into the jar opening. He stood shaking his head, watching her carrying the makeshift vase.

Chapter 4

The passing landscape at 30,000 feet from Indianapolis to New York had consumed the two hour flight. She had changed planes at JFK and now wanted to sit and think of what awaited her as she crossed the Atlantic, her first international travel.

The *Time* magazine she bought with Senator Dirksen on the cover was still in her travel bag tucked under her seat. It looked like something she wanted to read with the cover story about the impending Civil Rights Bill. Reading the latest progress of the legislation seemed imperative as she crossed an ocean to meet a man, Negro, and Sadie who had her own relationship with a man of color. Oh, Sadie, we have so much to discuss. She had also tried to read *Silent Spring*, which she knew was going to be scary because Bobbie had talked about it. All of the reading material, but she really wanted to watch her fellow passengers and the view.

Her seat mate, a business man, kept working with file folders in his briefcase. He pulled one out wrote notes then replaced it. He caught her looking and smiled, then casually said, "I want to talk to you, but give me a minute." She chuckled, his remark sounded as if she were a close friend. She thought him to be in his thirties. His curly blonde hair was long, well, longer than the crew cuts of the most popular style in Caylor. The brown eyes danced and darted, then became sincere as he asked her name. He loosened his navy blue tie that he wore with a white shirt, the initials embroidered on his shirt pocket –JTM.

"Jill Havlicek," she answered.

"How do you do Miss Havlicek? Any relation to John?"

"No." His Texas drawl prompted her to ask, "Your cowboy hat is in the overhead compartment?"

"Aw shucks, ma'am," he mocked, "How'd you know?" He held up a finger, "Please give me one more moment and I'll buy you a drink."

She placed the book in the seat pocket and stared out the window, then pulled down the shade. Night had come early. She left Caylor only a few hours before *in the morning*. She needed a whole day to recover from jet lag. William had taken fourteen hours "to catch up." Sleep one day? Sadie will not let me sleep one moment.

She'd had her interview at Southeastern. Mr. Sartoris, bushy black eyebrows and bald head, had been persuasive. He reviewed her references and talked of his conversation with Dr. Reader. "Yes, Mr. Sartoris, I would love to teach at Southeastern," she heard her words spill out knowing she had done something Henry wanted. Teaching, she sighed, I'm a teacher.

Jack. So old fashioned. He had asked for a second date, "May I take you to the movie and for ice cream?" As they watched, he held her hand. Their date felt like high school. They stopped for hot fudge sundaes at her favorite, The Frozen Custard. Caylor High School students came in, a steady stream from the local popular spot the Seascape public pool. He walked her to the front door and gave her a peck on the cheek, after which she grabbed him and really kissed him. He hesitated when she French kissed him, but he slowly relaxed and squeezed her tightly; then she said something to shock him.

She sat now trying to figure if she said it to entice him or discourage him or to test him. She'd looked him in the eyes, smiled, then said matter-of-factly, "I love hot fudge sundaes, but I love sex more." He looked stunned, and smiled sheepishly. He had cocked his head, she thought he might be waiting for her to say something else, but she turned away from him and darted into the house. He had called her first thing the next morning and thanked her for a "wonderful" date; he told her to have a safe trip, and looked forward to seeing her when she returned.

She lifted the oval shade of the airplane window, total darkness. Shifting in her seat, she pushed the seat button and leaned back. The ride seemed too long when she thought about seeing Sadie, but short when she tried to think about what to do with Jack or William who would be arriving a week from today.

JTM, she now thought, what does that stand for?

"May I buy you a drink?" he closed his briefcase and slid it under the seat in front of him. "I finally got that done. Do you want...well, tell me what you like?"

"I'll have what you have."

"A vodka martini."

The Texan explained he was a salesman, then offered her a business card. "Vice-President, European Sales Division. J.T. "Mac" MacLaughton." He explained that his territory was England and the continent. He prodded her about her plans.

"I'm going to visit my best friend; her husband is in the Army."

She did not mention William and the week she planned to spend at Lake Bodensee. At the reference to the Army, Mac expressed complete support for the American military in Viet Nam. He said it had been very good for business. His company supplied material for war machinery. He had been to Wiesbaden many times.

After the second martini, she said, "I lost my fiancé in Viet Nam."

"You should be proud he served his country." Listening to his pro-war stance he sounded more gung-ho about the military than William ever sounded.

"What a useless war fighting so far from America that has nothing to do with most people *in* America. The civil rights struggle seems more important and should concern everyone."

He responded, "You see we have to eliminate communism wherever we find it. Many of those civil rights groups are run by communists. If we don't stamp it out, it will destroy all of our freedoms."

"But a big group of Americans don't have these freedoms."

"You're talking about that Martin Luther King stuff. But they have the freedom to express their opinions. They march and have sit-ins..."

"And get beat unmercifully. I went to school with..."

A non-hostile argument drinking vodka was challenging. She wanted to lash out at his seeming dismissal of the tragedy unfolding on America's streets. The anger was hard to maintain because he had a deep wholesome laugh an antidote to her anger, disarming the heat, the Grandma Caitlin.

He asked, "Are you married?"

"No, I graduated from State University in Indiana a month ago. I want to see what life is like at twenty-two in Europe with my best friend."

"Could I help you discover Europe? I have my favorite places. Zurich is one. I can be in Wiesbaden in a couple of days. I can make a couple of calls."

"I can't promise..."

"For dinner? For drinks? For peace talks?" then he laughed. Could she record the laugh? And play it back on a sad day.

"I'll see. I must find out what Sadie, my friend has planned."

Before they landed at Heathrow, Mac had elicited a promise to have dinner with him in Bonn. He gave her the number of the field office in Frankfurt, Germany. She could call and leave a message. London was his home six months out of the year he explained, but "living out of a suitcase" was a better description of "home."

It was 4A.M. local time the captain said. Mac directed her toward the gate she would be leaving from. He handed her the card with the Germany telephone number scrawled on the back. She wobbled a bit and held tightly on his arm, walking toward her departure gate. The vodka martinis had made her light-headed.

In the first light of day she watched the crossing of the English Channel. 5A.M. What had happened to the night? With her twisting and turning in the small space allotted by the airlines, she never got comfortable and the political conversation kept her from sleep. She drank her coffee quickly as the stewardess gave directions in German and English to prepare for landing in Bonn.

The woods mushroomed as the rounded cauliflower tops became thick trunks. The plane jolted. When the tires skidded on the cement, the browns, greens, and gray concrete swished outside the window. The scene resembled a view from a car window. Would Sadie be at the gate? Pregnant? Amazing. Was Michael even around long enough to make that happen? Well they had been in Germany for almost a year, a year? Maybe nine months; Michael was sent here a year ago...And now she would be very fat, or did she manage to be the mother who did not gain any weight and still look gorgeous? Sadie always looks gorgeous.

William called in the confusing moments as she was leaving. Henry was honking. Lillian confirmed Jill had her tickets and passport. He was at Offutt and said he was flying himself over, delivering a plane replacement for one that was lost. He had exciting news, but wanted to tell her when he saw her. In the rush she wasn't able to hear his news. "See you in Germany, I'll figure out how to get to Sembach in the week before your arrival."

"My ETA is unchanged," he said.

The reverse thrusters now slowed the plane, shaking their seats. The sudden whoosh, rush, trembling of the jet caused her to have goose bumps. She asked William how it all works; his explanation of air pressure above the wings, pushing down, but flowing over the wings, actually lifting the heavy weight up, then the forward motion...she nodded and just concluded it worked.

Landing in Germany, pinch, pinch. I'm here, Siddhartha. And William, "They're gearing up for a bigger presence in Nam. They're deploying many fighter pilots. Chemical weapons on board. Death. War. The upside-I get to fly myself to Germany. Soon, taboo girl."

Nam. War. Hector, when? When will it not hurt?

Mac MacLaughton, should I call? I promised I would. Sadie will not let me take time away from her to have dinner with a strange man I met on the airplane. It was the vodka martinis that did it, flirting with a stranger and the trip to Europe. Caylor, Indiana was way across the ocean, such a long way from Germany. She had pointed it out on the globe to Luisa. Impossible to explain to a three year old, impossible to explain to a twenty-two year old. Germany.

Henry had managed to corner her about his conversation with William at the graduation party. After Lillian and Luisa had gone to Vacation Bible School, he was ready to head out to the job, but decided on one more cup of coffee. They sat at the kitchen table, eating strawberry shortcake.

"Princess," he started, "I talked to that Colonel fella."

"Dad, aren't you going to be late for the guys at the lumberyard?"

"You forget who your father is, Princess? The boss. Don't hedge. We are going to talk about this. Colonel Cunningham is on his way to an air base in Germany and my princess is on her way to an Army base in Germany and that's too close for coincidence. So drink your coffee and listen to your old man, for a change.

"You use your heart to make decisions and the Colonel seems to have captured a piece of your heart or at least he's begun to put some blueprints together. I saw it Princess. Your old man knows all the signs – the way he looked up when you walked by, the chuckle at your sarcastic snippets, and his attention to Luisa. Yep, the Colonel has plans for the Princess. And knowing the Princess the way I do, I would wager that you've been, ah…"

"Stop, Dad."

"That the two of you …"

"Dad! I'm your baby. You need to…"

"No, you need to listen. Your track record has been dismal. You two have become a tad more involved…Don't roll your eyes, Princess. I didn't get to be this age by not being able to see when a couple has tangled in the huckleberries. And you…I admit a chip off the old block, what could you hide? The long distance calls that sounded far away… two plus two equals four, always has, always will. So let's talk…"

"You know everything, what can I say?" Jill stared at her placemat, then over his shoulder at the kitchen clock. 7:30. She asked herself why had she not slept in. He smiled. She dropped her terry house slipper, pulled her leg under her butt and leaned forward, her elbows on the table's edge.

"Confirm," he said, holding up his hand, crooking his fingers, signaling her to answer.

"Okay, okay, he's picked out a lot; do you want to build us a house?" She answered, rubbing the edge of her coffee cup.

"And you? What is your investment in this 'house,' or should I say interest?"

"I like him, but…." she got up and poured more hot coffee. Sitting down she picked up her cup and smelled the aroma, "but any relationship with him would be strictly long distance and part-time, not ideal for a mother and a baby, and there is, the racial difference."

"It didn't seem to bother you with the migrant man." Henry put a big piece of shortcake in his mouth.

"Dad, I'm not going to sit here…."

Although she hadn't moved, he motioned her to stay seated. "You're going to sit right there until we reach an understanding of what is the status of my princess, the angel and a certain Negro Colonel. How do you plan to raise mixed race children in Caylor, Indiana?"

"The *Negro* Colonel and I have not discussed marriage let alone children."

"Now am I missing a chapter, midnight calls, international operators….why do you like someone so unlike you?"

"He is exciting, Dad…" She stopped and took a drink of coffee.

He swallowed and wiped strawberry juice from the side of his mouth, then spoke, "Exciting? Looking for a father for my angel shouldn't be like going over Niagara Falls in a barrel!"

"Oh, Dad. I don't like the part-time schedule." Henry nodded.

"We, I already told him that." Henry raised an eyebrow. Jill continued, "He's so intelligent and he's been so many places, so much experience in the ways of the world, the ways of women…."

Henry sliced another piece of biscuit dough and poured strawberries on top of it. "He's so *old* for you Princess."

"Like you Dad, mature. But I like that." She grinned.

Henry held his palms up and out in his mock surrender signal, "The plans are further along than you're admitting to your old man."

The Pan Am stewardess now spoke reminding the passengers to remain in their seats until the plane had come to a complete stop. "The plans are further along"…Germany. She held her breath and prayed. God thank you for a safe arrival. And let this all work out because you know Sadie and me.

ᲠᲔᲠ

"Jill, you deliberately picked the flight that got in the earliest…"

The friends raced down the autobahn. The interior of the Mercedes was gray leather with wood paneling. The quiet interior was neat and smooth much classier than the Chevy in Georgia.

Jill laughed; remembering that she told Henry, Sadie would have something to say about farmers' hours. "The Mercedes, Sadie? What a nice car for an Army person."

Sadie had cut her hair very short with pixie wisps outlining her face. She wore large gold hoops in her ears and several gold bangle bracelets with her Rolex watch. She had added another diamond ring wrapped with another stone Sadie identified as lapis lazuli. On Sadie's long fingers the chunky ring looked as if it was made for her.

"We needed a car. It is a quality car, and we'll ship it home when we leave...."

"You are so pregnant. I love it! My thin friend is now...."

"BWC," she said, "Michael's label, 'Big With Child.'" She wore a loose fitting sundress with a huge daisy appliqué across the chest; the long stem ended at the hemline. And she had the water buffalo sandals that she and Jill bought every summer. Sadie held up her foot wiggling her toes, "Ideal for pregnant, swollen, sore feet. Did you bring yours? We have to do a lot of walking."

"Sadie, you love the money." Jill rubbed the dash's paneling and touched Sadie's diamond ring.

"I love the money and hate the fuckin' Army."

"Oh, Mrs. Fredericks..."

They laughed. Sadie tried to explain the kilometer conversion to Jill as they passed highway signs indicating distances. Jill told about the graduation party, the night before and the night after when William had evoked the promise to spend a week with him. "He wants to take me to Lake Bodensee. Do you know where it is?" Sadie shook her head. "I had to look it up. It connects Germany, Switzerland and Austria."

"Are you in love, Jill?"

"With the money or the Air Force?"

"The black Major?" Sadie smiled broadly.

"The negro Colonel? Black?"

"Yes, black. T.J. says..."

"And you are asking me about love. T.J.? You're next to explain. William doesn't ever say 'love.' I want you to meet him, size him up...you'll see and we'll talk. Sadie, I'm so happy to be here. I have missed you. Let's don't stop talking until I pass out. I promised William I'd be with him...if I verified a conversation he had with Henry."

"The Colonel talked to Henry, oh jeez, please details. Pops? I'm surprised he let you come, but I am glad he let you, bribed you into coming. I so need my best friend."

They chuckled together.

"Germany, Dad said, it just wasn't coincidence we would all be here at the same time."

"Jill, this is *my* visit, not the colonel's. He can see you on his own time. We don't have that much time. I haven't seen you in almost year...not since Hector...sorry, I don't want any sadness."

"I think about him often. It helped to talk to William."

"See, you've had time with him, my turn. If he wants to fight over you, well this year in Germany, I have learned how to handle officers – the pricks!"

"Sadie!"

"I hate the fuckin' Army."

"Southeastern offered me the position and I said, 'yes.' No one was happy with the Boston trip. And...Bobbie, my connection, called her friend in Boston and it became too complicated, sleeping in their basement until I found my own place. It all started to feel like shoving square pegs in round holes. Plus she and Khalil are moving to Beirut. Khalil was offered a job at American University. You know her parents went crazy. I'm sure she will never go back to Gold Oak. But she was my link to Boston."

"Pops got what he wanted -you to stay in Indiana. I think we need to call him right away and ask for the summer, that way you can be with me when the baby is born *and* be with this pilot-spy-father of your friend Mo..."

"William, Sadie, just William. You'll meet him."

"You wrote of another guy, though, Jones?"

"Jack Jones."

"He wants to marry you?"

The conversation carried them to the base, through the gate where a military police officer saluted them and smiled as though recognizing Sadie. They shopped at the PX for groceries. Sadie picked vegetables, meat and promised Jill she knew how to cook now.

Jill tried to adjust to Sadie's bigness, a different size than her fat broken-heart days. Her height, the bold make-up and dress still caused men to turn at each stop. The friends pinched each other when they walked past the really cute soldiers. All the places, grocery aisles, military housing, soldiers, Army families, were secondary to their conversation. Jill tried to look at the military housing, office buildings, road signs as they passed, but Sadie and she laughed and interrupted each other at every sentence. Jill retold stories of her student teaching and its cast of characters, Ross Hass and Marge Merriweather. Sadie liked the story of the sex statues. Sadie told Jill of "Pig Alley" in Wiesbaden where prostitution was legal. Mike had told her a story of walking into the men's room at the park where guys stood masturbating, "the ever so neat Germans," Sadie said.

They made plans for three weeks. "No, Jill you are staying until August," Sadie ordered, "Call Pops, call Pan Am, get your flight changed. I know the Colonel-cum-thief will steal more of your time than his share, and all the guys at the NCO club, the Enlisted Men's Club…We are calling as soon as we get to the house. Anyway, Henry won't care, you agreed to teaching in his backyard and you will no doubt live in his house. Maybe you should just stay until Labor Day…."

"Sadie! We need to see what Michael has to say. He may want to throw us both out after two days. And my daughter won't recognize me if I stay away so long."

They pulled into the driveway of the plain duplex that matched all the duplexes on the street, on the last two streets, gray-beige, driveways to match, all the same design. She and Sadie grabbed the sacks of groceries and walked into the house. A jet rumbled in the distance muting their conversation. Sadie unlocked the door to the small two bedroom place.

Entering the living room was like stepping into a furniture store. She'd furnished it with antiques The parlor sofa looked stiff and uncomfortable with spindly legs. "Louis Fifteen or Sixteen," Sadie said, tossing her purse on one of the matching chairs. All were covered in the same broad stripes of maroon and beige silk. The coffee table and armoire were the same mahogany with polished curved carved legs and darkened brass hardware. A Persian rug completely covered the small living room floor surface. A leather topped desk and chair took up one corner. "Don't worry about sitting on any of it. When it gets too cluttered, we send some pieces home. Come see your bedroom."

"I think it's time to send something home." Jill teased.

"Right, the fuckin' Army housing. Some of the pieces were left by previous residents…yuck!"

Jill carried her bag into the small bedroom with the baby's crib, and carved oak furniture that looked like pieces from a gingerbread house, hand-painted with hearts and flowers. The baby's bassinette and chest were decorated to match the bed. The guest bed was dark wood with spun spindles for the headboard and four bedposts. A light-weight patchwork quilt lay stretched over a pink lace coverlet. The quilt was an interlocking-circle pattern of several shades of pink, red, and deep maroon on a white background.

Sadie said, "The double wedding ring pattern," and laughed. "Jill, shopping in Germany is great. I can hardly wait until we hit the cobblestone streets and the restaurants. Michael doesn't like German food, so I cook most of the time."

The pillowcases were white with pink crocheted lace cuffs matching the coverlet. The bed looked too pretty to sleep in. Sadie put her arm around Jill, "I'm so glad you're here. I planned for this, telling myself only one more week, only five more days. I made the bed this morning and said, 'Jill and I are going to sit right here and talk.'"

Sadie plopped down on the bed and watched Jill unpack. Jill hung dresses and blouses on the empty hangers in the closet. Sadie volunteered to get more if she needed them. Sadie talked about Michael's new found interest in European antiques. His father had written that Michael's grandmother had left Michael her house.

"The haunted house at the end of Vicksburg Road?" Jill asked, remembering the stone and red brick structure with turrets, gables and a wraparound porch built in the late 1800's. They had told each other ghost stories about people who lived there.

"Yes! I'm so excited. It will require a lot of work to upgrade the plumbing and roof. Some of the slate shingles need to be replaced and the leaks fixed. Mr. Fredericks said the squirrels, owls, bats and everything else had been living on the third floor and attic. But we can't move in until December when this fuckin' Army thing is over – four years at Thanksgiving. Maybe Henry can help me with the structural repairs."

Jill hugged her best friend and patted her stomach, "Boy or girl?"

"One of those. Some look at me and say the way you are carrying that baby it has to be a boy, others like Michael say it is a girl. Of course, what does he know? I just want healthy and…."

"And?" Jill said.

Sadie stood and headed for the kitchen, "*And*, do you want to take a nap? You've been in the plane all night. I would suggest staying awake until tonight if you can last that long and then wake up tomorrow ready to go, because we have people to see and places to go."

"Sure. Bring on the coffee, but the *and*…"

"We'll do the *and* later."

They moved to the kitchen a small linoleum floored space with steel cabinets. The base furnished the refrigerator and stove. Sadie left it unchanged; the contrast to the expensive furnishings of the other three rooms was startling. The ironing board was set up next to a bushel basket of sprinkled shirts ready for pressing. "Why," Sadie asked, "does Michael like the way I do his shirts better than the military dry cleaners? They are professionals."

"You need to do housewifely things…"

"Me? You have men asking you to marry you…one military, so you will be ironing them real soon."

"No," Jill shook her head, "No. William did not ask me. Jack Jones, yes, but jeez Sadie, Jack is handsome, you know Michael Landon? Think 'Bonanza,' he kind of looks like him, nice, too nice, great smile."

"And he wants to marry you? After one date?"

"No, the date wasn't even over. We walked to the car and standing by the door he proposed. Who does that Sadie?"

"Determined."

"Shouldn't I feel something?"

"Seems like it."

Sadie talked about Michael's plans to go to college and major in business administration. He had been able to accumulate two years worth of credits already. Michael definitely did not want to work for his father. His mother wanted her grandchild in Caylor as quickly as possible.

Sadie cut a piece of the linzer torte and poured Jill coffee. Sadie removed clothes from the dryer in the utility room next to the kitchen. She walked to her room with a laundry basket. Jill followed holding her coffee. They talked non-stop, all afternoon – Jack, to William, to Michael and around again.

They had written letters, but very few phone calls. Jill told her she missed the sound of her voice. They caught up on the last time Sadie and T.J. were together, right before Thanksgiving. She was with Michael here in Germany on Thanksgiving. Jill kept asking about the *and*, but putting Sadie's dates together of goodbye to one and hello to another involved using her fingers. When Sadie put her underwear into the drawer, she pulled out a letter that was tucked neatly into a buried pair of panties, "Here, Jill, read this while I start supper. Michael will be here in an hour. He is happy that you are here, because I've been driving him cuckoo. It will be your first meal prepared by Sadie in Germany. Remember how Hector used to cook and laugh as we tried to chop vegetables?"

"I hope you have learned to cook."

"Michael thinks Prayer taught me a lot. God, I didn't have anything else to do in that big old mansion. I sure didn't want to venture out into the madness of backwoods Georgia with the bears and panthers. Plus the two-legged creatures were scariest of all."

"I don't care if I ever go to Georgia again in my life, but we did have some happy times all those Sundays at 1254 Butler. You know I cried as I drove away for the last time?"

"Hector was great! Oh, so handsome and that wonderful sense of kindness. They just don't make many of those. He loved you Jill, I think that is what you will have to keep in your heart. Everything they talk about at the NCO club, oh, everywhere on this base is Viet Nam, 'Nam.' It is one horror story after another. Thank god Michael didn't go.

"Come with me to the kitchen, bring the letter. We have to figure out how to do this." She pointed to the letter she had handed Jill.

Blue linen stationery written with a fountain pen, the printed name at the top of the first page:

Thomas Jefferson Washington, Esq.

"Sadie?!"

Sadie laughed, "No, it's not the first one. Read on. You'll get a kick out of this letter. Michael is right; trouble follows us around like a lost puppy."

June 10, 1964

Dear Sadie,

   I love you. I'll let you do the deductive reasoning to figure out why.

   I was graduated from law school summa-cum-laude. The U.S. Army has a special place for special people – the Judge Advocate General Corps; I am grateful. Unfortunately, my man Hector was sent in for a direct hit. I hope to be able to defend soldiers against the institution that was responsible for his death. Maybe I'll save someone from the same fate.

   I have no way of knowing when you'll get this letter, but I hope you are still in Wiesbaden. I'll be there by the last week in June. Find me. You seem to be able to do that better than anyone.

   T.J.

꙳ξ꙳

The night like a set of parentheses enclosed them.

"The sound of the universe," William said, "the inky blackness with tiny unreachable promises of light." He turned the ignition off and rolled down the window. He had parked the dark blue military truck at the end of the flight line. He pushed the seat back, then leaned toward the passenger seat. He twisted Jill's curls around his finger and massaged the back of her neck. She faced him. The deafening roar of jet engines cut through the quiet. The four-wheel drive vehicle shook as the dart-shaped underbelly of the B-58 lifted up over them. The bombing pod and needle nose were clearly visible from their parking spot. The bomber's lights blinked, the wheels eased up into the metal capsule of the nose and locked under the wings. In the silent interlude, William spoke, "It takes a great deal of thrust to lift-off 163,000 pounds of bomber. A remarkable weapon system. They are on their way back home. Three men are needed to fly it. I flew in one in Arizona. No windows really, you watch the ground with radar screens." He whistled, then said, "Incredible."

"I can't imagine flying without looking out the window. I love the power..." Another plane leap-frogged over them, Jill continued, "What did you think of my friends?"

Sadie was on her best behavior with Michael and William sitting in their living room. Michael, tall, dirty blonde hair, as long as the Army would allow, thick in his chest and arms. Michael laughed easily and physically stroked Sadie whenever they passed each other or were in the same room. He tousled her hair, massaged her back and patted her stomach. He teased Sadie about her pregnant weight gain. When they stood together, they were an imposing couple. Michael's fullness had increased his attractiveness. In the four years since they graduated from high school, he had changed dramatically from teenager to man.

He and William talked basketball. Michael had played in high school. William brought up Wilt Chamberlain, and Michael teased Jill about her "cousin" John Havlicek and a new upcoming star Lew Alcindor from UCLA. Jill had turned up her nose at the mention of the university.

William and Michael talked in military jargon, sprinkled with some substance of war, Viet Nam, then Korea. The soldiers shared a dark German beer and laughed about the "flat-faced Korean women." They exchanged a quick glance and touched the beer bottle necks; Jill understood there was more to the story than they wanted to say. Michael became effusive describing the miserable gray cold mountains of his Korean post near the DMZ, a one year assignment.

Jill's thoughts of those 365 days raced like a 33⅓ record on 78: T.J. and Sadie in D.C.; T.J. and Sadie in New York; T.J. and Sadie at T.J's mom's in Indianapolis for one "glorious summer month," August 1962. T.J. had finished summer school and Hector had not left for Basic Training. We were all in honeymoon-nothing-can-stop-us mood. Sadie never mentioned even a thought that she would divorce Michael, never. T.J. seemed okay with having her on her own terms.

At least Sadie did not say she had been miserable in Michael's absence. And then Michael came back to the States, but the U.S. Army had promised him Germany and they sent him in September, September 1963. Sadie joined him in November.

And they all laughed at the backwards way the military did everything. William explained there were levels of incompetence, but some of the "stars"…they each told a general story – Michael's of encrypting a message from one general to another inviting him for a round of golf. Michael had to send the invitation under the highest security code. William told of casually walking into the wrong private room at the Hung Dao Hotel and seeing "this white ass humping a whore and two stars tattooed on his snow white cheek." From then on they all scrutinized each two-star they saw.

Although William was old enough to have fathered all of them, he was "at ease." Each time Jill met him the setting was different, but William comfortably performed, talked, reacted, and managed all of them.

"Michael is a refreshing antidote to my prejudice about white boys from the Midwest. I can appreciate his excitement on getting out of the *Army*. He seems happy and not at all interested in the Pentagon move. They'll pressure him to re-up."

"Re-up?"

"Enlist for another four years. They've talked to him about OTC, Officer Training," he paused and nodded, "a degree would qualify him."

"He really liked your inside information…"

"Experience, only. He knows most of what I told him, but Sadie," William paused, "I'm not sure about her taboo girl; she seems so at ease spending his money all those expensive antiques for furniture. I wonder if *he* gets his money's worth…"

The accelerating aircraft drowned all conversation. William leaned over and kissed her until stillness prevailed. After working an eight hour shift, he had driven to Sadie's to pick her up. In Kaiserslautern they had eaten in a small restaurant, all stone with clunky dark furniture. William ordered in German, no English spoken after a perfunctory "Good Evening." She had eaten vinegary sauce on roast pork, boiled red-skinned potatoes, sweet dessert chocolate, then she imagined Grandma Kohlhass in her German homeland. Lillian said, "Maybe some cousins" still lived in Berlin, but Jill was not venturing across the iron curtain. Sitting now watching supersonic bombers drill was too close, if only there were an "Iron Curtain."

"And now you know what happens at 0400 hours," William spoke, pointing at the oncoming lights of another plane, "however, I have a lot of faith in the Skunk Works to come up with something that will keep our intelligence people on the ground more, watching TV screens..." he stopped as the blasting noise muted his voice. He kissed her again.

She asked, "Skunk Works? I thought that was where Li'l Abner made moonshine?"

"The same idea except 'revenuers' actually pay the bills. Let's go. Are you ready?"

The thunderous rumble and shaking from the jet's afterburners provided the soundtrack for her nod. They drove parallel to the runway's pavement lights, "Will they keep you longer than a week?" Jill said, rubbing his thigh.

"It's Uncle Sam's agenda, but the taboo girl is on the European Continent..."

"Yeah, Uncle Sam needs to know *my* time is limited."

"I may not even be in Incirlik for a week. It could be a turnaround, but the base commander has requested my presence, so that could indicate any number of things. You could be making love with a full Colonel when I return."

"Well, making love with a Lt. Colonel was certainly better than a captain, so I will mark the days until your return."

He reached over and pinched her cheek.

She watched the passing base structures, office buildings, housing, barracks, hangars, like Wiesbaden, like Bunker Hill, like Ft. Benning. The base was utilitarian squares of concrete. Professor Tarkington's "red menace" brought the American bunkers, chunks of incongruous cement to the enemy's borders. Death and war were only moments from happening.

The same explosive mix had been a hairsbreadth from igniting in Cuba two years ago, Jill remembered. Caylor froze. In slow motion each person had evaluated their life. Lillian had called and talked calmly; they'd prayed together on the telephone. The churches opened for special prayer and meditation; the courthouse made public announcements of the bomb shelters in downtown basements. Bunker Hill Air Base was a known target for any Soviet nuclear attack. Henry went about the business of building, stating, "It is better to be where it hits than survive like those folks in Hiroshima." They had speculated on the warning time from Bunker Hill's first hit to Caylor's succumbing to the nuclear fallout – five minutes, ten minutes, no more than twelve minutes.

William spoke guardedly about his missions, watching the Soviets, "stealthy as cat's paws, without being detected, like chess, anticipating their next move, then being able to strike first. And all to allow you to sleep safe and sound, taboo girl." He had qualified that, saying only when she slept alone because he guaranteed neither when they were together. He made light, but it felt heavy in the night with the war machinery reverberating persistently.

They had talked in her guest bedroom at Sadie's as she put her clothes together to spend the night. He had pinned her down on the antique bed and threatened to take her clothes off so he could see her against the pink, red, and maroon. She laughed, refusing, saying she clashed with the color scheme. It had only been two weeks since graduation, but now in Germany it seemed miles and months ago. The walls were too thin for privacy. He said he would tell her his surprise when they drove to Kaiserslautern.

She now leaned over and outlined his lower jaw bone with her index finger, "mandible," she said. She traced upwards towards his ear, "temporal," then she pushed on the indention of the mandible joint, "glenoid fossa." She slid slowly down his rough cheek to his shadowed upper lip. She stopped at the space between his nose and bow-shaped mouth, "maxilla." He opened his mouth, snapping quickly, catching her finger.

"Sharp incisors," he said, "the better to eat you with."

Another war-bird sounded its song of power, fulfilling a commitment to freedom.

He parked in a small restricted lot. They walked into the visiting Officers' Quarters.

ᚱξᚱ

Jill spooned closer to William, his rhythmic breathing and snoring. The room was dark except for the crack of light from the slightly opened bathroom door, like a hotel room. His uniforms were all pressed and hung in the closet. His highly polished shoes sat precisely on the closet floor. The chest of drawers contained folded t-shirts, boxer shorts and socks, the web belts wound neatly. The army green jumpsuits for flying were hung next to the uniforms, each sewn with his name patch in blue and silver. Cunningham, Cunningham, Cunningham.

He snored. Why do men snore so loudly? She savored the sound; it meant she was in very close proximity to a man. Snoring, another item on the list of unique loves she and Sadie shared - the smell of gasoline, shoe polish, asphalt and mimeograph fluid; touching tarantulas and snakes; walking through the cemetery; balancing on the trestles of the train bridge as the creek flowed twenty feet below. And their Negro men – black men, she corrected herself thinking of T.J. "We're black men," he had told Sadie, "it is the language of the Civil Rights Movement, as you are white, we are black."

Black men? "Was it the rebellious thing to do?" William asked.

Henry's voice answered, "It depends on where you live, Princess. Paris might work. In America? Maybe New York, maybe Los Angeles, maybe San Francisco."

Or maybe a military base, Dad, where many men have married women of all cultures. Married? Yes, William had really said it, a serious proposal, his "surprise." She laughed at his first sentence, "Will you marry me?"

"A joke, right? We're sexual soul-mates. I like what you do, you like what I do. Can do? Remember Wes Montgomery? At the jazz joint in Indianapolis? My question, you're not serious?"

"I've never been more serious," he had answered, his dark eyes recorded each twitch on her face. He would know her answer without her words, but she spoke.

"It's the look Mo describes – Woe is me."

"I'm not woeful," he frowned, continuing, "I want no sympathy. I want you to be my wife."

"Now? Why now? You're a Recon man, flyboy and I'm not...I haven't changed. I refuse to be a military widow. Gary Powers, U-2 a recon man, what about poor Mrs. Powers? Her husband in a Soviet prison. No."

"Now? You're twenty-two, free, lost, mother of one, found by Jack Jones."

"Jack Jones is a dork, a handsome, but...stable, responsible, feet firmly planted on the ground, but...Her tone made each adjective distasteful. I don't love him, does that matter?"

"He is exactly right for you. Listen to what you said, and he is white, apt, decent. It is a 'tip.' I must react quickly." He raised one eyebrow, "I gracefully exited this scene before, *not this time*."

And it continued over light, white, Rhine wine, Blue Nun. One bottle, then the second and her tongue tripped over light, white, Rhine, wine. They laughed in the semi-darkness of candlelight with Richard Strauss playing on a scratchy recording. He continued, "In my area of expertise there are offers to work, work in places that don't change, places where you own a home, raise children and work normal hours, regular days with a two-week vacation."

"Live where?"

"I'm considering two places – Virginia or Los Angeles. Virginia if I stay in the military and work at the Pentagon or Langley. Los Angeles, if I go to the military contractors – Lockheed, Martin-Marietta, Hughes, TRW, the Skunk Works. I get letters all the time from those folks."

"Los Angeles? Henry had said it. But she had signed the contract with Southeastern."

"It takes time, taboo girl. We already work together. We see each other on a regular basis, but the change from military status to civilian employee....It takes time."

"How much time?"

"Maybe six months, maybe a year. Stars have to be briefed, clearance secured, re-evaluated, background checks updated, even you, taboo girl, you'll be questioned. They both vie for me to work for them."

"Who? Who would you work for?"

"The Central Intelligence Agency."

"The Bay of Pigs, the Cuban Missile Crisis, U-2's, Viet Nam?"

"Yes."

"Oh jeezus, and for me, if I say, yes?"

"Why would you say no?"

"More children?"

"Do you want more children, taboo girl? I have two, they are enough. If you want more children that is your decision."

"Not now, maybe no more, I don't know, but you are getting older, I know Bing Crosby and all that, but...I have no thoughts on another child at this point, maybe I don't want anymore, you're okay with no more?"

"Your decision."

"Your son? I don't know him."

"Melding families? Henry wants his daughter taken care of, someone to love and protect her as he always has, make sure she wants for nothing. I can do that, *Princess*, how about a bump in grade? Queen, I'll make you my queen."

William now rolled over slinging one arm across her chest, pulling her back against his chest. He was hard against her butt, still snoring.

ᴙξᴙ

Sadie made Jill a cup of coffee adding cream and sugar, something Jill never did. In their three weeks together, Jill was beginning to enjoy the taste of the sweeter drink. "You have to try my corn muffins. Tell me if Prayer would approve. Did I tell you Prayer wrote? James died and she moved to Cleveland or was it Columbus with their son Booker. She said she missed Georgia. How could anyone miss that god-awful place? Anyway, she asked how that young man of mine was doing in his civil rights marches?"

"What time, Mrs. Fredericks, are we going to the Judge Advocate Court?"

"I think 10A.M. will be just right to make my grand entrance. We'll ask T.J. what he thinks about your marrying a black Colonel."

"Mo's father is enough. It isn't like they haven't met."

"You're right. Look at the dress on the ironing board. Tell me what you think. I want to wear it. It is impossible to look attractive with this cow shape." The summery dress was sleeveless, creamy light cotton, expanding tiers of flounces, the bottom one trimmed with wide crocheted lace. The same lace formed a wide shawl collar that made coverlets over the shoulders. Sadie would be stunning. Jill held it up to her own neck and the hemline reached to her ankles. Sadie set her plate of muffins on the table. "Delicious, Mrs. Cunningham, you could be on the cover of *Bride's Magazine*." Jill laughed, quickly replacing the dress on the ironing board.

"Sadie, I don't know what to do. After last week at Bodensee…I feel like I had a honeymoon without a wedding."

"Yeah, you had to leave me and go off with *the* colonel."

"I lost a bet."

"It didn't seem like such a great loss," Sadie said as she rinsed the breakfast dishes.

Jill placed her plate in the dishwater and poured another cup of coffee. "We have to decide about this."

"Well, 'taboo girl,' what do you want me to say? He's too old for you? He seems like he is just about right because you need a daddy. He's black? What can *I* say about that? He can't afford you? He seems to be able to keep up. He's Mo's father? Your college roommate, you'll be her stepmother; it gives you an advantage. Many stepmothers are despised by their step-daughters for breaking up the marriage. Are you writing these down so we can keep score of the pros and cons? Luisa will have a sister, who could be her mother. It is starting to sound a bit Possum Hollerish."

Sadie dried her hands and hung the dish towel on a rack behind the door. She poured some bottled water into the iron and stretched her dress onto the covered board. "He has a very dangerous job, spying on the Russians and the Chinese. Henry will start WWIII, which might be more dangerous than flying a spy plane. Luisa will have a big brother. You're thinking with your crotch instead of your head. Sex with men of color…" She shook her head, "I don't need to comment." She paused. "T.J. says once you have the cola, you don't go back to the un-cola."

"Stop. I'm trying to enjoy this cup of coffee," Jill laughed. "Prayer would be proud of your muffins."

After their first week, they called Henry who said, "Yes, I'll wire enough money to keep you supplied for a month. Southeastern sent a letter saying they were having a meeting for first-year teachers Wednesday August tweny-sixth. Jack called and wanted Sadie's address."

Then Michael had come home in a rage, throwing the orders he had just been issued, sending him back to the States for the last four months. He was being stationed at the Pentagon. He had one week to get there, "No later than July 3!" The only explanation was the war was getting worse and they were sending more and more troops, creating too many vacancies at the Pentagon, so he was needed immediately. Communications. Sadie wailed about having a baby without her husband. He shrugged and said, "The fuckin' Army. What do they give a rat's ass about you or me or anybody? Four fuckin' months and I'm out of this piece of shit service. But Jill's here. She's had a baby; she can help."

They called Henry again. He moaned about the mother lode, and what had the U.S. Army ever done for him? Jill mumbled, "Freedom?"

Jill then left with William for a week at Lake Bodensee; Michael and Sadie had that time together. Her baby was due the last week in July. She would be given thirty days to move after that. "It was the best the Army could do for a pregnancy," Michael had said.

ᴦξᴦ

After Michael left, Jill and Sadie settled into a routine. Have breakfast, get dressed and walk, drive into town, shop, look for antiques, and eat lunch. William came every third day. Sadie called the Judge Advocate division on June twenty-sixth. Captain Washington would arrive in two weeks. Sadie immediately planned Bastille Day in Paris. Jill had objected. Sadie would have only two weeks before her due date. It might be too stressful and cause early delivery. Hardheaded Siddhartha had said, "Yes, then I can leave with you on August fifteenth." She had made up her mind and that was it and that was all.

Now as they walked down a gray hall, Jill asked how long it *actually* had been since Sadie had seen T.J.

"Too long," Sadie answered.

"Siddhartha, oh yeah, I said it, 'too long' is not a date. You know exactly when the last time you saw him."

"Thanksgiving week."

"Yeah, you already said that. I'm counting fingers…November to December, December to January…"

"Okay, okay, too close. Don't do it! I can't Jill. Stop."

Gray walls, gray linoleum, gray doors, darker gray and steel chairs lined the walls and outside certain doors. The soldier at the front desk had called somewhere then directed them down the

89

hallway, up the stairs at the end of the hallway. They started walking, but Sadie raced toward the door at the end of a long corridor, and then rushed into the room. Another, door another soldier, he stood, starched, stiff, crisp, hair trimmed, shoes polished. The soldier, "Amers" his name tag indicated, was young, dark shadows crossed his head where hair should be, fat cheeks and a flat dent at the bridge of his nose. Looking from Sadie's natural straw sun-hat with the white ribbon bow, down to her last lacy flounce, he sized them up. Sadie said, "Captain Washington," and Amers turned toward the door. "Come with me."

The gray door closed behind them. They entered a library. A long metal conference table dominated the center of the rectangular shape. Books covered the walls from door-to-door and from floor-to-ceiling. Four windowless doors opened into the room. Another soldier, this one with two bars on his collar, a captain, sat at the table with a semi-circle of opened books and a long yellow pad in front of him. He glanced up and smiled. Amers saluted the captain. The captain was tan with blonde almost transparent hair, a flat-top like newly mowed grass. He stood and looked from Sadie to Jill, "May I help you?" He had a slight accent, maybe Boston, Jill thought. His badge read – Crumpacker. His broad smile extended from ear-to-ear.

Sadie asked, "Captain Washington?"

Crumpacker talked rapidly to Amers who said, "Yessir" as one word and turned and left the room. The captain saluted Amers after Amers had left. Crumpacker then exited through the door behind him. As if on cue, T.J. came from the opposite side of the library. Sadie turned from Crumpacker's exit and rushed to T.J. They hugged each other.

T.J. laughed at Sadie's size, rubbing her tummy buried in gauzy flounces, "Remind me," he spoke, "not to get you pregnant, or should I say more of you to love?"

"I tried to cover it up. I was hoping you wouldn't notice."

He kissed her, and then held out one arm, "Come here Jill. You look terrific, the right size. My favorite constituent," he squeezed her next to him and she patted his brass buttons as he continued, "finally old enough to vote and here we are thousands of miles from Indiana." They all laughed and hugged each other.

Jill cried, "Oh, T.J., seeing you…how long it has been?"

"This is a joyous event. We're all together. P.R. would be happy I'm taking care of his woman. Let's go to my assigned cubicle.

90

Attorneys are not given much respect. Our furniture matches everyone else's. The same little elf makes them at HDQ. I know Sadie's crib has no gray vinyl or steel."

"None. T.J., every room, but the kitchen, looks like an antique store," Jill said.

Sadie laid out the plans, and told T.J. all that had happened with Michael's orders to return to the states. T.J. kept squeezing Sadie's hand as she talked. Jill had not seen Sadie so happy since she picked her up in Bonn. Jill thought it seemed like these two were the two who should be having the baby. And Jill liked both Michael and T.J. Michael was easy-going, talkative, smart. The men were similar in one more way – they both loved Sadie.

The women listened to T.J.'s basic training story, but Sadie and Jill both agreed the uniform and the fifteen pounds he said he lost were becoming. He objected, and then quoted his drill instructor, "Washington, now you're mean *and* lean."

Sadie looked for matches in their schedules, when he was off and where she would take him. Sadie filled in the squares on her pocket calendar. He got off at five and one of them would pick him up, maybe Jill because the Mercedes might be recognized.

"A Mercedes, Mrs. Fredericks? It will be easy to spot," T.J. said.

Sadie kissed him goodbye. Sex with men of color, kissing men of color, watching Sadie kiss T.J....She thought of William.

Kissing...in Bodensee; it had seemed incessant, but they were in a row boat and trying to make sure they stayed upright while laughing. The rented row boat allowed them to explore the shore line. Stone houses were built at the water's edge. Orange and red geraniums filled flower boxes and decorated windows and walkways. From the tiled roofs and outdoor restaurants, each turn on the cobblestone walks brought another Bavarian scene. How many times had she said, "Beautiful"? William would say 'yes' and kiss her. She would laugh and say, "No, William," and then she would point to a carved wood door, a church steeple, a stained glass window, a garden. With the softness of his mouth, the more he kissed her the more kisses she wanted. They shopped, took pictures, rode bikes, ate and talked and talked and kissed.

She now heard Sadie whisper, "I've missed you. T.J., I love you." Jill closed her eyes thinking of William's word SNAFU –

situation normal all fucked up. She and Sadie never got their lives to SN-situation normal, period.

They drove back to Sadie's small military quarters to find a blue Air Force truck parked in the driveway. "William," they said at the same time.

"I hope nothing is wrong," Jill said, "The military is so unpredictable. I don't know how you have managed all this time being a military wife. And now a double military wife."

"Oh god, don't I know it. Jill, it is part of the *and* you asked me about. Can we go to the piney woods and have a private conversation?"

William got out of his truck as they parked in the driveway. He kissed Jill and said, "Friday and I am officially unscheduled for the next three days. I hurried and left the base before they could change their minds. And...I decided to make dinner. I brought all the groceries and plan to burn for two problematic American women in Germany."

"I think they should make you a General for all your efforts," Jill said. They all chuckled.

Sadie and Jill interrupted each other with their retelling of going to meet T.J.

Sadie drank a 7-UP and left for the doctor. She said she would pick up T.J. and try to get him to leave early. Her parting words, "To hell with the fuckin' Army. I'm married to one and in love with another."

William cocked his head and motioned Jill to follow him, "They should have joined the Air Force."

"Fuckin' Air Force," Jill said, "They pull your string whenever they decide you're needed."

"Yes, ma'am. Now let's fix dinner unless you want to see if you match the quilt in your bedroom with that green dress you're wearing. We have the place to ourselves..."

William cut slices in the fatty side of the beef roast and stuffed each deep cut with spices and a white wine based sauce. "Jill, I have tried everything to get back to the states, but I don't think I can get back before December, close to Madeline's wedding. Maybe in and out of Offutt, but I think it's a tossup about a hop to Bunker Hill."

"Why does this sound like an opening line? And right after you've had your way with me." She stood next to him, watching each movement.

"Rosemary. You want to know the herbs, some sage, and whole peppercorns. When we go the American Embassy to get your visa for France…" he paused, taking his hands from the roast, he hooked one arm around her neck, then pulled her face to his. She reached around his shoulders pressing tightly against him. They kissed, his deep lips covering her mouth. He used his other arm to hold her tightly; he embraced her, pulling his face away from her face. Her mouth was soaked. He whispered, "When you get your visa, we could be married at the Embassy."

She slid her arms to the front of his chest, "You want me to be your wife, you don't say you love me…."

"Jill, I love you. I don't want you to leave Europe until I do. Stay with me…"

She looked down at his chest, the milk chocolate brown that made her want to taste him. The same reference, where he had started, on the rainy, windy, chilly afternoon in the Bodensee.

They had huddled in the corner of the terrace restaurant, a short distance from their hotel. The flower baskets surrounding the patio swung wildly in the gusts. She zipped up the windbreaker she wore with her sleeveless knit shirt and skirt. William insisted she wear a skirt or dress when they were together, "In public," he had said, "always dress decorously."

"Do you own blue jeans?" she asked.

"One pair, but I rarely wear them."

They discussed dressing before leaving in the rain-threatening day.

She had held his hand turning it over, rubbing each of his fingers; his hands were warm in the cool dry corner of the restaurant.

"What are you thinking?" he asked.

"Milk chocolate, melty chocolate…like…"

He had interrupted, "You say milk chocolate, 'exquisite Swiss milk chocolate' like we ate in St. Gallen. I like it that you think of me as something incredibly rich and edible, melt in your mouth delicious, but…I'm not a flavor. I'm a man of color."

The restaurant where they sat was built on the water in Lindau, the old city with white washed houses and aged brown and rust tile roofs. They cuddled in a corner protected from the heavy rains sweeping across the lake. Vertical sheets of silver, gray and white beat down on the water; the rough white-capped surface smacked against the heavy stone embankment of the restaurant's foundation. The air was rich with the rain. At the suggestion of the waiter, all the other diners had gone inside. William had explained in German they wanted to remain where they were and the waiter needed only to make sure they were supplied with hot coffee and cream. Jill watched William's dark eyes get darker as the sky got darker and more serious as he talked. He sipped coffee and looked from the water and the indiscernible horizon then back to her face.

"...I'm a Negro man, a black man, a man of African roots and a boy." He bristled when he said the word. "Yes, a boy, a white man's lackey. I'm thrown the keys and expected to fetch, expected to move with their derisive look and dismissive snarl. These acts of humiliation are all a part of what being with me, loving me, being my wife includes. As I'm treated, you can expect worse. I tease you, calling you taboo girl, but sleeping with a black man? Truly a taboo. There are places in America where even as Colonel and Mrs. Cunningham, we cannot share the same room, the same hotel, the same table at a restaurant, the same corner in a rainstorm." She saw the ugliness of Pekin, Georgia, and Montgomery, Alabama.

"And," he continued, "other places where we can, but people will stare as if we are freaks at a circus. You marry me and it encompasses all of that hate, the identity crisis that is America. Elke hid on the air bases rarely venturing into the prejudiced filled towns that were adjacent to them. And then there is the Air Force," he took a deep breath and a drink of coffee.

He lit a cigarette, "As a Colonel, I will walk into rooms where everyone stands and salutes me, where Generals with three stars listen to each word I say, wait for each word. Men I brief, use the information to brief POTUS, the President of the United States. I spin between these two dichotomous definitions. It is heady stuff, but at the core will be our marriage. You must be able to cope with these definitions of your husband. We will never be comfortable in Caylor. America is *deadly* serious about race. And as much as I am hated for something over which I have no control; you made a deliberate choice and you will be reviled for worse than unwed motherhood – fucking a nigger. The language? Yes. The names are shouted loudly. You already know what happened to your friend T.J. in Montgomery. No one is to muddy the purity of the white woman. And I will be found guilty of marrying one."

She sat staring. The clouds rolled and dissipated misting into the dark steel blue of the lake's surface. He watched her, but she knew he understood her reaction; it was what he did.

"Are you trying to scare me away from a battle?"

"No. There is no doubt in my mind that you can do battle with the ignorant and the ignominious. I am briefing you to guarantee you can prevail, inside, with me."

Now leaning against the kitchen cabinet his eyes moved slightly staring at her eyes, reading them, scrutinizing her facial expressions. "William, I'm torn over which side of this record to play. The A-side, I want to undress you and have sex on the kitchen table. I want to stay in Europe and live with you at Ramstein, but the big B-side, I've spent the last four years watching Sadie. Her husband left the day they were married; six months later she moves with him for six months. He leaves for basic; she has sex with T.J. and it's never stopped, like someone is pulling strings, Michael exits, T.J. enters. The fuckin' Army she calls it. She has never really been married. I've watched your life, heard Mo's stories, for crissakes, I have my own story. No. I want to be married and live together. You come home for dinner. We talk. We tuck the children in; you're home when there is a crisis. Sadie is getting ready to have a baby without the father...No. It's not how I want my marriage or a life for my daughter. And you have been down this road before."

He hugged her. She laid her face on his chest. He rested his chin on her head. He inhaled, pushing his chest tighter against hers, and then slowly exhaled.

"Okay, taboo girl, on your terms. And I won't ask again until all my planes are lined up, tip-to-tip. Now I'll finish the roast beef, so we can get to this kitchen table A-side."

She kissed him, "I love you, William."

Sadie had said, "Yes, I tell them both I love them because love is a feeling not a commitment."

Chapter 5

In Lillian's guest room the open windows held box fans, but the blades were unable to cut August's stickiness. The heat spun through, blowing the curtains and pages of the book Jill and Luisa read. Luisa sat on Jill's lap holding her mother tightly, her face pressed on Jill's chest. Luisa had danced around in the gray lederhosen and leather beanie. She'd paraded in front of the mirror smiling at her image. She alternately preened and concentrated on the story, looking from the mirror to the pages. Jill and she now used the room for their quarters. Jill stopped at each picture to talk of Germany.

Sadie had purchased hand knit cardigan sweaters, a red soldier nutcracker, and a Black Forest cuckoo clock for Lillian. Henry had looked at his red and brown plaid shirt and bright red-wool cardigan and said, "I've expanded some around the middle, and as much money as I spend, I could give the old geezer a good race on December twenty-fourth, but wait until Mrs. Fredericks arrives in

Caylor." Jill had told him Sadie said he was the closest thing to Santa Claus that she knew, so he should dress appropriately.

Jill and Luisa turned the pages of an illustrated copy of Grimm's Fairy Tales. "Mommy, you saw this?" Luisa asked, pointing to a large black bear.

"No, Luisa. Mommy saw this," and pointed to a wood frame house with rounded eaves and gingerbread wood trim. On the third time through the meticulously detailed pictures, Henry interrupted them. The souvenirs were spread out all over the bed.

"Grandpa! Come here! Look at what mommy saw!" As Henry walked to the bed, he pulled his glasses from his pocket to review the picture. Luisa's tiny finger traced a wood house in the Black Forest that had beckoned to Hansel and Gretel. Each shutter was open with bursts of light illuminating the dark woods. The window openings were carved with heart shapes and hung with wrought iron hinges. Geranium filled boxes decorated each window sill.

"Grandpa, will you make a house like this? For me and Mommy?"

"Sure, angel, where should I make this house?"

"By your garage. Right next. Like this grandpa," and Luisa held her hands out flat. Thumbs aligned, palms down, "one here and one here." She pushed her tiny hands parallel to one another.

"You've got it all figured out, just like your mother and grandma. They always have something for the old man to do, too."

"Come, grandpa, I'll take you." Luisa jumped off the bed and grabbed Henry's hand, "Let's go grandpa, come on."

"Okay, okay, but your grandma wants you to ride with her to go pick up some cucumbers for those pickles she makes. Edith Sigafoos has a mess this year. Jill, I wondered if you would like to drive out to the Ortmann's. Farren and Ferlin were supposed to have the shingling done, but I've got to make sure there's no child labor going on."

"In the raggedy truck?"

"Your mother is taking the car, plus I need to haul a couple of sawhorses out there. You need some fresh country air to clean out that German wiener schnitzel."

"Grandpa, come on," Luisa tugged on Henry's hand.

Jill knew schnitzel was an excuse, but decided a drive out to the country might help dispel the dull feeling that met her when she got back to Caylor. She kept seeing William waiting for her by the Embassy, saying, "Yes, let's just do it, here in Germany." Somehow she could not.

Ten weeks after she left Caylor, the plane landed in Indianapolis. The two to three weeks kept getting extended until baby Mike was born, "early," two weeks or three weeks early. The doctor said full-term to Sadie who swore Jill to secrecy, except Jill had to tell William and repeated his phrase, SNAFU.

Changing diapers and preparing bottles made her separation from Luisa unbearable. William helped and so, too, T.J., but she told Sadie she was going to have to do motherhood on her own. On August fifteenth, the baby's one month birthday, all the furniture had been packed and shipped. She and Sadie dropped off the car at the automobile shippers, then William drove them to Bonn. William had teased them saying they would need a C-130 to carry all their things.

On the plane Sadie had talked until baby Mike fell asleep, and then Sadie laid her head back, completely quiet, sound asleep. Baby Mike was so sweet and bald. William had told her in private that if he were to have some color, it would come later, but the mix of T.J. and Sadie would almost guarantee not much more than Sadie's olive skin. He should be able to pass. Pass? She asked. Pass for a child between Sadie and Michael.

She cried when William held her, promising only Christmas in New York for Mo's wedding. As the wheels retracted in the jet's belly, she separated from Europe and started her return to Indiana, the rest of her world. She wanted to go back, maybe the three of them, William, Luisa and her as tourists and a family. Maybe.

Jill stared out the window not seeing anything, recalling all the days of summer. The scenes flashed as pictures on Lillian's View Master – drinking and dancing at the officers' clubs, with William in Sembach, with T.J. at Wiesbaden and the first sight of the Eiffel Tower. William held her tightly in the crook of his arm, Paris the city of love and lights, bursting fireworks and kissing William. She had wanted to stop time like her favorite 45 record, play it over and over again. But with the bursting fireworks, Sadie started contractions. When the first red and white sparkles sprayed as if the cosmos had sneezed, Sadie screamed. They raced on the autobahn to the base hospital. T.J. stayed relatively calm, Jill thought. But neither of them was allowed to go in with her. They paced for two hours until the doctor announced the birth, a seven pound ten ounce boy. The doctor looked from T.J. to Jill. His expression was puzzled. "Husband?" he asked T.J.

T.J. shook his head.

"Then who's T.J.? She said, 'Tell T.J. I have a son and I love him.'"

"I am T.J."

The doctor shrugged, then said, "Well, if you're not...She'll be ready to see you in another hour."

William had not brought up marriage again, not anytime, until she was ready to walk on the plane. "Promise me you will think about everything we have discussed."

"Okay." She nodded.

"No, Jill, look at me and promise."

"I promise, Colonel Cunningham."

He reached into his pocket and pulled out a small ring box, containing an emerald and diamond ring, "When you decide that your answer is yes, then put it on your left hand."

She looked down at her right hand, Sadie and she decided that was the best option, sparkling green, no commitment yet. Many moments during the ten weeks felt like husband and wife interaction, shopping at the base exchange, waking up, cooking breakfast, saying goodbye at the door, saying hello at the end of the day, registering at the hotel in Paris as Mr. & Mrs. Cunningham. She kept the receipt. Then the View Master pictures ended, "that's all folks," she heard Woody Woodpecker's voice. No, it had been the captain's voice reminding them all to fasten their seat belts for their landing at J.F.K.

She and Sadie had parted company in New York. Sadie had gone to D.C. to show the proud father "his" son. Michael had called every day after the baby was born.

Now she stared down at the holes in the floorboard of Henry's GMC truck. He had patched it with small pieces of sheet metal, then covered the metal with rubber floor mats. The turn signal swung aimlessly from the steering column; the seat was ripped and sponge pieces flew out with each bounce. Henry upholstered the driver's seat with an old scrap of rug discarded by the flooring contractor. The cab was filled with bits and pieces of shingles, wood, marking chalk, nails of all sizes, tool aprons, blueprints, a staple gun and chunks of tar paper. The dashboard was thick with dust. His go-with-him everywhere Thermos rolled back and forth on the seat.

"Who's Mac, Princess?"

Jill spun around to face Henry, "Oh, no. Did he call already? I thought you told me every one who called."

"Ah, first the eyes, then the mind," Henry tapped his temple, "I talked to him. He sounded like a well-mannered chap. Said he'd call again. Who is he?" She looked at the stretch of gravel in front of them. A dust cloud warned of an oncoming car. "You're not answering," Henry said.

"A man I met going to Germany, from Texas but lives in London. Dad, this truck is disgusting. How can you stand it?"

"This truck helped me earn a lot of money so you could go to college, Germany and meet men from London..."

"I think it has nothing to do with money..."

"Well, I kind of like the old truck. It reminds me of myself, old, tired, broke down..."

"Enough. When was the last time you washed it?"

"It hasn't been cleaned since you and Sadie begged to wash it for money, for some juvenile delinquent behavior."

"Jeez-us that was seven or eight years ago. When are you getting a new one?"

"You sound like your mother. I had the last truck fifteen years, 'course they don't make them like they used to, and it's been twelve great years on *this* engine. But, I don't know if I can afford it, if I'm to build this gingerbread house for you and Luisa in the backyard. My women keep my nose to the proverbial grind stone or should I say ankle deep in sawdust?"

"I won't buy into that poor Henry stuff. I understand a bit about the world of finances. I did graduate from college..."

"Now you want to talk about finances," he banged the steering wheel with the palm of his hand, "and college?"

"No, but I will say, thank you a thousand times for letting me stay in Europe. You prescribed the right medicine. I needed it and I know Sadie needed me to be there. It made me realize how much I want to travel to even more places. So whenever you have extra cash...my passport is current."

"And built in babysitters, what more could my wild Princess ask for?"

Henry rattled on like his truck. He extolled his good luck at having Pete Givens, the vice-president of Caylor Bank as a close personal friend. Pete's daughter's college career paralleled Jill's and he and Henry commiserated for the last four years.

Jill stared at the scenery whisking pass the open window. The truck stirred up dust that sprayed the tall weeds on both sides of the narrow road. The small woods dotting the cornfields reminded her of the woods in Germany. It was no coincidence why so many of Indiana's inhabitants were of German descent. Home. She tuned out Henry's prattle about his costly granddaughter, not that he minded. The truck hit a chuckhole. Jill bounced up almost striking her head on the cab roof.

"Seems like you got a couple of men in your life. That Jack fellow called for you. He thought you'd be home two days ago. Any of these fellas smart? I had enough of Einstein. They all sound old."

"They have to be older. The president is killing all the young ones in the goddamned Viet Nam War, oh sorry, police action. Yes, my men are older. I'm older."

"Goddamned? Kinda strong for my princess."

"I just spent ten weeks with Sadie, whose favorite phrase was 'fuckin' Army.' And a whole bunch of soldiers who say worse."

"Any of these older men making a bid for my princess?"

"Dad, I don't know what to do. Jack asked me to marry him. William wants me to marry him and consider moving to Los Angeles. You know I wanted to go to Boston. Nothing seems to turn out the way I think it's going to. What am I going to do with the rest of my life? I hate Caylor, Dad. Jack is twenty years older than me. Twenty years. William is eighteen years older and constantly flying over the iron curtain. Just a little dangerous. They don't take kindly to strangers."

"Dangerous would be an understatement. Twenty years is a big range, twenty-two to forty-two, probably lost some spice by that age. I think too big for someone twenty-two, especially my twenty-two year old. But do you love either one of them? I mean Princess, you need to love someone otherwise you'll never make it through the rough spots. And there are more chuck holes in a marriage than in these country roads. 'Course staying here is important; your brothers took off…"

"You didn't pressure them to stay."

"No, no, they're boys, but you need, seem to need your old man more than the boys. I can watch out for you better when you're close."

"You are always trying to plant me in these god-forsaken cornfields! Southeastern is in the middle of Indiana in the middle of cornfields. Maybe I should go to Germany and wait for a certain pilot. It sounds more exciting than listening to corn grow at Southeastern High School."

"True for you, but it isn't just you anymore. Yes, you are single, but you're a mother. Luisa can't have her mother hanging out in Piccadilly Circus. She will be ready to start school in a couple of years. You have to…settle down, Princess."

Settle down at twenty-two? She shook her head as the truck slowed turning into a dirt driveway.

They pulled in front of the partially built home. Henry jumped from the truck, walked around to the back, and unloaded the sawhorses. The trees had been cleared to make room for the house, but the backyard was still a dense woods. The house was receiving its shingles from the two men that had helped Jill move from Elliston in April. They waved as Henry yelled instructions reminding them that his houses "must not leak." After several, "Have you done this's and that's," they assured him the work had been done just like he said. He turned toward the truck and signaled Jill to bring the Thermos and follow him to the house.

She walked through the framed wood rooms, squeezing through the 2" x 4" studs that would eventually be the walls. Henry pointed where the fireplaces would be, which was the family room, the kitchen, and master bedroom. Jill deliberately inhaled, soaking up the lumber smell and all the memories pine and turpentine evoked. Henry turned over an empty bucket that had been used to mix drywall putty and sat down. He poured coffee in the Thermos lid and handed it to her.

"I wanted to be a preacher when I was twenty-two. But here I am an old man, standing in the middle of my life's work. Oh Lord, Princess, I never wanted to build houses, never wanted to do much of what my old man wanted me to do. I had in mind college, a seminary. Your grandfather, a true old geezer, had other ideas. And this… the rest of my life?" He swept with his arm, encompassing the framed house, "No way. But when I walk through the house like this, I tell the old man, thanks." Henry shook his head and sipped the shared coffee.

Jill thought he was the best father and greatest husband. He enjoyed living his life, joking and arguing with his friends and fellow builders. She and Sadie had talked about what their "husbands" would do before they had any idea who their husbands would be. Jill had excluded builders, arguing against the dirt and rough hands. The inferior image of men who work with their hands instead of sitting in an office had made both girls turn up their noses. Now, looking at her father in the house he was building, his gnarled hands wrapped around his coffee cup, with split and broken fingernails, she was proud to have him as her father. She touched his hand appreciating the skill of men who create with materials that give them rough calloused hands.

"You're saying teach?"Jill said.

"I'm saying don't marry someone twenty years older than you. And wait for the right man. Your heart has not healed from that New Yorker doctor fella. Princess, be patient and take your days one at a time, like the Lord gives them to us, one sunrise and one sunset. You'll get there, but not by chasing around an exciting time. Believe your old Pops on this one. You will get there."

ᚱξᚱ

Jack called. How many times had Jack called? She had raced through the choices of what she would say, could say, when they did talk. She was going to marry a Colonel in the Air Force. Was she? He would have his planes lined tip-to-tip, but when? At least a year. William was trying to stay in the Air Force and work with the CIA. They had a place in El Segundo, California where he could be stationed. California? How many years ago had Klaus reminded her of the sun and surf, almost unreal as the horizon met the Pacific Ocean. She watched the Rose Bowl on New Year's Day with palm trees, 70° temperatures, and the mountains in the background. And all the movie stars…it seemed like…fantasyland in Disneyland where you could visit the enchanted castle of Cinderella.

Jill now slowly walked up the stairs to take Jack's call. What to say?

"Hello."

When she hung up, she had agreed to going to the Caylor County Fair to meet Beau and Robert and their wives and their children. She could bring Luisa if Jill thought Luisa would like to tromp through the livestock barns. Jack's two nieces and two nephews had each entered the 4-H animal contest. Melissa, Beau's daughter, had raised her own hog for her first competition.

"You truly have a farm family," Jill said.

"Swayzee, Indiana, I told you just a farm boy, then an engineer."

Jill fingered the receiver. She wanted to pick it up and call. Call where? William was in Turkey again. He had promised to let her know as soon as he knew when and where he would be in the States.

Call Sadie, later, Arlington, Virginia, a long distance call. If she called later, it would be cheaper. Henry would complain about the charges to his bill. Michael found an apartment with a short drive to the Pentagon. Only three more months and Sadie would be back in Caylor.

Jack was on his way to pick her up. Caylor County Fair, did I really say 'yes'? Would it have been hard to say, 'no'? She would see all her high school friends? Oh, god, see all my high school friends. Jack was big enough she could hide behind him if necessary. And Sadie swore that Jim lived in St. Louis. He had even married a girl from Webster Groves, Missouri. "*He is staying in Missouri*," Sadie repeated, trying to reassure her. And who else could be there? And maybe it would be her last August to go; she might be in California next August. William would never go to the Caylor County Fair. Yes, that will be my reason, *the last fair*.

She stared at the ring on her right finger, so delicate and dynamic at the same time. When they made him a full Colonel, he purchased it at Incirlik. He said, "Time to put the plane in the hangar." What hangar? He was in a plane in Turkey.

Could she call Jack and say she changed her mind? There was the food, always the food, elephant ears and roasting ears, cotton candy. It is August. Had she only been home a week?

Henry said he hoped she had enjoyed herself because, "the hole in my bank account would put the Grand Canyon to shame."

"Yes," she kept saying, "I had a wonderful time." Then to herself she said parts were wonderful, why did Sadie's relationship with T.J. confuse her so much? They both seemed comfortable with Sadie's husband; Sadie's marriage as a permanent part of their relationship.

Wouldn't Michael be suspicious?

"Michael loves me," Sadie had answered to each of Jill's objections.

But would he love you if he knew?

"Michael wouldn't believe it if someone told him because he loves me. And when I'm not BWC, we have great sex. Yes, Jill, and don't look stupid, you and William have great sex. You and Hector had it and don't forget, there was Luis, but we won't talk about that infamous roll in the straw."

ᚱξᚱ

Jack parked in the field of rutted dirt, smashed straw filler, and dried weeds that served as the parking lot for fairgoers. The farmers wore John Deere and Hybrid Seed Corn baseball caps and their scrubbed clean-cut sons all in jeans and heavy boots directed traffic. A farm tractor pulled wagon loads of attendees to the cordoned, trampled acreage, a corner of "Mrs. Winslow's farm." At one time Mrs. Winslow owned most of what made-up eastern Caylor County. Mrs. Winslow had died twenty years earlier, but all the farmers still referred to this section of the county as Mrs. Winslow's.

Mr. Sartoris had explained at her interview that the Southeastern School District bought the land for the complex of high school, junior high school and elementary school from a piece of "Mrs. Winslow's farm." Mrs. Winslow had set up a scholarship prize for the winners of the 4-H animal competition.

As they drove to the fair grounds and then walked through the oddly parked cars, Jack prepared Jill for his family. Melissa was a tomboy with two long blonde braids and broad man-like shoulders. She was big for thirteen, but her father Beau was the biggest of the brothers. Beau was, however, the most gentle-natured and quiet. "His wife Mary Ann is…" Jack paused.

"She's what, Jack?" Jill asked. Jack held her hand guiding her through the field turned parking lot. The sun cast an orange light on them. "She's…" Jack continued, "…strong-willed. I guess she needs to be to keep big Beau in line."

"Beau the gentle-natured? Or did you mean to say she is strongly opinionated, as in 'What's a tramp like you doing with my brother-in-law?'"

Jack stopped. He stared down at her, then his eyes swept across the expanse of fields now covered with tents and carnival rides. Stirred dust blew around as trucks and cars searched for an empty space to park.

"Jack?"

"Yes, Yes." He kicked at a rut in the grassy dirt.

Jill shrugged. "She'll like me or not. Jack, let me remind you I made a choice to have Luisa, if someone, anyone, everyone doesn't like my decision…I'm not going to lose sleep over it. We all make decisions, good ones and bad ones. It makes the world spicy. Let's go, aren't you supposed to feed me?"

Jack leaned over and hugged her, then spoke, "Yeah, I'm supposed to feed you." Jack patted his chest pocket where two ticket edges extended above the cuff.

They climbed over bent smashed barbed wires, the railing in an old fence. Jack had on his jeans, heavy leather hiking boots and a short-sleeved dark green knit shirt. A handsome square, she thought. Her tennis shoes were covered in dust, but her jeans and short-sleeved sweatshirt with the U.S. Air Force insignia were fair clothes. She remembered her last time at the fair, four years ago, wearing the senior cords. She squeezed Jack's hand.

The dust odor mingled with the animal manure and cooking grease. The rides lit up one end of the fairgrounds. The neon lights of the Ferris wheel made her pull Jack's hand again.

"Jack, I love the Ferris wheel."

He laughed, "Okay, after we meet the family we'll go. Anything else?"

"The merry-go-round and nickel pitch and maybe some cotton candy."

He shook his head, smiling broadly.

As they approached the first long white auction barn, Jack pulled her behind an International Harvester combine and a John Deere tractor with twelve rows of earth-tilling discs. The heavy machinery was on display; the salesmen walked among the farm equipment talking to farmers. The men of agriculture wore bib overalls, straw hats, and worn work boots. Many were sunburned, heavy, the big bellies Jill associated with wholesome country cooking of biscuits and sausage gravy. The farmers touched the pieces as if they were precious museum artworks, whistling, then asking questions. Jack and Jill took giant steps over electrical cords, the size of garden hoses that connected generators to the barns, tents and rides on the midway. They walked behind the barn to a spot that was away from the rest of the fair. Jack stopped.

"Jill, I want to tell you about Mary Ann. She is a church woman in almost every sense you can think of. She doesn't drink and allows no alcohol in her house. There is no cussing. She believes adultery is a sin. She has a heart of gold as in do unto others as you would have them do unto you. In many ways she is like your mother, probably like many women you've known at your church."

"And why have you brought me behind this barn to tell me she has strong church morals.? Beau is quiet and she runs the show. She will not approve of us and..."

"And I envision confrontation between you. I like the Caitlin, but..."

"They're your family Jack. I'm not going to...you didn't really think I'd..."

"No. I just know you and your friend Sadie, well just from your retelling of some of... well the things you say or have done..."

"Jack, stop! I understand. I won't tell her what I think until the next time we meet."

He visibly relaxed and squeezed her hand, "Okay, let's meet the Joneses."

"Wait. One question? How *did* you explain *me* to your family?"

"I said, 'I'm bringing the woman I'm going to marry.'" He just finished and there was a loud slamming behind them. One of the back doors of the barn had swung open and a teenage boy led a steer with huge legs and a broad white face with red fur. Jack pulled Jill's hand and walked her into the barn behind the steer.

"Jack, you keep saying that I'm going to be your wife. Don't you think we should be in love, love each other, make love, something?!"

"Sure all of the above. We will do all of the above. It is what husbands and wives do."

"Jack, stop, please stop saying we're getting married. I'm the one that has to say I do. And I don't."

He shrugged his shoulder. He held her hand and continued walking through the straw, dust, and manure covered concrete floor. Faucets with buckets under them lined two long rows of animal stalls. People sat on bales of straw and folding aluminum lawn chairs. Animals and owners were all living under the same roof. The names of local farmers hung from a clothesline strung precariously from stall to stall. Jill looked twice at the first black and white banner with an embroidered cow's head, "McKinnsey."

Jack stopped at her hesitation. "What? McKinnsey? They have a lot of cattle, tomatoes, hogs...They're from western Caylor County. We only meet this time of year to sell the 4-H beef. They are the biggest tomato farmers in the county, though. And now is their busy time with migrants coming to pick..."

Every day, driving to the migrant camp, as she made the last turn from the main road onto the gravel, she saw the giant black and white cow's head painting on the barn's side. From almost anywhere in the migrant area, the huge printed name McKinnsey was visible.

Jill had walked from the church, getting ready to leave at the end of the day. She tried to think of something in Imogene that she could give to Milagros as a present, then she'd seen Luis drive up in the truck. He pulled two bags of groceries from the seat.

Milagros sat in the door opening of the shack closest to Jill's car. Milagros jumped up from the doorway at the sight of Luis's truck. Milagros was the only one who seemed to have this happiness at his presence. He reached into his pocket as she ran to him. Luis pulled out something small. Jill recognized Milagros saying, "Papa Ochoa," but the rest of their conversation had all been in Spanish. Milagros hugged his knees. He patted her head and walked toward the shack where she had been sitting. Luis looked at the VW, then toward the church. He nodded to her, tapping the brim of his hat, then turned to climb the five wooden steps. He disappeared into the cabin.

Reverend Newsom had left a half hour earlier, letting her close the building's door automatically locking it. Jill reached her car and opened the door just as Luis whistled. She turned to look at the shack; he was signaling her to come to where he was. She threw her purse and bag onto the seat, then closed the car door. She walked only to the stairs. He leaned from the opening, then spoke, "Milagros' grandmother would like you to eat with us. Do you have time, Gringa?"

She looked at her watch. Her mother would expect her, sort of. Sometimes she stopped at Sadie's and stayed for dinner, "Sure, I have time." Dinner? Wash your hands before eating. The church bathroom, no she'd locked it. The cabins without plumbing, the outhouses. "Señor Ochoa, where do I wash?" she asked, but stopped.

Her face heated, the wrong question had been asked. She looked down at her feet.

"Soap, Gringa? You want soap?"

She blushed. The heat burned her face. She wanted to run and turned, walking toward the VW. Luis jumped down the steps; she heard his boots on the steps. He came up behind her and grabbed her arm.

"Gringa, stop."

She stood still. He walked in front of her, "Milagros' grandmother wants you to eat with us." He took each of her hands in his and holding on to her wrists turned them palms up, then down, then up. He lifted each one to his lips. His moustache tickled her. He licked each one, "They taste clean to me."

His eyes twinkled. She closed her eyes and took a breath.

"Okay, okay, my hands are clean."

She followed him into the dark house; the only light coming from a small window at the side of the cabin and the front and back doorways. There were sleeping bags spread on the floor. Luis handed her a metal plate from a box of plates and metal utensils, then introduced her to Rosa as she walked in from the back of the house. Jill had seen the older woman. She was round like a pumpkin, her shoulders hunched with the curved back from years of picking. Rosa motioned for them to follow her out the back door. Pots sat on three Coleman stoves and another big one on a charcoal pit dug in the ground and covered with a round barbecue grill.

Rosa now visible in the early evening sun pulled her hair from her face. Her facial skin hung in folds, over her eyelids, and her jowls to her chin. Everything sagged. Jill looked at her eyes, tired black eyes and saw only kindness. She bent and scooped refried beans and rice with twisted and abused hands. Her nails were cracked and packed with earth. And she had asked for soap? Jill bit her lip.

They sat on bushel baskets. Rosa had a folding chair with the back support missing. Milagros scooted her basket next to Jill. Luis placed three warm tortillas on Jill's plate. He started to fold one, scraping beans and rice onto the flour dough. Milagros took Jill's plate and quickly wrapped all her tortillas. Her little hands were swift and competent as Luis watched, waiting to assist.

No one talked during the meal. Milagros watched Jill as if she were an alien. She seemed to be memorizing every movement. When they finished, Milagros went into the house and came back with a large enamel pan. She walked to a pump located two cabins over and started to pump water. Jill followed her and grabbed the pump handle, pushing up and down until the water surged out the steel spout. She continued until the pan was filled with cold water.

Milagros pointed to a flat patch of grass, then motioned for Jill to put the pan down. Milagros dashed into the cabin and quickly returned with Joy liquid detergent. She opened the bottle and poured a cap full into her pan. She collected everyone's plates and silverware. After she had washed them all, she placed them neatly on a jellyroll pan.

Luis grabbed two rags from a make-shift clothesline between the corners of the houses, a rope strung from two nails. One large pot of water had been set on the grill over the charcoal. He picked up the heavy pot using the rags for pot holders, and poured the pot of scalding water over the utensils. He set the pot down and returned the rags to their line. He pulled a cigar from his pocket and using a small burning stick from the charcoal lit it.

Somewhere a few cabins away Jill heard a guitar being picked. She stood.

"Thank…Gracias, Señora Rosa…"

"Señora Sanchez," Luis interrupted. Jill glanced at him. He nodded.

"Gracias, Señora Sanchez," Jill continued. Holding her lips together, Rosa smiled, then glanced from Jill to Luis and responded quietly, "Si."

"Adios, mi amiga Milagros. Adios…" Jill said.

"Gringa," Luis said, but was interrupted by Rosa, "Por favor quedate."

"Please stay," Luis automatically said, translating Rosa's phrase. Jill looked at their faces. They watched her. She moved the few inches back to her basket, then sat. Luis smoked, turning to stare at the descending sun.

"Tu eres hermosa," Rosa began speaking slowly in a whispery low voice; she paused and waited for Luis to translate. Milagros stared at her grandmother.

Luis glanced at Jill, "You are beautiful," he spoke the words gruffly, quickly, and then looked away.

"Por dentro y por fuera. Tu tienes un corazón amoroso…" she paused to look at Luis.

"Inside and out. You have a loving heart." He puffed on the cigar; his eyes fixed on Jill.

"Tu quieres tanto ah los niños y eres tan bonita," she stopped. Milagros looked at Luis, waiting for him.

"You care so much for the children, she says, and you are so pretty."

"Tienes esposo?"

He shook his head, then spoke, "She wants to know if you have a husband."

Jill immediately shook her head, "No, Señora Sanchez, no husband."

"El Señor Ochoa es un hombre solitario," she looked at Luis, he stared at her. She moved her hand urging him to speak. He scowled at Rosa, her look changed to serious. She scowled back at him.

"She's saying that I'm a lonely man," he repeated matter-of-factly, then looked from Jill to Rosa to Milagros, who was nodding. He stood, walked away, then leaned against a tree.

Rosa continued, "El necesita una mujer como tu para llenar su spacio vacio."

He kicked the dirt, chewed on the cigar and paced not looking at anyone, "Rosa says I need a woman like you to fill this empty space." Luis sat down.

"El esta muy enojado con su dolorsa y hueca soledad." She patted her chest as she spoke the last few words.

Luis blew smoke slowly between his puckered lips. He took a puff, then slowly turned the cigar in his hands as if buying it new. He put it back in his mouth. Milagros patted his knee and spoke, "Papa Ochoa, mi maestra, English." The women waited.

He started speaking looking only at Jill, "I'm too angry because I have a hollow space, here." He made a swipe at his chest.

"El pisca tomates, pero es un hombre orgulloso, muy orgulloso." She stopped, turning to look at the thin slice of orange that the sun had become.

"He picks tomatoes," Luis spoke in the third person, "but he is a proud man, too proud."

Rosa, Jill spoke to the memory, I tried to enter his heart, to go with him. I begged. He was proud and maybe too protective of his Gringa. He did not want me to travel in that harsh no-place-is-home life. Maybe Rosa, probably Rosa, I will never know.

Jill now looked at the two Black Angus that were tied head first into the McKinnsey stalls. Straw was deep everywhere. There were no people at the McKinnsey space. Jack continued talking, "Mary Ann could tell you how many hundred thousands the McKinnsey's are worth. She keeps track of the wealthiest farmers in Caylor."

They walked slowly, Jack pointing out how the judges look into their eyes, their mouths, their ears. "I hated the farm when I had to work it, but when it's August and the tomatoes ripen and the migrants arrive, it feels like the completion of another of life's circles. On and on, each August all the planning, planting, spraying..."

"Every year...they come to pick tomatoes...." Jill said each word then stopped.

Jack stood still in the barn, watching a young girl brushing the hind quarters of her calf. She dipped the brush in a bucket of water. Large loud fans built in each end of the barn hummed, blending with small portable radios that played different stations.

"I'm sorry Jill, complete insensitivity on my part. I promise I won't make that mistake again. I want to be the best father I can be to Luisa. I didn't think, open mouth insert foot."

"It's okay Jack, she doesn't know...But we're how many hog stalls from meeting your family and you don't let me say anything about your marriage proposal. You're going to tell your family as if *we* have made this commitment."

"I will say one more thing and then we won't have to discuss it again. When the life cycle completes again, you'll be my wife."

"What about love?"

"Love is a decision and I have decided."

"Jack Jones, I have a few more things to say, one...love is a feeling not a decision. I am seeing another man."

"From Caylor?"

"No."

"From Indiana?"

She shook her head.

"Well, there it is. Indiana is in you. You're just one rebellious cornstalk, you've seen them, one cornstalk growing in the middle of the soybean field."

She shook her head and walked toward the door where they had entered. Indiana is in me. Indiana? Indiana is where I'm from, to *leave from*, not stay and grow, cornstalk? No.

"Jack, this conversation is crazy. In the middle of this goddamned barn at the Caylor County Fair!"

She turned and walked toward the door. He followed her. A young man with his Future Farmers of America jacket was returning with a black-faced steer. She ducked into a stall. Jack faced her, but backed her further in, backing her up against a bale of straw. She plopped down as if it had been placed there just for her.

"Oh, Jack." She knew without a mirror that her face was red. She blew air from the side of her mouth.

Jack sat next to her. She stood up; he grabbed her hand, "Sit down, please."

She sat on the crunchy seat. "There is," Jack spoke, "...Indiana. Smell it, close your eyes and smell it." Jack cocked his head, "Go on, close your eyes." The manure smell and a mooing cow dominated the darkness of her self-imposed blindness. She turned up her nose and frowned. He pulled some straw from their cushion, "Open your eyes, feel Indiana." He handed her the straw. Yeah, Sadie, the manger, making love in a straw-covered manger.

"Maybe I should have said, 'no.'" she said, twisting the shiny yellow stems.

"What is wrong?" He picked up her hand, turning it over in his.

"Four years away from the Caylor County Fair," she paused, letting out a sigh, "not enough time. I thought we were going to have dinner, meet your family, then you start, no, start and end, assuming we are going to be married."

"We are going to get married, but let's go to the Lions' Tent. I did ask you to dinner. And we'll meet the family later."

The county of Caylor was represented in shorts, jeans, t-shirts, square dance costumes, children with red and blue sticky faces from eating cotton candy. Paper cups and cones were smashed into the uneven dried grass field. Girls dressed in red gingham shirts and cowboy hats passed out politically stamped emery boards, fans, potholders, folded rain bonnets, pocket mirrors, then invited everyone to walk through the display tent. Jill waved and smiled at the recognizable Caylor High School classmates. She spotted Marcia, oh so many memories from the party when she broke up with Jim.

"Wait a minute Jack, I want to go talk to my friend from high school Marcia. We were friends, oh everyone was crazy about her. She was the life of our parties. Just wait on me."

Jill walked over to Marcia who was talking to another girl she didn't recognize.

"Marcia, is it still...."

"Jill, oh my god, you look great. I'm Marcia Webster now. I married Artie, can you believe it?"

"Artie, well he is lucky. You look gorgeous as ever. You live in Caylor?"

"Oh, yeah, we do. Call me. We're in the phone book on Hampton Lane. We have to catch up. The man you left over there...the one who looks like Michael Landon..."

Jill shook her head, "I'll call you. My life is... my life has become a long story."

"You know I love you. We have so many people to talk about, Kent, Creighton oh, on and on. You must call me. I guess you know Jim moved to Missouri, got married there."

Jill nodded and hugged Marcia. There were a lot of people she wanted to find out about. Marcia married Artie, why didn't Sadie tell her that one. Henry had called on occasion to tell of another high school friend who had married. Married? No, she wanted to work and then travel. Germany and Paris, yes, she had places she wanted to go. Marcia seemed happy, good –natured Marcia. Did she ever have a bad day? How many other guys besides Artie asked to marry her? Jill waved and walked back to where Jack stood.

"Your friend is so pretty," Jack said, nodding his head in Marcia's direction.

"And she is as sweet as she is pretty. She was popular in high school, all the guys liked her and she just told me she married Artie Webster and he *was* the most popular guy in his class. Strange, I never pictured the two of them together. Now I want to know the rest of the stories. Oh Caylor High School, I tried so hard to leave."

Yes, close her eyes and smell Indiana, the cotton candy blended with the broiled pork chops. The whirring generators and carnival music, the wholesome fat faces of farmers, nothing had changed in four years. Neighbors greeted each other; the county fair became an annual meeting place. Jill wondered which of these people had students at Southeastern.

"Come on let's get something to eat." Jack pulled her toward the food tents. The greasy smell of pork drippings splashing on charcoal floated in puffs of thick smoke. Some tents provided music from portable speakers. They walked underneath the canvas roof. Jack guided her to two empty chairs at one of the oil-cloth covered tables. Extra long tables made up a large square of dining space surrounding the servers and cooks. The diners chatted with the Lion's volunteers. Jack lifted out the wood folding chair, and then attempted to scoot the chair on the smashed grass closer to the table. They sat down with the fifty other people seated around the massive square.

Jack handed two tickets to a white-haired woman in a red apron. Her fat arms and hands peeked out from a house dress. She wore a soldier's garrison cap with the Lions' International logo. She smiled broadly, placing paper placemats in front of them.

"Lemonade or iced tea?" she said.

They ordered. She left, clearing the plates from the people sitting next to them.

"Does this other man want to marry you?" Jack spoke wiping their places at the table. He used the paper napkins, then crumpled them.

"Yes."

His eyes shifted from the table to her face. He straightened the silverware, "I don't want to pry into the yes, but you're sitting at the fair with me…it isn't the activity of someone planning to marry another man."

Jill picked up the stainless spoon and stirred her iced tea. "I said I had a few things to say. I'm not ready to marry anyone. I want to teach and see how I like it, how I like Southeastern. I want to work on a Master's Degree, but first I want to make sure teaching is the place for me. And last, but not least, I want to travel. I plan to go to New York at Christmas and maybe somewhere for Thanksgiving," she paused as the pork chops, fried apples and corn-on-the-cob were set in front of them.

The Lion's volunteer spoke, "This is what comes with your dinner, but we have many kinds of homemade pie for 25¢ a slice."

"Yes, come back and we'll see," Jack said.

"And the iced tea and coffee come with the meal." She smiled. Jill admired her wholesome complexion, wrinkled flawless skin. The older woman had kissable, pinchable cheeks.

"Thank you," Jack said, then looked at Jill as she buttered her corn, the butter sliding off her warm knife. "Here let me show you a trick," Jack grabbed her roasting ear. He thickly buttered the slice of bread that had topped his pork chop, then cupped the bread in one hand and rolled the cob in the curved slice, buttering it evenly. He handed it back to her, grinning, "There, now where in the world could you possibly want to go when the best food and hospitality is in front of you?

"Traveling? I'm satisfied with this neck of the woods. Johnson sends me to Chicago and Cleveland that is enough. People without roots don't last long in the woods. They can't handle the tough times, always running off, away from their problems." He cut his pork chop and stabbed a small chunk of the tender white meat on his fork, then used it to point, "And what about Luisa? She doesn't need a mother running around the world looking for god knows what. Her father…"

Jill stopped chewing and stared.

"Her father," Jack continued, "is a man of migration, always moving. She needs to stay put. What if he wanders back and she is as rootless as he is? What? You need to think about her. One of them has to have the place to come home to and it sure won't be him." He plopped the bite in his mouth.

A fly buzzed around her plate. She shooed it away. One of them has to have a place to come home to. "I have no home, right now," Luis had said. Jack cut another piece of pork chop. Married to a tree? A goddamned tree that knows how to butter corn-on-the-cob.

"Eat your dinner, Jill. We still have to meet the Joneses and ride the Ferris wheel." Jack winked at her as he used his fork to demonstrate that she should eat.

She shook her head. From 'taboo girl' to a 'rebellious cornstalk!' I guess I won't be playing Mother Mary in the church Christmas play. I have to tell Sadie.

Chapter 6

The long gravel driveway connected the square single story brick house to the paved country road. Mrs. Newsom saw the red flag of the mailbox still propped up. The mailman had not passed, had not picked up the letters she'd typed for Ned. She looked at the kitchen clock, one o'clock. Ample time to pinch the buds of the marigolds that were just beginning to get bushy. She picked up the scissors to cut some roses on her way back from the mailbox.

She pushed her hair under the straw sunbonnet. Her long, heavy, black hair made her head hot. The first-time Ned had touched it he whispered, "Raven-haired beauty." Her ancestors were so mixed she didn't know where she got her black hair. The only family she knew was her maternal grandmother who had raised her. Ned had said she was the most beautiful wife in the church's conference. Maybe eight years ago, but now? Well, perhaps she was still the most beautiful preacher's wife in the conference.

The parishioners had welcomed them to Emmaus Methodist Church and given them the three bedroom parsonage even though they were childless. The flowers were her children, each carefully attended and coddled. The women greeted her and politely asked if *she* wanted a family. A family? She wished, hoped, and prayed, but now in July 1965 after eight years of marriage and at age thirty, it seemed only a dream. She had written to an international organization, "Children for the Childless," about adoption, and waited for an answer each day. Ned had reluctantly agreed to sign the application. He was more concerned about his brother, Hugh, the army machine gunner, who was halfway through one year in Viet Nam, than having "curtain-climbers."

Ned would walk across the field from the church to the house at 2:30 to check the mail. It had been three weeks with no letter from Hugh, but the soldier's letters always came in spurts. They prayed for Hugh at each meal and during their private devotion before retiring. She also prayed that Ned would want to try and make a baby. Sometimes her prayers were answered, but not often enough.

She filled a large glass container with water and added a small teaspoon of the green crystal fertilizer that one of the farmer parishioners had told her would help her roses through the hot summer months, John Thurman. He was such a strong man with big square shoulders and a husky barrel chest that never quite fit under his white shirt and brown suit. He looked as if he could slay the enemy with the jawbone of the mule. His face stayed sunburned and sandy blonde curls danced across his forehead. He shared his pew with four children and Mrs. Thurman. Two of his children were born in the same year. She closed her eyes for a minute and calculated what she would have to do to have two children in one year. She shook her head as she shook the water jug, making sure all the crystals had dissolved. She put the gardening spade, water, and gloves into a big plastic bucket and walked out the front screen door.

The sun was hot, the sky cloudless. She felt the sweat forming on her face and her bosom. The front steps provided a wide view of the country road. The mailman was not visible. She shrugged. It could be an hour, an hour to weed around the mums, pinch the marigolds and fertilize.

Fertilize? The Christian literature on marriage had discussed fertilizing the egg, "The sperm must fertilize the egg for conception to begin." After Ned fertilized her egg, he would close his eyes as she wiped him off, like a baby, she cleaned him. Once she had asked him if she could taste it; he dripped and she wanted to see if it had a flavor, his fertilizer. He had had his eyes closed and made no comment. She leaned over to clean him with a sudsy rag. Her hair fell, covering her face, blocking her view as she licked the tip. He had flinched, but she did not look up and kept tasting, and rubbing his testicles with the washrag, then he had started to stiffen and she felt his hands on her head. She was not sure if he were trying to pull her off or push her down, but she had not stopped, putting more and more of his penis in her mouth until she felt her mouth get full and thought there could be no fertilization with this sperm.

He had lain still, eyes closed, breathing heavily. It had been like today, too hot to move and they had lain naked, sweating, not talking. He had not mentioned it for a week, but the following Sunday when they "retired" for their afternoon nap, he had said, "Mrs. Newsom, perhaps you will clean me before we begin." Now as she thought of it, her vagina sweat.

She had sent away for a sex manual that was advertised in *Redbook*. She had sneaked it from the mail, placing it at the bottom of her plastic bucket on the way back from the mailbox. On Saturday nights when he closed himself in his study to prepare his sermon, she pulled out her book and tried to figure out how to do what they said without alarming Ned. After he signed the application for the adoption, he had said, "Mrs. Newsom, I have decided that perhaps we need to know each other..." he had paused and closed his eyes, then continued not looking at her, but rubbing the back of her hand with his index finger, "...to know each other on Wednesday evenings after your women's circle meeting." He had then opened his eyes and exhaled, whistling. And slowly she introduced, "surprises" on Wednesday evening.

Now as she bent over the small dark green plants pinching the tiny flower buds, she rolled the buds between her thumb and index finger and remembered how he had enjoyed the first time she rubbed his rounded buds gently as he fertilized, but still no children, no special green crystals to mix with water. A car engine interrupted her thoughts. She stopped to look at the mailbox. She had ten more feet of flower patch to prune. Her timing had been almost precise, her watch said 2P.M. Her fingers smelled of dirt and marigolds. She breathed in the humid afternoon.

She watched as the mailman sat on the right side of his car, leaning out the window placing letters in the widely spaced boxes. He steered with a long extended left arm and leg. She had talked to him many times, calm, serious fat Jesse Huston. He had three children, all teenagers. His oldest daughter would be graduated next June, then his two boys. He would have three in college at the same time, well maybe only two; he had said his daughter wanted to get married. He had shared his fears with Mrs. Newsom. She had invited him to come to church. His family did not live in Swayzee, Jesse explained, but maybe he could get Rachel to drive out some Sunday. Then one Sunday, they came and continued attending the small country church.

"Emmaus is a friendly church," the district superintendent had explained to her and Ned when they asked to have a permanent church. In 1961 after five years in a roving ministry, they asked to be relieved from the summer migrant work. In June of 1962, at the annual conference they were given their first permanent church, Emmaus on the edge of Swayzee. The congregation was predominately local farmers, "A farmer gave us the house and land for the church," the district superintendent explained, "the same farmers who employed those migrants whom you cared for so deeply."

He had continued asking questions of Ned, then herself, "Janice, there is a very active Women's Society. I'm sure you may already know these women through their contributions of clothing and education materials for the migrant children. Do you think you will be able to continue your teaching and be a full-time preacher's wife?"

"Yes," she had told him, because she was a substitute teacher and did not work every day. And now she had two large bags of rags for the Indian Mission in New Mexico. She was to tear them in strips, sew them together, then crochet them into rugs. The recipients were the "least of these," she concluded, and wondered, if her work qualified for eternal redemption. She now rose from her crouch over the end of the marigolds' row and walked a few feet to the mailbox, the last moments of anticipation.

Anticipation, was that the best part? She had read that somewhere. It seemed so on Sundays when she finished drying the last lunch dish. She would close the cupboard, remove her apron and hang it on the utility closet door, before pulling the phone off the hook and laying it on the counter. Then she would walk slowly down the hallway, anticipating. With each step she pulled hairpins from her

French roll, squeezing them in her fist. When she opened the bedroom door, she dropped the pins on the dresser and unbuttoned her blouse.

In the dim light, she could see Ned lying on his back, naked, asleep, waiting to be awakened, "to know her" as he called it. His body was smooth and white, no suntanned face and arms like their farmer congregants. His head was almost hairless. It would not be long until he was as smooth there as everywhere else. He told his parishioners that "the Lord made a few perfect heads and wanted you to see them," then he rubbed his balding scalp. The congregation church-chuckled, a muffled heh-heh, and then restlessly switched their body weight in preparation for the serious, longer sermon.

On Wednesday evening she had slowly taught him what she had read, then on Sundays he would let her awaken him gently and he would "practice" what he had learned. He never spoke until they were finished, then he would ask, "Mrs. Newsom, am I a good pupil?" Like a deaf child, she guided his hand for speaking the language of sexual manipulation.

They had been at their church home for three years. She missed the migrant children. She paused, then spoke aloud to herself, "Ah, the children. Oh well, maybe today, I'll get something. At least it's Thursday, the weekly paper will be here." She now pulled the mailbox open. There were several letters, the paper and her August issue of *Good Housekeeping*. She quickly checked to see if the adoption agency had written or Hugh, then shrugged, dropping all of the mail into the bucket.

Her personal pruning created a colorful path of roses, pansies, impatiens, and marigolds. The impatiens withered in the sun and she had tried to plant them where they would receive the most shade from the big oak tree that grew on the north side of the driveway. The gravel crunched with each step she took. She waved to Ned as he walked on the path between the two cornfields that separated the church from the parsonage. The small brick church had no steeple, but a large sign carried his name, the time of the services and the name of his next sermon. Their driveway connected to another driveway that led to the parking lot of the church.

She stomped the dust from her shoes, wiping her soles on the welcome mat. She opened the front door. "Honey, here is the mail and the weekly newspaper. I hope they got our ad in there for the chili supper this Saturday. *The Swayzee Enquirer*, or should we say the Swayzee gossip Enquirer?" She placed the mail on the dining room table and proceeded into the kitchen. She removed all the gardening tools in her bucket and took off her sunbonnet, letting her hair fall on her shoulders. After washing her hands, she walked back into the dining room, picking up the paper, "I wonder what scandal they will feature this week?"

"Now Mrs. Newsom," Ned spoke from his host chair at the head of the mahogany table. He loosened his tie, then took it all the way off. He unbuttoned his shirt exposing his hairless chest and flat stomach. He yanked the tail from his pants, then took a long drink from a glass of iced tea, "You know these folks just like to keep track of each other." He reached for the small stack of letters. He put on his glasses, sorting the letters into two piles. "One for the church and one for us." He scrutinized the pieces and ah-hummed at each one. He stopped, holding one long envelope, "Mrs. Newsom, do you know anyone named Roy McKinnsey? Oh, wait, that was the last place we had the small summer migrant facility. M-m, strange."

"Perhaps, Ned, he is looking for help this summer. You know August is only three weeks away. What does he say?"

" 'Dear Pastor Newsom,

I guess a couple of months ago, maybe longer this letter came. The wife and I were vacationing in Texas and Florida, trying to pick a crew for Roy Jr. and myself for the summer. This letter was stuck at the bottom of another pile and I just came across it looking for something else. I apologize for this delay. I had to call the church to find your address. I hope this finds you and Mrs. Newsom in good health. We always appreciated the work you did for the pickers.' "

Mrs. Newsom looked across the table at the back of the envelope, with its small red and blue checked edge, "Honey, who is the letter from? It looks like one of those airmail air grams from a foreign country, kind of like Hugh's letters."

She opened the Swayzee paper and silently read. Turning the page, she spotted the church ad, "Chili Supper, Emmaus Methodist Church, Saturday 5-7P.M. $2.00 per person. All donations will be used for the mission work of the Women's Society of Christian Service.

"They put it on the page with the wedding announcements. Here is a picture of that sweet couple you married last week. They look so young and innocent. It reminds me of our wedding, remember? And you told me you were the luckiest man in the world? Do you still feel like that, Ned?"

She glanced up. His nipples were exposed. She wet her lips, thinking of the Wednesday night she had nursed them, then guided him to nurse her. She touched her breasts and felt her nipples harden; she unbuttoned the top button of her blouse. Ned concentrated on the letter and read silently. She looked back at the newspaper.

"Uh-huh," Ned said.

"Oh, look at this couple, Ned. It is that girl who used to come out and help with the migrant children. Listen, 'Mr. and Mrs. Henry Havlicek are pleased to announce the marriage of their daughter Jill to Jack Jones of Swayzee, Indiana.'

"Ned, it says she was graduated from State University and majored in education. She *is* teaching at Southeastern County High School. She took your advice, Honey, and became a teacher. Listen, 'Beau Jones and Robert Jones attended their brother as groomsmen.' Ned, that's Beau, our Beau from the church. Oh, listen to this interesting piece, 'Jill's *daughter* Luisa was the flower girl.' This gets even better...'The Matron of Honor was Siddhartha Fredericks,' what kind of name is Siddhartha? '...and Roberta Brenton Bashir of Lebanon, I wonder if that is the city in Indiana or the country, and Madeline McClendon of Washington, D.C. were bridesmaids.' This sounds like a United Nations meeting. Honey?"

"What, Mrs. Newsom?" He looked up at her from the thin stationery, "You said, '*Luisa*,' and I read, 'Sincerely, *Luis* Ochoa.' Now what did you say? I didn't hear it all. Beau Jones, what?"

"Here, look at this picture and read for yourself," Mrs. Newsom said, handing him the small newspaper. Ned gazed at the picture and read aloud, "Mr. and Mrs. Jack Jones, the former Jill Caitlin Havlicek." He took the enclosed small envelope and stared at the writing, then spoke, "Jill Habalchek, it is the phonetic spelling in Spanish."

"Honey, what does that letter from McKinnsey say? *Who* is it from?"

Ned handed the letter to his wife; she read aloud,

"March 12, 1965

Reverend Newsom,

We know of each other from the harvest of 1960 at the McKinnsey farm. I was the crew chief for the migrant workers. I am interested in finding the whereabouts of the young teacher, Maestra, the children called her. It has been a few years and what I ask may be impossible. If you know how to contact her, I have included a letter to her.

Mucho gracias, Señor.

Sincerely,
Luis Ochoa

"He signed his name with such thick letters. Interesting. And the postmark is smudged it is hard to read. The 'maestra' has just married."

"Mrs. Newsom, did you know she came looking for this man the next summer? I suppose the summer of '61."

"What did you say to her?"

"We were at Epworth Forest for church camp, but Reverend Sayers said he asked Roy McKinnsey and the workers, but no one knew of him, now this."

"Yes, now this. You do know the whereabouts of the maestra. What will you do?"

"I don't know. No news from Hugh, huh?" He laid the letter on top of the others, then arranged them neatly, corners and edges matching.

"No, Honey, not today."

Ned stood up and walked to the kitchen. He took the phone off the hook. "Mrs. Newsom, it is hot this afternoon. I want to take a nap. Do you think you could find a cool rag to sponge bathe me?"

Thursday afternoon, she thought, following him down the hallway unbuttoning her sleeveless blouse.

ȣ

Thursday July fifteenth, five weeks of wedded bliss, oh stop, Jill Caitlin. Sadie was working on her fifth year of marriage. She has reminded me, how many times? "You'll get used to it." Used to it? A year ago I was in Germany with William thinking of being a military wife, living in California or Virginia. Thinking, only thinking, William was too hard to pin down. Is it too late to visit a tomato farm? Oh, it hasn't worked for four years. I'm married that's it. Resignation? God, I hate that word. Settling. Settling down, she heard Lillian's voice, "Now Jill Caitlin, it is time for you to think of Luisa, what is best for her. You need to think about settling down." She shook her head as if Lillian were standing in front of her. It can't be in concrete not like some handprint in a newly poured driveway.

Wedding planning pushed the reality of resignation far away. A house, a farmhouse, a husband, not Dr. Andujar, but Luisa. All of this marital bliss...bliss? All of this marital space, yes, I'm here, in this box and it's time to think of my baby and her life. I did make that decision, "be the best mom I could be." Jack couldn't be a better father, gentle and understanding. Yes, Sadie, I can do this, I have you to call, to drink with...and Mo, my friends. Bobbie, when will I ever get to Beirut to see her? I promised her at the wedding I would come.

She sighed staring at the John Deere calendar Jack had thumb tacked to the corkboard by the telephone. Their farm house sat on a small rise, up from the surrounding acres of corn. Each direction she looked – out the window over the sink, out the doorway to the screened back porch where Luisa sat, out the bay window of the breakfast nook, rows and rows of symmetrically aligned stalks of corn, green ribbons that rippled, then converged into a solid line at the horizon. Cornfields. She sang, "I'm as corny as Kansas in August... Kansas?" I'm surrounded by these damned Indiana cornfields.

"Chutes and Ladders, please Mommy, Chutes and Ladders," Luisa begged from her seat at the table on the porch.

Luisa opened the game box and put the cards in their places on the board. The screened porch was used for eating evening dinner, reading the paper, relaxing and watching the sun set. It was the coolest place in the 100-year-old farm house, "Only parts are 100 years old, Honey," Jack had repeated several times in the three months it took her to decide to move.

Her kitchen was large with the sink and cabinets included in the 100 year old part. Jack was building new cabinets and each week some of the old ones were removed and replaced with new pieces. He started the project before they moved in. The new cabinets were cherry finished in smooth rich reddish-brown with white enamel fixtures. Jack insisted the house was hers to decorate. She sat at the square table soon to be replaced with a round oak one. Jack was refinishing it in his garage turned woodworking shop.

She cut pieces of crinkle ribbon and slid the narrow blue strands across the sharp edge of the scissors. It curled and she added it to the small pile of already curled pieces. She'd wrapped a small box in blue teddy bear paper. The large present was a Fisher-Price popcorn-popper push-toy. She had tried it at the store, the small plastic balls popped and pinged creating an annoying noise. Luisa had run it all over the hallway, turning into the living room, cutting across the dining room, then back down the hallway to the kitchen until Jill had screamed for her to stop. She smiled thinking of the miles of hallways at the big house on Vicksburg where Little Mikey would have space to run with the pop-pop-pop. Sadie would be ready to kill her! But that was okay; Sadie threatened her for any number of reasons, always. She teased her about being a farmer's wife, living in a farmhouse, in the middle of cornfields. The list went on and on.

The two-story farmhouse sat atop grounds that swept down and away from the gingerbread decorated front porch. The three-sided porch was a selling point for Jill. The hooks were in place for a porch swing. Jack had not found one in any of the outlying buildings, so promised to have one hanging when they moved in. And so it was. The house had oak floors throughout. Henry had his flooring contractor Floyd Burns come and refinish the floors and put new linoleum in the kitchen and bathrooms.

All four bedrooms were upstairs. Jack used one for an office and his closet. He kept his clothes neatly lined up. He organized his shirts and pants in two rows with shoes all polished and placed carefully in their own wood cabinet.

She had furnished the guest bedroom with Jack's old bedroom furniture. She and Sadie shopped for American antiques to decorate the room Jill wanted to be the library. They found fairy-tale furniture for Luisa's room, a canopied bed and Jill's favorite, a four-poster mahogany bed, for their bedroom. Piece by piece, drape by drape, accessory by accessory, she made the old structure comfortable. Two large wooden rocking chairs occupied the front porch, "ideal for watching the corn grow," she told Jack.

They came to their farm home the night of their wedding. Her wedding dress belonged to Lillian, silk cream chemise, very simple, no lace or ruffles and only caps on her shoulders for sleeves. She wore a flower head band with a small lace veil. Jack said she looked Heaven-sent. Everyone agreed except Sadie whose comment had to do with a tramp trying to look virginal.

Sadie gave her something old to wear, a pair of crystal earrings from Grandma Fredericks whose house she now lived in. Bobbie provided the blue garter, and Mo let her borrow a gold bracelet William had given her for her birthday. She sent the bridesmaids pictures of her dress and said dress accordingly; she requested they buy a dress they could wear again. "Color would be helpful, something to liven up the place." She told Henry she only wanted flowers in bloom from anyone's garden, roses, peonies, wild flowers, nothing from the florist. Henry could spend *his* money on champagne. And Jack picked her bouquet of Black-eyed Susans and daisies on his way to the church.

Jill told him, "I do not want a diamond ring. Diamonds are overrated and overpriced! I hate them, hate the whole concept of DeBeers. They control the number of diamonds released, guaranteeing high prices. And they use black slave labor to mine the diamonds in a country governed with apartheid. Jack, have you seen how they treat their black people? It is…."

Jack stopped her mid-argument, "Yes, dear, I understand, no diamonds for Jill Jones."

"I only want a simple gold band, a rose gold band like Sadie's."

The wedding had been a ball; they ate and made merry. She did not want it to end because she thought they would never all be together again. Bobbie lived in Lebanon and Mo in D.C., and each married husbands whose work could take them anywhere in the world. So she drank too much champagne and Jack carried her across the threshold of their farm house, where she passed out on the couch in her wedding dress. She did manage to get up the stairs sometime during the night and lay next to Jack before getting sick. Later the next day, after 7-Up and saltines, she had sex with her husband. It had not been their first time, but perhaps their fourth. Jack expressed discomfort having sex without being married.

The yard was a full acre with an almost new garden shed; Jack had bought the riding lawnmower, garden tools, and rotor-tiller.

He squared off one large section of the backyard for his garden. "You can't take the farm out of the boy," she teased him as he plowed the small plot and planted the vegetable seeds.

Jack made their relationship easy. He was calm, listening to her fears of marriage to a man twenty years older. He would think she was childish. *No, he liked her spunk.* He would want her to stay home "an old farmer's wife." *No, she could participate in farming as much or as little as she wanted.* She would never get to leave, imprisoned by cornfields. *No, during her vacation breaks from school, she could travel.*

What about his family? They were all church-going, upright folks. Yes, there was Chick, but no one...*No, he interrupted, they would accept her as part of them, including Mary Ann.* His patience and understanding with Luisa supported his argument that they should be married. Jill watched them together as they planted seeds; he bent over with her and explained about chemicals in the soil. Jill reminded him Luisa was only four years old, but Luisa said, "Mommy, the vegetables need nitrogen. It is the dirt; they eat dirt, like Mikey put dirt in his mouth and Aunt Sadie said, 'No!'" They had all laughed and Luisa continued, "To hide the seeds and let them eat in the dark."

And finally, Jill had asked, "But what of Luis, will he be thrown in my face?" Jack had held both her hands, kissed her fingertips, then said, "As I'm sitting here with you, I promise never to mention his name as long as I live." Reassured, she had said 'yes.'

After the wedding, the seeds had sprouted and his patience with Luisa was steadfast. Luisa would awaken scared in their new home; he would place her in the bed with Jill, before going to the guest room to sleep. In the morning, he would talk to Luisa and ask what frightened her. He would examine all the parts of her room and explain each piece in the daylight.

"Okay, one game. I must start dinner. Jack will be home." Jill now glanced at the clock, 3P.M., then again at the calendar, July fifteenth. They were to go to Sadie's for cake and ice cream with all the Fredericks for Mickey's first birthday. She had told Jack dinner would be simple because Sadie would have more than cake and ice cream. Sadie seemed ready to impress her in-laws with all the ways she could spend the family money. And they seemed pleased that she did it so well.

Jill fixed iced tea. Luisa wanted the leaves in it, the mint. Jill told her to go pick some and wash it off. Jill transplanted a few stalks from Lillian's patch that had been from hers in Elliston.

A year ago, July fourteenth, Bastille Day, Paris, William. It had been everything a summer could be, love and people and places. In December they had met in New York for Mo's wedding just as he had said. They'd danced, laughed, made love, so fantastic making love with William. Hugging closely in the cold air, they rode the Staten Island Ferry. They visited the Empire State Building, and talked about the great romance of Cary Grant and Deborah Kerr. "Such love," she said, "Do people really have such love in their life?"

He had said, "Yes, they do," and kissed her.

She wore her emerald ring on her right finger during the whole trip. "There is love," he had said, "and then there is the construction of relationship. Husbands and wives must build from lovers, or men and women can remain lovers."

"Lovers?"

"Yes, the simplicity, to just enjoy what is; not molding or making it do more than this, meet, love, laugh."

"Mommy, you first." Jill picked up the card, turning it so Luisa could see, "Five."

Jill moved five spaces and read the instructions, "Pick up one card."

"Three, mommy."

Jill moved to a ladder and bypassed a curve in the path. Luisa moved and landed on the chute, back four spaces. The game board of zigzagged chutes and ladders, forward, then backward, this way, then that way. They mimicked the pattern of the cars on the highway, that March night five months ago. The weather had been awful, a full ice-storm. William had phoned the school, and she returned his call.

"All flights are grounded; I will be here an extra day and night. Please come when you get off work."

William had perfected how to be in love, she concluded in the steely, cold sleet-filled evening. She had crept along the ice-slickened highway to Bunker Hill Air Base, passing cars that had slid onto the shoulders, a treacherous day and being in love with William was treacherous. He never mentioned marriage exactly as he had promised.

He did mention months, "...a few months, Jill. The Air Force is trying this out and they've asked me to..." He would call and she would be asked to move to Europe for six months. Impossible request, she knew he knew. When she reached Bunker Hill base's main gate without mishap, all the way from Southeastern, thirty-five miles, she wanted a drink. They drank, maybe too much. She talked, "Stability, a home, one place with him."

He listened, then he talked, "The Air Force is working on a permanent position that would be in one place, a job created just for me. It takes…Stars must approve, Secretaries of the Service, advisers. Jill, to get the government agencies to use the same co-ordinates takes…"

"Months," she had answered.

As he watched her dress at 2A.M. to drive back to Caylor, she admitted their relationship would only ever be these meetings, momentary at an Air Base or fine hotel. The intermittent rendezvous appealed to her womanly singleness, but she wanted stability for Luisa. William could not give her that, not in March in an ice-storm, not in the mellow glow of alcohol, or the lubricating wetness of love-making. Like always with William, she wanted to suspend time. But she had dressed, then kissed him not knowing when the next time would be. Maybe in a few months on a hop or a pass. Always again, but *not* for long. At 2:30A.M., in the cold, in the dark, inching along the icy plate of asphalt, it was as if a warning sign had been posted, "Dangerous Curves Ahead." Can I be Paul Bunyan's ox and make the twisted straight? "No, not even close," she had answered herself, aloud, "Not in an ice storm, not ever."

Jill now turned over the small Chutes and Ladders' playing card. "Four," Luisa said.

Jill moved four spaces, a ladder. "Pick up one card," Jill read the instructions on the square. "Three" She counted with Luisa, "Eight, nine, ten, Mommy wins."

"One more game, mommy, please, one more."

"No, baby, let's go get the mail. Jack will call and want to know if anything important came."

The farmhouse was fifty yards from the mailbox. They walked and talked; Luisa picked Black-eyed Susans. Jill liked the wild-weed look. "It's natural," she had argued with Jack. She wanted wildflowers to grow wherever they and mother earth thought they should. At the hardware store, she purchased wildflower seeds and sprinkled them among the weeds. She hoped they could take their place next to the "strongmen of the fields."

"The bullhorns and dandelions will take over the yard," Jack had said, then tried to get her to plant flowers in the space on either side of the driveway. He had suggested roses for the area in front of the porch, "Like your mother's geraniums in pots," by the banisters. Not this summer, she had said. She now stopped to take in the view, and remembered Henry standing with her after he had driven with her to the house. He had promised Jack to check the foundation, the soundness of the structure, decide what needed to be done, and ask Jill what configuration changes she wanted. When they were finished, Henry was to give the list to Jack and an estimate of the cost.

She and Henry inspected the house, then walked out the front to leave. On the April afternoon, they faced the spring sun while Henry held her arm. A fruit tree was at one corner, "Apple," Henry had said. The maples and oak trees were tipped with yellow green buds, she thought of Robert Frost, "Nature's first hue is gold, her hardest one to hold." The grass was changing from the brown winter cover to green. In the distance a farmer slowly dug deep black ruts in the tangle of dead soy stalks and weeds. Henry had taken an exaggerated breath and said, "Ain't God good to Indiana?"

The front yard was the only place that was uncultivated. A sea of bullhorns, dandelions, Queen Anne's lace, milkweed, and bright yellow fluffy pods of seeds were everywhere, growing more defiant and prolific every day. Prolific? Jack had surprised her. She had expected methodical as he did everything in his life, a checklist, always #1, first before she could do #2, or #3. She had a list tacked on the refrigerator each day. Before he went to work, he sat, drank his coffee, consulted his pocket calendar, then composed his list. He left it so she would know when to expect a call, if he had an appointment, if he was going to Beau's, to Robert's, the bank, his entire day on a list. But in their bedroom he relaxed. Spontaneous. She had encouraged all his tentative movements, pushing his hand or fingers, positioning his head. Lying in bed, worn down they had discussed children. Jack wanted a son, but only if she wanted another child, "Maybe in a couple of years, when Luisa is in school all day," she had answered quickly.

She and Sadie talked about babies a lot. Sadie wanted another one, maybe two. Sadie was trying every month to get pregnant again "Would Michael be the father this time?" Jill teased. Mikey looked like Sadie so far, same dark eyes, same olive skin, maybe slightly darker as he got older, "very Greek looking" Sadie explained to everyone. His hair was curly. He was gorgeous, a fat baby boy who had no Fredericks in him. Luckily, the family found him to be 100% Fredericks. Old man Fredericks pulled Sadie aside and said his grandmother had been dark-skinned, "Well, olive-skinned, dark olive, Irish, dark Irish." He saw the grandmother only when he was young. She had died when he was six years old. Old father Fredericks was apologetic, but said he never understood so personally what was meant when they argued about eugenics and the influence of one's ancestors.

No one knew except Jill and Sadie. Sadie decided not to tell T.J. after she saw how much the Fredericks worshipped "their" grandson. Mr. Fredericks said it was one of those skeletons, but now looking at his grandson, he realized these skeletons sometimes emerge. Jill and Sadie had chuckled at the story. "Amazing how people come up with reasons, when there are none," Sadie had said.

"Plausible, acceptable, undisputable reason," Jill had responded shaking her head while sitting at Sadie's kitchen table.

Luisa ran several steps ahead of Jill. She stopped to look at her watch. Jack would call in thirty minutes to ask about today's mail. Luisa opened the mailbox, but couldn't see in. She reached with her small fingers. Jill pulled the stack of letters and two magazines, *Popular Science* and *National Geographic*. She handed the *National Geographic* to Luisa.

Jill opened the thick letter from the county clerk's office. "On July thirteenth....Luisa Havlicek has been declared the legal...of Jack Walton Jones, to bear his name..." The attorney had said it would not take long once they were married because the identity and location of her true father were unknown. Jill had squirmed when he said the word, "unknown," but for legal purposes he had to use the term. Jack wanted his women to have his name. If anything happened to him or to him and Jill, Luisa should not be abandoned or left to the "wiles of fortune, or some small print in a legal document." He was adamant; the school would know this was his daughter. Luisa's kindergarten started soon. "Jones" would be a part of her and she would never know another name, "Luisa Jones." Jill looked at the letters written in bold type, no middle name, then she stared at the dark hair parted and plaited with the tendrils outlining her face, dancing on her forehead. Luisa held the *National Geographic* open to a river with a huge flock of soaring birds, filling the space where the sky should have been.

Luisa Jones, Jill would explain that when people asked Luisa her name, she would now say Jones.

As they reached the front porch the phone was ringing. Luisa ran up the steps and into the house banging the screen door.

"It's daddy, mommy," Luisa met her in the hall.

"Hi, Honey," Jack spoke cheerfully. He was a happy man, she thought. He made her feel as if their marriage was the piece of his puzzle he'd been seeking. "Was that Luisa Jones who answered the phone?"

"How did you know? I'm just reading this thick bunch of court papers."

"I had to call Randy on this thing with Chick; Robert with some searching found an address for Hawk. We all need to meet with Randy - Beau, Robert and me because Chick is in Idaho and Hawk is in Florida."

"Meet about what, Jack?"

He explained Chick's most recent demand to extract his percentage of the farm at the current market value so he could start a business. He wanted his brothers to buy him out or sell the property completely and divide it four ways. Beau and Robert were furious. Chick had hired an attorney to help with his latest "hare-brained scheme." She only detected slight irritation in Jack's voice. Knowing his lists, this problem had not been on there, and he was rearranging numbers.

"After our meeting, next week, I'll know for sure, but Robert believes we'll have to talk to Hawk, and he wants me to do that."

"You'll call him?"

"No. We, as in you and I, will pay him a visit."

"Us? Why not Mary Ann and Beau? Mary Ann always says she wants to tear Hawk apart, piece by piece, the Christian way, right?"

"Jill, I thought you'd want to go."

"No Robert and Sally?"

"Sally couldn't handle Hawk. He's too unpredictable, too vulgar for Sally."

"Vulgar? Old man Busching said, 'Vulgarity is the only uncorrupted form of moral discourse.'"

"Honey, we can discuss vulgarity and morality driving to Florida."

"I'm familiar with both," Jill said.

"The second week in August, during Hurricane season."

"How appropriate."

"Jill?"

"Yes."

"You do want to go, don't you?" Jack said.

"I hadn't thought about it – Hawk, Florida, hurricanes, m-m-m, yes, those sound like all the ingredients for a calamity. Calamities are my strong suit, right up there with my chocolate chip cookies."

"I love you and your chocolate chip cookies. We'll take a belated honeymoon. We'll relax and watch the sun set in the ocean."

A belated honeymoon? Honeymoons were sex and romance, candlelight dinners and room service – William. He had always taken her on a honeymoon.

"Sure, Jack, a belated honeymoon."

She hung up and told Luisa to get the stepstool, in order to reach the countertop. They would sign the cards for Mikey. The phone rang again. Jill answered as Luisa reached for the receiver.

"Hello, Jill?" Mo said.

"Mo, please tell me you've called to…"

"I've called because soon we won't be able to talk on the phone and I hate writing letters."

"What?!! How will I ever learn all the joys of married life?"

"I tried to whisper in your ear there were other suitors out there if you just waited, patience. Remember?"

"I do. But why? Tell me, why we can't keep talking? I need to hear your voice."

"We're moving. Stewart got his first overseas assignment. I put my resignation in at Justice."

"Moving? Where? Just now, when I might need some help with marriage 101."

"Oh, is the honeymoon over? You'll get it."

"Okay tell me where in world you'll be and I can't call."

"You'll have to get out the map, I did. Sumatra. You know Stewart wanted to go without me, the scoundrel. I explained to him that Foreign Service did not mean servicing the foreign."

"Oh, Mo, you sound terrific. I want to visit you in Sumatra."

"Sure, sure, anytime. We will probably be there for two years, and I have just the person to fly you."

There was a slight pause. Jill heard muffled sounds as if a hand were covering the receiver.

"Hi, *Mrs*. Jones."

"Colonel Cunningham, how are you?" Jill wiped her hands on a towel and leaned against the wall, closing her eyes for a minute. She felt him as if he were standing behind her, rubbing her neck, not five hundred miles away in Washington, D.C.

"Wait until my daughter closes the door, then I'll tell you." Hearing his honeyed voice, Jill tingled as if blood were rushing to a limb that had fallen asleep, prickly and warm. And Mo had done this. She was leaving for the other side of the world, so she could not get a proper tongue lashing.

"I feel," William continued, "One hundred percent better now that I have you on the phone. Madeline dialed and refused to give me this number and threatened me if I found out on my own. May I take you to Sumatra, Mrs. Jones?"

"William..."

"I know you are married and it's not what married women do, except there is Mrs. Fredericks..."

"Oh Sadie, she has the Fredericks giving her all kinds of reasons why that little boy is dark." He chuckled, the familiar low confirming chuckle. She missed his voice, and imagined him on the phone, the hands, the shoulders, oh the shoulders as she grabbed them and held on, as if the simple motion could change his scheduled departure, change his scheduled life.

"Sumatra? You know the answer..." Jill said.

"My taboo girl, I heard this song and now every time I hear it I think of you, please listen, "My Girl" by the Temptations, I dubbed it 'our song.' I've got so much love...a sweeter song..." he sang in a low whispery voice, "I've got all the riches one man can claim,...I guess you'd say what can make me feel this way...my taboo girl."

"I've heard it, 'sunshine on a cloudy day,' now it will sound...okay, I'll remember 'our song.'"

"How is the angel?"

"Luisa Jones?"

"The circle is complete," William said.

"M-m, circles are always complete, but marriage is the road taken, straight or curved, but not a circle."

"God, I miss you, taboo girl. Sumatra? Palm trees and sand, making love on the beach."

"A year ago today, remember?"

"Paris, and then you were Mrs. Cunningham. I should not have let you go."

"No, William, you understand…"

"Completely. Jill, Madeline *always* knows how to reach me. If you ever need me, anything. I am serious about this - get in touch with me. Life changes, what a cliché, let me start again. The present has a momentary life span about the length of snowflakes on a warm windshield. Find me. Promise?"

"Yes."

"No, promise."

"I promise, Colonel Cunningham."

Chapter 7

Jill pushed the radio buttons of Jack's Cadillac, "our Cadillac" he responded at each of her references. She argued she was "a Volkswagen kind of person." And the next car they buy would be hers, a new VW Bug; she wanted a white one. The Delco radio of the Cadillac was set for his favorite station, 1350AM in Kokomo, Indiana. Now winding through the mountains of Tennessee...the DJ announced, "That was Johnny Cash, folks, and now one of my all-time fave-o-rites..." Not fave-o-rites, oh, jeez. "...from one country boy, Tennessee Ernie Ford, named after our great state..." The first bars of "16 Tons" were played. Nothing changed on the radio in how many years? "'61 to '62, '62 to '63, '63 to '64. She used her fingers tapping time to "...oh St. Peter don't you call me, 'cause..." '64 to '65...four years, four years and I thought, okay, I did not want to ever travel these mountain roads, again.

The car drove smoothly and handled easily. The driver's seat adjusted automatically with a few touches of a button. She moved it closer to the pedals from Jack's position for his long legs. With a pillow wedged between his shoulder and the window, Jack slept peacefully on comfortable white leather. The windows were rolled down. She pulled the button to raise the back windows slightly. The car had air conditioning, but Jack hated air conditioning. The warm summer afternoon whipped through the wide blue car, ice blue. Jack waxed and polished it, a luxurious car, maybe like a Hollywood movie star's car. The first time Jill drove it, Sadie had teased her, "nice car for a farmer's wife." Yeah, a nice car, not hers, but nice. She wanted Imogene II.

After the meeting with Randy, Jack explained the legal wrangling had become more complicated. Hawk was alive and probably in good health and therefore the property could not be bought/sold/leased/transferred until Hawk relinquished his claim to it. Hawk's parents had specifically made him sole heir and beneficiary. He was their only child. "They had no choice," Jack harrumphed.

When the brothers sorted through abstracts, and deeds, Randy suggested they meet with Hawk and buy the land from him, making payments as if he were retired. They would then own it and Hawk would enjoy some financial benefit. Jill interjected that Mary Ann would never agree to such an arrangement. She had told Jill from their first encounter at the county fair to the wedding reception that Hawk was a disgrace to the family, "a despicable human being," and should be purged. Jill had laughed, imitating the particular evil inflection Mary Ann used when saying purged.

Jack drove to Bowling Green, Kentucky, then turned the driving over to her. She used the quiet time to trace the horror she experienced driving through these same mountains with T.J. bandaged and bruised. It had been dark when she drove, although the temperature was the same – hot and sticky.

Jack had left the roadmap on the back seat; the pages slapped in the wind. She couldn't reach over the front seat to throw it on the floor. But the smack-smack-smack of the paper created a rhythm, a backdrop.

Hawk she did not know. There were family pictures from when the boys were small. He appeared stern, upright like the pictures in her history book of miners during the gold rush. His eyes were covered by heavy unkempt eye brows. His lower face was hidden under a full beard and his large head rested on a thin frame with muscular arms. He seemed tall, but the boys were all young and small.

As with most old-time pictures of men, their grim unsmiling faces made it hard to see if he were handsome.

She liked his face. It intrigued her as a black-bearded pirate character. She imagined him with a gold earring and knife gripped between his teeth. Jack dismissed all of it, "He was mean and used the strap especially on me as an example to my younger brothers."

Jack told her, "I promised myself if I ever had children I would never even spank them." His gentleness with Luisa seemed to prove that point. But still, Jill argued with herself, there must be something redeeming about Hawk. Mary Ann's disapproval alone convinced her that he could not be all bad. And why had they all wanted Jack to go to Florida?

The highway cut through slices of stone mountains and deciduous forests. The road twisted and a vista would open to a panoramic view like a religious calendar picture of God's work. Endless deep-green broad leaved trees clung to white granite walls with long narrow waterfalls. "Beware of Falling Rocks," signs stood among sprinkled chunks of gray rock. With the clear blue sunny sky, she now saw the reason for the postings.

But the night, with T.J. asleep she had been more afraid of his waking than falling rocks. She'd pushed the gas pedal out of fear, the last leg of the journey home. Home called to her. Indiana cornfields sounded like a big hug and then there was Hector. He was pulling her then, requesting she leave T.J. at the Medical Center where he worked and studied. He had called Sadie, but Jill was also a part of the rescue team and she had raced to uphold her promise to Mrs. Washington, to bring her son home. Home. How did a person bring their son home? Sadie brought Mickey home. The government brought Hector home.

And she brought T.J. home. She drove the Buick, running from all that hate. She pushed the big V-8 engine into the zone of illegal mph's. All those cubic inches as Jim Bancroft would have called them, hot and racing. She had accelerated hard in the curves, then let off the gas pedal, holding onto the steering wheel against the inertia. "No brakes," she had heard Jim's instructions. In the middle of the night on mountainous roads, Jim's advice came in handy. The steep downgrades only helped her go faster. Jim taught her how to drive. He had had an affair with speed and his four-speed '58 Pontiac Bonneville. 120 mph in the country was his goal, but the curves - that was her Indy 500 lesson. She drove radically and was lucky to be alive. Hector's direction to Sadie, "Be careful."

She risked the possibility of getting arrested. Oh, Hector. She had thought of him all the way to Indianapolis, then and now, a thousand times in as many ways. Sadie kept it up like a Girl Scout, stoking the fire, blowing on it, keeping it alive. "Jill, T.J. just sent clippings from a German paper; it tells about the U.S. Army lying to the American people about G.I's who have been killed, *actually* killed and the rest who are just missing in action, unreported, swept under the rug because they don't know. They are listed as killed. It is easier than finding out where they are. Jill, you have to find out! You're going to New York, next week to Mo's wedding. Go see Hector's mom. See if you can find out something. You have to Sweetie."

On Sadie's insistence she had taken the extra time and gone to E. 178th. Saying the area was too rough for her to go alone, William wanted to go. "I know what military paperwork looks like. I know what it should say, read between the lines."

"No. I must do this myself."

He'd dropped her off and said he would be back in one hour exactly. "Let's synch our watches."

He double parked in the street, and kissed her, "Are you sure you don't want me to go?" She shook her head and touched his hand.

"You have sixty minutes, not one minute more," he spoke tapping his watch.

The cold winter smacked her, blowing up her legs. She had shivered, wondering if she should have stayed in the heated car. William was just at the corner; she could signal him. No. She climbed the broken concrete steps and opened the tall narrow door. The foyer was unheated. Mounting the three sets of stairs, she smelled onions cooking, Pine Sol, old musty wood, a dirty bathroom odor, rotten food. She held her breath. The hand railing was pulled away from the wall; many of the balusters were broken or missing. The wood steps had been patched with sheet metal. She heard Hector's voice, "tenement."

He lived here? She thought and kept repeating it as a question then an answer. He lived here? He lived here. He climbed these steps, how many times? Thousands. Did he notice the dirt and cigarette butts? A door opened and a female voice screamed, "Pinchy bruha!" A teenage girl, heavily made up with black lines on her eyelids, red lipstick and black hair that had been bleached reddish-brown, stomped out of an apartment.

Jill hurried up the last flight of stairs; she had called, explaining to Juanita that she only wanted to read the papers the Army had sent. Juanita had said, "Si, come." Damn Sadie, another one of her crazy ideas.

Jill had knocked and the door opened immediately. Three small faces, brown faces, Luisa faces, all dark-haired with black eyes peeked around the door's edge. They would have been Luisa's cousins...And at once several voices said, "Jill, come in," in Spanish and English.

The apartment smelled of cooking beans and chilies. "Spicy," she told Hector the day he cooked the same menu. The smell transported her to 1254 Butler and his "Puerto Rican specialties." She inhaled savoring the odor. Could the smell put him in the kitchen, the bandana and his apron, stirring, smiling?

Could they take her coat? No, she was not staying that long. She unbuttoned it and put her gloves in her pocket. One of his sisters hugged her, then said, "Guadalupé, Lupé, Hector always called me." Lupé was pulling Jill by the hand down the hallway. Lupé was heavy as if seven-months' pregnant, although she was not. Juanita called after them. "Jill, do you want water or anything to eat?" No, no she had answered, following Lupé.

The two women entered Juanita's room. Pictures of Hector covered one section of the wall. Jill stared at each one. His school pictures from first grade to senior pictures, one with his diploma and a short man with thick glasses, bushy hair and moustache grinning proudly. It had to be Buzzy.

Hector and his curls, a gapped-tooth smile, short hair, and the Army picture with the American flag. The tears formed. "Our place is just too small to hide heartache and happiness," Hector's voice reminded her.

"Jill, it's okay to cry. I look at these pictures and feel like he is just away and he'll be back, then we can take more pictures. I cry when I make myself say, 'Lupé, he is not coming home.' He's not, Jill."

Jill reached in her pocket for a Kleenex. Lupé was Hector's baby sister, the last daughter Juanita had. She was the mother of three, "and only three," she had told Jill. "I promised Hector no more," Lupé said as she patted her stomach. Lupé now pulled a large manila envelope from Juanita's drawer. She handed it to Jill and invited her to sit on Juanita's bed. The dog tags fell onto the rose quilt that covered the double bed. Jill picked them up; the metal was cold, but burnt her hand. She dropped them. Bad idea, Sadie.

She closed her eyes taking a deep breath, pulling her lips between her teeth. Why did it feel like he was now in the room with her? She felt him, on the bed watching; she smelled him, his dimples. He touched her fingers, rubbing her hands like when he encouraged her to talk. She leafed through the papers his handwriting on the white envelopes with the shaded blue, like hers in the storage box at Lillian's.

She shoved the personal letters back into the envelope saving the notice from the Secretary of the Army. She opened it and read slowly, on paper Sadie, "in service to his country…Lieutenant Hector Alonso Andujar was killed in action on August 6, 1963."

No missing in action, Sadie, killed. "They lie Jill, they lie about many of the guys, the places they send them, what their mission is. You can ask Michael. He heard it from the guys who'd been. He read those memos from General to General, coding and encoding all that jargon." The letter from Arlington Cemetery confirming the date of internment, September 3, 1963.

"They lie Jill. Read it carefully." Jill glanced at her watch, five minutes to be at the curb. She jumped up from the bed, then ran out of the room down the hall. Lupé rushed behind her.

Jill crossed in front of the couch and into the kitchen where she put her arms around Juanita's shoulders as she stood over the stove, "Gracias, Señora Martinez." Juanita turned from cooking and hugged Jill tightly in her soft heavy chest.

"Jill, my son loved you and you're welcome in his home, here, anytime. Our home is your home."

Jill mumbled she would come again, the next time she was in New York. Hector, could you please be here when I come again? Jill hugged the little ones, then opened the door and turned to face the small place, "Remember your Uncle Hector would want you to study and to speak English. He cherished each of you. He talked and talked of becoming a doctor, right here, because he wanted to be with you.…"

"Honey," Jack now spoke, "you look so sad. Are these roads giving you problems?"

"No, no. Sad? Really?" She tried to see in the rearview mirror; Jack reached and pulled her sun visor. She glanced in its mirror; the mascara was smudged under her lower lashes, she pushed the leather shield against the window, "I guess I am ready for some coffee. I think the last sign said twenty miles to Chattanooga. So you want to change drivers there?"

"Sure, Honey. Are you certain you're okay?" Jack reached and touched her shoulder, then pulled gently on a piece of curl.

"Yes, I'm fine. I just had this feeling about digging up our past…revisiting, a place, people…it seems that it is probably not always the best thing to do, you know?"

"We have to find Hawk, make sure he isn't a corpse. And yes, I know. Hey, where do you want to stay tonight? A nice pool, champagne?"

"A cold beer sounds better."

ฯ๎๎๎๎

Two hours on the road, not far from Valdosta, the "Best Country Kitchen in South Georgia" sat off the road. Semis competed for space with pick-ups in the truck parking section. Jack pulled the Cadillac into a space close to the door. The morning was hot and thick. Jill gauged the humidity high because her natural curls were tight and fuzzy. After their wedding she had cut her hair. Jack said, "Whatever makes you happy."

"Midge's Country Cookin'" was near the junction that led to Columbus. Jack had seen the sign and asked if she wanted to stop. She said 'yes,' but wondered if anything had changed in four years. The TV and newspapers were full of marches, protests, sit-ins. Dr. Martin Luther King, Jr. was everywhere, urging people to have strength to fight non-violently.

Walking through the doors to the large restaurant, she did not see a black-faced customer. Four or five black men worked in the kitchen. A honey-haired hostess took them to a booth and she placed the plastic covered breakfast menu in front of them. She asked in a syrupy accent if they wanted coffee. Jack picked up the small stainless steel clip that sat in the center of the table advertising "Midge's Country Biscuits and Gravy." He switched back to the menu, "Biscuits and gravy. Sounds yummy as Luisa would say. It's been awhile since I've had biscuits and gravy."

143

Jill watched him as he frowned, something in the 'it's been awhile,' she heard pain.

"And," Jill said, "it will be a longer time before you get them from Jill's country kitchen. I don't like them. They'll probably serve them with grits and I hate those."

"Good morning, Jill Jones," Jack spoke, sardonically.

The waitress placed brown heavy mugs in front of them with a cream pitcher. She was in her forties, Jill guessed, rounded hips, chest, face, round brown curls around her face, a porky-pig nose. And bright red chipped nail polish.

"Thank you ma'am. You must know I have to have cream," Jack said.

She took their order.

"Why," Jill spoke, "do they talk like that? 'Yes, suh, how ya'll doin'?"

"Okay, Jill, that's the second snip of the meal, it's written all over your face, your lips are pursed. Mrs. Jones is disgusted?"

"The South, I hate the South. Jeezus, Jack, it's all over the news. They hate black people, call them that disgusting n-word, send the dogs after them, spray them with fire hoses...."

"Stop. We'll eat our breakfast and go."

"You smile at her, 'Good Morning, ma'am, thank you, ma'am.'"

"You know nothing about her. You are generalizing about all Southerners. They are not all alike."

"If she weren't like them, she'd move out of this area so no one would know. Why would anyone want to be labeled a Southerner? Talk about vulgar and immoral!" Her face heated and she knew Grandma Caitlin was about to explode.

"Honey, I'm not defending prejudice or discrimination, but I believe firmly in assessing each person as an individual. I remember your Cynthia stories about her disliking you just because you were white. And you were angry about it."

Jill stirred her coffee. The room was outlined in booths. One area next to the kitchen was designated "Truckers Only," then there was a long counter. She tried to see the men leaning against the counter in Dickie work clothes and t-shirts, jeans. Most wore cowboy boots or leather work boots. They were the faces she saw on TV, standing, jeering as they turned hoses on black people. She shrugged her shoulders, "I had a baby. I guess I can do anything."

Jack shook his head.

She said, "Do you want to change your mind? We can't get an annulment because we've consummated..."

"Quite well, let me stop you there..." Jack said, smiling as if catching his first big fish.

She picked up her coffee mug as the waitress placed their breakfast in front of them. The servings were large, taking up the entire heavy oval china plate. The waitress set two small bowls of grits by them. She put the green ticket on the table; a broken front tooth distinguished her face.

"Where y'all on your way to? You're not from these parts."

"Florida. We're quickly passing through, "Jack answered, winking at Jill.

"Georgia's a lovely place, but the TV people are trying their damndest to make us seem like we hate our Ne..black folks. I've been around blacks all my life. I can't imagine livin' without my best friend Sarah. We couldn't go to school together, but we studied together. If it hadn't been for Sarah, I wouldn't have passed English. Sarah moved to Atlanta and went to college, a Nee...a black college. She calls me every Saturday afternoon when I get off work...I better get back...sorry about bendin' your ear. Ya'll have a safe trip."

When they stood to leave, Jill reached in her billfold and pulled out two dollars and left them on the table.

"Honey," Jack said, "I already tipped her..."

"I don't want her to think all Northerners are alike." Jill smiled, and then walked hurriedly toward the door. Picking up the roadmap, Jill slid into the passenger side, "A whole book of places to go," she said reverently touching the cover.

"We need to get only to St. Petersburg today."

"How were your biscuits and gravy? I couldn't decide by the look on your face if you were enjoying them or cleaning your plate because you're supposed to."

"Okay." Jack said, leaning forward to turn on the radio. He moved the needle up and down the dial.

"I didn't mean to sound impossible in there. If you like biscuits and gravy, I'll make them for you. Luisa might like them. Prayer fed her some grits when she was two months old. I never fix them. She might like those, too."

Jack was quiet. He adjusted his seat and the side view mirror and rear view mirror. Jill removed her sandals and turned to face him.

He reached over and pulled her to slide closer to him in the seat. He rubbed her thigh under her skirt. Jack preferred her in skirts, like William, she thought it made her appear older. She wondered, but did not ask Jack why. Some things Jack did not explain. She and Sadie talked a lot about May Rose, Jack's mom. They tried to figure what kind of mother she was, but Jack never talked about her.

"Jack, will Hawk ask about May Rose? Or does he know she died?"

"He tried to kill her so many times, he doesn't care about her."

She opened the road map. "Whew! Maybe we should go somewhere else for our honeymoon. Ft.Walton Beach? Mobile? New Orleans? The French Quarter? Interstate 10 goes all the way west, to Los Angeles. We can still turn. I hate the South, you hate your father, and you just accused him of attempted murder. Jack?"

Jack slowed the car down and pulled onto the shoulder.

"Oh," Jill said, "I suppose it's my turn to drive, after fifteen minutes...I'll drive." She slid back to her door. He put the car in park and left the engine running.

"Honey, stop. I don't want you to drive. Come over next to me." She scooted back to where he was. He frowned as sadness fell over his face like a veil. He leaned one arm on the steering wheel and the other one on the back of the seat. "You're probably starting to think I'm crazy, but there are just things about my family I don't talk about, never talk about. Like a box of old pictures on a shelf, I never take them down. But I want you to know and I don't know how you can unless I tell you.

"First, I want to make a promise to you. I'll never strike you..."

She pulled away from him, moving slightly toward the door. He stared at her as a tear rolled down his cheek. She reached and turned the ignition off, this gentle lover, who touched her delicately as if she were a porcelain doll. He needed reassurance for each intimate touch, pinch, massage, nibble. She coaxed love-making out of him, when he had lain on top of her the first time, he asked repeatedly, "Am I hurting you?"

"No," she whispered, squeezing him tighter on her, reaching her hips up to meet him so he would know, she hoped, how comfortable she was with his love-making.

"You're okay? This is all right?" he had asked.

146

She had locked her legs around his and said, "Okay," then yelled, "Jack, tell me how I feel to you!" His face had broken, dissolved into pleasure.

Her husband now faced her with a tear on his cheek. They were stopped somewhere near the Georgia/Florida border on the shoulder of Interstate 75 with a dense pine forest as the backdrop. Slowly, one picture at a time, he told of the beatings, always after Hawk drank. He made all the boys watch, except Chick who was not to be disturbed.

"Like a macabre show, he made us sit in the kitchen doorway, huddled together in our pajamas. We couldn't move or speak. If we closed our eyes, he slapped our face. So we sat with our eyes open and our minds closed, seeing, but not seeing.

"He slapped her with his palm, cursing and asking her if she liked it. If she nodded, she was smacked across the face with the back of his hand. If she said 'yes,' so we could hear her, he'd say she was lying and smack her with his palm. Back and forth, back and forth, his flesh on her face. The sound made me cringe.

"I begged for God to make him stop. He would. Never a reason that we could understand why, he would just stop and pick her up, like a bag of potatoes over his shoulder. God he was strong. Then he'd carry her through the kitchen to their bedroom, but we couldn't leave until he'd come back and given us his fatherly advice, the bastard."

"Jack, it sounds awful. I don't think I want to know what he said."

"I want you to know how awful he was, how truly brutal…he wasn't profound, just disgusting vulgar trash about our mother."

"Don't make this worse on yourself, just stop Honey. We can talk…"

Jack put his finger on her lips, "'Boys,' he'd start, 'if you don't remember anything else about your wife, remember this – you got to show her who's boss.' And always the next morning mom would be in the kitchen making biscuits and gravy. They tasted great and Hawk would eat a big plate full. When he was finished, he'd rub his stomach and say, 'Boys, if you want this kind of cookin' from your wives, you beat 'em, then fuck 'em. Make their pussy purr and your meals…' he'd laugh a disgusting evil laugh."

"You never tried to stop him. I don't understand," Jill interrupted.

"When Beau was thirteen or fourteen, he got his first burst of that big size. Beau never said anything. He still doesn't talk much. Anyway, Robert and I didn't know Beau had a plan. Hawk called us from our beds and he had mom at the table, she was saying, "No, Hawk, not in front of the boys, they've seen…" he backhanded her, but it was the last time. Beau jumped over Robert and me and punched Hawk. Hawk slid into the refrigerator. Beau turned into a punching machine. Mom was screaming that he was going to kill Hawk. We didn't care if he did, but we knew mom didn't want that. Robert and I grabbed Beau and took him outside. We got in Hawk's truck and drove around for hours, all over those country roads, talking. And we promised each other never to hit, never to do any of it." Jack took a deep breath, and stroked Jill's cheek with the back of his hand.

"But your mom, May Rose, why didn't she leave?"

"Now that I am forty-three, now that I have some adult perspective, I think she didn't know she could. She married Hawk when she was sixteen and he was nineteen. Then all of us, one right after the other, stair-steps. Her father was furious she got pregnant; he may have beaten her, too. She never talked about her parents. She died so soon after Hawk left, we weren't grown enough to ask. I think she had died long before Hawk left. He killed her spirit.

"Gram and Pop Jones acted like they didn't know what went on at our house. I remember Robert asked Gram once when she took us shopping for school clothes. She just shushed him saying, 'Now Bobby, a marriage is a private affair. Pop and I don't meddle.' And Hawk was their only son; maybe he learned it from his father. They disregarded everything Hawk did. He would leave us and stay gone two or three days. But when he came home, he was always angry and mom would get a beating. What a twisted, backwards…" Jack sat quietly touching her face and hair. She leaned over and hugged him.

"Honey," he spoke in a hoarse whisper, "I've thought about this, thought about it a lot. I was afraid, maybe still am, thinking that if I became a husband…" he bit his lip, and held his breath, then let all his air out. "…If I became a husband that something would happen, silly, I suppose like becoming a vampire after being bitten by one. Am I like alcoholics, one slap away from being a wife-beater?"

"Jack, you don't have to worry about that because if you ever raise your hand in a threatening way, I'll kick you where you're not supposed to be kicked. Henry taught me that, and when you bend over, I'll take the palm of my hand like this," she held her hand flat moving it toward his face, "then ram your nose up into your face. Think Grandma Caitlin doing karate."

He shook his head, and then kissed her. He held her face on his chest. The steering wheel pushed against her back.

"I love you, Jill. I promise I'll never do anything to hurt you or our daughter."

ჯღჯ

Bradenton, Florida was part new developments, part old wood frame houses. Henry had given them addresses for the houses he had built; Jack and Jill had driven by them. Forty years and the white framed bungalows still stood without evidence of much ware. She found Henry and Lillian's winter cottage in their quiet community of retirees. The sandy lawns and heavy trees with their Spanish moss represented the romantic South of *Gone With the Wind*, but she and Jack now drove to Ocala for their last planned stop in Florida. They spent most of the week at Treasure Island, staying at a motel on the beach. Henry pressured them to stay there, "It will be a romantic honeymoon hotel, Princess."

She was sunburned. Prayer had been so right, summer in Florida was not the time to sunbathe, but the ocean and sand were seductive. Once or twice she allowed herself a thought about love-making on a beach in Sumatra. Was there such a beach? Even closing her eyes, there was no imagining Jack was William.

The thick jungle forests of Central Florida broke into cleared grassy horse farms. Bright white fences separated the plantations from their wilderness, swamp surroundings.

"The address Jack, are you sure? This looks like a land lost in time. Maybe an alligator will crawl out of the woods."

"Yes, Jill. We're headed for Hawk. Robert and Randy verified his address and drew this map on how to get there. Hawk would pick an out-of-the-way place. He's not a friendly, neighborly person."

"We can still go back to the main road and go home…"

"This issue has to be settled. I could give less than a damn about making a social call, but my brothers need me to do this. And if they came, they might end up with blood on their hands."

149

A white crushed gravel road led them between two parallel white fences. Peaceful. Pastoral. It smelled of newly mown grass. Pastures and riding tracks extended as far as she could see. All outlined with the painted wood fences. Horses grazed on the lush green grass plotted in precise squares.

"How does Hawk fit into the serenity of this horse farm?"

"I don't know, but soon we should know something." Jack answered.

Jack parked directly in front of the two-story white brick farm home built along a semi-circular driveway. Columns from the ground to the roof held up a large overhanging porch. White wrought iron furniture and huge molded concrete planters decorated the ground floor veranda. The planters brimmed with red geraniums and tumbling vines. The veranda was surrounded with thick bushes of pink and white blooms, well-kept, like Lillian's flowers. He got out of the car and walked up to the front entrance, white double doors with brass handles.

Saturday morning, the end of their honeymoon week, and this stop Jack promised, "...will not take all day." They would head home, trying to get as close to Atlanta as possible, then drive the rest of the way on Sunday. Jack had stressed diplomacy and speed. How could anyone be diplomatic with a violent person? As she waited, the colorful character descriptions intrigued scared her. Where does Hawk Jones fit into this thoroughbred horse ranch?

Another road veered around the house and into a pine woods. Behind their car a secondary road led to garages and a screened box that housed a tennis court. Two sleek black horses were tied to a hitching post beside the house.

Hawk could not live here. Jack must have received the wrong information. He banged the knocker and waited. The door was opened by a short, fat man wearing yellow Bermuda shorts and a navy blue golf shirt. Jill could not hear what he said to Jack. The man seemed friendly gesturing with his hands in the general direction of the deep woods behind the house. They talked for a moment, and then the man peered toward the car and waved at Jill, smiling. He shook Jack's hand and watched as Jack walked down the sidewalk to the car.

Jack with his khaki pants, madras shirt, and loafers with no socks dressed like the *Esquire* models. Where did he get his excellent taste in clothes? She shrugged, watching her handsome husband return to the car. He'd been exceedingly gentle in their love-making this week and spontaneous. One afternoon, he dragged her from sunbathing covered in oil and sand, insisting he wanted to make love while she was oiled and sweaty from the sun.

Jack now slid under the steering wheel explaining that Hawk did live here, but had his own trailer. He drove past the house onto a paved road, no more decorative white gravel. Another small lane branched to their left following a white fence that surrounded a large oval track and two long rows of stables. In the distance a black horse and jockey paced slowly around the track. A semi with an attached horse trailer was parked next to the stables. The painted sign on the truck door was a horse's head and read, "Fine Arabians." She could not read the address until it said "Ocala, Florida." A teenage boy stood hosing out an open stall.

"He has the coolest job today," Jill said.

Jack said nothing. He frowned and the ridge between his eyebrows deepened with each of the turns past the pieces of the horse farm. She noticed he clenched the steering wheel. The narrow lane made a slight curve into a thick clump of trees and then to a cleared area. Tall pines made an alcove for an Airstream aluminum trailer. Paved parking spaces for three cars were carved from the woods. A sandy patch of grass next to the trees allowed for two more cars. A gutted pickup sat on concrete blocks. Jack braked, staring at the rusted shell.

"God, that looks like the old truck! No, no, it must be another one. He always swore by the old Ford, he kept telling us the Ford truck would take him wherever he wanted to go. We always prayed that it would hurry and take him."

Jack let out a deep breath and parked in the space between an old black cockroach looking Hudson and another Ford truck, a newer model, but still beat up. The sand had blown in tiny drifts under the wheels and pine needles covered the roofs and windshields. The new Cadillac stood out in the space between the dingy cars.

"Are you sure, Jack?"

Behind the trailer a tangled jungle of Spanish moss covered oaks seemed ready to take over the metal hulk. The trees blocked the sun. The clear, sky blue day was now dark in this spot of shaded oak and pine. The clearing was quiet, a muted silence as if light and noise had been extinguished. "I thought," Jill continued after no response from Jack, "that you said Hawk was a hobo. Nothing around here seems to move."

"Jill, it's been almost twenty years; maybe he's changed in his old age. That man," Jack pointed back towards the large home, "...funny we laughed about having the same name, Jack. Jack Lassiter, he said that Hawk was in charge of his stables, but had Saturdays off and we'd find him here. Come."

Jill got goose bumps as she held Jack's hand for the short walk to the trailer door. As Jack knocked, they heard a rustling sound from under the trailer, but nothing appeared. They saw only the scratchy palm fronds brushing against each other. She stepped closer to Jack.

His second knock made a padded thud on the door. Instantly the inner door was opened. A tall black woman, the color of devil's food cake, with large eyes and a white rag tied around her head scowled at them. "Yes?" she asked in a velvety low tone. She stared from Jill to Jack and back, then over their shoulders. Her inspection continued like a bouncer in an old speakeasy, peering through the screen at their shoes, their arms, hands and faces. The woman did not move. Her body was sinewy, sleek in her light cotton dress.

"Jack Jones, for Hawk Jones. Mr. Lassiter said we would find him here."

"Yes," the woman said, then closed the door. Jill squeezed Jack's hand, peering around the end of the trailer, a small space with a butane tank and what looked like a doghouse, but there was no dog. The inner door opened, then the outer door was opened, forcing Jack and Jill to take one step backward to accommodate the swing. A man almost Jack's height stood ram-rod straight, staring with the friendly blue eyes that had enamored Jill at her first meeting with Jack.

"Come in. Come in." Hawk's face was baked red-brick brown, like Henry's; the color of white skin exposed to years of sunshine. His eyes crinkled with deep crow's feet. Close up the whites were bloodshot. The old man's cheeks veined like some geology cartography map all swirling asymmetrical lines. Hawk's gray Dickie pants, pressed with a polished crease, were held up with suspenders. The sleeveless v-neck undershirt covered a muscular chest. Rough scarred arthritic hands reflected his age, but his defined arms were like a young man's. Seeing him, Jill saw clearly how much Jack must resemble his mother and Robert, who had always seemed unrelated to the others, was the image of Hawk. Did Hawk know this about his son Robert?

Jill shook his outstretched hand. Hawk pulled her next to him, giving her a hug. He smelled of Palmolive shaving cream, soapy, clean, Henry before the Old Spice.

"Jack, introduce me. Is this *your* Mrs. Jones?"

"Hawk, this is my wife, Jill."

"When did you stop working those columns long enough to find this pretty piece of horse flesh?" He asked, but immediately laughed, a deep hearty laugh.

The small trailer was neat, trim, ship-shape. Starched white doilies protected highly polished mahogany end tables. Equestrian statues and trophies dominated the tops of all the flat surfaces. The linoleum floor was waxed to a mirror finish, no rugs. A small black and white TV sat in one corner on a brass rack, a ceramic horse, rearing on its haunches competed for space with the twisted antenna. Hawk walked to the TV, turning it off, "Damned nuisance, can't hardly see it anyway in the middle of the jungle. Have a seat. Have a seat."

He motioned towards a small couch upholstered in a spotless cream colored slipcover, the only place to sit in their miniature living room. Hawk seated himself in a large dark brown leather recliner which overwhelmed the space. He was stocking footed and the footrest touched the arm of the couch. Two pairs of well-worn, but highly shined boots sat on a sheet of newspaper by the door. The woman left the small living area down a short narrow hallway. Jill heard a door close. Almost instantly as if the closed sound were his cue Hawk yelled, "Louisiana get in here. We have company. My son and his wife are here. I told you I had sons."

Louisiana quickly reappeared. Her head rag was removed, revealing braided hair, the black and gray plait started on both sides of her center part and clung to the edge of her scalp. Her dress was fitted at the waist. She stood at least two inches taller than Hawk. She was expressionless except for her eyes; they watched with intensity. She had a wide mouth with bittersweet chocolate colored lips, a flat nose spread between high cheekbones, tough, strong hands with short nails, and no jewelry. Jill caught herself staring at Louisiana. How different from the other state-named friend Madeline Missouri McClendon.

Hawk snapped at Louisiana to get his children something to drink. There was a large clock in a horse statue that hung in the kitchen, the space an extension of the small living room.

"May I," Jill started toward the kitchen, "help…"

"Sit your frisky ass down. Louisiana can handle this. You're my guests."

Hawk offered bourbon straight or on ice. Jack refused. Jill accepted; the clock said 11A.M. Jack frowned at her. She shrugged.

Louisiana handed him his drink and placed Jill's drink on a tiny end table. "Jack, Mrs. Jones, forgive my bad manners," Hawk winked at Jill, then continued, "Honestly, I've tried to lose such civilized things as manners and formalities, but as far as I run, deep as I hide, there's always some bastard shows up. Reminds me I ain't alone in this garden. Meet Louisiana, meanest black bitch south of the Mason-Dixon. Horse looks at her and stops in his tracks. They don't like to see her climb over the fence. I met her in Wyoming, didn't know she was a woman at first, all buried in chaps and flannel. Bam! I got the clothes off. Tamed the flesh." He shook his head and hummed, "M-m-m-m, oh yeah, going to *do* Louisiana with a banjo on my knee."

Louisiana sat without moving on a barstool wedged between the kitchen and living area. Her eyes stay fixed on Hawk's face as he laughed at his remade lyric. "But," Hawk took a large drink from his glass, "I want to know about this red-head..."

"Hawk, this is Jill *Havlicek* Jones of Caylor..."

Hawk stopped still, then twisted in his seat and stared at Jill. He pursed his lips and furrowed his brows, never taking his eyes from her face. He rubbed his chin and squeezed his mouth in his hand. Finally, he took another drink and hoarsely said. "Lillian Kohlhass? Mother-fucking-Christ! You married her daughter. Mother-fucking-Christ, Jack. You married *her* daughter! You're her mother-fucking son-in-law, my son is her son. Mother-fuck! Louisiana get me another drink!"

Her daughter? Jill shivered, the goose flesh appeared on her arms, this was, no impossible, not this grizzled rude, irresponsible...Swayzee, mom said her boyfriend was from Swayzee, no, impossible. She rubbed her forearms, then spoke, "Most people say I'm like my father..."

"Hank Havlicek, good son-of-a-bitch, damned good, but Hank Sr. ....he could have been hitched to a wagon, no different between him and a mule, but your mama was a fine woman. Jack's mama..." He drank a big swallow, his shoulders fell forward; he stared at the ice cubes, "no matter how much bourbon..." he rattled the ice against the glass. He stared at Jill. His eyes, studied her, struggling, then sadness washed his face. He used the back of his hand to take a quick swipe at his eyes. Could he cry?

He shook his head, answering her silent question, "Jill, it was a different time, virgins, good girls, bad girls. You sowed your oats and hoped you didn't get caught. Oh, how Lillian cried, that wonderful woman never did nothin' to deserve those tears. She loved me so... Jesus, it hurt. I hated all of it, hated life, hated May Rose, hated her, and she was..." He emptied his glass.

"Hawk, "Jack spoke, "it was a long time ago..."

"No, Jack! It was fucking yesterday! Louisiana, more bourbon, no ice! And give my daughter-in-law some more. Caylor was different then, well, maybe not. I haven't been in twenty-five years. You like it?" He stopped, glancing at Jill, and then continued, "Naw, you don't like it. I can tell by your face." He paused as Louisiana poured bourbon into his glass, then refilled Jill's glass. "How'd you end up with the engineer?"

With the last question his tone changed. Cynicism replaced his sadness.

She started to tell of her first introduction to Jack. Hawk nodded as she told of teaching, the farm, "I have a four year old daughter. I traveled a different road, Hawk, maybe times have changed in Caylor after all."

"Not Jack's daughter, I guess..." he half-asked, half-stated.

"Yes and no..." Jack said, "I've adopted her."

"He couldn't," Jill interrupted, "be a better father, really, he gets a gold star for patience and love."

Hawk stared from Jill to Jack. "Well, you made an honest woman out of her, for the right reasons."

"Jack did not make an honest woman out of me. I was honest before I ever met Jack..."

"Hey, feisty filly, Jack. I'll drink to that." He raised his glass.

"Yeah, lots of Irish in her genes..." Jack started, "Her grand..."

"Caitlin Galway Havlicek," Hawk said, "talk about feisty bitches. Jeezus she used to turn bar stools over huntin' for Hank." Hawk threw his head back laughing. "And Hank would crawl behind her...now all of 'em dead, raisin' hell with the devil." He laughed again. He caught his breath and addressed Jill, "I'd like to see you go off on those Bible totin' philanderers of Caylor! I bet you got enough Galway in you."

Jill laughed and raised her glass, "To Bible totin' philanderers." She laughed again as Hawk laughed heartily.

Louisiana prepared supper in the small kitchen. She leaned over the counter that divided the living room from the cooking area, "Will you eat with us?" Her voice was seductive.

Jill turned to face her, opened her mouth, but Hawk spoke, "'Course, they're stayin'. Louisiana cooks better than she ropes a bull."

"Hawk," Jack said, "we can't impose..."

"Impose? For Chris sake, you're my son."

Soon the tiny space was filled with the smell of baking corn bread and frying chicken. The bourbon never stopped flowing. Hawk told stories as if trying to catch up on his years of absence. He told of rodeo days in Montana and nights spent under railroad trestles, of working ranches as men went to war. Hawk alternately pulled a pouch from his pocket, patiently rolling cigarettes, then drank bourbon. Louisiana filled plates and handed them to all the Joneses. They ate where they sat.

Jack looked at the clock then his watch. Jill picked up their dishes and carried them to the tiny counter. She had just volunteered to help clean when Jack asked her to get the papers for Hawk from her purse. She walked by the bar and bent to retrieve her purse by the side of the couch. The room spun as she stood straight.

"Here, I need to sit down. I feel dizzy."

"Can't hold your liquor?" Hawk laughed.

Jack unfolded the sheaf of papers, "Hawk, Chick has put us in a legal bind, us, I mean Robert, Beau and myself..." Hawk set his glass on the table and started the process of rolling a cigarette.

Jack continued, "...we've sent you letters...our attorney...the abstract company said...we were thinking about a trust fund, you'd be paid monthly. This way you'd enjoy your inheritance now instead of never. Chick and you....well, he'd get a lump sum..."

"You're talking of taken' my property from me. I read your damn letters. I ain't a moron; I scratched through that legal shit! You look like fuckin' May Rose, now you're actin' like her...takin' my life away..." Hawk threw the cigarette toward a saddle-shaped ashtray.

"Hawk, you know enough about the numbers to know we are *taking* nothing; we'll be paying you the market price. Robert has..."

"My sons takin' my property..."

"We can challenge you in court, possession is nine-tenths..." Jack said.

Hawk leaped from his chair and punched Jack on the side of his face. Jill screamed. Jack reached for his face; a drip of blood was at the corner of his lip. He took a deep breath, and stepped toward Hawk, then backed away, shaking his head. Jack pulled a handkerchief from his pocket, then glanced at Jill. He stepped away from her, staring. He glared at Hawk. Jack drew back his fist, readying a punch. Hawk had inched away his right arm bent, his fist clenched, then as he started his forward thrust, Louisiana grabbed his arm. Hawk in one motion turned and slapped her with his left hand, knocking her on the couch. Hawk yelled, "Leave me alone, bitch!"

Jill planted her feet and pushed Jack toward the door, then turned to face her father-in-law, "Who the hell do you think you are?! Hitting a woman and your son? No wonder you left your family. You're a weak piece of man! Jack told me you'd been brutal, but I wanted to meet you. I have and he was right. You're disgusting. My grandfather may have been a mule, and my grandmother feisty, but you, you're a horse's ass!" With her arm she took a full sweeping motion of the trailer, "Sorry that was an insult to horses!"

Her face flushed. She pushed past Jack, yanking his hand as she reached the door. Hawk whooped. As Jack took the first step down, Hawk yelled, "You finally did something smart, Jack, you married you a feisty bitch!"

Jack whirled, pulling away from Jill's grasp, clenching his fist. Louisiana stepped between the two men, "Go now and don't come back to our home!"

Hawk yelled from behind Louisiana's shoulder, "You'll never be able to satisfy that feisty bitch! Hank never could Cat!" Then his laugh boomed through the jungle cul-de-sac.

Jill sat silently in the car. Jack had brought her to meet this devil, her mother's boyfriend from Swayzee, the boyfriend who...The white fences became blurred lines buckling the dark green swamps, then the humid green wall separated them from the evil. The wind blew through the Cadillac. She tried to breathe deep, closing her eyes.

"When were you going to tell me about Hawk and my mom? When did *you* know?"

"I hoped never. I grew up hating your mom. Everything that was wrong with my mom...he never stopped reminding her of the goodness of Lillian Kohlhass. I did not know Lillian, but I prayed she would die."

"And when...Jack, don't you think this is something I should know?"

"No, not something you should know. It is so painful. I didn't want you to know any of this pain ever. See what is going on here in this car between us."

"When Jack? When did you know?"

"Maybe..." he sighed, "Last year when I took you to the Crabapple. Your mom has an old wedding picture of her and Henry in your hallway with their marriage license. Two plus two. Honey, I struggled with the information."

"But you asked me to marry you that night."

"I wanted to marry the woman I fell in love with. My entire childhood, over and over again I heard of the woman, Lilly, the one not married, but should have, the big regret of his life. I couldn't let that happen, not a never ending story, like a country song of unrequited love. I decided I would not, could not follow in his footsteps."

Jill stared out the window; her hair blew, she pulled the curls from her eyes, "Sumatra."

"Sumatra? Indonesia?"

"Mo moved there last month and said I should visit. I think I need to go. Please stop me if I ever mention going anywhere south of the Mason-Dixon Line; Lincoln should have let them secede."

"Sumatra?"

"Maybe. I have a few weeks left of my summer vacation."

"Sumatra?"

"Yes, Jack. One, you said I could travel, and two, after that bullshit you just put me through...Sumatra sounds so inviting."

Chapter 8

Grass, trimmed, fertilized, "Mr. and Mrs. Suburb," Jill had said to Jack who countered that they lived eight miles from the closest suburb. Eight miles, not seven and a half. After four years of marriage to Jack, she knew when to give up the fight. Now the front yard looked as if it had been carpeted like "a goddamned golf course." Jack had cussed at the weeds one too many times. He plowed and sprayed, then seeded the front yard to match the back. Jill planted the rose bushes. They grew thicker and richer each summer. The oak tree was bigger in spite of losing two large branches during the ice storm in March. Now in August full of leaves and birds, the scarred bark of the lost limbs was difficult to see. The tree shaded the porch and the small tea table and chairs where Luisa sat. Her dolls faced her in their own chairs, listening while she read the story of Cinderella. She showed them pictures from a Golden Book and explained the details of the glass slipper. Their closest neighbor, and only girl playmate near to the farm, had left on vacation.

Jill planned special activities for Luisa, Vacation Bible School, craft classes at the YWCA, day camp at the park, but at eight years old and living on the farm, Luisa had learned to play alone. At the moment, Jill wanted to sit on the porch swing and get away from the heat of the kitchen. Jack had taken them on vacation for their fourth wedding anniversary in June. They had stayed at her Aunt's cottage on Lake Macatawa in Michigan. The cool breeze of Lake Michigan and the channel that hosted freighters in and out of Holland, Michigan, was a welcome change from the farm. She did not tell Jack about the déjà vu she experienced when they passed the sign to Benton Harbor and St. Joe.

Four years, married to Jack…had it been that long? Spring, summer, fall, winter again and again, the days that filled the months became rote. After he was told a small cyst on his prostate could be treated with radiation, the doctor severed his vas deferens as a safety precaution. But it had made a "vast difference" as Sadie and she had said. Thank goodness. Luisa was the only child she wanted. And why didn't she want more children? It didn't matter why, she just didn't.

Sadie had become a baby machine for both of them. After little Mike, there was Claudine who looked like Michael and was named after Michael's grandmother. Claudine had dirty blond stringy curls and large blue eyes, Michael's with his long lashes, and olive skin like Sadie. She had a plain prettiness, like a girl of the prairie. Sadie wanted to keep her in dresses because "girls wear dresses." And last spring, four months ago, Sadie gave birth to Caitlin. "I had to name her after you Jill, she was born on your birthday." My twenty-seventh birthday present, baby Caitlin.

Baby Kate had no hair yet, Sadie's large dark eyes and very pale almost translucent skin. Sadie had decided one more try for another boy and she would be done, "maybe in a year or two." Jill had suggested a trip to Indianapolis to see T.J., that he seemed better at making male children. They laughed and drank cold beer. Sadie labeled Jill "blasphemous." Luisa usually begged to go to Aunt Sadie's every day because there were so many places to play and real life babies to read to. After each pregnancy, Sadie returned to her slim figure, saying, "Chasing curtain climbers keeps me thin."

The Joneses settled. Who would want to keep up with them? "A happily married couple." Teaching nine months, working in the garden, sewing clothes for the fall and winter, going to church,

Luisa's classes – gymnastics, swimming, children's choir- a basic monotonous existence. What happened to…?

Mo sent a letter a week after arriving in Sumatra with her address and the current mailing address for her father. He made Mo promise him to make sure, "Jill always knows how to reach one of us. I tried to tell him you were married to a successful man who was quite capable of taking care of you…He only said, 'Do this for me Madeline.' He loves to give orders, the military and all. And the rest of the story, well, we are all adults now, so I will let that ship sail." And for all these four years, whenever Mo moved or William got a new mailing address, Mo sent a short note with the current information. And why did "My Girl" become such a popular song? They still played it.

On occasion Jill wrote him and he returned her correspondence. The return envelope said Bob Smith and went to Sadie. Maybe she wanted to know she could if she needed to. Sumatra became her standard line to Jack when she had had enough, "One day," she kept saying to herself.

Southeastern took so much of her time. Teaching rewarded her in ways she never imagined. The kids coming in after school, talking about sexual problems, things they didn't want to discuss with their parents about dating. After school she worked with students struggling to learn English It gave her the most satisfaction. Elena Zambrano taught an English for Spanish-speakers class on Saturday mornings. Jill assisted her. It kept her Spanish from becoming too rusty. Jack and Luisa used the time to go visit Beau at the farm. Luisa fed and brushed the animals. Mary Ann made them big breakfasts.

Lillian was shocked at the story of Hawk; although Jill never told the whole story of all the beatings and the constant reference to Lillian as the reason Hawk was miserable. Lillian did say that even though he only lived a couple of hours from them in Florida she did not have the "least bit of interest" in seeing him. "Too long ago," Lillian said, not the "fucking yesterday," of Hawk's rant.

Henry and Lillian welcomed Jack like their sons. Lillian always asked how Jack was before mentioning Jill. Jack was Mr. Nice Guy. Jill fought everything in her power not to be a bitch just to see if she could shake him. She reminded herself that sometimes decisions made for all the right reasons left her feeling hollow and just at those moments she would sit and write William.

The smell of baking peach pie, sugary nutmeg mixed with the scent of the roses surrounding the porch. The rag rug felt mushy against her bare toes as she swung. She sipped iced tea, then pressed the cold glass against her forehead. Jack had said no air conditioning, "Just open the windows; the natural airflow will keep it cool." Kept it stuffy, she had said to herself. Arguing with an engineer about airflow was useless. Jack would be happy she had canned all the peaches he picked at Robert's.

Jack was easy to please. He liked to have the house in order and dinner in the oven when he came home from work. He wanted to make love a couple of times a week, never two times in a row, but at least twice a week. Well until about a year ago, then he got into the routine of every Saturday night. In the summer he would mow the grass, riding his John Deere. Saturday evening was "Girls Night Out" and he would take her and Luisa out to dinner at Caylor's finest, Mrs. Meigs. He ordered Salisbury steak and old fashioned cream pie. They'd stop at Henry and Lillian's, then home. Tuck in Luisa and watch television, then to bed. He was gentle, passionless. "How could he be passionless?" Sadie asked. He was mechanical, do this, then that, then he was done.

She closed her eyes. August. The locusts had started their buzz. Yes, she had driven by McKinnsey's, yes very slowly, but nothing. Her August ritual. Sadie always called to tease her, "Been there yet?"

The church newsletter had said Reverend and Mrs. Newsom were taking a church in Logansport a move from their church in Swayzee. Did Reverend Newsom ever hear...no, he would never have heard about Luis Ochoa. Oh, Luis, Luis, we made a baby. The first kiss more passion in that one moment...nine years ago...it's the heat and humidity. The condensed water dripped down her bare thigh; she wiped the cool water, then rubbed the glass against her legs. The sun brightened the cornfields; the green ended at the blue...it had been Luis, his mouth...she licked her lips and pushed against the rug. The chain creaked on the hooks, Luis.

Saturday morning nine years ago, a day off from going to the migrant camp. She woke up early and rode her bike by Sadie's, trying to roust the dead. Sadie slept soundly, not budging when Jill pulled off her sheet. Sadie cursed in the pre-dawn light, but never opened her eyes. "Only love or madness," Sadie had said "awakened people before the sun rose," and then she mumbled, "too early to make that decision. Go my little red-headed friend and call me when you get back." It had been a whole conversation, and Sadie had not moved, dead asleep. Jill then rode her bike alone beyond her usual boundaries. She was curious, and the thought that she might see Luis overruled all objections – Lillian's shoulds – she called them. He had told her they work six days a week, not like her "easy" schedule.

His seriousness and an occasional look intrigued her. Did he like her? She had not been around a *man* who liked her, but had a hunch if she presented herself in a certain way, not really knowing what that was, he might respond. Convinced, with Sadie's help, and not wanting to be only "Miss Church," she rode by the McKinnsey's tomato farm.

Hiding from her small charges, who played closer to the church, she cycled in back of the farm cabins. The early morning sun brought the fog to the top of the tomato fields. The gray-yellow mist of dawn hid the workers bent over the bushes moving slowly, steadily through the rows. The bike tires crunched on the asphalt as she passed the silent field hands. She tried to distinguish them from *him*, any unique movement or visible sign. The vast expanse of tomato plants and workers blended, obscuring the individuals. She stopped on the tractor path to the open field, and drank from the small water jug she carried in her basket. Sweat ran down her face; even at this early hour the humidity held the heat. Later in the day it would be oppressive, the bike ride impossible.

The bent backs of the migrants moved in deliberate procession, one or another occasionally standing to stretch and rewrap a bandana or neckerchief. Several trucks drove in and out of the fields between the end rows and the main road, hauling tomatoes to the canneries. She scanned the open field, but did not see Luis or at least she could not identify him from all the others. After finishing her drink, she poured some on her face. The rivulets ran down her neck soaking into her top.

She turned her bike slowly retracing her path towards Caylor. As she came to a four-way stop, a pick-up approached. She stopped, waiting for the driver to see her. Tall corn stalks and weeds lined all sides of the intersection. The driver would have to stop at the 4-Way. Caution taught her to wait and make eye contact before she crossed in front of an oncoming car. She faced the truck, staring at the windshield. The sun reflected off the glass making it impossible to see if the driver had seen her.

The truck stopped; the visor was pushed up. Luis's hazel-green eyes frowned under his straw hat. Caught, she froze. He motioned from his window, beckoning her to come to him. At that moment she wished she had listened to Sadie. Could she melt in the heat? Disappear in a wavy mirage? She rode the short distance to the truck. Luis stared, then said, "Jill, it is too early and it is Saturday. I know you are not lost. You wanted to see me?" His stare was a challenge. To look away? To move? To flinch?

She rolled her eyes, took a deep breath, held still, then answered, "I was riding my bike..."she paused. The blue chain guard had "Schwinn Tornado" stamped on it; the basket was bent from a drop. "You said you worked on Saturday," she fingered the black handlebar grip and small holes where the multi-colored plastic streamers had been, "I was checking." She closed her eyes. Why didn't I prepare a story?

"You questioned me?" His eyes underlined his demand. "Let me put your bike in the truck. I'll take you home." He bounded out of the truck. He handed her the water bottle, then stepped in front of her, grabbing the front handlebars in one hand and the seat in the other. He hoisted her bike into the bed of his truck. His deft actions startled her. She had not counted on this reaction. She had not counted on anything; and tried to figure out what she should do or say.

He turned towards her, so she now stood directly in front of him, "Luis, I can take myself home. I got this far. I know my way back."

The truck was used for hauling supplies to the workers. Bushel baskets, new, used and dirty, were stacked haphazardly from the floorboard to the passenger door and on the passenger seat. The only empty space to sit was the driver's seat. He brusquely lifted her, setting her down in the truck like a rag doll. His hands felt rough on her bare arms. He slid in next to her. She rested her feet on the large hump in the center of the truck's floorboard. They occupied almost the same space his shoulder brushing against her shoulder. She had worn short shorts to ride in the eighty degree heat; the vinyl seat cover burned her bare legs. The intimacy of physically touching Luis intensified her curiosity. He smelled of the ever-present rotten odor of tomatoes mixed with the smell of earth and fresh plants. She cringed and breathed deeply. Her bare thigh and shoulder touched this man she hardly knew. She tried to relax, but the heat of his body added to her discomfort.

The truck was new, but battered.

"It got hot so quickly this morning," she said, using her hand to wipe her forehead.

Luis frowned, "Indiana, August."

While the truck bounced along the country road, she tried to think about a serious question, not the weather. She wanted to ask him about his life; she repeated it, Luis do you have a girlfriend, then could not say it aloud.

"Can you leave them to work alone? I mean you don't have to stay here?"

"Jill, I will need directions. This is too far for you to ride your bicycle. You are too young to be alone on these back roads, anything could happen to you. Why did you want to see me?"

"I just did. I don't know why," she whispered.

"Do your parents know you ride alone in the country?"

She looked down at her hands. She used her index finger to trace her knee scars from a fall she took learning to ride the bike. "No," she paused, "Well, sort of..."

"Don't. Tell me you won't do this again."

"But I ride my bike all the time."

"Tell me you won't do *this* again."

"Luis..."

He stared at her. She shrugged, "Okay." Her concession broke the tension.

"I only come," Luis spoke, "to this place once a year, but the truck drivers in Indiana, Ohio, Oklahoma are the same."

"Where *is* your home?"

"I live in Texas, but only a few months out of the year. We constantly move. I have no permanent home, at least now."

"How do you get your mail?"

"You rode your bike out here to ask me how I receive mail?"

"I guess I just wanted to talk to you. You come and go, but you don't stop to talk. I wanted to know who you are. And that's why I rode my bike out here."

"You little gringa, your curiosity could be dangerous."

"But how can I know unless I ask?"

"What if I stop this truck out here on the country road and take you?" She heard the seriousness in his voice, but he smiled.

"No, you wouldn't do that," she shifted in the seat, causing friction between her bare leg and his jeans.

"But I'm not the only one driving a truck on this road. You make yourself a target. Your clothes expose you and make you tempting. Did you think of that?"

"No," she answered, but she sat up straight and turned her face toward him, trying to match her shoulder to his. "You are treating me like your daughter and you're not old enough to be my father!" She flipped her ponytail as he faced forward.

He slammed the brakes. She put her hand on the dash, catching herself. He pulled the truck to the grassy shoulder. She opened her eyes wide and opened her mouth to speak. He pushed her chin up with his index finger and tenderly kissed her. Her lips tingled from the brush of his moustache. She grabbed his shirt collar, reflexively hanging onto him; he pulled away, "Si, I'm not your father. I will stop because I think you understand."

She sat back squeezing slightly closer to him; the sudden stop had shifted the empty baskets. He eased back on the road, "Please go on about this conversation you wanted to have with me." He leaned over her; his arm rested on her knee as he reached for a cigar that lay in the ashtray. The pungent odor mixed with the tomato smell and filled the cab.

Startled by his stop, then the impulsive kiss and now his arm on her leg, she reached toward the door handle. "Stop the truck! I want to get out."

He slowed. She pushed against him, nudging him. He drove completely off the road, then put the gearshift in neutral. He yanked on the emergency brake. She tried to move him.

Facing her he put one arm on the seat behind her and the other around the back of her head. He leaned forward and kissed her, separating her lips. She tasted the cigar on his tongue. Her chest pushed against his, her thin top stuck to his sweaty shirt. She thought he would let her out, but he wrapped his other arm around her shoulder, his tongue still in her mouth. She stopped pushing and gripped his tongue between her lips. His moustache scratched her lip, a tickly scratch. He held her in a half-hug, pulling his tongue from her mouth.

He gently pecked the end of her nose, as he opened his eyes. "Whew!" he whispered, shaking his head. He pinched her cheek, then turned and put both hands on the steering wheel. He shifted gears, released the brake and headed onto the road. Something had changed in the cab, but she didn't know what. Her voice trembled, "I really, honestly, don't talk to strange men or kiss them. I don't talk to men at all. You're from another world, a long way from Caylor. I just wanted to know you." She saw the city limits sign.

"I won't drive through town with you. I've read the 'No Mexicans Served' signs. These are your home folks, you should be safe."

The truck stirred the dust in the parking lot of an abandoned grain elevator. He helped her down, then quickly took her bike from the back of the truck. His shirt clung to his muscled chest, as he handed her the bicycle.

"Luis, thanks."

He stared down at her, pushing his hat off his forehead. He placed his hand on her hand as she gripped the handlebar.

"'We dance around in a ring and suppose, But the secret sits in the middle and knows.' Your Señor Frost." He leaned over and kissed her on the tip of her nose.

She mounted her bike glancing towards the truck; he was making a U-Turn, a gravel dust cloud obscured her view.

"But the secret sits in the middle and knows?" Jill now idly pushed the porch floor, swinging in the afternoon heat. Is it possible to ever feel that way? No, her past, a time…the heat and innocence dancing, twisted in some rite of passage. Who are you Luis? Where are you? Can I please see you again? Why do I do this to myself? "The secret sits in the middle and knows." And I dance around this ring…She drank all of her iced tea and sucked on an ice cube.

"Mom?"

Jill looked down at Luisa who now stood with a brush, rubber band and ribbons.

"Oh, I forgot. I did say I wanted to braid your hair." Jill pulled Luisa toward her lap and had her stand in front of her. She brushed Luisa's long curled black hair. "Did I ever tell you about Milagros at the migrant camp?"

"I like that story, mom. Tell me again, and how she had hair like mine."

"Milagros was very shy…"Jill started.

"What kind of name is Milagros?"

"It is Spanish for miracle." Jill parted Luisa's hair.

"Why did you name me Luisa? Was there a girl named Luisa?"

"No. I named you after…"

"After who, mom? You stopped."

"After a very special person. Now Milagros, she would hide from me…"

The phone rang. Jill got up from the swing and hurried to the kitchen phone.

"Jill," Sadie said, "what are you doing? Come to the club and meet me for drinks by the pool. Someone is here, I want you to see. Please, please?"

"Hi Sadie! Bored again? Surely the babies are keeping you busy…"

"Why is it when I have something extraordinary to share, you make some sarcastic reference to my procreation skills?"

They laughed. Jill explained pie and dinner.

"Stop Jill! I know how long it takes a pie to bake. Get off that miserable farm and get in here!"

Jill just mentioned Sadie and Luisa jumped up and down. Jill told her to clean up the dolls and get her swimsuit and towel. Luisa swam like a fish and stayed in the water until her fingertips looked like raisins. She and Jack had discussed putting in a pool, but the maintenance made Jill shudder, too much work. She decided to piggyback Sadie's Country Club membership and use the Caylor Public Pool. When the heat got unbearable, they went to Beau's cottage at Lake Manitou.

Mary Ann, what a nosey, phony, "Jill, I don't think Bob McKinnsey has the same pickers every year, why do you ask?" Mary Ann what would you know of love and passion? Mary Ann left in June for the lake and came back in August or was it Labor Day? Jill was sure Beau looked forward to his summers without her. He did go up there occasionally. Beau made Jack promise to go to their cottage whenever they wanted. "Inn-Over-Our-Heads" they called the two-story five bedroom place.

Jill changed quickly; putting on her swimsuit, then threw on a sundress cover-up. She pulled suntan oil from the cabinet. The phone rang. No doubt, Sadie saying hurry up. She is so impatient. She told Luisa to get her swim toys and put them in her canvas pool bag.

"Hello?" Jill said.

168

"Jill Havlicek?" a female voice asked.

"Yes, well no, Jill Havlicek Jones, who is this?"

"You'll never guess…Cynthia Ferguson Chandler."

"Oh, my god, Cynthia! I am shocked. Where are you? What? It's been nine years or eight, too many. A voice from the past."

"I know you are probably in the middle of something, but I have a specific reason for calling, and then we can catch up. You know the problems they're having in Kokomo this summer, my hometown, and I'm disgusted."

"A riot in Kokomo. I was surprised. The whole world seems to be coming apart…oh Cynthia, it's awful, but if racial problems are the reason…"

"I married Reggie Chandler. Do you remember him?"

"Sure I do, the best looking guy in the Class of '56. You lucky thing…"

"I think so, but Reggie and I have been working hard at the church trying to figure out something positive we could do, something for Caylor to cross these boundaries, Eastside-Westside, black-white. We decided to start with the women – an interracial group, a place to discuss issues and be socially comfortable. I tried to think of women who might be interested. I called your mom and she said she thought for sure you would like to be a part of something like this and gave me your number. Reggie and I sat down with another friend from school, T.J., remember him? T.J. Washington?"

"Yes, oh gosh, you all still see him? I can't stand it Cynthia. I want to know everything. Yes, yes, when can we get together?"

"We are having our first meeting next Tuesday at 7P.M. I am not a Caylor native, so if you have someone, anyone who you think would like to be a part, bring them. I hate it that we are so segregated in this small town. I'll never forget Mo's father trying to set my arrogant freshman-self straight. He was right about tolerance."

"Colonel Cunningham. Mo keeps in touch with me; she is in Bombay, India. Her husband Stewart's specialty is Asia, so they put him in all those places. They started in Sumatra, then Bangkok. We always talk about the race madness in America and of course Viet Nam. My best friend here in Caylor, Sadie, would love to come. We shake our heads about the separation. This is so exciting."

"Bring her. T.J. is coming from Indianapolis. He's running for State Representative from his district and has organized many community groups…"

Jill smiled. T.J. She always told Sadie that if he ever saw little Mike, he would claim him. Cynthia continued, "Bring your children. You have any more than your daughter, Luisa, right?"

"Right, Luisa, and no, only one, Sadie has three."

"Me, too. Me, a mother of three, can you believe it? I practice law part-time and change diapers full-time. The fathers, Reggie and my friend Bitsy's husband, George, they will take the kids to the park. You may remember George Foster, he played football with your old boyfriend – Jim Bancroft he told me."

"Yeah, sure George Foster, sure…"

"Bring the kids. We live right up against Carver Park. They'll have fun."

"Should I bring something?" Jill asked.

"Bitsy and I thought we'd do refreshments this time. We can decide how we want to do it next time."

The conversation ended with many questions unanswered, but Jill had to get to the club and tell Sadie. T.J. When Jill tried to encourage Sadie to make a telephone call, Sadie evaded. "Out-of-sight, out-of-mind. He's moved on with his life and so have I."

Sadie lacked sincerity in her protestations about calling. Jill was convinced, T.J and Sadie had talked. But she believed Sadie was being honest when she said, "T.J. has no suspicions about little Mike."

Jill now left the pie on the counter with a note for Jack, then climbed in the car with Luisa. Sadie certainly had something up her sleeve, but now with Cynthia's call she could tease Sadie if her surprise was too crazy. Jack hated notes on the refrigerator, but she had explained long ago that she needed to be with Sadie to keep from dying of isolation in her "pumpkin shell" made of cornstalks. Usually she came home excited from being with her best friend and made up to Jack for her "waywardness." She would treat Jack to his favorite – sexual aggressiveness. Sadie would tease her, "Jack should find out what a tramp you really are by teaching him some of the things William taught you. Sex on the kitchen table, wasn't it?"

The Caylor Country Club was situated in the middle of the golf course. It had a restricted membership, but Jill told the valet she was Sadie Fredericks' guest. Jill and Luisa walked through the women's locker room and emerged onto the large patio and pool area. She and Sadie called the members, "big frogs in a little pond." Jill and

Sadie flaunted the fact that Michael's name admitted them, two Southside girls, into this exclusive club.

A trimmed bronzed Sadie waved from her lounger. She looked unlike the mother of three children, one of whom was a wild five year old boy. He now grabbed Luisa and dragged her to the shallow children's pool. Sadie ordered Jill a vodka-lemonade, the summer special at the club.

"Okay, Sadie. I'm here, where is this person you want me to meet?"Jill glanced around the lounge chairs.

"I put that chair under the umbrella, just for you. I know how you feel about too much sun."

"Sadie, the person to meet, you are changing the subject."

"No, not until you are half-drunk. I want you to react without all that goddamned Jack hanging over you. I hate what he does to you. You're the exact imitation of the farmer's wife!"

"How many vodka-lemonades have you had? Anyway, there were some very famous farmer's wives in American history." Jill removed her cover-up and set her bag next to the chair. She spread Coppertone oil on her legs.

"Sure, Jill. Try to rationalize."

The turquoise pool was filled with kids splashing and yelling. A couple of the mothers she recognized, but not girls she had been friends with in high school. The scene of kids, pool furniture, mothers and waiters did not reveal anyone out of the ordinary, just the usual Caylor.

A young man walked up, looking like a California surfer. He wore swim shorts and a tank top with the Caylor Country Club emblem on the front, a golf putting green with a flag sticking in the hole. Sadie ordered, then initialed the receipt. "Michael loves picking up this stack at the end of the month. He always says something about my being a lush. But, I remind him that I don't drink alone." Sadie winked at Jill.

"You always put me in the middle of your mischief. But now I am going to get even."

"What are you talking about?" Sadie said, then took a drink of the icy lemonade. "Take a long drink, Mrs. Jones."

"Oh, Siddhartha Stephanopoulos Fredericks, do I have a surprise for you."

"Yeah, hurry up and say that name while you're sober…"

"But where is this person you want to show me?" Jill said, taking a sweep with her hand, "Nothing but the regulars. Hiding in the Stag Bar, perhaps?"

The waiter placed two frosty glasses on the small plastic table between their lounge chairs. Sadie held up her glass, laying the orange slice on a napkin. "Here's to my best friend – the farmer's wife." Sadie touched the edge of Jill's glass. They drank and they giggled like they had been doing for almost eighteen years.

"Sadie, we are twenty-seven, what are we going to do for the rest of our lives? Have you thought about that?"

"Besides raise these children and keep our husbands thinking they won the jackpot in Las Vegas? Is that what you mean? Vodka's working, you don't start this conversation until your tongue is loose."

Sadie had a new diamond, a pumpkin seed sized stone and about that shape. Her passion for expensive jewelry was fueled by Mike's bank account. She wore five separate gold neck chains each a different length and link style. On her wrist five clanking bangle bracelets, and a thin gold anklet graced her long legs. Against her tanned olive skin the gold jewelry was at "home," but she often wore the same set in sterling silver.

The teenage babysitter Sadie had hired for the summer now walked up with three year old Claudine in tow. Baby Kate was usually left at Vicksburg with the housekeeper. The babysitter, Tanya, with the long scraggly hair and barely budding breasts was deeply tanned from spending the summer with Sadie at the pool. Tanya was a Zambrano, but Jill was not sure which of Elena's brothers was her father. Jill saw Elena in the dark-haired girl.

Sadie ordered sandwiches and chips, and signed another receipt. Claudine's olive skin was the same darkness as Sadie's.

"Jill, I'm ordering you one more lemonade. Are you ready? And Tanya, please put more suntan lotion on Claudine and Mike."

"No, Sadie, are you ready?" Jill interrupted and told Sadie about the conversation with Cynthia. Sadie lay back and pulled her sunhat over her face. Jill picked up the brim and stared into her glasses, "So Mrs. Fredericks next Tuesday, you'll have a chance to talk all that tough-guy, love 'em and leave 'em bullshit..."

"Oh, *bullshit*, is it? Now you've had enough to drink. Wholesome farmer's wives don't cuss. Here it's time for you to meet your someone.... Oh, I love how life is so circular. Bullshit, huh?

Okay, tell me if this is bullshit." Sadie reached into her large straw bag and pulled out a printed booklet.

"Tell you if *what* is bullshit?" Jill said, reaching for the booklet. Sadie evaded her reach.

"First, Michael brought this home," Sadie used the corner of the small booklet to point at Jill, "last night and asked me to look through it and see if I were interested in this trip. I picked it up on my way out the door this afternoon. So as I sipped my vodka-lemonade…let's have one more. Jack will just have to be pissed…"

"Come on Sadie, what you talking about?"

Sadie signaled for the pool waiter to bring them another drink, then continued, "So I'm sitting here in the sun, minding my own business, trying not be grossed out by Nancy Bloodstone in that awful green suit and her varicose veins and…well, I started reading and I had to walk into the clubhouse and call you. Good, here are our drinks. Let's toast and you better take a big swallow…"

"Sadie, I think the vodka and sun are getting to you, but I'll toast to your insanity…it is what keeps us sane." They laughed and touched their glasses.

The pamphlet featured the round insignia of the U.S. Chamber of Commerce. The printed title: "Business Knows No Boundaries." The next line was written in smaller letters – "Introducing," then **"CONFERENCE OF THE AMERICAS,"** the next line – "North, Central, South," and then the dates, "November 4-9, The Fontainebleau, Miami Beach. Call for Reservations: 538-8811."

Jill opened the front page. There was a picture of the Chief Executive Officer of the U.S. Chamber Commerce and the letter:

Dear Members:

As the boundaries of our world diffuse and the oceans become bridgeable rivers, our mission is to develop vital communication links in our hemisphere. The current problems in Southeast Asia underscore the importance of increasing these links between our business community and those of our Latin American neighbors.

For years some of you have been doing business with countries from Mexico to Chile and have created sister cities with communities in these countries. We are trying to build on these foundations and establish a strong network of trade in products and ideas between our continents.

We have established this conference as an introduction for those of you considering expansion in new markets and as a forum to exchange goodwill between our countries and their businesses – agricultural, industrial, service.

Please join us for this vital and important conference.

Registration forms must be received in our office by September 15.

The enclosed guide will acquaint you with some of the representatives who will be attending. You may want to make contact with these people before the conference to guarantee appointments.

Thank you for participating in this very important exchange.

Jill paused and peered over the pamphlet to look at Sadie, "Siddhartha Fredericks, you look like the cat that ate the canary. Why? You said you had someone you wanted me to meet. At the international conference?"

"Go on Sweetie, just keep turning those pages."

"Yes," Jill said, turning each page deliberately looking at each picture, pausing to read the description of the person's business background and government affiliation. "Jorge Sanchez, Chief Operating Officer, National Bank of Panama..."

"Turn to page ten!" Sadie sat on the edge of the chair, drinking and motioning with her hand.

Jill flipped through the pages; she stopped at page ten and read, "Colombia." She stopped reading and gasped, "Oh god, Sadie! Oh, god!"

"I knew it! I knew it! Read it!"

"Luis Ochoa," Jill barely managed a whisper. Sadie motioned her to continue. Jill read, "Chairman of the International Agricultural Department of Colombia, Mr. Ochoa, President of L.O. Coffee Ltd.," Jill fingered the tiny picture like a blind person reading Braille. She was covered in goose bumps in the hot afternoon. She paused, then sucked on the straw in the lemonade and vodka. The noise of the pool became silence. He was older, or was he younger? He looked younger, maybe the short hair, and no curls. His eyes were deep under his eyebrows, a smile, a tiny smile, maybe a smirk. Yeah, more like a smirk. Same moustache. Where was the rest of him? What did it all look like? "Oh, god, Sadie, what am I going to do?"

"I guess see if there is a shed in Miami near the hotel."

"Go? Is that what crazy thing you are suggesting?" Jill looked at Sadie who drank her lemonade, but had closed her eyes under her sunglasses.

"Of course we're going, Jill. It is time to go on one of our international adventures."

"No. I have a job, a husband, a daughter..."

"Yeah, that's what I was thinking...a daughter and her father."

"You should be thinking about a son and his father."

"Okay, Sweetie, you want to play that game. I'll see T.J. next Tuesday and you and I will head for Miami in November."

"Oh, Sadie, I'm shaking. I think I'm going to cry. We can't just show up."

"Sure we can. You just need to think of an excuse to tell Jack and the school why you will be out of town November fourth through the ninth.

"Sadie, stop. What would I say? Hi, remember me? Picture my face in the straw?"

"Yeah, and take him a tomato. It might all come back to him." Sadie laughed.

"You are truly and completely nuts! Go to Miami? Just go to Miami, Florida?" Jill said it twice aloud, but her mind played a chant with the phrase, go to Miami, go to Miami. The picture. She wanted it to speak, to smile, to frown. Luis Ochoa...Chairman of the International Agricultural... "Sadie, I want to see him," Jill whispered.

Sadie pulled her sunglasses off and leaned over the aluminum arm of the lounger and winked, "Sure you do, Sweetie. You've never stopped wanting to see him; now we are going to. You better brush up on your Spanish. We may have to talk to a few body guards to wiggle our way through. Oh, this is going to be better than one of our Nancy Drew detective adventures! Where is the Colombian delegation? Specifically, the Agricultural Director? We haven't done anything this exciting since...Germany."

"Paris, Bastille Day..." Jill said.

"Montgomery..."

"Hardly an international stop, but okay. Look out, Miami, or should I say next week at Cynthia's with T.J.?"

"I did make a deal, huh?" Sadie frowned.

The friends laughed and drank. The children ran up splashing cold water on them.

"Sadie, we're mothers now. Older? Wiser? Maybe we should stop and think this through. We have a few more responsibilities now."

"Jill, try that bullshit on someone who doesn't know you."

"I have to think about this. Jack..."

"Okay, today you can think, tomorrow we plan."

"Stop. Sadie, promise me you won't say anything to anyone about this, not even Michael. No especially Michael. It has to be another one of our secrets."

Jill sank back in the lounger remembering the face of the migrant worker Luis and now the picture of the agricultural minister. Colombia? She held the booklet open to page ten. Was he married? Colombia? From Texas to Colombia? I thought, assumed, yeah, assumed. Oh, god, Luis, August, September, October – three months, plan...Yeah, we must plan this. She shivered in the heat of the afternoon. She peeked one eye open to see if Sadie was looking at her. Sadie met her glance, laughed and gave her a thumbs up.

"You've found your Luis, Jill. And thank god we didn't have to go to Texas to do it."

ﯼﯖﯼ

Twice a day for the last seven Sadie and Jill practiced going to Cynthia's. Jill and Luisa arrived at Vicksburg in the early afternoon with Sadie's plea, "Please come early. I'm too nervous to get the kids ready." And they did. Jill sat at Sadie's desk in her bedroom and wrote ideas for the interracial club and Sadie tried on clothes. Jill had invited a woman from her church and talked to Lillian about coming, but Jill did not know who or even what the club would do. The ideas had been only secondary to the ongoing discussion they were having about little Mike, T.J., Michael, and the girls, Claudine and Kate.

Sadie had admitted, "I'm afraid of T.J.'s reaction. He demanded to know what the doctor was talking about in Germany when he said, "father." I told him the doctor, "assumed.""

"And you thought that would satisfy him?"

"I was so emotional I just had his baby and I blurted it out to the doctor. T.J. is his father. When I saw you two I was breathing normally, recovered. Oh, Jill, we met in October and again in November before I left for Germany."

"Sadie, you never stopped, did you?"

"A one night stand, okay, okay, a two night stay. Mike was TDY in Italy when I got to Germany. He was in Italy my first two weeks in Germany. I sat there wondering if I should not have stayed longer in New York."

"It sounds like you did stay or did you mean *not leave*?"

Their conversation resolved nothing and continued. "I didn't have my period oh, god, that sounds so weak, but it had seemed simple six years ago. If Mike objected, I was going to leave him, but it did not turn out that way. Mike was Mike -sweet and unsuspecting, innocent."

Sadie now washed her hair for the second time. The first time she had made Jill roll it so the ends curled slightly, then changed her mind. The clothes were scattered all over the bedroom, walk-in closet and ironing board. Sadie wrapped the towel around her head as Luisa came in followed by Claudine.

"Mom, Claudine won't sit at her tea table. She won't listen to me. And Mike threw his truck at us. Mom, come help me. Aunt Sadie's children are…"

"Are what?" Sadie said, looking down at Luisa who stood with her hand on her hip. Sadie bit her lip, suppressing a smile.

"Aunt Sadie, your children are…my grandpa said like wild animals."

Sadie raised one eyebrow, "Henry ought to know, his daughter…"

Jill laughed, then grabbed Luisa's hand, "Come Lo, let me see if I can talk to Mike. Aunt Sadie needs to get ready. We're leaving in thirty minutes." She pointed to her watch and winked at Sadie, "Thirty minutes."

ɤξɤ

The Mercedes station wagon was filled, three children in the back seat and a few toys. Sadie's house was on the very west edge of Caylor. Cynthia's address was east, but right in the city. Carver Park had been created during a separate-but-equal phase in the Caylor Parks Department. Jill attended meetings at the YWCA when plans for programming were discussed. At the meetings she learned more about the checkerboard history of blacks and whites in Caylor. The entire Civil Rights Movement took the front page headlines of the Caylor fish wrapper. She tried now to talk of these historical phases to Sadie, but Sadie was too nervous.

"Sadie, how am I going to go to Miami? You've at least talked to T.J. in the last five years…"

"Not for four years, and nothing about a son, you know that!"

"Okay, okay four years, but…"

"Jill, you know I want to turn this car around. I can't believe I'm doing this. It's crazy."

"We're almost there and crazy is something we are famous for, right? The last address was 500 and Cynthia's address is 817 E. Tulip."

They drove to a two-story brick and wood frame house. It appeared to be newer than the houses on either side of it, both wood-framed like Henry and Lillian's. Sadie parked in the street under a huge tree. Four cars were tightly parked in the driveway. The one closest to the sidewalk was a dark blue Buick 225. Jill thought of Henry's dependable Buick that brought T.J. back to Indiana safely. A bumper sticker read "Washington in '69."

Sadie clutched the steering wheel. "Why did I say yes? Kids you must act like when we go to Grandma Fredericks. Understand?"

The kids jumped out of the car and ran up the sidewalk.

The grassy lawn was precisely landscaped. Evergreen bushes provided a fence from the public sidewalk. A tall maple grew in the tree lawn. Planted shrubs lined the front of Cynthia's. Jill recognized the landscaping for a new house. The trees had to be removed to dig the basement; they were replanted, but took years to grow.

When Cynthia and Jill talked, Cynthia seemed settled. The prospect of building this bridge between their segregated neighborhoods reminded Jill of her conversation in Bodensee with William. Her desire to break down the racial barriers perpetrated over and over again because of skin color started so long ago. Having Luisa, was her one act of defiance, but only one small voice. Jill ignored her need to amplify this inner small voice. Their minister recently quoted Gandhi in a sermon. The minister's voice stirred again the place in her heart where she wanted to go for Luisa's sake. She'd come home and made a small sign for her desk, "Be the change you want to see in the world." Now she was acting on her beliefs.

The inside door was open and Jill heard voices. She rang the door bell. The chime played Big Ben's tune. Jill squeezed Sadie's hand. Luisa held tightly onto Jill's other hand.

Cynthia came to the door. She was heavier, but not much. She held a healthy fat baby in one arm, maybe six months old Jill concluded. The baby had a full head of tiny black curls. He wore plastic pants and t-shirt with a Cincinnati Reds emblem on the front. And the tiniest tennis shoes. He had big brown eyes; he buried his face in his mother's chest. Cynthia hugged Jill, "It's great to see you. This is Timmy, my latest and last. I told Reggie he wasn't getting close to me again." She laughed. Jill remembered how much she'd liked her laugh as soon as she heard it, but also how rarely Cynthia had laughed at school. Jill introduced Cynthia to Sadie.

"I heard about you a lot from Jill and Mo. I'm happy you came. Come I want to show you the path to the park where the guys are. It is just out my backyard. Reggie and I were lucky to be able to build this house here. Caylor and their zoning laws, but in the end they were happy I wanted to stay in the ghetto…oh, don't get me started on the Caylor Zoning Committee and the red-lining banks."

Mike tugged on Sadie's hand and told her he had to use the bathroom. Sadie shrugged, then spoke, "He doesn't care, whenever we get anywhere he has to use the bathroom…"

"Sure, sure," Cynthia said, "Let me show you. With three kids, dining out is a real test and the restaurant bathrooms…" Cynthia paused to roll her eyes and switch Timmy from one hip to the other. Jill offered to hold him. He held out his arms. Jill took him, as Cynthia spoke, "The bathroom is down the hallway, the second door on the left." She put her now free arm on Sadie's shoulder and directed her, then turned back to Jill, "Come with me and let me introduce you to the other women."

The living room where they stood was light blue and dark blue. A gray velvet couch and two chairs with blue throw pillows took up most of the living room. A limestone fireplace built with a limestone slab seat separated the family room from the living room. Glass doors on both sides made it possible to see one room from the other. The stone seat was fitted with gray velvet cushions. A built-in bookcase next to the fireplace held family pictures. Reggie, looked as handsome as ever, surrounded by family receiving some award. There were framed degrees and several trophies.

Jill guided Luisa and Claudine as they stepped through the opening to the family room. The walls were paneled in rough cedar stained pale gray. Folding chairs were arranged in a circle that included a couch. Three black women sat talking, but looked up as Jill and Cynthia came in. Cynthia quickly introduced Bitsy, Vickie and Janet. Bitsy and Janet, Jill recognized, although Bitsy was much heavier than she'd been in high school. She still had a round cherubic face, with baby fat dimples. In their high school conversations, Bitsy was sunshiny, a smile to light up the day. They had done decorations for the Mother-Daughter Tea, maybe their junior year, but Jill remembered how pleasant Bitsy had been during the long hours after school.

Janet was thin and had been thin in high school, too. She was as quiet as Bitsy was talkative. They both wore their hair like the Supremes' page boy with the straight across bangs. Vickie had her hair in the natural slightly fluffed-out Afro style. Vicki, tall and serious, sat straight in the chair as Bitsy giggled with Janet. Vickie wore an African print top and long skirt. Several bracelets of red, black and green beads graced her thin arm.

As Jill reached to shake Vickie's hand, she noted an orange button, "Free Omar, Leon and Don." Vickie dressed like many of the protesters pictured in *Life* magazine and on television.

"Janet Brown..." Jill spoke, holding her hand.

"It was Brown. I married Louie Flowers..."

"Flowers' Barbeque? Louie, do I remember him?"

"He graduated a couple of years before us and didn't play ball so you probably don't..."

Jill decided to look at her freshman *Connection* and find Louie. "I do remember you and I were in Sampson's history class," Jill said. The women laughed recalling "Führer Sampson," as they called him. Bitsy said she had him when she went, and Vickie said it sounded like she was lucky not to have gone to Caylor High. "They probably weren't ready for the Rosa Parks thing in Caylor then, anyway."

"Were you?" Jill asked, "In high school? I seemed to be preoccupied with boys and after game dances."

Vickie grimaced as Jill spoke. Jill continued, "But here I am older and wiser, ready to do something more meaningful, something so my daughter will have more social consciousness than I did."

Cynthia clapped, "Very good. It's exactly why we are all here. Yes, Vickie?"

Vickie nodded.

They talked, but Jill switched from watching the group to looking down the hall. Sadie should be returning any moment with Mike. Jill wanted to see the park before they started the meeting, and to say 'Hi' to Reggie. Would he even recognize her as the scared freshman who asked for his senior picture? Cynthia looked toward the living room door opening as she went to the kitchen to get Jill lemonade.

The women in the family room talked of children. Each introduced their non-present children. Vickie had two daughters, one eight like Luisa and another one three like Claudine. Cynthia came back with the lemonade and took Timmy from Jill. Cynthia said her oldest was four year old Evie, then the terrible two year old, Karen. Vickie said hers were playing in the park and probably driving Reggie and George crazy.

"Not to worry," Cynthia said, "Reggie has the patience of Job. He married me and stayed that ought to tell you everything you need to know." She laughed.

Shifting Timmy from one side to the other, she started to talk of her plans for the group. She looked towards the living room speaking of the hope she and Reggie had for a successful interracial community group. They envisioned a unique group dedicated to making change. They would discuss any problems, but have activities for interaction. Jill agreed. The other women thanked Cynthia for thinking of this way to meet. The doorbell rang and Cynthia stood to answer it. Jill hoped it would be her friend from church, June.

Jill sipped her lemonade and stared through the fireplace into the living room. There was no movement. She heard Cynthia introduce herself and she recognized June's voice. Where was Sadie? Did she get cold feet and leave out of the back door? Jill shifted in her chair. Luisa patted her knee. Jill looked down at Luisa who was pointing at the opening between the kitchen and the family room. In a white polo shirt and navy sports slacks, chubbier than Germany, with soft afro curls, was T.J. holding Mike. Sadie was holding a Kleenex to her eye.

Jill jumped from the chair and walked to the doorway. T.J. put Mike down. Mike grabbed Luisa's hand.

"Jill, my favorite constituent. Come, come, and give me a hug." It was *the* bear hug; her last one was in Germany the night before they flew out. His strong arms encompassed her, she closed her eyes, oh T.J., so many of these T.J. hugs when I needed them most. His cologne, she took a deep breath, and the memory of a hug at 1254 Butler so many years ago, when Hector had abandoned her. T.J was using the same scent. He had to be the first president of color, for all of us, to bring these racial walls down.

He whispered, "We have to talk. *You* should have...*she* should have..."

Chapter 9

The hot dry afternoon breeze swept through the large study hall, rattling the venetian blinds. All the Southeastern Consolidated School District teachers were seated for the presentation by the Superintendent of Schools. The message came and went. Jill sat in the classroom, but it became all the classrooms of September – the newly polished floors; freshly painted walls, the bottom half shellacked to protect the paint from hand prints, but yellowing the brighter beige topcoat. The marble floors of Caylor High were now the thickly waxed linoleum of Southeastern High. The black chalkboards converted to green; wood desks transitioned to four-legged Formica tops with matching metal and plastic chairs. Last year's mistakes switched to improved lesson plans.

The beginning of the year started in September with school, not in January at the depths of cold and darkness. Labor Day was the first day of the New Year. September carried promises of new beginnings. Dry heat and crunchy, burning leaves smelled of the transition from summer to autumn. The humidity stopped on some private signal from Mother Nature; the clear skies prevailed, defining the season. Time to take a deep breath, tie your shoes and start a new race. The new football team found hope for a winning season in September.

Bonfires, fresh apple cider, sweater-weather, defined this month and the anticipation of love. Love? Yes, September. Those were Caylor High School days. I met Hector in September. Now I am all settled, was settled, well trying to settle. November is only two months away, very *un*settling. Sadie called everyday with a new plan on how to crash the Chamber of Commerce Conference in Miami.

She stared out the window, the endless cornfields. The harvest season arrived and demanded canning and canning required time over the stove cooking and stewing tomatoes. Jack had brought home two bushels from Beau's farm on Sunday and all week they had sat in the corner of the kitchen; their bright red skins reminding her of the thick dark hands that picked them so deftly. She shook her head, trying to stop the picture of the shed in the heat.

When her department chairman Don Kippenburg touched her elbow to pass the umpteenth mimeograph handout, she jumped. The purple ink and mimeo fluid smell brought her back to the ongoing meeting. She checked her watch, 12:30P.M. She planned to take some time in her room to decorate the bulletin boards before leaving to pick up Luisa.

Superintendant O'Malley's speech, the same one he had given for the last five years with the other members of her department. Superintendant O'Malley once had red hair, now he had a sandy point at the top of his head. His face stayed flushed, his belly seemed to get bigger or his shirts were smaller; the buttons stretched in their holes. He wore his September seersucker – the summer suit. His other suit was gray flannel. Before he started, he took off his coat. He now used a crinkled handkerchief to wipe the perspiration from his face. "The students of today present us with special challenges, their needs.... You have seen the long hair, fringed vests and their disregard for authority...we will be doing everything we can to make sure our students are disciplined and well-groomed...at least this hasn't been the 'summer of love.'"

Jill sighed audibly. Don looked over at her. He nodded, affirming her sigh by mouthing the word "boring." Did Don associate September with love?

When she started teaching five years ago, Don had more hair. Attempting to be stylish he now bravely sported a moustache and long sideburns. At thirty-nine he was too old to be hip, and the hip preached not to trust anyone his age. Jill concluded he was trying to display the only hair he had. His summer tan had begun to fade from his square face. He was a golfer and talked non-stop of his favorite holes, drives, putts, clubs, traps, the matches he had or should have won at the American Legion, Elks, and Country Club. He had played all the courses in the state. And if they built a new one…yeah, that was love for Don. His wife played, but preferred golfing with her girlfriends.

Don repeatedly told Jill to call his wife and they could play golf. She and Sadie had signed up for beginner's lessons one summer, but the game did not appeal to her. Don had returned this summer with news of the "Newest course in Caylor County," encompassing a section of Cougar Creek, the stream that fed into the reservoir. He was negotiating for a lot abutting the course. Henry had built Don's first house and Don had talked to Jill about his second home – the dream home – a golf course in the back yard. Thank goodness Jack did not like golf, hearing Don talk all school year was enough. She was sure he would play in the snow if the balls came in colors.

Oh, Don, do we suppress love, switch our passions to hobbies? Why doesn't crocheting rugs feel like straw on the backside in a shed?

At last the lecture ended. Jill talked briefly with her co-workers before returning to her room. *National Geographic* provided world maps that she wanted to post in preparation for her geography and history classes. In her room alone, she stapled the construction paper background for her homeroom bulletin board. She tacked the stenciled titles where the mimeos would be hung each day. Being alone once the semester started was nearly impossible because her students liked to come early and stay late. She liked her interaction with her students. It reminded her of Reverend Newsom's advice to become a teacher.

In these rare moments of quiet time, she remembered Margie Merriweather's admonition of how sweet the sounds of empty classrooms were. Many Fridays she considered driving over to Marion to see if they had their TGIF meeting at the Gondola, but there was canning, bad weather, Luisa's gymnastics lesson, always something.

The pictures were tacked on the bulletin board. She had outlined the maps in postcards from Lillian's collection, places in the United States from Niagara Falls to Death Valley. They would be the starting point for the first discussion on the geographical features of where her students spent their vacations. She would ask them why these features encouraged the type of settlements that took place there. School.

She dressed casually today for the conference. The conservative country school board that employed her demanded rigid standards for their teachers. She knew if it had not been for Dr. Reader and his friendship with the retired Mr.Sartoris, she would not have been hired. She considered this day still officially vacation and wore a tie-dyed blue sun dress; the shoulders were spaghetti straps that tied. And sandals, the end of summer, but she did not want to wear stockings just yet. Her whole outfit was a violation of the regular dress code, no bare arms or legs.

After two hours, the room, desk, storage cabinet and bulletin board were finished. She now closed the cabinet that contained all of her supplies and opened the closet door for her personal things. Removing her large canvas bag containing the lesson plan folders and textbooks, she threw it and her purse over her shoulder. A quick glance in the full-length mirror attached to the inside of the door-twenty-seven, older than the hippies, younger than...oh, she had a youthful face in spite of Sadie's constant reminder that she was an *old* farmer's wife. She smiled at her reflection, the teacher, the maestra. The association of classroom to teacher was with her old sinister teachers who had disparaged her school activities. What would Miss Gottschalk, that old narrow-faced hag, say if she saw Mrs. Jill Havlicek Jones, teacher? Now she was one of them. One day I'll look in this mirror and see the wrinkles and pearl necklace...no, never. She slammed the door.

The building was completely still as she left. Most teachers had chosen Don's method – two hours for Southeastern and four hours for the golf links. A sunny Thursday, September afternoon, people would be at work, "great for a round, nine holes before dinner." The last long weekend before school started. Yeah, Don, almost time. ...Was the big ball inching toward the start? Nine, eight, seven...No, she would not sing "Auld Lang Syne." She chuckled, no, not "should old acquaintances be forgotten"? Impossible.

The clanging of the lockers had not started. The whistling, shouting students changing their classes were absent. Her footsteps echoed in the clean silent hallway. She inhaled the smell of fresh wax and paint. She walked outside toward the parking lot. The heavy wood school door clunked closed. She smiled, three days and it would all begin again.

Her car and the football coach's were the only ones left in the parking lot. She looked at her watch. 2:30. Did she have time to stop by Sadie's? Pick up Luisa and drive to Sadie's…an hour from now by the time she got from Southeastern, visit Lillian for awhile, then head west to Sadie's haunted house. Jack would be home at six. Yeah, always time for Sadie. She would not cook, and tell him to take Luisa for pizza, so she could can the tomatoes. A plan.

Too far to be clearly heard, the football team practiced. There was a mono-hum of boys yelling and the coach's whistle. They had their first game tomorrow. The locusts buzzed in full force, shouting their final hurrah before the frost. Yes, summer was ending and now time for the beginning of…of whatever happens. The New Year… five, four, three, two. The light breeze blew dried leaves and dust devils across the parking lot. September, crisp, bright, clear…September.

She opened the trunk of her Oldsmobile and shuddered at the mess. Lillian's voice reprimanded her for not being neat, "but…" she argued with the motherly conscience. She arranged the boxes of jars she had picked up at Sadie's a week ago. Sadie insisted Jill fill them with her "special homemade tomato sauce."

"Damn it Sadie, you make me feel guilty, but guilt is a useless emotion!" She sighed, hearing a car pull up in the parking lot. The car's door slammed as she laid her bag on top of the jars, her weekend work now safely covered up. Thank goodness for large trunks, she could hide her responsibilities. She closed the trunk and dismissed the thought of boiling tomatoes and steamy kettles of Ball jars. I'll go laugh with Sadie first, maybe a cold beer to get motivated.

She turned from the closed trunk and faced Luis.

"Luis! Oh my god. Where did you come from? September. Michigan? No. Where? Oh my god, where?" She glanced around the parking lot. He drove a new Mercedes, no truck. "Tomatoes. To pick? No."

Jill stood silent, a ghost, a mirage. Unable to say all the things she had daydreamed, if. His chest covered not in a plaid shirt, but a starched oxford white shirt, half-way unbuttoned, exposing his curly hair. She remembered his chest in the shed pressed against him. There was gray in his wavy hair, cut shorter, and gray strands in his moustache; no curls peeked from a straw hat, but the hazel-green eyes were unchanged, impassioned as they had been. She caught her breath.

"Jill."

His heavy accent so foreign and familiar, the voice…her name.

"Luis, oh my god…" her voice barely audible, had anything come out? His name, Luis, not the miniature one she called Luisa. "Here in the middle of these corn fields at my school. You're here, just today. How? How did you know? Nine years? And here? Luis how did you find me? How did you know today? Oh my god…." She reached to touch him, a quick feel, like testing a hot iron. She'd wanted to touch him for nine years, now he stood within reach. Her eyes widened, she needed to pinch him, pinch herself, pinch something. His trousers were dark brown gabardine; cut fully with tucks, the work of tailors? Oh, god, the body, flesh, him, not her imagination. His face was serious, but his eyes seemed to welcome her.

"Gringa, you did not move. There is much to say. We have to talk. I know of you. I am here. I want to see my daughter. I want to see my daughter this evening." *His* daughter? He knows. She shivered. No. My daughter. Our daughter. Jack's daughter.

"But Luis…" Her planned afternoon, canning tomatoes. He grabbed her, hugged her, kissed her. Pressed against him, heat, the heat…the straw, the truck, the rainy afternoon, his mouth, the way he kissed, pumping his tongue, the taste of cigar, the brush of his moustache, the pieces like cake batter filling an empty pan.

He slowly released her, "You may ask all your questions, I know your curiosity, but I want to see my daughter. This is your town and we know the local gringos don't take kindly to strangers, especially dark-skinned ones."

Her hands eased down the front of his shirt. She touched his tummy, his side, rubbing his shirt, outlining the pocket, the monogram in dark brown, "L.O.", Luisa's nickname. She took a deep breath and stepped backward. He held onto her elbows. She tapped his chest lightly, exploring the buttons, the hair, the just visible scar, the tanned neck, the face, one color, rich brown. His face had a five o'clock shadow. When did his day start? Where did it start?

She wanted a fan for the heat in her face. She thought, "Mrs. Jones was seen kissing a dark stranger in the teacher's parking lot."

He stared. "You blush, Gringa, are you embarrassed? No one is here, but us." He cocked his head indicating the lot. His tone was deadly serious. The lines around his eyes and brow were deeply grooved.

Her mind raced, reassembling her agenda, "You?" she whispered, "And here? I feel caught. I didn't know..."

"You were being hunted?"

"Luis, I'm married."

He held her chin up with one hand.

"Si. This is not a problem, is it? I want to see *my* daughter."

"Yes. No, not a problem, he's not... She is at my mother's in town. We must meet somewhere. Do you have a hotel room? Can we meet where you are staying?"

"This visit is short. I am not staying in Caylor."

"Okay, okay. We can go to my friend Sadie's."

"The woman with the binta mark on her forehead?"

Jill met his eyes, the hypnotic look, back and forth, one green pool to the other, the autumn colors green to dying brown the critical change not summer, not winter. "Yes. Her husband is away on a sales trip to Iowa. Sadie would want to meet you anyway. Kill me, if I didn't ...Oh, Luis." She took a handful of his side and squeezed; his love handles taut. The body.

He glanced around the immediate surroundings. Jill continued, "It is okay, really, Sadie is not like anyone in Caylor."

He frowned and nodded, a half shake of his head, "Where?" he demanded.

She retrieved a notebook from the car, writing directions, on a piece of paper. She told him it would take her at least a half an hour to get to her mother's, and another ten minutes to Sadie's. She circled her arms around him, linking her thumbs in his belt loops. She said, "You will not leave me this time?"

"I traveled too far down this road, Gringa, to leave you again." He pulled her close to him, squeezing her, and his chest and shirt buttons pressed on her skin. His scented aftershave smelled of spice and dusky plants. He wrapped one arm under hers, the other held her head. He kissed the space in front of her ears, then her cheeks, and her mouth. As he hugged her, she laced her fingers in his hair. Could she have him on her? She hugged him, and he responded with a crushing hold.

The afternoon warmth and space exploded. Heat surged through her, the empty parking lot now full of his presence. He freed her, kissing her nose, "My little Gringa, you're not the girl I left. We must talk." He wrapped one of her curls around his finger; tugging it slightly, then he slid his hand down her neck, and pinched her earlobe. She grasped his hand and kissed the palm, no calluses. Pulling his hand from hers, he abruptly turned, and walked to his car. He opened the door, leaned in and picked something from the seat. He backed out and stood up, "Jill, I have something for you."

She walked around the back of his Mercedes. He handed her a paper sack. She opened it, as he spoke, "Indiana tomatoes, the best kind. And for my daughter," he handed her a stuffed gray elephant with a pink bow, "Like her mother in this way?"

She nodded, "Si, Señor Ochoa, but more like her father in most other ways."

"Si, I want to meet Señorita Ochoa." He shook his head, smiling.

"Luisa," Jill said.

"You have questions." Questions? Oh, god was the map clear enough? Is he leaving again? Where did he come from? Colombia? Today? Not staying in Caylor? He picked tomatoes, and now what? His daughter? How did he know *his* daughter? He found me. How did he know? Yes, Luis, I have questions, please find Sadie's, please.

She now drove with Luisa through the west side. The west side, his Mercedes would be at home, only the rich folks in Caylor drove Mercedes, the big frogs, and not many of them. But his clothes, the shoes, leather loafers, casual, but not faddish, classic trousers, full, custom-made; and the shirt monogrammed like Stewart and Mac on the way to Germany, but no one at Southeastern, oh they were hicks, what did they know? More of the *Gentleman's Quarterly* fashion, but the Latin accent and the scent, what was the cologne?

Who was Luis Ochoa? Migrant worker? What was that experience? How do you jump from the fields to an international director of agriculture? Questions? Yes, I can't stop.

She turned off Vicksburg and onto the road that led to Sadie's semi-circular driveway. The huge Italian cypress met the road at

Vicksburg; the white pines on each side completely obscured the house. She told him, "It looks like a woods, but keep driving."

Vicksburg was a cul-de-sac and Sadie's house the only one on the street for half a mile. Black walnut trees forested the acre between Vicksburg and the house. Michael liked to remind Sadie and Jill of the bank in his front yard, the woods. The native hardwood supply steadily declined and the price rose. As the last large stand in Caylor, each year they became more valuable. Some of the walnut had been used for decorative flooring in the dining room and the downstairs library. The third floor ballroom with its intricate inlaid wood had been home to squirrels, birds and spiders. Before Sadie moved in, Henry had fixed the roof and other structural problems. "They don't build 'em like this anymore," he told Sadie and Michael.

Jill parked by the slate steps that were part of the slate walk to the museum house. Built on a huge basement the mansion rose to three stories. Two seventy-five year old white pines stood sentry in the front yard. The porch was stone and concrete. The arched porch roof supported the second story and had been made with red bricks and limestone. The uneven bricks were all stamped with "Kokomo," the closest foundry when Old Gramp Fredericks had built the place. Toys littered the front porch in disarray and disrespect to the elegance of the mansion. Dolls, trucks, crayons, Play-doh...Claudine and Mike. Caitlin was too young to make the mess.

Jill had called Sadie from Lillian's just to say she and Luisa were coming. Sadie said, "I'm in the middle of stripping woodwork in the laundry room and doing laundry. Thursday and Friday are Hilda's days off. Michael's gone, let's just drink and you can stay all night."

Jill called Jack at work, "I'm taking Luisa to Sadie's. She asked us to stay all night. Michael is out of town and she'll be alone...." True, not the whole truth, but the truth.

"Knowing you two and vodka, it is probably better you stay all night. I don't suppose you considered I might be sleeping alone...."

"Jack, maybe you'll miss me. You know you have to have deprivation in order to have appreciation."

Luisa now jumped from the car. She ran through the house, down the long hall. Jill followed her reminding her to slow down. Luisa charged through the family room and out double French doors to the backyard. The swings, slide, sandbox, tree house, and jungle gym resembled a park. Sadie had volunteered to have the next interracial women's group with the children. The group decided the children were the key to change and were to be included whenever possible.

Jill followed the path Luisa had run, past the kitchen to the end of the hallway, descending three steps to a small door that opened into the laundry room. Sadie sat with a rag tied around her hair, pedal pushers and torn holey sweatshirt, holey tennis shoes, her baby toes poked through the sides. Her eyes were fully made up with purple eyeliner and thick mascara. Stunning Sadie, all tanned, even in the worst condition she was attractive.

"Sadie, get up. You are not going to believe who is following me..."

"Following? Probably the police. What have you done now?"

Jill pulled on Sadie's arm, "No, this is serious. Come. Come. Where's the baby? Where's Claudine?"

"Oh, it must be a child molester..." Sadie laughed, standing. She put the lid on the stripper, "I'm sick of the smell. Let's get something to drink. Rum tea and stripper that ought about do it. It is just about time for Caitlin to wake up." She pulled off her rubber gloves, dropping them on the newspapers that were covering the entire floor. "One thing about this house, there is always something to do. I think the plumbers are starting tomorrow to replace..."

Jill clenched Sadie's arm, "Sadie stop, he's here..."

"What's wrong? Your eyes are... the plumber's here? No, he's coming tomorrow."

"No, dummy, Luis! Luis! Luis! Come! He's here and he's here!" Jill pointed to the floor. Sadie stopped and stared. Her mouth dropped; she shook her head, "I don't believe it, you've lost your..."

The door bell rang. Sadie whipped around to face the door as if he were standing on the other side of the laundry room door, "Who's...?"

"Sadie, it's Luis! I'm trying to tell you...Oh, god, Sadie, what do I say? What do I do? A drink? Vodka? Come!" Jill danced back and forth clinging to Sadie.

"Slow down Sarah B. You can do this. How does he look?"

Jill hesitated, took a deep breath and relaxed. "He's older, m-m sexy though and thick, do I smell like him?" She paused to rub her front, "Big. Oh, god, I forgot how big, chest, arms, oh Sadie. I melted when he kissed me."

"Wait, you a married woman, Miss Church..."

"Sadie, we'll talk about that later, Luis is here."

The doorbell rang again. Jill squeezed Sadie's hand and stood still. Sadie pulled her up the laundry room steps, down the hallway, past the kitchen until they stood in the arched opening of the foyer, fifteen steps to the screen door, the only thing separating them from Luis. Sadie walked, yanking Jill with her across the parquet floor. "Luis Ochoa," Sadie said, "Come in. My friend was just telling me how she found you hiding under a bridge…"

"Sadie!" Jill turned toward her friend who laughed. Luis opened the extra wide wood screen door, the kind that banged when it closed. Sadie said it helped her hear little Mike when he ran in and out. Jill rushed to meet him, holding out her hand.

"Come, Luis. Your wild child is playing in the back. Please meet my best friend Siddhartha Fredericks. Sadie, Luis."

Sadie held out her hand, "Thank god you've come. I hope you're here to restore order in this madness." Sadie pointed to Jill.

Luis used both hands to hold Sadie's, "How do you do Siddhartha? After the male child who taught peace of mind. You have not created the order in her madness?"

"Tried, Luis, tried." Sadie laughed, shaking her head.

"Your friendship," Luis said, "with my gringa has helped her through these many years of my absence." He dropped her hand and touched Jill's arm.

"Uh, Luis, she's been…she's helped me through my madness…" Sadie reached and put her arm around Jill, hugging her, "You're not taking her…"

Luis shook his head, "I already have," he patted his heart. "I want to see my daughter."

"Sure, sure," Sadie said, "Come, oh, let me fix you both something to drink, then I must change these clothes."

Sadie walked down the hall quickly, dodging into the swinging kitchen door. Luis hesitated, taking a full 360° turn in the foyer. The square oak staircase climbed three floors. Balconies of wood balusters were at each floor. Pictures of people from another era decorated the walls along the stairs. Family pictures of strangers, but Sadie described them as "Gramp Fredericks'people." The pictures in various wood and gilt frames were vintage black and white or sepia. Sadie collected them in antique shops, estate auctions and secondhand junk stores. The hallway walls below the "family gallery" were wainscoted. At the corners the molding was cut to resemble twisted candles with a teardrop shaped flame at the tip. Above the paneling Sadie had used bold maroon and cream striped wallpaper. Sconces decorated both sides of each opening from the foyer, two by the sliding wood doors of the living room, two by the hallway and two by the dining room entrance. A hand painted globe light was built into the end of the banister; glass crystals hung around the bottom edge. There was no overhead light. A large Persian rug covered the inner square of the foyer.

"English," Luis said.

"And Early American plus pre-historic Sadie. The place is a hodge-podge of what she likes and what Michael will tolerate. We grew up calling it a haunted house because it has so many nooks and crannies. It is…"

"Intriguing. You like this, Gringa?"

She liked hearing his name for her, like the way he said it. "I like to visit, but it is much too big for me. My house…Oh, I don't want to talk about the farm…"

"A farm, Gringa?" He stared at her.

"Farmhouse, actually, you know the kind, typical white-framed, quaint, old and comfortable, Indiana."

He paused as if seeing something she couldn't see. He nodded without speaking.

"Come," she said, deciding he seemed to have completed his thought. "The kitchen is one of my favorite rooms. Sadie has modernized it. Come." She held his hand as they walked the short distance from the foyer to the heart of Sadie's home. Sadie had set drinks of her spicy tea on the table. The west wall that extended to meet the family room was entirely paned windows. A counter ran under the windows and ended at the breakfast nook. A heavily used, nicked and oiled cherry wood table jutted in a bay window shape, the original one made for this half-octagon space. It separated the kitchen from the family room.

Luis walked to the counter and stared into the backyard.

Luisa and Mike were climbing the jungle gym. Luisa hung upside down by her knees. Mike yanked on one of her two ponytails that brushed against the ground. She grabbed the bar in her hands, dropped to her feet and ran after Mike. Claudine sat with a bucket in a fenced area by the sandbox. Luisa was dressed in blue jeans and a blue and white striped t-shirt. One ponytail had a blue ribbon tied in a bow, the other an untied white ribbon. Mike laughed and Luisa screeched, giggled and ran in the playground. Jill leaned against Luis. He reached and laid his hand on top of hers.

"Luis," Sadie spoke, "Would you like to sit down? I make this spicy iced tea. Jill loves it, but if you want something, stronger…we have a full liquor cabinet. Sometimes Jill adds vodka…please tell me if…"

"Si, gracias. Tea is fine." He squeezed Jill's hand, "Gringa, she is," he paused, "As beautiful as her mother. An angel in blue jeans." He walked to the table and seated himself where he could watch the backyard.

Sadie walked down the steps to the family room and out the French doors to the backyard. She opened the fenced-in area where Claudine sat. Retrieving her daughter, she headed back to the house.

Luis spoke, "Your friend," he nodded in Sadie's direction, "her children, they have different fathers?"

Jill looked at Luis. He waited, taking a drink of tea.

"Uh-um," Jill said, "Yes."

Sadie came in. Claudine was covered in sand and dirt. Her face, hands, and clothes were filthy. She held her hands to show Jill and Luis.

"Poor pitiful, Pearl," Jill said, laughing. Claudine hid her face on Sadie's shoulder, getting the dirt on Sadie's already dirty sweatshirt. Sadie excused herself to clean Claudine and herself.

She had just left the room when Luisa and Michael came running in. "Mommy, Mike said his dad is putting a pool in his backyard. He's teasing me," Luisa's voice was soft. She looked up at Luis, "Who are you?"

Jill made a move to speak, but Luis said, "Luis Ochoa." He looked Luisa straight in the eye.

"How do you do? Your name sounds like my name. My mommy said I was named after a very special person, were you?" She stared back, not intimidated, demanding an answer. She had Jill's mouth and her smile, but his nose, his hair. Jill thought how much they were alike, viewing both of them this closely together. He smiled broadly. She stood with one hand on her hip, waiting for an answer.

"Si, yes, yes, Luisa," Luis said, "we have similar names." He glanced at Jill, extending his hand. "May I shake the hand of someone named after a special person?" Luisa looked at Jill, who nodded. Luisa thrust her small hand into Luis's large palm.

"Where are you from?" Luisa asked, "You say your words different."

Jill interrupted before Luis could answer, asking if she and Mike wanted something to drink. They said "Yes!" in unison, and clamored after Jill to a small children's refrigerator in the family room. Sadie kept miniature cans of root beer that she ordered from some place in New Jersey. She had discovered it on one of her shopping trips to New York.

Sadie came back to the kitchen with a clean Claudine. The children refreshed ran out to the backyard.

"Luis," Sadie spoke, "I just want you to know Jill and I were coming to Colombia." Sadie walked into the family room and pulled some toys from a high shelf and sat Claudine in the middle of them.

"Stop, Sadie," Jill said.

"No, Siddhartha, go on, please," Luis said, sitting back in his captain's chair. Jill stared and shifted in her seat. Sadie walked back into the kitchen. Luis looked at Jill, but asked, "Siddhartha, how did you come to decide to go to Colombia?"

Sadie took a baby bottle filled with formula from the refrigerator, then removed a pan from many that hung on the wall surrounding the stove, all with highly polished copper bottoms. She turned to the sink and filled it with water, setting it on the stove. She pushed the range buttons and answered Luis, "Jill begged me to go with her after she saw your name in the U.S. Chamber of Commerce pamphlet," Sadie laughed, "Wait, and I'll get the pamphlet and show you how she drooled on it. Jill, keep an eye on Claudine," Sadie spoke, as she left the kitchen.

"Luis," Jill spoke, "please don't believe her, she talks nonsense. She wanted to go to Colombia, well, Florida actually to the conference."

"The conference, Gringa? What conference?"

"The international one, you are one of the guests of the United States Chamber of Conference in Miami, the first week of November. You know about this?"

"Si. That's Jorge. I have no time for that in November. I must be in the mountains."

"And we had planned, talked actually of finding you. If we didn't find you...well, we might have considered a trip to Colombia. I guess we were going to ask the local police if they knew you."

"Si, they know me. I'm Colombia's most famous citizen," Luis' eyes sparkled as she tried to read his face, his movements. "However," he continued, "they are suspicious of gringos looking for Colombian citizens. You can understand?"

Sadie returned, holding Caitlin in one arm and the pamphlet in the other. She handed the booklet to Luis. "We've looked up a few famous people in our past. We were getting ready to…"

"Feed Caitlin, Sadie, her bottle is ready," Jill interrupted, "Luis doesn't need to know how bad *you* are."

"No, continue. I want to hear about *my* gringa."

Jill blushed. He rubbed her hand as he thumbed through the pamphlet. "Jorge did this. His job is to rob the U.S Treasury, like your Dale Carnegie, win friends and influence people. Jorge is not so… handsome, he used my picture and title." He shook his head, closing the booklet. "I will not be in Miami."

He squeezed each of Jill's fingers, gently tracing the joints, and rubbing her wedding ring. She put her other hand on top of his. His hands were scarred as she remembered, but his nails were trimmed. A manicure? The nails were buffed, no rough hang nails or splits. She turned her palm up and grabbed his hand, interlacing her fingers with his. He wore a gold band on his left hand. Was he married? Did he have other children? Was his wife Colombian? His palm now felt sweaty in hers, but she held onto him.

The conversation between them progressed effortlessly. Sadie fed Caitlin and talked about Michael's company International Harvester and their farm production equipment. Luis interjected his crops required hand labor, human judgment at each step. He explained the picking, that each bean was meticulously inspected. Sadie told of International Harvester expanding into global markets as Michael called them, and lamented that Michael had been to South America, but only to Argentina. He had promised her under penalty of possible divorce that the next time International Harvester sent him, Sadie was going.

Caitlin started to cry. Sadie left the kitchen with both of her daughters.

"Jill, your face looks at me, but you are thinking of questions. Ask me, it is why I'm here."

Jill battled her thoughts and questions. What did he really want coming to Caylor? Was it part of the promise he made nine years ago? Did he have plans for Luisa? His conversation on coffee was the most she had heard him talk, except for lambasting the bracero program. She did not want him to go, yet he seemed to be in a rush, not relaxed, soliciting information taking mental notes. "How," Jill hesitated, "do you want me to explain you to your daughter?"

"Until you can talk to her in a way she understands," he paused, releasing her hand, and crossing his arms on his chest. "She will know I am her father, but for *this* time you may decide."

Sadie walked back into the kitchen with Caitlin's diaper bag. She looked from Jill to Luis and back again, "I think I'll take the wild bunch for pizza. I have to swing by Michael's mom's. She has a piece of furniture she wants me to look at. She thinks I can refinish it because with three small children and an ancient house that needs constant attention, I must have time on my hands for her. I'll be gone at least a couple of hours. That's enough time for what is happening at the kitchen table?" Sadie chuckled, shaking her head, as she tapped on the window that faced the backyard.

"What is transpiring," Luis spoke in a serious tone, "at your kitchen table… will take the rest of our lives, but we'll start with two hours."

Sadie winked, "Jill, show Luis the house. And be sure to take him to your special green room, the Princess Suite."

"The Princess Suite?" Luis asked, "Siddhartha, am I making you uncomfortable?"

"Uncomfortable? In my own kitchen? It feels like a transformer struck by lightning in a thunderstorm. Yes, uncomfortable, not because of you Luis, but Jill. She's wanted to have this conversation with you for a long, long time. I must leave before she runs me out of my own house."

"Get out Sadie!" Jill yelled.

Sadie laughed as she held her palm up, "See what I mean Luis? Your Gringa. The madness…nine years…nine long years." Sadie talked as she opened the French back doors and then yelled at Mike and Luisa, "Time for pizza!"

"It's time for you to go." Jill called to Sadie.

Luis watched the two friends as Jill got up to greet Mike and Luisa who came running in. "Hey, whoa, I want hugs." Jill said. She hugged Claudine, Mike and Luisa. Jill kissed Luisa goodbye. Luisa turned to Luis and said, "Nice to meet you, Mr....."

"Ochoa."

"Would you like a hug, too?" Luisa said.

"Si, yes."

"Mike, come back! We have one more hug," Luisa demanded.

Jill heard the order, just like him. The children hugged him. Luisa said, "Bye, Luis Ochoa."

Mike yelled at Luisa, "Come on Lo, I'll race you to the car. The last one…" Mike was three years younger, but almost the same size as Luisa. The screen door slammed; Sadie's car started, the sound disappeared through the woods.

Luis reached for Jill's cheek, pinching it between his knuckles. "Thank you. I wanted to hold her. Gracias. Now what do you want to know? We're alone, ask."

The questions, the answers, she said, "Do you want more tea?"

"Gringa, are you asking what *I* want?" He grasped each of her shoulders, then kissed her. She shivered and burned at the same time. She spoke catching her breath, "Would you like to sit here and talk? Would you like to see the house? Or…"

"The Princess Suite?"

"Come, I'll ask questions as we walk." She took a deep breath. They climbed the stairs to the second floor, and then peaked in doors. She became the museum director, pointing out the antique lighting fixtures converted from gas lamps. He asked questions about certain pieces, corrected her when she said, "Louis the Fourteenth."

"Louis the Fifteenth."

She laughed, "Luis Ochoa, the first." He tackled her gently in the hall and nibbled on her neck.

She held his head, "See it is a haunted house, you're turning into a vampire."

They walked to the back wing of the house; he touched her bare back, yanked on the string, untying one shoulder strap.

She stopped and faced him. "Where do you live in Colombia?"

"How do you know I *live* in Colombia?"

Jill stood still, "Please Luis, I've had this conversation with you a thousand times, but never with you. Who are you? I see you in my baby's face. I deal with a serious personality, an intensity when she is in school. She frowns as she does her arithmetic. You have excellent math skills?"

"Who am I? You ask the question, but it isn't the question for the information you want."

She walked a few steps and stopped. "My green room, the Princess Suite, so named because my dad calls me his princess, and when I stay all night with Sadie…"

"Your husband lets you stay all night…"

She turned and kissed him. He reached behind her, plucking the skeleton key from a hook.

"Siddhartha locks her green room?"

"The furniture is very expensive, irreplaceable and she can keep Mike out of here. There are too many rooms for him to get lost in."

She took the key then unlocked the door to her favorite bedroom in Sadie's house. Just the clunky turning of the key made her feel as if she were entering her own secret garden. Sadie called the room her concession to the European antiques that Michael preferred to her early American pioneer tastes. Jill walked into the Cinderella fantasy castle. Silk velvets dominated the room. The drapes were heavy brocade emerald green, the Persian carpeting, emerald green, forest green and rose. The centerpiece of the room an oversize four-poster mahogany bed had been prominently placed on a large platform. Mosquito netting hung ornately from post-to-post. The room had an attached bathroom with brass fixtures and a four-legged bathtub and four-legged sink.

"I fantasize I'm a fairytale princess like Snow White. And when I go to sleep, I hope my handsome prince will wake me up with a kiss. Usually, though it is Mike and Luisa coming in to jump on the bed and throw pillows. We camped out here for five days last winter during a blizzard."

"Five days with a Princess, we will try to do that." Luis grabbed her, yanking the wood stick and leather barrette from her hair. Her shoulders were instantly covered with curls. He laced his fingers through the strands, keeping his face locked on hers. He kissed her, his tongue in and out, deeper, tracing her inner lips. He tasted of tea, but she detected the smell of cigar smoke on his moustache. His cologne again; she squeezed him tighter deliberately inhaling deeply to remember the scent.

"No, tomatoes, Gringa. Men also wear cologne when they want to be undressed."

She leaned away from him, smiling slightly. She began unbuttoning his shirt, "Like this?" She continued, undoing the buckle, unhooking the waist band, then unzipping his fly. He wore black silk boxers. She paused and looked at his face. Using the back of her hand, she rubbed the front of his shorts.

He slipped the other strap from her shoulder. The loose fitting dress with the low waist fell to the floor. He picked her up and threw her gently on the bed. Her head swirled, had Sadie put rum in her tea? She was on top of him, under him. He said phrases in Spanish. They sounded familiar, too familiar; she heard Hector's voice, then Luis's. She closed her eyes and stopped thinking, instead feeling her body's response to Luis's stimulation. He was so deep in her; she held her breath and exhaled his name. He asked her again, and again, "What do you want? Tell me. Tell Papito what you want."

"Just you," she whispered, "just you."

Her legs quivered. She smelled him, tasted him. He took her as before and she only wanted him to take her again. She wrapped her legs around him not wanting to let go. He gently slapped her butt, "Come let's put your green room back in order. It doesn't look like a Princess slept here, perhaps a tiger." He smiled.

She washed him gently with the green wash cloth and towel. He slowly patted her arm and she blushed at his soft touch. He pulled her down and kissed her nose, cheeks and neck; then, he held her next to him. She pulled away crying.

"Gringa, why the tears?"

"It's like we're starting the pain all over again. I could get pregnant. My husband has been sterilized, and you, in and out of me, in and out of my life only the straw is missing." With the towel she wiped the tears from her cheeks.

"There is no similarity. No straw, Gringa, only the silk sheet touched you. Pregnancy? Let's wait. We will be making love again. You need to plan. Not in and out. *In* your life. In. Remember you belong to me. Hasta que la muerte no separe. I will never have you *out* of my life, not until my death."

"Luis, *who* are you? My head is spinning. You left in a beat-up truck for Benton Harbor, and come back in a Mercedes…."

"I rented the car. Gringa, the only thing that matters is you are the mother of my daughter and we will share her. I must know how to call you, to reach you whenever I need to."

"My husband…"

"You have mentioned this man now, three or four times, I do not sense love, and the tiger had been in the cage much too long." He raised one eyebrow, sat up and started to dress. She hugged him and reached around to help him zip up his pants. As he buttoned his shirt, he said, "You can think about this, but I'm leaving here in a matter of hours. I have a plane...I'll be out of your country before the night is over. I hate this goddamned country!"

For a moment his hostility stunned her.

"Okay, Jack, my husband, leaves the house at 7AM and never comes home before six in the evening. You can set your watch by these times. Luisa and I are usually home by four-thirty, but no one else will answer. And Sadie's telephone."

After locking the door and then putting the key back on its hook, they walked to the stairs, she stopped at the top step, "Please go to the bottom, I want to walk down and have you catch me."

He smiled, "Catch a tiger?"

"Si, catch a red-headed tiger," she laughed.

And he did, holding her and turning her around, "Is this part of your fairytale?"

"I wanted my prince to do that, thought about it so many times walking down this grand stairway. Thank you. Now I can write 'happily ever after.'"

They returned to the kitchen. She put fresh ice cubes in their glasses while he walked to the outside patio. She wrote down Sadie's number and hers and their addresses.

"I think you may know this information."

With a nod, and a smirk, he pocketed the paper. The sun had set. Now peach twilight illuminated the brick and slate. Luis leaned on the waist-high patio wall, staring at the horizon. He puffed slowly on a long cigar, "Cartagena, Colombia," he said matter-of-factly. "I'm a coffee farmer. The price of green beans is about to fall, so profit margins must be adjusted to account for the difference. Mathematics? The numbers decide my existence; I must know mine to keep the accountants accurate. You need a post office box. You need a bank account in another city, Indianapolis? Jones or is it Havlicek-Jones?"

"Coffee farming? From tomatoes, peaches, apples to coffee? Why do I need *another* account?"

He turned towards her, "Si, tomatoes to coffee. You don't understand and don't have to right now, but listen to what I'm saying."

She stood and gazed straight into his face, "Yes, Luis, you have my undivided attention," she spoke sarcastically.

"You and Luisa will be a *consistent* part of my life. You need to think about how you would like this to happen. In six months I will call to hear your plan and then we will spend a week together." With a quick twist, he turned his back to her, and viewed the sunset.

She watched this one person with so much presence commandeering the space. The cigar smoke mingled with his cologne. She floated from reality, Jack, the farm, canning tomatoes, teaching, Caylor, to Luis – Colombian coffee farmer, her prince or a ghost?

"You ask much of me," she said.

He glanced away from sun's afterglow and stared at her. He relit his cigar, putting the match in the concrete urn ashtray.

She continued, "I never knew you were coming back. I never stopped hoping," she touched the buttons on his shirt, "even my annual pilgrimage to McKinnsey's just to see…" She stepped two steps back from him, "…but I had to make a life for Luisa. I had to make difficult choices, not things based on what I wanted, the irresponsible, 'Just do it, no regrets.'" She thought of William jetting all over the world. "I wanted to go state-to-state, to Michigan, to Texas, knock on doors, but Luisa *needed* stability. I chose stability. I chose a husband…who is very predictable, dependable, *reliable.* Now like lightning, you've struck. Sadie said it, a thunderstorm."

He cocked his head, making a zigzag with his index finger on her chest.

"Luisa, can't be torn between, what? Colombia and America? I want her to grow up stable, secure. No one is going to disrupt what I've established for my daughter. I have parameters that no one will violate. *No* one."

She took a drink of tea, then placed the cold glass on her cheeks. His back was to the gold crease of the sunset, the ochre glow haloed his head and shoulders. With a knotted brow, he inhaled the cigar, slowly exhaling. He twisted it in his fingers, staring at the tobacco leaf.

"This is your season, Gringa, the copper red…" With the back of his hand, he brushed her breast, hardening her nipple.

She stepped back from his touch. He turned his head slightly, smoking. He examined her toes, up her legs to her breasts, stopping at her eyes. Was it the snake coming from its basket? The skin flared at the neck, moving ever so slightly, weaving? He puffed, blowing the smoke deliberately.

"'They would not find me changed from him they know; only more sure of all I thought was true.' Señor Frost. Jill Jones, meet Luis Ochoa. Who? You ask, 'Who are you?' The someone who defies parameters. I will not upset the balance in our daughter's life. Six months, Gringa."

She shook her head jerkily, subconsciously saying no, but unable to form the word. He grabbed her hand. She hesitated and put his hand to her lips. She fingered his gold band, "Luis, are you married?"

"Si."

"To whom?"

He was silent, withdrawing his hand from hers, looking past her at the sunset.

"Yes?" she asked. "Something is wrong?"

"You," he whispered.

"Something is wrong with me?"

"No, you are prefect."

He snuffed his cigar in the concrete urn. "Your friend is very nice. I need her. Can she be trusted?"

His abruptness made Jill feel eighteen all over again, how many times had he walked away at the migrant camp when she asked a pointed question. "Sadie? With my life."

"Please tell Señora Siddhartha, gracias, and the Princess Suite...home of the red-headed tiger, si? Thank her." He leaned down and kissed her on the tip of her nose, "Our daughter...like her mother, mahogany eyes."

He turned; she reached for his arm.

"Si, Gringa?"

"Again I want to go with you, Luis."

"Six months and we will discuss this request. We are no longer traveling separate roads, Gringa."

He walked quickly across the patio and through the patio doors. She listened to the locusts and then the sound of his car engine. The dry evening air chilled her. She picked up the cigar from the ashtray, smelling it. Luis. He was really here. She touched the wet end to her lips, licking the tip that had been in his mouth. Luis. Six months.

Chapter 10

The freezing November rain pelted the windshield of Jill's Oldsmobile. The usual twenty minute drive had taken forty-five. She'd driven the ten miles from Southeastern, and now splashed through Caylor's flooded streets. Ice covered the country roads. When she complained of the cold at the farm, Henry reminded her, "Always warmer in town." The buses had come early to pick up the students, the blessings of working at a country school. Freezing rain? Call the busses. Thanksgiving tomorrow meant only twenty-eight days until Christmas. Not quite winter, but getting close. The slush slowed the wipers. Water stood in huge puddles from curb to curb and storm drains overflowed. Jill drove cautiously through the center of the street.

She looked at her watch, glad to be on time to meet Sadie for their annual, "the Wednesday before," celebration. The tradition started in their first year of friendship. Sadie had just met Jill in grade school. They walked home together every day.

Back then as Thanksgiving vacation loomed, Sadie's unhappiness dominated their conversations. Jill and Sadie sat on the broken concrete steps to Mrs. Minnix's porch, and talked about Emma Sue's Thanksgiving plans. She wanted to drive to Possum Holler, Tennessee to see Jennie Sue's father and grandmother. Sadie had been miserable thinking of four days without Jill in the hills of Tennessee. The people called her cousin, but seemed so "backasswards," she used Emma Sue's term. They promised at Thanksgiving "no matter what, we'll be together on the Wednesday before." In the past 18 years, they had only missed twice - Jill refused to return to Georgia after the summer with T.J., and when Sadie was in Germany.

Flip-flap, flip-flap, flip-flap the rubber blades squeegeed the rain, helping for a brief moment. What was the point of ineffective windshield wipers? As the heavy Olds plowed through the puddles, an arc of muddy water covered the sidewalks.

Sadie and Michael had gone to the convention in Miami... nice, balmy, sunny, but Luis did not go, had not planned on going. Sadie searched diligently for Jorge, "But," she lamented, "The event was too big, so many conference rooms and displays, and too many places were out of bounds for spouses." She ended up just relaxing on the beach and working on her tan. She smiled, "There were a lot of very handsome Latin men."

But in two and half months... nothing from Luis. Nothing. Strange? She questioned if this was how he would conduct his interaction. He promised to be in her life. "In," he declared very clearly. Okay, Luis, tell me, *in* where? *In* how?

On the other hand, he did say six months. He lived in Colombia, Cartagena. Later she'd looked it up on the map, but what? Nothing. How do you get mail Luis? He left, not leaving any way for her to reach him. Gringos looking for him in Colombia? No, not an option, even though going to Colombia with Sadie did have a certain element of adventure.

The radio station forecast more rain as the "low pressure trough is...what you see is what you get." The D.J. laughed. "Duck Soup for Turkey Day." Thanksgiving travel would be difficult. She and Jack traditionally spent part of the day at the church with Lillian and Henry helping feed those with nowhere to go. Then they ate a late afternoon meal at Beau's with the brothers. She would be smiling at Mary Ann, Beau's wife, talking family small talk.

Jill wished she could say one thing to Mary Ann about Luis, a piece, a subtle hint of information that Jill was no longer the *abandoned tramp* that Mary Ann liked to insinuate. One day, Jack Jones, I will let your sister-in-law know. One day. Oh, maybe one day, when I know. Jeez, Luis, what do I know? "You will not be out of my life again?"

This miserable rainy cold November day and still all I know is your absence. Happy Thanksgiving to me. At least I could write William a letter. Could? Still if I wanted.

The parking lot of the Caylor Country Club was empty. She drove to the front entrance. The club looked closed except for the valet who sat under the awning reading. The rain poured all around him. In his bright yellow slicker he resembled a school crossing guard. Jill recognized him, Harold Winston. He'd worked at Caylor Country Club for as long as she could remember. He spoke with a British accent and acted like a gentleman. He carried himself as she imagined British Royalty, not much smiling and a lot of peering down the nose. Last summer he helped Sadie chase Mike through this same wet parking lot yelling, "Master Fredericks!" The little wild one laughed as the old man finally corralled him at the wire fence separating the parking lot from the first fairway. "Master Fredericks?" He should have said, "Master Washington."

Thomas Jefferson Washington, Master Washington's father, won his first election on November 4, three weeks ago. T.J. would serve a half term to fill in for the local councilman who had suffered a heart attack. A special election was required to fill his space. T.J. had been temporarily appointed, but the law stated an election be held as soon as the ballots could be printed and within certain time lines. T.J. campaigned against two other contenders in order to complete the term. T.J. called Sadie and invited her and Jill to Indianapolis to meet his campaign crew. As his first official election, he wanted to share it with his "favorite constituents."

Jill couldn't get away from school, but Sadie said yes; she was flying to Miami the next morning to meet Michael at the Chamber of Commerce Convention. After some discussion, they decided Sadie needed to talk to T.J. alone, if possible. Later, when the margin widened, making T.J. an early evening winner, Sadie drove to his campaign headquarters. She talked to T.J. and confessed to Jill, "Okay, I had a drink or two; well I'm not sure how many. Emma Sue calls it liquid courage."

As soon as she got back from Miami, Jill drove to Sadie's to hear the election night story and about her search for Jorge.

"I met his fiancé, bubbly, she hugged me and said she'd heard so much about me. Right. You know she didn't know anything. Her name is Penny, and she is shorter than you, real short. Cute, round and shapely. Said she graduated from Howard, too."

"Were you nice?"

"I think so, greeters and strangers talking to each other. They were all friends who had worked together to elect T.J. I wanted to run out of there, a fiancé?"

"What did you think, *Mrs.* Fredericks?"

"T.J. said he wanted to give me some materials for the interracial group. We went to his office which was just across the street from the celebration."

They spent an hour away from the festivities. In the five years since Mike's birth, they had not been alone. T.J. had carefully explained politics to Sadie and the sacrifices necessary to be successful. The great fear of politicians was "skeletons in the closet." He "demanded" Sadie had said, that she needed to declare Mike's paternity "now or never."

T.J. said, "Now in the beginning of my political career or never. It can be damaging now, but not devastating, not career altering. Later as I move up the ranks any unknown family secret becomes lethal, destroying my chances politically. It is why I am getting married, it's so much better to campaign with a 'perfect wife.'"

"Perfect wife? What does that mean? Black?" Sadie said.

"Sadie, you know exactly what that means. My wife can't be the wife of another man. We aren't Mormons. You also know that when we met you had already chosen a husband. It didn't keep me from loving you. I loved you. I love you. It is a 'feeling' as you so often reminded me."

Sadie cried as he continued.

"You're the mother of my son. What can we do with that? You know I wanted to be a politician and affairs with married women are not part of my job description. *You know this.* We are now where we must make this decision. So tell me Sadie, now or never?"

They had then promised to keep this secret between them, the "never."

T.J. had held her, hugging her tightly "I thought I was not going to breathe again and at that moment I considered it. Just squeeze me to death."

T.J. said, "I feel as if I'm losing an arm, my son, my first born son will never know me as his father. But Sadie you must make the next decision. If he ever comes to me and asks me if I'm his father, I will not deny him. I will say, 'Yes, you are my son.'"

Sadie had whimpered and shed enough tears to use up a travel pack of Kleenex. And then she told T.J. where she was staying close to Weir Cook Airport because she was flying to Miami first thing in the morning.

Sadie kept asking, "What do you think, Jill? Did I do the right thing?"

"Right?! There are no right or wrong answers only responses. My minister told me that when he counseled me about marrying Jack. But what about the hotel by the airport did he come?"

Sadie nodded.

Jill wiped Sadie's tears and hugged her, but she knew T.J. and Sadie had done this to themselves. Sadie, hard-headed, independent, made now or never decisions, like marrying Michael in the first place.

"Remember, Dad always reminded us that decisions have consequences..."

Sadie cried in the retelling, "Little Mike will never know, never want for anything, ever..." as if that rationalization would satisfy her empty heart.

Jill stopped her, saying, "Never say never. We don't know what is going to happen. Look at Luis just appearing. It would have been easy to think never, but even Jack had said one of them - Luis or Luisa – has to stay in one place. Maybe he kind of knew. And you, Mrs. Fredericks, don't know what will happen."

Sadie had stopped sniffling and said, "Okay."

Jill now parked under the country club awning, and Harold opened her door. He smiled, his kind face with droopy eyes and bulldog jowls. Rain dripped off the brim of his yellow hood and onto his cauliflower shaped nose, he shook his head, but continued to greet her, "Lovely day, ma'am."

She stopped as he helped her jump the mini-stream, pouring down the driveway.

"Always the optimist, Mr. Winston. Is Mrs. Fredericks here?"

"The senior Mrs. Fredericks?"

"No. Master Fredericks' mother."

Harold chuckled, shaking his head, then answered, Mrs. Michael Fredericks *is* here. How are you Mrs. Jones?"

"I'm happy that I have a four day break from teaching, but this weather…" She held her hand, palm up, then shook her head.

"It's November, Mrs. Jones, not unseasonable." Jill nodded as he continued, "She said you will be dining upstairs and excuse me, let me quote, ma'am, 'Act like you have had some home training.'"

"Home training? Miss Emily Post, really? I'll choke her when I see her."

"What?"

"Thank you, Mr. Winston."

The rain dripped from crevices in the awning. A large drop fell on her cheek, creating a giant tear. Crying? Was it an omen? Sadie said she had a surprise. A surprise for Sadie could mean anything.

Sadie constantly bought her presents; some like the butter churn were for the house; some like the fresh flowers in October were "just because"; still others were very expensive like the diamond and onyx broach that had belonged to Grandma Fredericks, the first Claudine. The pin was an antique filigree mounting with diamonds shaped into a star design on a smooth black background. Sadie said it looked too "school teachery" for her, but she knew a school teacher. Jill lightly touched the pin that she had worn on the gray crepe dress with the high collar, long sleeves, lace cuffs and tucked bodice. She said to the dead English teacher, Miss Horn, "Yes, Jill Havlicek, now you look like a teacher."

Jill climbed the wide concrete stairway to the lobby, coatroom, and main dining room. The predominant decorating color was light gray, with pastels. Mauve, pink, peach splashes of abstract flowers created murals on the walls. No one was in the lobby. Two-story windows provided the only light in the bi-level entrance. The lower level led to the locker room, and swimming pool, their summer haunt. The rain dripped against these long windows each recessed in a block and brick exterior wall.

Jill hung her raincoat on a cloak room hook, and walked through the wide opening to the elegant eating area. The same long vertical windows used in the lobby surrounded the restaurant, like the lobby, another empty room. A small parquet dance floor and stage carved out an interior corner space. Gray cushy carpeting covered the dining room floor. Jill thought a full-time person would be needed to keep the light carpet clean.

She started walking towards Sadie when Sadie called out, "Take your muddy boots off!" Ah, the carpet cleaner's assistant.

"Hi, Siddhartha. I thought this was a high class place? Keep your voice down, someone might be disturbed."

"There is no one in this entire dining room," Sadie retorted, making a sweeping motion with her arm. It looked as if the entire place was ready to serve 200 people to a sit-down dinner. The tables some seating eight or nine people others four and the most intimate for two people were covered in linen tablecloths. Four-foot tall boxes held silk flower arrangements in the pastel accents of the lobby.

Jill took off her boots and carried them to cloak room. She returned stocking-footed. Her feet sunk into the deep pile carpeting as she padded to Sadie's table.

"I love this view," Jill looked toward the third hole's fairway with its rolling hills and stands of trees. Twisted stalks of charcoal gray brush dotted the golf course. The impenetrable rain, darkness and winter blocked the view of the horizon. "Better in the summer, but still amazing in the rain."

The waiter brought two hot brandy-laced spicy cider drinks with cinnamon-candy swizzle sticks. "Hello. I'm Bobby your transition waiter. I'm waiting on Greg to relieve me, but he is delayed in this storm."

"Yes, Bobby, I remember you from last summer at the pool," Jill said.

"He's Linda's young brother, remember Linda Higbie? She's now Linda Stevens, Brad Stevens, remember?"

"Sure. You look like your dad, Coach Higbie."

Sadie smiled, "Bobby, please bring us some of those snack crackers with cheese and two more ciders. We have some things to talk about that need coaxing, a freeing up of inhibitions." She winked at Jill.

"Oh, no, Sadie, what have you kept from me? You only said surprise. You didn't say what. T.J.?"

"No, you know we ended that…" Sadie glanced out at the rain-soaked afternoon.

"Paused? Let's just say pause because we don't know…"

"Okay, pause," Sadie said.

"He may lose an election, and that would change a lot of things..."Jill said.

"I know; never say never."

"I'm sorry; I didn't mean to say a sad thing. Open mouth, insert foot. I guess I hoped T.J. wouldn't be so tough. Sadie..." Jill reached to touch Sadie's elbow.

Sadie turned and half-smiled at Jill, then spoke, "Sometimes, me too, but you know this is better for all of us. Michael, after nine years of marriage? He's been...oh he loves me so," she sighed heavily. "And his family? They love little Mike, the heir apparent's heir; in her own way Mrs. Fredericks has learned to handle her daughter-in-law. But hey, this surprise is for you." Sadie tapped the top of Jill's hand.

Jill shivered and curled her legs under her in the big blue velvet chair. The huge marble fireplace crackled. The flames cast a golden glow in the cold formal room.

"You look like a drowned puppy," Sadie said. "Did your hair look better when you started this day?"

Jill reached and touched her own frizzy hair, "I feel like I've been swimming."

"The weather is miserable, but I like the grays, outdoors and indoors. They cheer me up. Look around. Yes, I was on the renovation committee. Michael always tells me I'm a nut case, but I ignore him."

"Okay, to cheer." Jill picked up her crystal tumbler, "I could use some and for sure you could too. Are we counting days on the calendar since November fourth? Another son would be nice."

"Don't forget my five days immediately after with Michael and I do take the pill. Three munchkins is about the right number. But this is your day, Mrs. Jones." Sadie tipped her glass against Jill's, "A toast to another Thanksgiving dinner," Jill raised her glass and drank as Sadie continued, "To my best friend who knows me and still loves me." Sadie took a big drink.

"Sadie, did I have a choice? And one more toast, Mrs. Fredericks, your wedding anniversary, two days ago, nine perfect years and three children later..."

"Stop. I love Michael and some years have been more perfect than others." They touched glasses and laughed.

Tingled and warmed by their drinks they reminisced about Thanksgivings past. When Sadie finished her second hot cider, she opened her purse, "Let's see what Sadie Claus can find in her bag of goodies for Mrs. Jones. You have been naughty or nice this year?"

"Come on Sadie. What have you got? Not another pamphlet? Your bag is beginning to scare me."

Sadie deliberately removed a nail file, then a bottle of copper-colored nail polish, then a pacifier, and placed each item on the table. Dramatically, she pulled three envelopes from a rubber band, "Let's see…Mrs. Michael Fredericks from Public Service of Indiana, I guess you don't want that. Caylor Gas and Fuel, they should give it to us free as long as Gramp Fredericks was their Chairman."

Sadie looked up from the envelopes, grinning. Jill reached for them, but Sadie laughed as she pulled them back, "Do you know anyone at the National Coffee Federation in Bogota, Colombia? M-m, Colombia, isn't that in South America? Where they grow dark…rich…coffee?" She winked at Jill, "And men with green eyes?"

"Sadie!" Jill reached across the table, trying to grab the envelope.

Sadie laughed, "Okay Miss Curious," and handed the envelope to Jill.

Jill tore open the envelope, "Is this our worst adventure yet?"

"I'll let you know when we are finished. You know it will be one of the shuffleboard court discussions when we retire at St. Petersburg. Read it!"

"'Dear Mrs. Jones…'" Jill read, "Oh please, Luis, Mrs. Jones?"

"Go on," Sadie interrupted, "He's just trying to be polite. Well, actually, he is polite and well-mannered. You on the other hand, have major Amy Vanderbilt needs…"

"Stop! Why are you defending him? He wants to control me."

"See? That's good," Sadie spoke, "if that's his mission, Luis has all my support. Man on a mission. You are out of control, just ask Jack."

"Out of control? I wasn't the one shacking up with a politician in Indianapolis, what two weeks ago?"

"Yes, Mrs. Jones, we do have our secrets. Let's drink to that."

They touched glasses and drank. The heavy rain darkened the late afternoon. Bobby walked through the room lighting centerpiece candles. Two other waiters shuffled silently through the tables, placing glasses, fresh flowers, polished silverware and bread & butter plates on each table.

Jill continued reading, "'An account in the name of Jill Jones has been opened at Merchant's National Bank. In order to access this account, you must use the following numbers in all transactions. All records will be retained at the bank. If you have questions, please contact Mr. Charles Nye, the Vice-President in charge of the International Division.'"

"Well, Jill, Indianapolis is the only place with a Merchant's Bank. When are we going? I wonder how much it costs to fly to Colombia?"

"Colombia? No." Jill laid the letter on the table; she traced the edges shaking her head. Sadie pulled it out from her hand.

"Let's have another cider," Jill whispered. "What am I going to do? How will I explain this to Jack?"

"Oh, Jeezus H. Christ, Jill, Jack? You always accuse me of marrying too soon; maybe that comment should be applied to you. Let's go and see what they tell you about how much money you have, then we can see if passports are in order. Or we can go shopping. The biggest shopping day is in two days. Tell Jack we are going shopping for Christmas." Sadie bit into a cheese covered cracker.

"Sadie, what? My rich uncle died?"

"Oh, is that the homosexual one, the famous New York designer? No, I don't think so. Jack could easily ask your mom and dad. More creative, Mrs. Jones."

"We know honesty is out. Hector said it is hard to improve on the truth. But no, there will be no truth-telling here."

"Don't worry it is probably just a couple of hundred dollars. You can buy Luisa some clothes, an extra pair of boots. He's missed out on nine years of child support."

"This man is mucking up my life royally."

"Ah, Miss Sarah B. you're here. I've found extra money is not something that messes up my life. I propose a toast to the Colombian connection!"

"Why do you toast my calamities?" Jill asked.

They drained their glasses and Greg quickly refilled them. Greg wore the club's evening dress, black pants and white shirt.

Jill tapped her finger on the letter, "What am I going to do about this man?"

"Do you have a choice? I mean I don't think you have too many options."

"Exactly. But Sadie, I don't want to tell him to go away."

"No shit, Sherlock. I don't have a degree in psychology, but I do know you like these globe-trotting men, in and out of your life, here today for play time, a fix, and then gone tomorrow. And it's been awhile, since when? Mo's wedding, New York? And a certain...Captain."

"Colonel, Sadie, colonel."

Mo's wedding; New York had been cold, colder than she could remember it being on her New Year's Eve with Hector. She could almost see Hector climbing in and out of Imogene or in and out of the subway trains. Then, William who went by cab or drove himself. They danced at the rehearsal dinner in Long Island at East Hampton, Elke's home. The home's windows opened to the ocean. The white marble fireplace blazed and illuminated the cathedral-ceilinged living area.

The four days had taken on a dreamlike quality. The church, an Episcopalian Gothic building in Manhattan, held the holiday wedding. The cavernous sanctuary was lit with candles placed at the end of the rows. Christmas greens decorated the arched vestibules and hung on each of the pews. The church smelled of pine incense.

Stewart's family and their friends came largely from the world of finance, real estate and medicine. Jill experienced her first exposure to the black upper class. It had been exciting. She kept hoping her "cornfields" weren't showing.

She still had her forest green velvet dress with the long leg-of-mutton sleeves and cream colored lace cuffs. The sleeves reminded her of fencing scenes in old movies, the cuffs covering her hands. The silk velvet was heavy and soft. William rubbed her back when they danced or stood next to each other. The fitted bodice and scoop neck exposed the top of her breasts and some cleavage. Mo's dress with the same neckline had an upper collar of lace and pearls. Mo had frosted her light brown hair, so she looked blonde like Elke.

She and William flirted like the lovers they had been. He was irresistible in his tux. They were lovers going nowhere together, but embracing the playfulness as children in a school yard. And when the bell rang, recess was over.

When she met Mo's brother, she understood how he was able to deceive people about his heritage. He was light, barely tan, had sandy-colored hair and resembled Elke -thin lips, narrow nose, blue eyes. As Mo looked like William, Christian Cunningham resembled his mother. He was fifteen and tall. William remarked, "In another year he'll be taller than his old man."

"And ready to earn my wings, father," Christian had answered in what Jill thought was the most respectful response she had ever heard from a teenage boy. She spent her days with teenage boys who had to be reminded of where they were and to whom they spoke.

The charm of the father, Jill decided, as she watched Christian flirting with the girls at the reception – Stewart's eighteen year old sister, Christian's step-sisters' friends, cousins, so many young women.

"New York," William said more than once in response to her quizzical look, "only in New York. Ostentatious – it is and they are." William flirted. Jill saw the William Mo hated, prowling? The rogue, warmly interested in young women. When she got home, she stored the emerald ring, his gift in Germany, and told herself it would be Luisa's when it fit.

Jill now shook her head at Sadie. William, she mused, then said to Sadie, "Colonel Cunningham."

"Yeah, a Colonel at the Waldorf Astoria, wasn't it? Room service? No, sorry, you were the room service. I forgot Mrs. Jones."

"Sadie, you've had...My life has changed in five years, dramatically. I teach. I'm a wife, a mother..."

"Rationalizing? Luis doesn't seem the type to give you much choice in this affair."

"It isn't an affair!" Jill smacked her hand on the table.

"Shish. Didn't I wash the sheets from the green room after your guided tour? No, no, not you Mrs. Jones. This is me, Sadie. Cut the bull...Only time, Jill. You are not on a slow boat to China with *this* Colombian."

"Why aren't you telling me, 'Jill, you're married with a nice home and a decent husband, a lovely daughter? No you say 'affair.'"

"I can only tell you what I see. Yes, list the bullshit, oh sorry, I broke my own rule, but you have stepped into another dimension. I saw and heard him in my kitchen. He's serious. But Jill he's been serious from the moment you met him."

"An affair? Adultery? It all sounds so sinful. Lillian will be disappointed. Oh, god, Sadie, did you hear me? I just accepted your term and this relationship."

"Lillian will be disappointed? Come on Sweetie, we've been through thick and thin *and* Lillian's disapproval followed us like a bad penny."

"What did Henry tell us in one of his better moments, 'some women shouldn't have been born with wombs.' I think that was a cut, but you know Henry, there is always some raw truth in his sarcasm. It's wrong, but it feels right being with Luis. I mean he is the first, oh, Sadie. I want to see him again. I told him parameters. There are all these people to consider, Jack, I have to...let's do Jack last. There's Luisa. Does she know her real father? Or Jack who she believes is her father? Jack is her father. I mean he couldn't be any more... Sadie help!"

"We have to work on the scheduling. There are certain times when Jack would never know. He wouldn't miss you. You could travel to some clandestine place. He trusts you. He is so in love with his little woman...disgusting, but suits the Colombian's plan. We also need to know how flexible Luis is about your marriage."

"Listen to you. It sounds like a business – travel, scheduling, flexibility," Jill said.

"Maybe, but if we don't plan, horrible things could happen, I mean things we don't want to happen."

"Michael's right, together we would rob a bank. But I don't want us playing shuffleboard, saying 'What if...' Dad says 'we only make this life trek once; make the experience without regrets.' It is a bigger fear than losing Jack. Did I really dismiss Jack, just like that?"

"My friend, you dismissed him just like," Sadie snapped her fingers, "the day you said, 'I do.' What did the Colonel always ask you in his letters about Hector? Love? For certain that was *not* the reason you married Jack."

"Sadie, that's cynical. I do love Jack...okay, okay in a sort of way," Jill sighed. "Gotta go, Sadie. Let's go Friday and find out what chaos Luis Ochoa created. We can meet Mr. Nye. I'll drive."

Jill said she had to make pies to take to the church and for the Jones's. Jack would be worrying about her drive in the wet weather and her timing. His clock would be running.

Jill and Sadie now hugged barefoot in the candlelight. Nearby a harpist tuned his strings in preparation for the evening diners. "Listen Sadie, the angels are playing…"

"Angels playing for the devils," Sadie answered, with a grin and threw her head back laughing. The huge crystal chandeliers were turned to brightness just as Sadie laughed, but dimmed, as the waiter presented her their ticket to sign.

"Happy Thanksgiving, Sadie. Thanks for you."

"Happy Thanksgiving, Jill. Friday we'll do this," she held up her receipt, "Compliments of Luis Ochoa."

ïξï

Jill sat on the living room rug surrounded by boxes of Christmas decorations and strings of lights. She substituted bulbs determining which ones were burned out on the chain. She paused and took a drink of cinnamon tea, Sadie's recipe, only hot this time. Christmas? In a matter of days. Thanksgiving? It sped by. The last log Jack added to the fire glowed red.

Luisa had been asleep for an hour and Jack almost as long. Why hadn't she been able to fall asleep? Jack's promise to take Luisa to chop down their Christmas tree first thing in the morning? The excitement of the interracial club's first annual Christmas party? Would Luis remember her at Christmas? Remember how? A present? A call? Card? A letter from the National Coffee Federation?

Sadie had given her two boxes of Christmas decorations she'd found in the attic at Vicksburg. They were dusty, but none had been broken - tiny hand-blown glass balls, see-through pastel globes, six different porcelain angels with musical instruments and hand-painted faces. "Too many rug rats at this house for something so delicate. Besides, Michael's buying Mike a golden retriever puppy for Christmas. No, Jill, you can use them," Sadie said. After a sudsy gentle bath, Jill laid them all on towels on the kitchen counter, but she still had not been sleepy.

It had been three weeks since she and Sadie had gone to Indianapolis, but still no call from Luis. She assumed the bank would notify him she'd been there. But nothing.

Tonight's Interracial Club Christmas party put her in the mood for the season —not only the planning, and shopping, but also baking with Luisa. They decorated Christmas cookies to hang on the tree. Planning the event built the bridges Cynthia had hoped for. Bitsy and she were co-chairmen for the refreshments. The club invited children recommended by the Salvation Army to a Christmas party. They chose the YWCA to host the event and the "Y" allowed them to decorate. When she and Jack drove home after the party, she hoped all the smiles and laughter would carry everyone through the holidays. The kids of the group's families getting together, planning, and preparing saw no color. The club's fathers met and talked. Jack sat huddled in a corner with a father who had brought his young sons. How many people said, "Jill, your husband is such a nice man"?

Bitsy had talked about Caylor – from her perspective. Jill listened to stories of the black guys she'd known only in passing, but whom Bitsy knew as best friends. John Ferguson moved to Indianapolis, a basketball star at Caylor High School. When he could not get a contract with any of the National Basketball Association teams, John had moved to Italy to play. Jill thought he was the most well-known black guy in their class.

"Did you know," Bitsy asked, "that John, 'the Swan,' gosh he was so graceful shooting baskets, exciting to watch, anyway, he dated Sarah Bowman?"

Jill was shocked. Sarah's father was Dr. Bowman, *the* Dr. Bowman, everyone's pediatrician, west-side, white, lived in the park.

Bitsy nodded, "They came to our parties together, many times."

"What happened to Sarah, anyway?"

"I don't know, just a lot of talk, maybe she was pregnant. No one knew for sure, but John did go to Italy. Dr. Bowman had enough money to send Sarah anywhere."

Jill asked, "Mimi Scoggins?"

"She definitely was pregnant. Did you know that part? Jimmy Dunn, remember him?"

Jill nodded thinking of the half-back that received most of Jim Bancroft's football passes. As they talked, Jill thought how much fun their class reunion would be next summer. Ten years since high school, where had all the time gone? And now she heard new stories about her former classmates. Did Marcia Webster know all this gossip? She'd call her after the holidays, maybe she would like to join the interracial club.

She tossed a green light bulb into the discard pile, then continued winding and unwinding the bulbs. The club's work and friendships joined the families in only four months. Cynthia and Sadie went toe-to-toe on certain decisions: where the party was to be, catered food, the guest list (mayor, city attorney, pastors), but they argued to a certain point, then stopped, agreed and laughed. The other members said, "Let Sadie and Cynthia decide, but lock them in the padded room while they do it!" But at this evening's party as they cleaned up, they all decided to make it an annual affair and ask more to participate.

The children's laughter enlivened all of them. The club mothers had taken their children shopping and each bought a toy and clothing for the name they had been given. The club's children gave presents to the guests. The young guests excitedly opened the presents. Smiles and laughter the whole evening and a few tears of surprise and joy. Merry Christmas.

She drank tea and laid her head on a couch cushion. The fire and Jack's reading lamp lit the living room. The floor lamp stood by his old overstuffed chair and footstool, the only piece left from his move to the farmhouse. She'd reupholstered the worn-out tufted weave. The chair blended with their Ethan Allen early American furniture. Sadie gave her two discarded high back chairs. Jack re-glued the legs and stained the scratches, they looked new, well, old and new. She crocheted two oval living room rugs. The large weave fit her old hardwood floors. Lillian had said most houses had been built with pine floors and women prided themselves on scrubbing them without getting splinters.

Their front bay window reminded her of 1254 Butler. The three sides sat atop a storage area with a place large enough to sit. She'd removed the seating pad until after the holidays. Jack would hang the lights there if she ever got them all to work. Before going to bed, he had laid the newspaper on the end table, and instructed her to use extra logs to keep the fire going.

She sat alone in her cozy living room, listening to the quiet creaks of the old house. The last burning log popped. I should get up and put on a new log. The brass mantel clock would soon chime the midnight hour.

She opened her eyes; Jack had leaned down and kissed her.

"Honey, you need to come to bed if you are going to sleep." He closed the glass door on the fireplace, the log now white ash. He unplugged the string of lights lying next to her, then helped her to her feet. Her flannel gown covered her bare legs. She straightened out her fuzzy chenille robe.

"The children," Jack said, "were so special this evening. I wish I could give you more of your own. When you are surrounded by them, you seem like these decorations, all bright and glowing."

"Luisa is plenty of children for me. You forget I have 120 every semester as well as the ones at church. It is nice to come home and relax." She was relieved she'd had her period in October, the month after her visit from Luis, and she started taking birth control pills again. She told Jack the doctor had suggested them for what he thought was a preventative health measure. Yeah, preventative.

Jack wrapped his arms around her and kissed her. "Jill Jones, you're a special person. I love you." He kissed her again as he reached to turn out the floor lamp. He took her hand as they walked to the stairs, "I think the program you introduced, well Cynthia and you introduced this evening will be a great success."

"The Christmas party for the children?"

"No, no, the idea of setting up a fund to help people in need pay their heating bills."

They walked into their darkened bedroom. She sat on the edge of the bed and dropped her slippers on the floor and threw her robe toward the chair.

"Some people," Jill spoke, "have to choose between eating and keeping warm. There is something wrong with that. We all agreed this was a problem that happens to all colors and we could help as a group."

"When I pay the bills, I will write a check to the foundation. I suppose Sadie and Michael were the ones who gave the $5,000 to start the fund."

"They said it was anonymous, Jack."

"I know, but it is well, I'm not sure who else can afford that kind of money in Caylor. I mean who would want to?"

In the dark, she smiled. Someone, someone. Luisa could only wear so many boots and winter coats. The money was more than her and Jack's down payment to buy the farmhouse, three times more than Henry had paid to buy Imogene, enough for a year or maybe two at State, and too much for Luisa. And when he called...he would call, he did say "in," her life, she would tell him.

Chapter 11

Luisa jumped from Jill's car and ran to their large front yard. The winter view of the cornfields extended panoramically like so much divinity candy, softly shaped snow and more coming down. March was the time for the snow to melt. The crocuses would soon peek from the frozen dirt for their first kiss from the sun. This would surely be the last winter storm of the year. Well, they had not had *the* ice storm. March was only four days old; there was plenty of time. Sadie would be twenty-eight this month. Twenty-eight? Are we getting that old? Ten years ago they graduated from Caylor High School, Class of 1960.

Jill turned off the ignition and reached across the seat to pick up Luisa's lunch box and books. She pulled her bag of papers from the backseat. The storm would reduce her school week; she could catch up on grading papers. She missed her Volkswagen in the snow. With its heavy rear engine, it had been so easy to push from a snow bank.

Luisa flung herself on her back, moving her arms and legs back and forth, leaving the "snow angel" imprint. She watched, and felt a pang remembering the snow angels she and Hector had made. The Lillian in her curtailed the thought, "Luisa, get up you still have on your school clothes! And now look at you, all covered in snow. If you want to play out here go inside and change."

They trudged through their un-shoveled walk. Jack would not be home to clear the path for another hour at least, maybe longer if the roads weren't cleared. They stomped snow from their boots on the still visible doormat. The porch was protected and the heat of the house usually kept it snow free. The wind created drifts along the porch railing. There would be no school at Southeastern tomorrow, but Luisa…if possible, Jack would have to drive her to Lillian's. Caylor's city schools rarely closed because of inclement weather. When? One time in her twelve years of attendance, when they were buried in twenty-four inches in that many hours.

When they opened the front door, the warmth of the house hugged them. Her front foyer and hall had become a coat check room with boots, gloves, hats, snowsuits and scarves. The winter outerwear hung on the hooks of the hall tree or was scattered and dropped on the rag rug. The closet meant to keep the pieces organized was full of winter coats, three for each of them. Jill's small family had certain garments for the special demands of winter. Jack wore insulated coveralls to shovel snow. Luisa had five pairs of mittens and gloves to change when one pair got wet.

Jill dusted snow from Luisa's hair and shook the snow from her own coat. The phone rang. The grandfather clock at the end of the hall said 4:30. Sadie, she decided. The phone rang again as Luisa took off all her snowy clothes in the hallway. Jill rushed toward the kitchen. On the third ring she picked up the phone.

"Jill Jones?" an unfamiliar female voice with a thick accent asked.

"Yes."

"Please hold for Señor Ochoa."

Jill called to Luisa to turn on the television, and cautioned her it would only be for few minutes; Jill closed the kitchen door. Luisa squealed in the living room, "TV in the afternoon."

Jill heard the sound and returned to the phone. "Yes," she answered haltingly thinking of the fly entering the spider's parlor.

"How's my daughter?" He sounded happy.

"She's fine, Luis. She just made a snow angel, her favorite. I thought you would call sooner." She heard Sadie chiding her about when is your Colombian connection going to call you.

"But you have heard from me, si?"

"Yes." She smiled, looking at her ring. The large emerald was positioned in a gold leaf with tiny diamonds mounted in twisted stems that turned into the band like a grape arbor. She and Sadie had never seen a ring with such detail. The inside band showed signs of wear; the tarnish had enhanced definitions in the leaves and stems. Jill wore it on her right hand. She explained the unique ring to Jack, "Isn't it gorgeous? A present from Sadie. She bought it on her antique shopping trip to Georgia, and insisted I needed it." Sadie recognized the setting as antique and encouraged Jill to find out its origin.

"It's European, Jill," Sadie had said, "I just know it, but ask. It must have a story."

Jill had opened the package at Sadie's house Christmas Eve morning over coffee and Sadie's version of fruit cake lots of rum and fruit, not much cake or dough.

"Thank you," she now said to Luis, "it is amazing, unusual…"

He interrupted, "From the Spanish court, Queen Isabella, Columbus's patron. It was as close as I could find to a European princess. You must tell Siddhartha, I know she asked you to ask me."

For months Jill had dreaded this conversation, yet she'd wanted to talk to him. She paused momentarily to recall the rehearsed speech she had planned. Luis, I believe this will not work even though I want to see you. I cannot figure a logical way to explain to an almost nine-year-old who you are. She'd initially considered this call "remote." He lived in Colombia, South America for criminey sakes, how often could he call or much less come to Caylor? But then he'd opened the account in Indianapolis and he became a presence squarely in her life. He'd said, "Six months." Without looking at a calendar, she had reasoned sometime in the winter.

The emerald ring came at Christmas, December. In January another deposit, sixty days after the first one. In February as Jack assembled their receipts for their taxes, she had driven to Indianapolis to talk to Mr. Nye. He said the accountants at the bank handled joint international accounts "differently" and nothing would be sent to her house or to the Internal Revenue Service. As the evidence arrived, piece by piece, she had concluded this conversation with Luis was inevitable.

"Luis, you want my parameters, I know."

"Gringa, your word. There are few boundaries I do not cross and fewer places I do not go."

"Please listen," she took a deep breath, "You have not been a part of my life for nine almost ten years, well not directly a part. I accept that you are with me through your daughter every hour of the day. I wanted to make a life for her that provided her with the most stability. I hate Caylor, but it's a small community where she is free to grow up without big city problems. She has her grandparents and cousins and friends. It is a great world for your daughter. I don't want anything or anyone to upset that."

"Si."

"She takes ballet lessons; she is in swim classes, gymnastics. I've tried to make life ideal for her because she didn't have a quite normal beginning." He hadn't stopped her and she'd presented most of her planned argument. She exhaled.

"Is that all?" he spoke brusquely.

She cringed, pulled on the curled telephone cord and stared at the red and white squares of her kitchen floor. "It looks like a checked picnic table cover, Miss. Good Housekeeping, where is your taste?" Sadie commented when she first saw it.

Luis continued, "Your spring vacation is Friday April 3 through April 12. Your tickets for Curaçao and your itinerary will be arriving at Sadie's. You can do this. Your husband approves of your vacations. I will see you and my daughter there. We can talk international banking on the Dutch Island. It seems to have fallen within your *parameters*." He chuckled, a short laugh. "Adios, Gringa."

The line clicked. She slammed down the phone. "Damn him, he didn't listen."

Luisa peeked her head through the kitchen door. "Mom, may I have some milk and Nestlé's?"

"You have been watching TV. No Nestlé's. Milk, yes. I'll start dinner in a minute or two. I have to call Sadie."

"Who was on the phone? Grandpa or Grandma?"

Jill poured a glass of milk, speaking as she handed it to Luisa, "An old friend. Go turn off the TV and read the book you brought home from school. I am going to call Aunt Sadie."

"Aunt Sadie? Are we going to see her?"

"No, it is a blizzard outside, remember?"

Holding her milk, Luisa walked out of the kitchen with her head down.

Jill dialed Sadie's number. "Sadie, I hate him. He doesn't listen. He ignored everything I said."

"Hello, Miss Sarah B. Let me guess, you're talking about Señor Ochoa? Jack doesn't have the heart not to listen or to ignore you, or was it Henry? He has the guts, but doesn't exercise those options."

"Are you listening? He ignored me, Sadie! He says I am going to meet him in Curaçao with *his* daughter. He makes me...."

"Curaçao? You need to stop, Sarah B. You're going to Curaçao, when? You probably shouldn't be going someplace with somebody you hate, but I'm not so sure you *hate* the dark foreigner with the large international bank account..."

"Sadie, you sound like him. Why didn't he listen? It's his daughter, too. Doesn't he want what's best for her?"

"You, of course, know what's best for your daughter? and his daughter? *not* the enigmatic Latin?"

"Jack never says what I'm doing is wrong."

"Jack? Who thinks you are a gift from God? I don't think I would make that comparison. There is none. And you know it. Now do you want to drive in here to get this letter from the 'National Coffee Federation' in Bogotá, Colombia?"

"Are you serious? I have a letter?"

"Yes. I tromped out in eighteen feet of snow to get the mail and didn't he say you'd be getting something? He seems to be a man of his word. I'm not looking at the dates, but I'd be willing to bet we're real close to the six month deadline he gave you last September. I know you remember that date in my green room, the way *you* remember numbers."

"September Fourth."

"Bingo! My calendar says this snowy day is Wednesday, March Fourth."

"Sadie..."

"Are you coming for the letter?"

"In this snow? For that damned Colombian? Not no, but hell no!"

"Lillian, your pride and joy is cussing." Sadie laughed uncontrollably.

"Oh, Sadie, straighten up! Why me?"

"You know why. Your dad says you never do anything the easy way. Henry is right again. I wish he knew about all of this. He would be teasing the daylights out of you."

"Stop, Sadie, or I'll tell Michael what you did the last time he was out of town on business."

"You cannot blackmail me, Mrs. Jones. I have Colonel Cunningham stories that would make Jack's toes curls…Mr. and Mrs. Cunningham, a taste of bigamy…or maybe Luis would like to know the real life adventures of his daughter's mother, his gringa?" Sadie, laughed and continued, "Fix yourself some coffee and we'll work on this Caribbean thing. Where is Curaçao exactly?"

Covering fields and frosting the trees, layer upon layer the snow fell.

ᴙξᴙ

"Jeezus, Sadie, we're going to be late!" Jill said. The airport entrance road was blocked with construction equipment, trucks dumping asphalt as steamrollers pressed it into place.

"Hold on. We have forty-five minutes and they are signaling us to come on. Hey, the signal guy's kind of cute. Look Jill." They inched from two lanes to one. Blinking yellow lights, and free standing signs with orange fluorescent flags littered the blocked lanes. Traffic cones were sprawled where they had been knocked down by oncoming cars. A young college-age boy with bleached blond hair, muscular arms in tight jeans waved them to move into a single lane.

"We should've called…" Jill said, looking at her watch. "8:30A.M. And all this commotion."

"Jill, we have time. You know the mayor and his cronies are trying to win votes…maybe we should have called T.J. and asked him to stop construction because Sadie and Jill are…"

"Sadie, I see the door for American Airlines. Maybe you should just let us out. We can check the bags and…"

"I'll park and run back because I'm walking you to the gate. I don't want you to get weak in the knees. You need those legs strong for other things." Sadie reached across Luisa, sitting between them,

227

and pinched Jill's legs. Jill smacked her hand. Luisa grabbed each of their hands and shook her head. They all laughed.

"Sadie, you better not worry about my legs and figure out where we are going to park."

The signs for parking took them away from the construction. Sadie eased to the curb. A valet, an old man with curved shoulders that had carried too many suitcases, opened their door. He smiled a false teeth smile.

Jill slammed the door as Sadie left her and Luisa at the curb. The early spring morning with its heavy dew and clear sunshine relaxed Jill. The lilacs would be blooming soon. Spring pushed the winter dreariness back into the closet. She buttoned Luisa's coat, handing the valet her ticket. He opened it and checked his watch.

"Ma'am, you have plenty of time. Let's go inside and you can check your luggage." Plenty of time? In hours she would be seeing Luis; there was not enough time to prepare for that. Seven months since the Princess Suite. The green room, why did she and Sadie call that single event "the green room?" Did he think of it as *the* green room? or the red-headed princess? or an afternoon in Caylor? or the tiger princess? What did he think about period? Seven days, twenty-four hour days, hour after hour with Luis Ochoa, what would that be like? Luisa pulled her hand, "Mom, I need to go to the bathroom, but why are there so many people in line?"

"It's spring break, Lo, everyone wants to go some place, just like us."

There was a line in the restroom and a line at the airline check-in. The valet held their spot and promised to look for Sadie. When they got back to the American Airlines passenger line, they presented their tickets.

They walked quickly to the gate. Luisa held her gray elephant in one hand and Jill's hand in the other. Sadie carried their jet tote. As they walked to the gate ramp, Sadie handed the bag to Jill and hugged her.

"Don't forget, Sadie, right back here in seven days."

"I hope so. I don't want you to decide life with Luis beats your Hoosier farm."

Jill shook her head and walked down the ramp.

Sadie wiped her eyes.

Jill turned and held up seven fingers, her last gesture before she and Luisa walked through the entry doors. They boarded for the first leg of their flight to Miami, then on to Curaçao on ALM. The flight attendant helped them find their seats in first-class. She took their carry-on bag.

The plane taxied for takeoff. Jill lay back in the seat as Luisa stared out the window. Indianapolis was beginning to turn spring green. In one month, March to April, she and Sadie had managed to get everything done, including buying some sexy seductive clothes and studying travel brochures.

She so wanted to go to the tropics and tried to contain her excitement in front of Jack, but she hummed and smiled involuntarily. Memories of the green room, and the shed, the fantasies of Luis in Curaçao caused Jack to say, "You're so sensual." She was, she knew. Her thoughts of Luis kept her physically reacting, jagged heat from inside up and through.

Jill and Luisa had driven to the Federal Building in Indianapolis to get their passports and to buy traveler's checks from her account at Merchant's Bank. The letter from Bogotá instructed her to buy Luisa clothes for the trip. Luisa had gotten her first passport and Jill had to renew hers from when she went to Germany. Looking at her old passport picture, Jill decided she looked better now. Older was agreeing with her. Jill's memories of flying spilled over one another. She smiled now flying to her newest adventure. She had planned the tourist trips, "the landhuis" or local Dutch plantation houses with antiques. Sadie said buy what she could and she would pay her when she got back. She wanted to go to the Curaçao museum and ride around St. Michael's Bay. She had no idea what would happen with Luis, and wondered if he even liked to do touristy things.

While she was away, Henry had volunteered to bring his "two fellas" and help Jack re-shingle the farm house roof. Jack insisted the dusty, noisy job should only be done if Jill were not at home; the remodeling would ruin her vacation. Jack had explained his reasoning to Henry who reprimanded him in front of Jill, "You're too easy on her. She needs to be around to clean up our mess, not gallivanting in the West Indies."

Jack shared Luisa's questions about the place she would be visiting and the trip to a totally different country. Luisa talked almost non-stop of flying to an island in a big blue sea. They checked out a book about Curaçao. Jack read to her, "A 500-year old island that has shifted from Spanish to Dutch occupation. It lays in the southern most part of the Netherland Antilles only sixty miles from Venezuela. The quaint Dutch outpost is bathed in the Caribbean sun. Many people go there for snorkeling and deep sea diving."

Jill listened and said to herself, about 500 miles to Cartagena, Colombia, but only an hour's flight.

Now in the comfort of the first-class cabin, she sipped coffee; even in a china cup it still tasted like dirt. She could hear Henry ranting about "residue from an oil change," his phrase for the worst tasting brew. Oh, dad, I have to tell you about this man in my life, want to tell you, but how? Maybe after a week he won't be in my life. He may decide seven days is seven too many.

The planning for the trip had worked at the farm. Jack accepted the trip as Spring Break, but in Lillian's kitchen over pie and coffee, she and Sadie had a close call. She shook her head remembering the conversation.

"How are you paying for a trip like this, Jill?" Lillian asked skeptically, precluding almost any answer Jill would give. "Jack can't afford the Caribbean trip *and* remodeling the farm," Lillian looked down as she cut green beans for dinner.

Lillian filled a big stainless bowl with washed raw beans. Jill reached into the bowl and pulled three or four from the pile. She bit into one, crunching it. She stared at Lillian, who stared back. Lillian frowned as she waited for Jill. Under the table, Jill kicked Sadie's leg. Sadie was on her third bite of blackberry pie. They acted like naughty school girls under the teacher's scowl. Sadie looked from Jill to Lillian, then back to Jill as Jill spoke, "Mom, Jack insists he is one cent away from being broke, but he has money. He just doesn't like to spend it, well, spend it traveling."

"He wants to make sure you and Luisa will be well taken care if anything happens..." Lillian said, defending Jack like always. Hawk's son, Jill thought, but never repeated the phrase to her mother. Jill kicked Sadie, again.

"Oh, please Mom," It had been Jill's contemptuous tone when Lillian started the "Jack Bullshit." "But paying for the trip was...well, it..."

"Not necessary," Sadie had interrupted, gaining her command of the conspiracy. Sadie went on to explain to Lillian that she and Michael had promised Mike and Claudine a trip to Disneyland during Spring Break, but the Curaçao trip, a top sales reward, needed to be used.

Lillian continued chopping the beans, "Why doesn't Jack go with you and Luisa. It seems like a family trip and far better than a week with Henry shingling the farmhouse roof. Jack is going to be miserable with Henry's insistence on faultless construction, no cutting corners."

Jill smiled at the vision of the two men trying to outdo each other. "Jack hates going too far from his home and hearth. After the trip to see Hawk, I'm not sure he's going to want to go too far ever again. Last summer he made it to Aunt Mindy's cottage, four years after Florida, and then only to Holland, Michigan. No mom, you know Jack, he loves that farm."

When they moved to the farm, she had wanted to save their moving boxes. Jack had told her flatly that there was no need because it would be their last move. "You're home now," he stated.

She swallowed his declaration with great difficulty, calling Henry and crying about being stuck forever and ever in a cornfield. Henry told Lillian, who tried to talk to her son-in-law, hoping to pry him from his concrete boots.

ฯ๕ฯ

The plane touched down in Miami. Jill took a deep breath. Her daughter, their daughter, had only two hours to learn of the "friend" who would be meeting them in Curaçao. She and Sadie ironed out the rough edges, but Luisa's sense of who was who in her world was firmly established. The introduction to a new person, and this particular strong presence, needed some carefully worded, acceptable definitions. They disembarked. From a cool 40° in Indiana to a sunny 75° in Miami, she smiled, soaking up the sunshine.

Luisa laughed, "Mommy it's summer. We got on the plane in winter. I want to do that again. I must tell Dad winter to summer."

Jill shook her head, precocious intelligent daughter, this was not going to be easy.

They switched planes, boarded the flight to Curaçao, and settled into their seats. Luisa asked about Curaçao all over again. "Where are we staying?" Luisa turned to Jill, chewing the complimentary peanuts and continued, "Not a hotel, a house, a beach house, right? Aunt Sadie said a private place."

Jill drank the Caribbean punch the attendant gave her. She tried to suppress her internal furnace thinking of Luis caused. The letter had only said their accommodations would be in a private residence. Jill had ignored her marriage vows in the green room. It seemed so right, being with Luis, but she knew her heart dictated those words.

"The love thing" as Henry teased her. But Luis made a vow, long ago in the shed, "until death separates us," the vow before Jack, and William and Hector. She sat next to his daughter, their daughter, their exchange made the vow whole. The consequences of their choice would come. Luis controlled her life, could he protect her from the unintended consequences? Affair? The heart has its reasons, deeper, much deeper, okay Dad, it is a "love thing."

"Luisa, we are staying with a friend of mine in Curaçao. He lives close to the island and promised to take us to some special places."

Luisa listened. Jill fidgeted and paused with each word, deliberately putting them together in terms that made sense to her not quite nine-year old daughter. "He is the man you met at Sadie's last fall. Do you remember?"

"He talked funny and had a name like mine?"

"Honey, he's from South America. He speaks Spanish. You heard his accent; it's not funny, just the way he speaks."

"Does he know daddy?" Luisa looked at her mother as she chewed peanuts.

Jill shifted in the wide leather seat. She took another drink of the rum and fruit punch, then called on the spirit of Sadie to help her respond to this hurdle. Certainly a friend of Jill's would know her "daddy," Jack. Sadie, what? Jill evaluated each word, "Sweetie, you know when you ask me why Sadie and I laugh sometimes and no one else laughs?"

"M-hmm," Luisa set the empty peanut package on her serving tray. The attendant leaned over to pick up Luisa's empty glass, package and napkin, and deftly, folded the tray table into the seat.

"We laugh," Jill continued, rubbing Luisa's cheek, "because we have a special secret that no one knows only Sadie and me. I want you and I have to have special secrets that no one knows but us, okay?"

"Not tell Daddy or Grandpa or Grandma?"

Jill nodded, "Not tell anyone, just you and me."

Luisa turned her head to look at her mother. She fingered the buckle of the seat belt, and the button that adjusted the seat, then returned to her mother's face, "Like when we stopped for chocolate sodas at Shelby's and didn't tell daddy because he had fixed dinner? And we acted like we were hungry?"

"And we were miserable. Yes, a secret between us." Jill leaned over and kissed Luisa's forehead.

"Oh, Mom, Teresa and I tell secrets all the time, so Darcie won't know what we are talking about. Can I buy Teresa a present from Curaçao?"

Jill squeezed Luisa's hand and patted her long curls. Could she keep a secret? Would she want to keep Luis a secret? She struggled keeping it from Jack. He checked her itinerary and asked her where she would be staying.

"International Harvester," she had answered, "made arrangements with a hotel. I do not know the name. They are picking everyone up in a van, but we will be greeted by name."

She and Sadie told Michael their concocted story. He had to know because he and Jack spent time together over dinner occasionally. They were not best friends, but they talked. It had become so complicated. In six months the "farmer's wife" simple lifestyle had been blown to smithereens. Oh, Jack, when will you know? Sooner rather than later? How will you know? A slip of the tongue from Luisa? Yes, Luisa, tell your daddy, how easy, how impossible. Well, I won't be the first one to be divorced in the Class of 1960, Marcia said Barbara McHale and Ronnie had divorced and Ronnie married Shelly Thomas. Oh Caylor High School, will I ever get out of the gossip column? Divorcing Jack and marrying a Colombian?

"If we're careful," Sadie had promised, "we can do this." As Luisa grew, the more her features resembled Luis's. I wonder how long before she notices?

When Jill had said 'yes' to Jack's marriage proposal, she said it for one reason – Luisa. Jack's stability would provide the environment she wanted for her daughter. Stability ran smack into the wandering-star syndrome Henry accused her of having. She had her own standards for the pursuit of happiness. These two factors, to stay and to go, shifted back and forth like hairpin curves on a mountain road. Having Luisa in secure surroundings was a dream realized, but her heart told her secure surroundings were only part of the equation. She wanted more, a small piece of the radical adventures, okay, passion that had been.

She could hear Sadie laughing, "Come on Jill, are you trying be the prima donna of drama? Joan Crawford?" Sadie told her to relax and enjoy herself without getting bogged down in the morality of sleeping with a man who wasn't her husband. Sadie dismissed all of Jill's apprehension with the snap of her fingers, "Sadie's hedonism," the ultimate rationale for all things forbidden. They had been at Sam's Subway in Indianapolis after the Curaçao shopping trip. They laughed and toasted the adventure, but now the pilot announced their descent into Curaçao International Airport, the local time was 4:32P.M., and the local temperature was 84°. The pilot paused and Jill added where Luis Ochoa is waiting to turn Jill Jones's world upside down.

Jill leaned over Luisa's shoulder as the plane eased down to the tiny island surrounded by azure sea. It looked just like the brochures, a green island with endless blue. Luisa pointed and asked, "What is that mom? Where is the tiny ship going? Isn't it too small for our airplane? Mom, will we go in the water?"

She had repeated them too quickly to respond, Jill uh-hummed as her stomach floated inside her like a feather in freefall. Would he be there? He hadn't called or written since the snowstorm edict, and if he weren't there? Thanks to him she had plenty of money to stay wherever she wanted. At least they could have a wonderful spring...no, he would be there. "In your life," he had said. *In.*

The plane taxied to a standstill. As they descended the steps Jill scanned the terminal entrance and spotted a smiling Luis. Jill and Luisa crossed the white coral reef-like runway. The sun shone brilliantly in the late afternoon. Jill reached in her purse for her sunglasses, and waved to Luis, who walked to meet them. "In your life, Gringa," she saw him and heard his phrase race through her head. Deep breath.

Luis now put his arm around her shoulder in a simple hug, then bent down to greet Luisa, "Welcome to Curaçao. How nice to see both of you again, si?" He discreetly winked at Jill. Luisa stared from her mother to her father, and then frowned. An airplane engine drowned out all sound and Luisa turned to see it take off.

When quiet returned Jill answered, "Si, yes, Luis. How nice."

She glanced down at Luisa, who was watching a single engine plane land. Luis did not stop smiling. His relaxed face, the delight dancing in his greener than usual eyes, said welcome to Curaçao more clearly than his greeting. His baggy pants and sandals were beachcomber clothes. Jack never wore sandals. The breeze and close proximity kept his spicy fresh cologne scent all around them. The seductive smell brought back the green room memory. Her sundress smelled like it and she refused to wash it, instead pulling it out of the closet, smelling and remembering. She and Sadie had sniffed all the bottles at Ayres' men counter, trying to find it when they were buying cologne for Michael.

Jill had asked Jack if he wanted some, but he said, "I don't wear anything that comes from a bottle. Soap and water is all I need. You don't want me to smell like a French whore, do you?" Their conversation ended, but the man who filled this moment with himself and his scent was definitely not a French whore.

The sun, clear blue sky and eighty degrees, nirvana or heaven? Pinch me Luis, so I know I'm not dreaming. Jill swirled around, stretching as she absorbed the palm trees, the small European cars, the people in a Crayola range of colors from tan, sepia, beige, burnt umber to brown-black. The plants seemed at once tropical palms and desert cacti. A desert tropic? Yes, that was the picture painted in the brochure. She shivered. Caylor, the farm, and Jack were thousands of miles from her and this moment. Is this what it feels like to be touched by Tinkerbell's dust and travel to an enchanted land?

"You look like a native, Luis," she spoke, touching the front buttons of his shirt.

"I am. I have a home here." A devilish half-smile curled under his moustache. He did not say more as he reached for her hand. He squeezed tightly, the same grip as the day they were introduced, but his palm now soft. She wanted to stop in their walk through the airport and hug him. Luis dropped her hand. Putting his arm around her shoulder, he led her through the front door of the airport. His chest on her back, the muscular chest brushing and pushing, her sexual heat rushed through her.

Luisa walked in front of them, pattering about the trip. The age of innocence? Could she really keep this secret, but more could Jill keep the much deeper relationship *from* Luisa? Her family was all together in Curaçao, so complicated and so exciting. Luisa read her moods as well as any trained professional, much better than Jack. Luisa now proudly displayed the ALM wings the stewardess had given her for her first flight. She turned to Luis, "I want to show my daddy. He has never been on a plane. Mr. Ochoa, do you like planes?"

He had flinched when Luisa mentioned Jack, but smiled at her question, "Si, yes. Luisa. I have one parked in the hangar over there." He pointed to a row of hangars on the far end of the runway.

"Your own plane, Mr. Ochoa? Can we go see it?" Luisa smiled at him.

"Si, señorita, if your mama says, okay." He looked at Jill. Jill shrugged, then nodded as they both looked at her.

Jill inhaled the balmy air; she wanted to be as relaxed as Luis. Luis directed them to look at the hangars, and assured them they would get a closer inspection later. He turned and signaled to a man in a flower print shirt and the same style draw string pants as Luis. The man, with a shaved head was not much taller than Jill. He sported a gold earring. Luisa stared until Jill grabbed her shoulder. The man's full black beard made him seem to be a West Indian pirate. Jill guessed an ethnic mix of black and Spanish, but the people in Curaçao appeared to be racially mixed. Luis introduced him as "Caz, the driver."

Caz drove to pick them up. The car was large compared to the other European autos darting through the airport drive. It was a gray Mercedes limousine. Luis spoke to Caz in Spanish. Taking the luggage tags and their passports, Caz left them and went into the terminal.

"He will get you checked in with the Dutch." Luis pointed over his shoulder at a group of uniformed officers standing behind a desk at the airport entrance. Luis smiled broadly and listened patiently to Luisa's running commentary of the first–class service, coloring books, peanuts, rum-punch for children and a deck of cards with a picture of their plane.

"Mom and I played 'War.' She lost. Mr. Ochoa do you play cards?"

"At the casinos."

"Casinos?" Luisa asked.

"Casino, a large place where you can spend money quickly on a deck of cards," he said.

"Do you play cards with your daughter?"

Luis looked at Jill then back to Luisa, who frowned slightly waiting for his answer. He said, "I don't have time to play cards. But if *you* want, I will play this game with you, 'War?'" He patted her head as she smiled.

Caz loaded their luggage and handed the passports to Luis. They drove away from the airport, looking through tinted glass windows at the passing landscape. The bright sunlight shone on an expanse of desert hills, strange twisted trees, tortured by wind and dry air, vying with the cacti on both sides of the road. She viewed a seemingly deserted huge home built on a bluff. The landhuis? It was yellow with white trim. She wanted to stop and take a picture, but knew there would be time. She smiled at Luis as he caught her staring at the house. He nodded toward the house and said, "Later."

Luisa inched closer to the window. Luis leaned to share her view and explained that the kadushi were like the saguaro in Arizona, a tall stately cactus that was used to make a delicious soup. Luisa turned up her nose, "Mom, have you had cactus soup?"

"No," Jill said, "but I have had cactus jelly." When Luisa frowned again, Luis and Jill both laughed. The ground was crunchy looking, red dirt and rocks mixed with mushroom shaped cacti. A whole new place, thank you Luis. He tapped her knuckles and she thanked him in her thoughts.

Caz turned sharply and pulled into a curved driveway, the foliage changed abruptly. Wedged between palms, feathery pines and bougainvillea was a large stucco one story house. The bright white residence with a blue-tiled roof was surrounded by a patio. Amoeba shaped flagstones, a mix of concrete and tiny shells, provided a walkway to the front door. Under the roof overhang were white painted wood shutters, the same broad wood slats covered all the windows.

Luis opened the polished teak front door that was side lighted with teak slats. As they stepped into the foyer, Jill heard a whispering swish like a mother calming her baby, shush, shush, shush. Wood slats formed the upper walls. The dancing breeze created an irregular rhythmic rustling. She paused as Luis whispered in her ear, "The trades, the language of island love," then in a normal voice, "Let me take you on a tour of your vacation home." He winked at Jill. Luisa ran in front of them as if she knew where she was going.

They walked down a hallway to the living area facing the sea. The house sat on a rocky point up from the turquoise water. The ocean facing walls were combinations of narrow plaster frames and long wood shuttered casements. Dense bushes, cacti and tropical pines surrounded the sides of his home. Jasmine and wisteria hung over the outer stucco walls; gardenia bushes sat in clay pots. The furniture was a western style of leather and light ash, maybe Arizona something? She would ask Sadie. Each room was accented with dusty blue – couch pillows and ceramic vases. The house was light and alive.

On the one living room wall facing the sea hung a huge oil painting. It featured a rich blue sea, a mirror reflection of the water crashing outside the room. The colors were intense, an original oil. She looked at it a long time, while Caz carried their bags down a short hall to their room. The picture was of the ocean, but the water had an urgent, almost painful motion, as if pushed and shoved by a sinister force. She shook her head. Luis came up behind her, tracing her back with his finger.

"Obregon," he said, "Alejandro Obregon, a part of the Abstract Expressionist Movement. You like it?"

"M-m, I think so," she answered.

"It is how I spend my money. Later we will discuss how *you* spend my money." He laughed. She turned to face him; he walked across the braided sisal rug to the outdoor patio where Luisa had planted herself. The ocean's ebb and crash could be heard as constant background sound.

ᴦξᴦ

The intermix of the overhead fans' swap-swap-swap with the ocean's non-stop splash and scratch on the rocks had swept Luisa into an early sleep. Jill kicked off her shoes, removed her strapless bra and tied on a crinkle cotton gauzy sundress, sky blue with darker blue embroidered flowers on the four rows of flounces. When they tried on all the summer fashions, Sadie said, "Sexy-sexy." Jill turned around in front of their bedroom's full length mirror. The flounces spun out like a square dancer's full skirt. She rubbed Chanel #5 on her neck and between her breasts; the flowery smell took her back to their dance at the migrant camp.

How could she know she wasn't dreaming? Here now in Luis's house exploring all the nooks and private pieces that were him. Who is Luis Ochoa? She shrugged, "Maybe I will get an answer."

The sun had set, but its afterglow lit the bedroom as Luisa cuddled asleep with her elephant. Jill walked barefoot down the hall, a railing separated it from the rest of the house. The terra cotta floor was cool on her feet. The sisal and jute prickly.

Sunshine flooded the house during the day. The lighting was controlled through opening and closing the wood slats with the twist of long-handled cranks that extended to the floor. At night Luis used kerosene lamps of painted antique glass. Chains and pulleys lowered them for lighting.

When she asked questions on her tour, Luis explained, "The antique lighting of the early island plantation owners makes it possible to live without electricity during the hurricane season. Hurricanes usually take a more northerly route, but I like the self-sufficiency." The gabled roof and teak-beamed ceilings allowed the fans and slats to keep the house breezy and cool. The gables were also part of the water recovery system that gave him a means to collect rainwater in a cistern for storage.

She now smelled the aromatic scent of fresh coffee. Alone in the large living room, she faced the ocean. The kerosene lights cast a gold glow to the beiges of the room. Primitively painted small ceramic handleless cups were arranged on an alcove shelf. She turned one upside down as Luis came through the kitchen door, carrying two cups of coffee. Shirtless, wearing only the drawstring pants, he bent and kissed her. The moustache, wavy dark hair with the silver temples that contrasted with his tan face, all of it – the thickness of his hairy chest, how would she be able to do this? From Luis to Jack? She put the ceramic cup back in its place as he handed her the coffee.

"Taste this Gringa, and tell me what you think. Should I fire the farmer who grew these beans, or keep him?"

She sipped the coffee; it tasted like all the coffee advertisements – full-flavored, rich, robust. "Keep him. This is delicious. I haven't ever…"

"And probably never will. Come." Luis held out his hand, he pulled her to him. "A toast to many cups of coffee with my gringa." He led her from the outdoor patio past the pool through gauzy curtains to the master bedroom.

"And my daughter?"

"The trades have put her asleep after a long day from Indiana to paradise."

৵ξ৵

Luis's bedroom felt heavier than the rest of his house. The bed, desk, and armoire were mahogany. His chair, obviously *his* chair, was deep cordovan leather with brass brads. The back, seat and footstool were contoured to his frame. He walked naked from the bed to the small bar that was part of his large entertainment center – television, stereo, speakers, shelves of music albums and books. Jill had the sheet pulled over her. The breeze floated across the room both high through the teak rafters and low from the patio opening.

He poured a drink and spoke, "Gringa, what would you like? I'm having absinthe on ice and a cigar."

"Licorice flavored? No. Kahlúa?"

"Si," he turned and made the drinks.

Jill picked up the coffee cups on the end table by the large bed. She turned them upside down.

"Is there a hole in your cup Gringa?"

She smiled and shook her head, "The cups are antiques. Sadie has made me ever vigilant for them. Are they European, Curaçaoian...?"

"Before your tongue gets knotted, they are Colombian. They belong to Mamacita. She packed them several years ago. I used her furnishings here, hoping to make her feel at home. You're lying in her bed."

"Luis, stop. You've just told the middle of something. Mamacita? Like Papito?" Her stomach twinged. Did he call someone this term of endearment? He cocked his head, and sipped the liqueur.

"Jealousy? I like that, but not necessary this time." He smirked as he walked to the bed. He set the glasses on the table, leaning to kiss her. She turned her head, swishing his face with her hair. He chuckled.

"Mamacita? A joke?" She scooted to the other side of his bed. He fell onto the bed next to her, tackling her across the shoulders and throwing her on her back. He held her pinned down as he spoke, "You love Papito?" He smiled, his face close to her face.

"In *her* bed, you're asking if I love you. Maybe it's not the place to ask that question. Luis," she spoke, his eyes sparkled like the man who caught the one that usually gets away, "you mention a woman, and *her* furniture, *her* bed," she squirmed loose under the sheet, "making *her* feel at home...does this have anything to do with the gold band that you wear?"

He released his grip on her, "Gringa, Gringa, Gringa, follow me to the patio, away from *her* bed, although it seems to now have become *your* bed, the territorial tiger." He tousled her hair, and pinched her ear lobe between his fingers. "Come, I will have a cigar and absinthe and we will go to the mountains, to Mamacita." He sat up, picked up their glasses, and not dressing, he walked out through the sheer curtains to the night. She tied her dress back on her shoulders, and followed him.

They sat on cushions placed on built-in concrete benches. She sat cross-legged; her dress spread around her like a decorative doll on a child's bed. The ships passed in the distance, a quiet parade like so many fireflies on a summer night. The clear black sky and sea were one, a backdrop with chopped, diced and sprinkled crystals of light. The jasmine and gardenia smells blended with the intermittent puffs of cigar. He picked a gardenia and put it behind her ear. "Channel #5 and gardenia, my flower in my sanctum."

"Mamacita, the story, please Luis."

He reached and held her hand, "Si, the story, not a happily ever after story like your prince on the stairway landing.

"Mamacita was stout, dark-haired, fair-skinned," he stopped and touched Jill's chest, "like this fair Gringa. Each time they came to our home, they made a demand or killed someone. But the soldiers and scavengers never stopped coming." He lit his cigar and leaned back against the patio wall. He stared at the sky, and slowly the smoke drifted. Jill rubbed his bare thigh. He looked at her, shook his head and turned back to staring at the sky.

He started with a whisper, "The mountains," his reverential tone coated the phrase as he described the lush, wet, green impenetrable steep land. It sounded like a holy place where one's soul would reside. When she had asked at Sadie's about his attendance at the conference, he'd mentioned the mountains, but his spoken word this time resonated with pain.

"The mountains," he said the word again, then closed his eyes.

His father had protected him. He sent him to school, away from the farm trying to avoid the critical point of Luis's life, the age when he would be expected to join and fight. His father had tried to have a father-son talk, starting and stopping. The sheer ignorance of men who killed one another for such reasons as politics had infuriated and disgusted the elder Ochoa. Luis's father had avoided the expression of anger at all costs because within him there was an anger like a beast that had been locked away. If it escaped from his father's control, he became a mad man, a tornado with directions only from God. Luis remembered his father's clenched fists, tight lips and the deep crease in his forehead, but not madness. Mamacita spoke of it in hushed tones, "Do not unleash the bull."

His father was not there *that day*. Mamacita had told the story of *the* day to explain her feelings, her reasoning for sending him far away from the farm. "Mamacita," was the woman who would have been his mother-in-law.

Mamacita's porch faced the emerald mountains that enclosed and composed her world. She patted the small bundle, a baby boy lying on her lap. She concentrated on two things – mountains and baby. She had tried to block out all that had happened, but under her porch in a cellar, Luis sat silently in the darkness waiting for her to call him, to make a signal that he could return to the house. He and the baby were all that was left of her family. Her husband had been killed, her daughter raped, and killed; her brother long ago left the uncertainty for Mexico. Now she must send the young man, barely sixteen, to join him.

She had stared at the mountains, her father had read to her of the promise from God to look to the mountains for help. They provided the coffee that was her family's plantation. In Bogotá, the politicians who did not understand the country or the relationship of the peasants to their fincas (farms) talked of redistributing plantations, "land reform." They knew nothing of her "family." They only wanted to separate children from parents and she too, would have to let go of Luis, but not the baby, his son, her grandson.

No one had come to talk to her, no they came only with guns… strangers, and said her husband was a "slave owner," robbing the workers of what was theirs. They talked of taking away these mountains and giving the pieces to *her* field hands. But her land had been in her family, many, many years. Her grandfather taught her to pick beans and know when the cherries were best. And now she knew *she* could not leave alive, but the young man, he would have to be released to the river, to the ocean, to a current that could take him to safety, perhaps like Moses to return under different circumstances. "Perhaps," she had whispered in a hopeless plea to a God that seemingly had forsaken her, but He had forsaken Job, taken his land from him, too.

242

She held Luis as he cried over the death of his child sweetheart. She described the soldiers to him. "Scraggly armed-bandits, peasant workers with ammunition rounds strapped in bandoliers." They had ransacked the large plantation over and over again while he was at school. They shouted obscenities, disrespecting Mamacita. Luis came home and argued with Mamacita, begged her to seek them out and avenge the deaths of the mother of his son and her father.

Mamacita refused, "No, no, no." She said again and again.

Luis must leave Colombia or he too, would be killed in the violence, his sense of honor and age allowed no other choices. The freedom fighters had told Mamacita to pack her things and go, proclaiming what was hers now theirs. Luis pleaded with Mamacita to let him protect his young son and stay with her.

"They are bandits, but they will not kill an old woman and a baby, no, Luis you will go."

Luis knew she wasn't old, the violence was making her old, but he accepted her refusal to let him stay.

She gave him money to buy a ticket to Mexico City – a long way from the turmoil of La Violencia. She made him promise to write her and she promised to call him home to her mountains when they were safe again.

He booked passage from Cartagena to Veracruz on an old ship crowded with hundreds of others fleeing for their lives. His stomach had turned at every swell. He dozed sitting up in the cramped, hot, rodent-infested under-deck. Hardened bread and dried meat sustained him through his trip. His arrival in Veracruz and the train ride to Mexico City overshadowed the dank depressing boat trip. Mamacita's brother welcomed Luis as if he were the prodigal son.

"Luis is to be educated," Mamacita had instructed in her letter. She recognized his intellect and did not want it wasted. She had asked the priests at Luis's school in Manizales to write a letter of reference for him to St. Francis, the school he would attend. They had. Luis walked into a rigorous program of English, economics, mathematics and government. His small country school had not prepared him for this intensive curriculum. St. Francis expected their boys to go to college and become Mexico's leaders. He fought homesickness, but the longing slowly faded as he buried himself in his books. He played catch up to his fellow students. They rejected *the* Colombian; and he spent some evenings nursing a black eye or cut lip. On the long walk home his only consolation was that his opponents could not walk home. They had to be helped.

English came easily to him. He studied political science. Father Ibarra a counselor-teacher pushed his Colombian student during after-school tutoring sessions. Luis had told Father Ibarra he had only one goal – to return to Colombia to his son and the coffee farm of his family. "The world," Father Ibarra countered, "is shrinking and you must know it and use it. Otherwise, you will spend your life running." The global homogeneity the priest talked of did not entice him, but Father Ibarra lectured and questioned in the hot Mexico City afternoons, and Luis listened.

Luis learned of world geography, of political wars and religious wars. He began to understand the forces that had killed his family. He accepted that his place was not in his homeland. "Timing, as with Christ's coming, is the most important factor in any life equation. When it is right, you can smash the walls of Jericho or part the Red Sea. 'Timing.'" Father Ibarra repeated the word, giving it a mystical cadence.

Luis began to make the connection with the tentacles he saw emanating from his existence to the greater world community. Father Ibarra demanded independent study in philosophy and literature, encouraging Luis to read Robert Frost. The teacher had cajoled him about his seriousness, his intensity. He tried unsuccessfully to coax Luis into joining the soccer team. Luis's impatience was in a need to know, to consume all that was available. St. Francis was only a stop like the hero in Homer's epic poem; Luis knew his journey home would take time. It would be up to Mamacita to tell him when. Timing.

With his cigar now smoked, he snuffed it in the ashtray's white sand. "Ah, Gringa, you made me talk of my childhood."

"Sixteen is not childhood. I was barely eighteen when I met you."

"Those times in Mexico, it feels like another person, another life-time, twenty, almost twenty-five years ago."

"How long exactly?"

"M-m, twenty-three. You were born?" He chuckled, tousling her hair.

"I was five," she sat up straight, putting her hands on her knees.

"A child with a child's curiosity," he reached under her chin and lifted it towards him "your face always begs, 'Papito.' The questions Gringa, always the questions. First you feel," he released her chin and hugged her, pressing tightly, "feel like this, feel me against you, my nakedness next to yours, in yours as a man and woman, then," he pulled away and stared at her face, "then you know. You ask, 'Who are you, Luis?' Feel me, then know me. Si?"

"Philosophy? Am I beginning to understand the enigmatic Latin as Sadie calls you?"

"Do you feel, or do you know?" He asked, as he sipped his absinthe.

"I know more. I feel closer." She rubbed his belly, combing the hair between her fingers.

"Come closer, Gringa and tell me what you feel."

"Luis, please tell me her name."

"Who?"

"The mother of your son."

He hesitated, sipping his drink, and whispered, "Lourdes."

"Lour-des." Jill took his hands between hers and kissed his fingers. "Tell me about her, what did she look like? Do you have a picture?" His hand jerked slightly, but she held it tightly.

"She is dead."

"Well, not quite; I feel like she is here with us," Jill said.

He set his glass down and pursed his lips, staring at her. He spoke in a barely audible voice, "What you feel…."

She waited. His shoulders fell as he looked at the sea. His power diminished as a toy truck whose battery died. Had she asked one too many questions? She did not want him to hurt from an emotional wound. She scooted next to him, placing his arm around her. He was compliant and he hugged her. She laid her head on his chest, listening to his heart. He stroked her hair.

"They raped her," his voice was a hoarse whisper as if speaking to himself, "then killed her." His chest heaved at each period. "I was…at school. When I got home Mamacita was rocking my baby son, chanting, praying, and singing words that made no sense. Her blank eyes stared at me without seeing. She made me hide in the cellar. Finally, she let me come up and told the story of *the day*."

Mamacita told of screaming and crying, two bandits held Mamacita in the house. Her husband had begged, "Please not the child," his plea was the last thing she ever heard him say, and then the pop-pop of bullets. And her daughter crying, "Papa," then a slap. Lourdes had cried out again, "Mama," and another slap, then the sound of men arguing who would be first. It seemed like forever as they took turns laughing and arguing, before two more pops. Silence.

Instantly, she was released to God. Lourdes lay in the grass with a ripped bloody dress exposing her bare scratched legs.

"Twenty-three years ago, and I still ask what if I had been there that day?" He squeezed Jill tighter, "She was only fifteen." Jill's hair was wet with his perspiration.

"I buried both of them. Her father was 'el hombre de siempre' (men of always). She named our son David."

He gave each piece of information like a bricklayer, one piece down, precisely placed, tapped parallel with the others, cement wiped clean, then the groove pressed by hand. "I wanted to name him Hector after my father..." He stopped. "Gringa, that bothered you. I felt you react."

"No," she whispered, shaking her head involuntarily.

"Si, you cannot lie to your Papito, you don't have the heart," he held her tighter, his hands now pressing her face and breasts against his chest, and continued, "Hector Ochoa." He repeated the name. He released her completely, pulling away. She limply fell forward. "Gringa, stand away from me," he ordered, gesturing with his arm toward the middle of the patio, "and say that."

She stood and walked a few steps in front of him. The rumbling splashing inky sea pounded the rocks. Neptune let his percussion be her soundtrack.

"Say it," he said.

The concrete floor was cool on her bare feet; she stepped on a sisal rug. She shook the flounces; they fell in fluffy rows to her ankles. "What?" she spoke, "You're being...."

He stared. The breeze cooled the sweat on her right cheek where she had pressed against him. This distance between them was too far. Could she go back and hide in his hug? Would the sea answer? There were never answers from tenement stairways, to cornfields, nothing, only this feeling of pain.

"Say - Hector Ochoa," he said, crossing his arms on his chest. He was brown all over. The confidence to be naked comfortably, Hector had said, "It's just the body, Babe, we all have the same parts." Luis's penis lay limp between his legs, the round chest crossed by the muscular forearms, he stared at her face. The tears welled up and she bit her lips, closing her eyes. She rubbed the spot between her eyebrows, covering her eyes with one hand. "Hector," she struggled to whisper, she wiped the tear on her cheek, "Ochoa."

"I don't know this Hector you speak of, but he too, is here with us."

"Yes, he too, is in this space. I buried him seven years ago."

"Come here." He held out his arms. She sat on his lap. He held her back against his chest, his hands in her lap, her hands on his. "There is," he spoke, "too much pain on this beautiful night, Gringa. These people have come and gone, but the shadows of their deaths will come and go like those clouds passing over the moon. They move on and the moon is bright again. It is life that shadows of death should come and go. I know your shadow, when it blocks the light, we will talk again."

Chapter 12

    Luisa awoke and looked at her sleeping mother. She whispered, "Mommy." She patted her mom's back side, "Mommy, I have to go to the bathroom." Jill pointed toward the door. Sunshine poured in their bedroom from the wall of glass sliding doors. A gentle breeze and the sound of the ocean floated through the room's open slats. Luisa scooted out of the bed, walking to the bathroom where her mother had put their toothbrushes. I'll brush my teeth and...When she opened the bathroom door, it squeaked. Her bare feet stepped on cool brown floor tiles decorated with big blue daisies. The bathtub, sink and toilet were blue with brass handles.

    Pulling out a small step-stool placed under the sink, she reached for her toothbrush. It hung in a brass holder. Where is the toothpaste, maybe I should ask mom. She looked around, but did not see the cosmetic case her mother had packed with her brush, hair ribbons, barrettes and toothpaste. She struggled on tip-toes to open the wood medicine chest and found her toothpaste. She quickly brushed her teeth and used the toilet. A brass holder held blue toilet paper. Blue toilet paper, mom will have to buy some. Hanging down between the toilet and a towel rack was a handle that opened and closed the vents. I have to tell grandpa about these turn things. Luisa turned the handle and watched the blinds.

Luisa walked back to her bedroom. "Mommy, I'm hungry."

Jill opened one eye, "Go to the kitchen, see if Mr. Ochoa is in there. Come back and get me if you don't see him."

Luisa found her pink satin slippers under the bed, next to her mother's. Someone had unpacked the suitcase. Her robe hung on a corner chair, but she left the room in her pajamas. She rubbed the front of the pink cotton shirt that she had picked "vacation shopping" with Aunt Sadie. Aunt Sadie buys lots of things and makes mom laugh and buy me things.

After closing the bedroom door quietly, she cautiously eased down the hall. She stepped down the few steps into the living room. An ocean right outside, I hope I can go swimming today. The ocean's breeze and splashing came through the open doors, but she heard a man singing and smelled breakfast. She followed her nose and ears across the living room's scratchy rug. Who's singing? The open dining room was empty. The voice is low, is it Mr. Ochoa or Caz? The singing grew louder as she pushed open the swinging door of the kitchen.

"Luisa," Luis spoke, "Buenos Dias, Chiquita." Luis used a blender on the counter. It whirred.

Luisa smiled. "Mr. Ochoa, what language is that? It isn't pig Latin. My stupid cousin Harold is always talking pig Latin, so I don't know what he says. He tells me, 'Girls aren't supposed to know what boys say.'"

"Spanish. I said, 'Good morning little girl.' Try it, Buenos Dias."

"Bwen-us, dee –us," Luisa repeated.

"Si. And tell your cousin that girls know what boys say even when they don't talk. Is your mother still asleep?"

"Yes, Mr. Ochoa. What are you making?"

"Your breakfast. Here, come and see. You're here just in time to tell me how you like your heuvos." Luis picked her up and sat her on a bar stool at the counter across from where he cooked. He put a straw placemat on the tile-covered counter. She watched, "These tiles look like my bathroom, did you pick them?"

"Si," he said, standing close to the refrigerator. He wore a large white apron over his casual draw string pants. He stirred a clear glass pitcher of fruit juice, then poured a small glass for Luisa and a larger glass for him.

As he set the small glass on her mat, he said, "Luisa, do you know what a toast is?"

"Yes, Mr. Ochoa. We toast at New Year's Eve, and sometimes mom and dad toast on their anniversary." She smelled her juice.

He looked down at the frying pan, putting his lips together as if kissing, then pulled his top lip into his mouth. He removed strips of bacon and placed them on a metal rack. The rack hung over a pan filled with paper towels. He laid a fork next to the bacon and smiled at her, "A toast," he spoke, "to your first day in Curaçao." And he touched the edge of her glass.

"I came yesterday, remember?"

"Si, to your first breakfast with Luis Ochoa." He touched her glass again.

She smiled, then drank the sweet gold liquid, "Mr. Ochoa, this isn't orange juice. What is it?"

"It is my special recipe, a secret. Do you like it?"

Luisa took another drink emptying half of her glass, "Yes. Will you give mom your special recipe so she can make some for me and dad?"

Luis turned away going to the sink, and staring out the window to the sea. He squeezed the counter's edge.

"Mr. Ochoa, May I have some more, please? What time did you get up to make my breakfast?"

Luis turned around. He shook his head and smiled. "Si, Luisa. Like your mother you have many questions. You may have more juice. Here," he poured more into her glass, "now tell me how you like your heuvos."

"Way-vos? Mr. Ochoa, I don't know what that is."

Luis chuckled, "Eggs. Say it again, heuvos."

"Way-vos?"

"Si."

"My mom takes a fork and stirs like this," Luisa held her hand and shook it back and forth imitating a rapid stirring motion, "Stirred eggs, Mr. Ochoa. I like them all mixed real fast."

"Heuvos – stirred fast, coming up." The black iron skillet sizzled with bacon. Luis dropped a pat of butter into another smaller frying pan, and then cracked the shells of the eggs, two at the same time on the sides. He let them hit the hot butter and stirred quickly, mimicking Luisa's movement. He looked up from the pan; she smiled and nodded.

"Mr. Ochoa, would you cut up my bacon, like this? I don't like big bacon." She used her hand to make slicing motions.

"Si." He cut the bacon and pulled gold-plated silverware from a drawer and placed it next to her.

"I never saw gold silverware, are you rich Mr. Ochoa? My Aunt Sadie is rich and she doesn't have gold silverware."

He chuckled, "Si. I am rich I have a house full of people I love."

Luisa frowned and said, "I think rich means money."

"Okay, rich means money and si, I have money. Now would you like leche?" He dropped two pieces of bread into a toaster.

"Let-chee, Mr. Ochoa?"

"Milk, say it, leche."

"Let-chee, please," she repeated.

"Si." He poured a glass and set the tumbler in front of her.

He poured himself a cup of coffee from a glass carafe, then walked to Luisa's side of the counter and sat on the barstool next to her. "You asked when I wake up," he said, then took a drink of coffee.

Luisa nodded, her mouth full.

The toaster popped two pieces of toast. He removed the golden brown bread, buttered it, and spooned on strawberry jam. "I wake up in time to wake up the sun," Luis smiled, placing the toast on her plate. He used her knife to slice the bread into bite-size quarters. "No big toast?"

"Yes, si?"

He laughed.

Luisa stopped eating, shook her head and narrowed her eyebrows, "Mr. Ochoa, you do not wake up the sun. God wakes up the sun. Don't you read the *Bible*? God made the world and the sun."

Luis laughed, "Si, Luisa, God made it all. Now you can stop frowning. Do you have enough to eat?"

She nodded. She had a milk moustache and her cheeks were spotted with strawberry jam. Luis picked up a cloth napkin from a stack in a basket on the counter, reached under her chin with one hand, and lifted her face, to wipe her mouth and cheeks. She grabbed the napkin from him and tucked it in her collar making a bib, "Mom will be mad if I spill strawberry jam on my new pajamas."

"Mom will be what?" Jill said, entering the kitchen.

"Bewn-us, dee-us," Luisa said, then looked at Luis.

Jill looked at Luis who shrugged and smiled.

"Good morning, Luisa. I see you found something to eat. Where is your robe?"

"Good morning, Gringa. Cómo estás? Te vey muy bonita hoy." (How are you? You look pretty)

"Muy bien. Gracias." Jill answered. Luisa looked from Jill to Luis.

"What are you saying, mom?" Luisa asked. "Mr. Ochoa fixed my way-vos just like you. And he made a special juice. Mom get…Mr. Ochoa, please pour mom some juice." Luisa smiled at Luis. She pointed to the pitcher. Luis shrugged and smiled. "Breakfast is in your parameters, Mrs. Jones?"

Luis and Luisa faced her, each cocking their head slightly to the left, then Luis and Luisa looked at each other and smiled.

"Mom, tell Mr. Ochoa how you like your way-vos and he fixed bacon. Mr. Ochoa, you didn't tell me how to say bacon…."

"Tocino," Jill and Luis answered in unison, then laughed.

"Tocino. And coffee, mom. I didn't have coffee, but I am sure it is yummy because Mr. Ochoa made it, too."

Luis nodded. "Ah, Mrs. Jones, have a seat," Luis directed her to a barstool and put a placemat in front of her. He reached into the drawer and withdrew another place setting of the silverware.

"Mr. Ochoa, may I go swimming in your pool?" Luisa asked.

"Si, Luisa, I want you to swim in the pool before we try snorkeling in the ocean."

"Mom, I'm changing my pajamas. I want to swim in the ocean." Luisa jumped down from the barstool and ran out of the kitchen.

Luis's back was to them, as he removed a plate from a stack in the cupboard. His muscles were as clearly defined as the day in the shed. Jill closed her eyes briefly and smelled the coffee and bacon. Their relationship was so brief, but how could she have known then, that now in this place, this kitchen, Luis's place, that she would be with him? She wanted to be in this place then, his life, her long ago dream come true.

Luis walked to where Jill sat. He placed her plate on the mat. As he reached in front of her, she touched his shoulders. He turned to face her, then hugged and kissed her. He released her, kissing the end of her nose. "Your parameters, Mrs. Jones, how am I doing?"

"Luis, you look like the cat that ate the canary."

With the back of his hand he brushed her breast, "I have my canary in my cage now. That's what you see." His eyes crinkled; the intensity completely gone. She had not seen him so relaxed. Did he have a family life? People with whom he relaxed and smiled? She reached around his shoulder to kiss him again.

"Maybe we should have breakfast in bed, Mrs. Jones." He pulled away, cocking his head in the direction of his bedroom.

They finished breakfast and she stacked the dishes by the sink and offered to wash them.

"No, Gringa. Conchita will be here later. She can do this."

"I can do dishes Luis. And I want to do *your* dishes, but would you tell me about Mexico City? The rest of it. Did you finish school? How long did you stay? Did you go to college? Or did you go back to Colombia?"

He shook his head, "Gringa, let me make some more coffee, then...I'll finish, not finish, continue, but Luisa and I are going snorkeling in the pool. I want her to learn how to use the equipment before we go to the sea."

He removed green coffee beans from a rubber-sealed glass jar. He dropped them in a heavy iron skillet, and laid the beans in one layer. He turned the burner on medium high and put a lid on the pan, then spoke, "Mexico City, 1949. Is that what you want to hear?"

"Uh-hum," she said, wiping the hand painted tiles of the counter."Wait, just a moment. I must check on Luisa."

"If she wants to swim, Caz will watch her, or swim with her if you want him to."

"She's quite the little fish, but yes, please call Caz."

With the sound of splashing water and the laughing voices of Luisa and Caz in the background, Luis continued his story.

"I got a job building the subway, hot, dark, miserable work. I thought death by armed bandits would be better compared to those bastards, slave bosses. In case we wanted to quit, they had a steady stream of men willing to work for the pesos, better pay than many jobs. I kept writing Mamacita and she kept saying, 'no, not yet.' I was going to work through the summer until I started at the university.

"I wrote and told her I was miserable in the city. You gringos have a saying about taking the boy out of the country, but not the country out of the boy."

As he stirred the beans on the stove, they turned brown. He took an hour glass container on the counter and laid a cloth in the top half, then removed the beans from the skillet, pouring them into another pan. "They need to cool for a minute."

He opened a cupboard and pulled out a dark green jug resembling a wine bottle, "The water, it must be soft, naturally soft to bring out the best flavor of the beans. Water ruins the best coffee." He heated the water in a pot, "you have to be careful that the pan itself doesn't leach into the water, no aluminum, only glass or stainless steel." He emptied the carafe and handed it to Jill to wash.

"Mamacita must have known I was ready to come back to Colombia," he continued his story, "and risk everything because she wrote and sent me the name and address of an uncle I never knew I had."

Luis sprinkled the cooled beans into a grinder, an old-fashioned wood box with a crank on top. It looked like one Sadie used for decoration in her kitchen. He twisted the handle, then offered the job to Jill. Gradually she turned the beans into the grounds she recognized when she made her own coffee. He took six scoops of the grounds putting them into the cloth filter.

"Luis, an uncle? Your uncle or Mamacita's?"

"My father's brother. I didn't know my father had a brother." He slowly poured the heated water over the grounds. The coffee dripped into the bottom. He waited and then added more water.

"That's strange. You had an uncle you didn't know?"

"Mamacita wrote he was a farmer near Veracruz where I had landed in that broken down boat three years earlier. But farming…Get a cup and you will have some of L.O. Limited's top of the specialty line."

"Luis…"

"Gringa, my father never mentioned his own brother. My father viewed the land as life, farming. He responded to the land as if he were a coffee bush, hated going to the city, hated being away from the coffee. So strange, he had a brother who was also a farmer? Mamacita said only 'They were different men.' My father and I spent every day together and he hadn't said a word about another farmer in the family, nothing about Veracruz. Mamacita refused to write anything more. Taste it."

She sipped. "The coffee is…delicious, almost as wonderful as it smells…strong, full, oh jeez I sound like a Folgers' commercial. I've never had coffee that tasted so…fresh, I guess, yeah, fresh."

He nodded and smiled proudly as he poured some in his mug.

"Gringa, if people drank coffee fixed this way, Folgers would be out of business, well, so would I. They buy a lot of beans from me. But you Americans, you like your Folgers, basura (garbage). Your beer is weak, yellow. And such bland java!"

"And you left Mexico City?"

He chuckled. "You did not want to hear about damn jankees? Si. At 19, from my perspective, Mexico City was just a place on a map. I had no connection with any of it. My 'family' wanted me to go to university. I was enrolled, but I hated the city and thought only of going to the mountains, even the Mexican mountains…I said goodbye to those kind people who'd been gracious and followed Mamacita's instructions to get me educated. Why do people make decisions at 19 that seem…?"

"Absolutely profound, the way life should be. I know."

With his hand he touched her cheek., "Si, absolutely profound. I had to go to the farm, to the land."

Through the open kitchen window he stared at the sea, then turned to face her, "Remember, when we talked at the church building in the rain? There is in me something that draws me to the dirt. God created us out of the dirt." He shook his head, then leaned and kissed the end of her nose. "I was going to the university, but the possibility of farming with my father's brother. I was curious and *he* owned a farm. It seduced me like the Gringa, the siren calling me." He frowned and closed his eyes for a moment.

"Siren? Odysseus was tied to the ship…"

"Si. I should have been tied to the ship."

"What was his name?" She drank. The flavor was powerful, seductive. Would it be possible to drink other coffee again?

"Who?"

"The siren, male siren in this case, the call from the uncle, his name."

"Ramos," he turned away from her completely, the breeze floated through the kitchen, he looked at his hands, turning them over, palms up, then palms down. He used both hands to grab his coffee mug, His gaze stayed now on the ocean, endless blue from the sea water to the horizon, and it flowed from aqua to dark blue to the sky's cloudless blue.

Luisa came through the kitchen door, "Mr. Ochoa, please, I want to learn to snorkel."

૪ξ૪

His bedroom emanated a warm yellow glow, day or night. During the day the curtains filtered the bright sunlight, turning the room and furniture ochre. The evening light imitated the natural filtered sun. She lay next to him, leaning on one elbow, touching him as if buying a new mattress. She pinched his skin between her knuckles, starting with the stubbles on his cheeks, then the flesh under his chin.

"Skin," she said, "is the largest organ in the body."

"The most sensitive. Gringa, what are you doing to protect yourself from pregnancy?"

"Well, let's see Señor Ochoa, we've made love how many times in the last five days and you are now asking? Nothing. I'm doing nothing. I thought you wanted more children." She smiled.

He sat up, "I told you…"

"And you think I do everything you tell me? Besides, you only said 'in my life,' that might include more children, si? I am not quite twenty-eight; I think I could have more children, at least one."

He lay back on the pillows, folding his arms under his head. He stared at the ceiling. The kerosene light on the nightstand flickered; he rolled onto his side, then turned up the wick. He returned to lying on his back. Absently he brushed her breast with the back of his hand before once again locking his hands behind his head.

"My children," he said slowly, "have been taken from me, grown up away from me. It is too painful. You're taking this angel, my angel, back to the United States. I can't be her father. She says 'daddy' and it's a punch to my chest. You board the plane, wave goodbye and I must stand and know she will be older, days missed, another month, bigger…"

"You seem in control of all of it. Are you suggesting Luisa and I return to Colombia with you?"

"No, it's not possible, not now." He closed his eyes.

"Wasn't that Mamacita's phrase, no, not now?" She traced the welt of the scar on his chest, "But I want to go with you."

He turned on his side, facing her. He placed his finger on her lips, then outlined her face ear-to-ear, "I know Mrs. Jones. You've told me that every time you look at me."

"No more children ever?" She said it and fantasized of doing pregnancy with him, a happy couple pushing a stroller. Luis feeding a baby with a little spoon? She grasped his thick fingers. Diapers? No.

He shook his head, and spoke softly, "You've done the right thing."

"What Luis? Taking birth control pills?"

He shook his head.

She continued, "You know and I don't?"

He nodded, "Luisa's cousin Harold said girls aren't supposed to know what boys say. Harold may be right." He chuckled.

She pulled the hair on his chest. He feigned pain.

"Luis, what? I've done what right?"

He held her hand, rubbing her wedding band, and whispered, "Jack, married Jack Jones."

ɣξɣ

Luisa called Señor Ochoa their special friend. Luis accepted Jill's parameters as a school boy agreeing not to use his sling shot again. He treated his daughter as a special treasure. He laughed with her, educated her, and responded physically, patting her head, holding her hand, giving her piggy-back rides. Luis worked at being non-intrusive. Jill noticed the overarching gentleness never visible with the migrant children. She anxiously awaited his reaction to Luisa's questions and familiarity, expecting her daughter to be scolded or denounced, but Luis remained the ingratiating father. At moments she saw him physically turn away as though recovering his composure. He listened, offered suggestions, waited patiently as mother and daughter dressed, argued, and shopped.

He left them alone on the fourth day of their visit. He told of business at "home," papers that required his signature, "an authorization" for a shipment to be received. Jill and Luisa spent the day swimming in his pool and shopping. They bought a souvenir for

Jack. Luis insisted on doing the touristy things with them – ride the glass bottom boat, inspecting the Hato Caves, exploring the forts; Amsterdam, Beckenburg, Nassau and the ruins of Waakzaamheid, all the places Jill studied in the brochures.

Now their last day in Curaçao, Jill sat in a converted plantation home, waiting for lunch. Luis and Luisa were together at the port. She leafed through the postcards she bought. The postcards were all pictures of the "Landhuis." Sadie would want to see pictures, postcard photographs, "always better than a camera," as Lillian explained her huge collection. She took a piece of hotel stationery, her souvenir to show Jack the nice hotel "where they stayed," and began to write.

Dear Sadie,

These are the Landhuises(sp.). I bought all these postcards to mail, but decided to put them in an envelope instead, I promised to send them and now we are leaving in the morning, and your sorry ass better be at the airport. You'll see me before you get these, but at least you won't be able to say I didn't send them to you.

I don't want to come home. This is a man I don't know. Stop laughing, I mean understand, not know in the Biblical sense, as we have managed to get to know each other pretty well. He is friendly (surprise) and talkative. He does the whole father routine with Luisa. She calls him Mr. Ochoa or Señor Ochoa, but together...well they're together today in Willemstad.

She stopped and crinkled the paper. Sadie will know all of it tomorrow when she picks us up. Well, some of it. Luis, ten years ago, I was so different, enamored with a migrant worker, a wandering nomad, and now piercing that invention is you. Who are you? Gentle, kind, friendly, but the fire, the anger? Is it the place? Curaçao? Trade winds? Did you blow this Luis in from somewhere else? Change him? Or is this him? Oh, that we could stay here...'No, not now.'"

ɤξɤ

Luis sat Luisa on the patio wall of the fort that was now a restaurant. He had brought his binoculars and held the heavy glasses for her as they watched the ships coming in and out of St. Ann's Bay. He told her in what countries they were registered and what their cargo was. He explained tonnage and guessed their probable destinations. She began to recognize certain flags, "Which one is that?" he now asked her.

"Valenzuela," she answered. When she made a mistake, he frowned. "Argentina?" she asked, then frowned back as he answered with a deeper disapproving look. He knew this face, but tried not to laugh when she frowned back, her face almost a mirror image of his.

"Are you married?" she asked.

"Si," he answered, looking down at the gold ring on his left hand, to your mother, he could only say to himself.

"Do you have children?"

"Si." He resisted hugging her.

"How many children?"

"All I want." He winked.

"Do you live here?" She picked up the binoculars and he reached to steady the heavy lenses as she tried to move them.

"Sometimes," he said.

"You have another home?"

They had eaten fish and now were walking and then stopping to look at the sea. They talked, 'letting their lunch settle' as he had explained.

"Si." He lit a cigar and identified ships, "Oil tanker, Liberia." She stopped him and pulled the glasses from him.

"I want to see." She held the unwieldy glasses, and spoke with them covering most of her face. "I see the American flag, Señor Ochoa."

"Jankee? Let me see."

"Yankee, Señor Ochoa, say Yankee."

259

"Jankee, Señor Ochoa," he mimicked her, looking through the binoculars, "A cruise ship, only human tonnage."

"No, not Jankee, Señor Ochoa."

"No, not Jankee Señor Ochoa," he said, then laughed.

She put her hand to his mouth, shaking her head and frowning. "Stop."

"Alto?" he asked.

"Alto?" she repeated the word, her big brown eyes stared at him.

"Si. Come my maestra, I will buy you an ice cream," Luis said.

"May-ester?"

"May-estra, teacher. You're my teacher. I must learn proper English."

"Si, Señor Ochoa, proper English."

"Luisa, my son calls me 'Papa,' you may call me Papa, not Señor Ochoa." He patted her head, "Proper Spanish."

"Papa?" she cocked her head and pursed her lips.

"Si."

"Papa, si," she responded, then asked, "Papa, do you have a little girl?"

"Si, a little girl who speaks proper English."

"Papa, does she like ice cream?"

"Si."

"I love strawberry, does she?"

"It's her favorite."

"Papa, can I meet your daughter?"

"Si, next time."

Their separate afternoons had passed quickly; they now sat around Luis's dining room table. It had been formally set with a white linen tablecloth and crystal etched with a bird of paradise flower design. The stems of the goblets were frosted and hexagon shaped. The flatware was the same gold-plated ware he used every day. The china was Spode. Jill had already read the name when she washed the dishes, the same china for all the meals. She realized he had no everyday ware like her hand-me-down mismatched pieces from Lillian and Caitlin's china. The dinner table glowed ochre in the candlelight duplicating the exact golden moment the sun sets. Luis's skin mellowed with the lighting. The thudded arrhythmic clap-clap-clap of the window slats added to the mellow flow of conversation.

Luis and Luisa talked, interrupting each other with stories of the fish they had seen. One swam up to Luisa as if giving her a kiss, another large fluorescent-orange school had surrounded Caz. Luisa described the fish as the ones she had seen in aquariums at the pet store. Luisa listed her favorite things on their trip, Señor Ochoa's plane, swimming with the rainbow colored fish and playing War with Caz who taught her the card suits' Spanish names.

Connie cleared away the dishes and brought them dessert forks. Luis had promised them Connie's special Dutch apple pie for their farewell dinner.

"Mrs. Jones," Connie asked in her slightly gruff ex-smoker's voice. She had explained quitting the habit in one of her stories. "Would you like da ice cream on your pie?"

She smiled at Jill, the roundest fat cheeks to match her big-rounded chest and full hips, the whole body like a Macy's Thanksgiving Day parade balloon. She talked non-stop about everything, but her boss. When she arrived on Monday afternoon, Jill listened and tried to find pieces of the Luis puzzle. Connie disappeared in the evenings, after the dishes and kitchen were immaculately cleaned. Luis swore she was in the house, but Jill never saw or heard her. Connie talked of Holland and the canals, the tulips and her cousins whom she rarely visited. She had only one remnant of her Dutch; she used the sound "da" instead of the word "the." She spoke the native "Papiamento," with Caz.

Caz spoke Spanish. "No, English, Gringa. You'll have to speak Spanish with him." But Caz was fluent in Papiamento. Jill liked to listen when Connie and Caz argued. They seemed disagreeable most of the time, but Connie would look at Jill and say Caz was some sort of Cuban-Voodoo crazy man. She laughed heartily and Jill was sure that Connie repeated the name in Papiamento because she and Caz then laughed. Caz would hold up his hands or pull a small stick from his pocket and gesture as if throwing a curse her way. Luis explained, "They argue like a sister and brother over things that don't matter – green bananas or ripe bananas make the best piña coladas, plant by the full moon or new moon."

"No, thank you, Connie," Jill now answered. "I want to enjoy my last few cups of Señor Ochoa's coffee. It is too rich for pie with ice cream."

"Gracias, Gringa." Luis winked at her.

"Mom, we saw this huge ship today, a Liberian tanker," Luisa paused to look at Luis who nodded, then she continued, "Liberia is a country in Africa, right Papa?"

Jill froze. Connie placed the plate with a slice of warm apple pie in front of her.

"Luisa," Connie spoke, "would you like a piece da size of your mother's?"

"Uh-m-m, smaller, Mrs. Vanderkwast, this size," Luisa held her index fingers two inches apart.

Connie smiled every time Luisa said her whole name. She had commented that she had wished Luisa met her when she was married to her first husband, "da no-count Captain *Crane*, so much easier for da sweet girl to say." He had been the one who left her in Curaçao, "forty years ago, left me like some empty bottle, just tossed out, broke." He had called her a whore and told her to sell her "wares" if she wanted to eat. She talked of these personal experiences freely, easily, but when Jill asked how long Connie had worked in the house for Luis, Connie, said, "No questions about da master." Connie had smiled and continued, talking, telling of the first bar where she worked.

"Si," Luis now answered Luisa, "Liberia was the country founded by Señor Sam to accommodate all those slaves that were taken from ships after slave trading became illegal, at least illegal in your Washington, D.C. It really meant someone wanted to make more money off human flesh and increased the ante."

"Liberia, Papa?" Jill asked.

Luis shrugged, "Si," he said, his eyes twinkled like a boy trying to hide a frog in his pocket, a frog that had just croaked.

"Mom, do we have to go tomorrow? There is going to be an Easter festival with dances and bands…"

"Yes, Lo, we have to leave tomorrow morning. Aunt Sadie will be waiting for us in Indianapolis." She spoke to Luisa, but watched as Luis avoided her stare and prepared a cigar.

Connie put an ashtray next to Luis and took the dessert plates to the kitchen.

ϒξϒ

Jill packed their suitcases and laid out the clothes Luisa would wear on the plane. Luis had said the temperature in Indianapolis was forecast to be only 50°. They would carry their coats. Luisa was sound asleep after a long day with Luis.

Taking one last look in the mirror she was pink from the sun, and her stomach was poochy, a little like Lillian's. Oh not yet, Lillian, I don't want that yet. The dry heat of Curaçao helped her hair stay loosely curled. The extra touch of mascara made her eyes stand out as Mo had told her years before. She smiled at her reflection. She was not Attila the Hun, but she was going to have a battle with Luis. "Papa?" No, that would not work, not one slip of the tongue around Jack. Oh, jeezus, Jack. Was it even possible to do this? Meet Luis and Jack couldn't or wouldn't find out? Papa? No, Luis.

Let's get this over. She closed the bedroom door. She had waited until Luisa slept to put on the black sexy gown that had embarrassed her from the moment Sadie held it up in the store. "He'll think I'm some sort of trollop, just like Lillian said we were."

Sadie had dismissed it all saying, "He took your virginity, so he can't call you a trollop. However, sleeping with a married woman would give you some chance to label him."

Now she walked barely covered. Her nipples hardened as the shimmering satin slid back and forth across her chest. The gown was long and tied at the shoulders, but split at the side from the waist to the hem. "Easy access," she had said to Sadie.

"Exactly what you want, Gringa," Sadie said.

When she walked, her left leg was exposed. The tiny lace bottom revealed her entire pubic area. She had argued with Sadie that the panties were a waste, "I might as well be naked," but they matched the long lace robe and Sadie said she must consider it a complete outfit, "not pieces to be worn individually."

As she entered through the slightly ajar door, Luis sat at his heavy mahogany desk. He placed some papers in a briefcase, closing it quickly as she approached him. He walked to meet her at the foot of his bed, reaching to hug her. She jerked back. He paused, "You may leave the way you came in." He pointed behind her to the door.

"I'll leave when I'm finished."

A smile played at one corner of his mouth, "Okay, Gringa, say what you came in here to say before I have my way with you, or is it the same purpose?"

"'Liberia is in Africa, *Papa!*'"

He shook his head, "Gringa, Gringa, Gringa."

She recognized now the patronizing expression, her name in triplicate.

"Señor Ochoa!" Her face heated as she turned red, "You told her to call you Papa?"

"Si," he shrugged.

"You agreed, Luis."

"For the moment, but moments change." His tone had turned serious, his frown returned as if a switch had been flipped.

"And men change? And men's *words*? I want a man who is as good as his word. I don't come from a place where a man's word cannot be trusted! I refuse to be part of such a place! I established parameters for Luisa. I made that decision without you. The day I said goodbye to Milagros, I formed a value for raising children, children I didn't have. Permanence, place, no uprooting. But now...You've denied us being a permanent part of *your* life – married to goddamned Jack Jones, 'the right thing.' She says Papa one time...and then what *Papa* Ochoa? A plan? You have a plan for that moment? Words for it?" She turned away from him, her satin gown brushing his bare feet. He grabbed her wrist, she tried to pull from his clench.

"Jill," the cold tone burnt her heart like a branding iron on flesh. He held her until she stopped resisting. The sweat beaded on her lip and moistened her forehead, her scalp sweat; the blood flushed her face. His eyes were ice and fire.

"A man of his words? Words? Is that what you want? Words that don't change?"

She stood still as if lightning had struck within touching distance.

He released his tight hold; her arm dropped limply to her side. A tear of frustration ran down her cheek, but she did not move, recording the tick on his cheek and the full veins in the bull neck as the blood filled his face.

"Luisa...belongs...to *me*," his calm carefully spaced wording belied the fury in his entire body. With each breathed word his chest expanded. His hands clenched and unclenched making the muscles in his arms expand and contract.

She closed her eyes, bit her lips and shook her head.

He reached and lifted her chin, "But Gringa, you belong to me, also."

She opened her eyes. The eyes of the devil – green, shifting from one of hers to the other. His nose, nostrils fanning moved by the devil's breath. She looked up, white slats and teak beams, the ceiling of the devil's house. Then down to her coppery polish on each toe. The devil sucked them, their nerve endings connected to her crotch. The power was now in his face, the moustache neatly trimmed, thick between the nostrils and upper lip. Stop breathing fire, Luis. Belong to you? Have I sold my soul to the devil?

The silence became the noise of rustling palm fronds in the patio, the grinding of sea on coral reef, the whisp-whisp-whisp of the wood slats, the rhythmic ceiling fan. She shuddered all over again, the sound of blades against thick air, the pain of Columbus, Georgia. She took deep expansive sups of air. The time inched. The ochre calmed. She sensed them returning to their battle lines of demarcation. He breathed normally, his hands opened, the eyebrows separated, his chest relaxed.

"I'm having absinthe over ice and you?" He spoke, turning away from her. His breakaway instantly relieved the pressure. She walked through the gauzy curtain to the clear night. Cooler air. He mixed liquor and ice, the cubes tinkled with the stirring.

Over her shoulder she said, "I think the local poison would be fitting – Curaçao on ice," then stared away from him. Why did ownership sound so romantic when he said it in whispered tones between the sheets, telling her of his love in Spanish, but now so painful? He joined her on the patio. There was a kerosene lamp burning on a wrought iron table. She leaned against the retaining wall that was wide enough to sit comfortably. He had an uncluttered view, no visible neighbors and no windows or doors opened onto his private patio.

"Socrates, your hemlock." He handed her the drinks and reached into his pocket, pulling out a small wrapped box. "Here, for my hard-headed Jankee."

"You hand me a glass of death juice and then a present. Something to take with me when I cross the River Styx?"

"Si," he smiled.

The Grandpa Havlicek in her wanted to walk out the door and throw his present at him.

He told her calmly of the old Dutchman who answered Luisa's thousand questions as they argued over each item as the best choice for her mother. "The shopkeeper said, 'If you're her daughter, she must be a beautiful woman.' I said, 'She is her Aunt Sadie's daughter because she likes expensive things.'"

Jill kept her eyes focused on the small box and opened it slowly deliberately, appreciating that Luisa picked it out. She removed a dainty gold link bracelet with a single gold charm, a miniature Dutch shoe inscribed on the bottom, "Remember Curaçao."

"Gringa, you like it, I can tell by your face. Did Luisa tell you?" Jill answered with a shake of her head.

"Bueno, mi chiquita (good, my little girl) she knows how to keep a secret."

"Your daughter, Señor Ochoa. Thank you for my bracelet *and* my daughter. I will never forget Curaçao."

Curaçao, the midnight sky and busy night sea, heaven with the devil, tomorrow Indiana, home. Home is where your heart is. Sadie had given her that phrase on an embroidered pillow. My heart is with the devil. My home...the cornfields. How would that look with embroidered daisies and red ribbon? She fingered the gold octagon links the shape of the landhuis where they had eaten delicious broiled fish. Remember Curaçao?

"Gringa, will you vacation with your Señor Ochoa again?" He stood next to her watching the ocean.

She clinked the ice cubes against the glass and took a big swallow, "Is it a choice I make?"

"The *words*?"

She nodded.

"Mrs. Jones, you will meet me whenever I ask you. It is a choice you will make because it is a choice I have made." He tipped his glass to the edge of hers, "Hasta que la muerte nos separe."

They drank, then he plucked her glass gently, setting it on the patio wall. He drew her to him, sliding his hand across her breasts, around her back, then down to her ass. He slipped his hand underneath her gown at the slit. His touch was soft, fingering her lace panties, crushing her against his chest as he kissed her. She sucked on his tongue while untying the drawstring pants, the loose cotton fell to his feet. He kicked them away and scooped her into his arms. His chest smelled of spicy clean cologne. He whispered, "We need to do this inside." He carried her to the bed, the white sheets pale gold in the light. He slipped the ribbon ties from her shoulders. He nursed her breasts, squeezing the tip as he moved from one side to the other. She grabbed his head, pulling his face to hers. He kissed her while removing the gown, and then tossing it. His mouth never left hers. His back shadow-danced with her legs on the walls. The kerosene lights created art images, peaks of knees, valleys of elbows and ridges of shoulders.

He pushed her gently down and rolled half-way on top of her, pecking at her like a pigeon in the park, picking, nipping. He pinned her down. "You're exquisite Jill Caitlin Jones, when you…what do they say? 'Have your Irish up?'" He threw his head back and laughed heartily. She heard Hawk's voice, "You'll never be able to satisfy that feisty bitch!" The bitch is satisfied, Hawk.

"Mrs. Jones, you've gotten what you wanted, a rare achievement with Luis Ochoa."

"What did I want?" She tried to get up, but his weight kept her immobile.

"Where are you going? You cannot get away from your Papito. If you keep squirming, I'll have my way with you again."

She shifted under him, raising her leg lacing it with his. He stopped nibbling playfully and rolled completely on top of her, supporting his weight on his forearms. She separated her legs and kissed him, holding tightly around his chest.

In breath whispers the trades murmured. She wanted to take the moment and do it all over, to feel her whole body burn and suck him into the heat. He gave her his plucky half smile, "Let's go to the patio and finish our, what did you call it? War of Words. And wear the black silk uniform. I like the battle outfit, the one the Jankees' enemies wear in the rice paddies." He chuckled, getting up, then walking to his bathroom. Facing the sink he spoke to her, "Gringa, you're very tempting, tempt me into this struggle and get me a cigar from the drawer. Cigars among generals can bring peace. An old Indian custom."

"Pipes, Luis, peace pipes." She opened the night stand drawer, reaching for the cigar box. She touched a cold metal and pulled the drawer farther open. She screamed.

Luis rushed from the bathroom holding a towel. "What, Gringa? You saw a ghost? What?"

"Luis, there's a gun in that drawer!" She pointed as if it would jump out.

"Si, generals have guns. Now get me a cigar."

She gingerly reached again into the drawer. He walked to the bed and handed her the towel as he took the cigar. He removed a small metal cutter, snipped the end of the tobacco, then closed the drawer. "Come," he said, cocking his head toward the patio, "I'm ready for a tough Colombian-Irish skirmish."

Chapter 13

"Married Jack Jones." Like a record with a scratch over and over she heard Luis's declaration played again and again. When she woke up next to Jack; when he called to remind her about his list; when he stood smiling, pointing out the beauty of the new shingles; and when he made his passionless love. "Married Jack Jones." Jack did say the tropical climate must have worked some "magic" on her. "Married Jack Jones." No Luis, to be with you..."I know, Mrs. Jones, you've said that every time you look at me."

Walking back into the farm lifestyle provided no magic. Where did Jack get that word? It had been awful. She worked on her emotional doldrums by cleaning. Henry and Jack's shingling job shook out the "mummy dust" as she called the dirt of the ancient farmhouse inhabitants. Jack said he ran out of time to clean. More time, she could have stayed. "No, not now," Luis answered.

And spring break ended. Thank God for teaching; the busyness of school after a week off provided a return to normalcy. Her students immediately demanded the usual - stay after school to work on their debate speeches, and their term papers. She graded their papers and helped them create more. They continued writing about Viet Nam and the peace movement. Hector was one of the first ones to die in the war, for what noble cause?

Only six weeks until summer vacation and her senior students' grades were to be completed in three weeks. Their whole time schedule was accelerated to get ready for graduation. Bobbie, you were right so long ago, "keep moving on Jill." Dwelling in the past, she accepted, was not getting her anywhere except depressed. Yeah, school kept her moving on.

She drove now to Lillian's to pick up Luisa, then on to Sadie's. Daily, since returning, Sadie called, "You have to get here and show me pictures. And I need all the juicy details of tropical life with a certain Colombian. Come to Vicksburg and stop avoiding me!"

Jill said, "A picture is worth a thousand words and mine are not developed."

"For sure, you are in development and so is your affair, but get over here. I've waited long enough."

Eads' Photos said her pictures would be ready today. She and Luisa would stop and pick them up, then drive to Sadie's. Jill was anxious to see them though Luis was in none of them, "No evidence, Mrs. Jones," he explained.

Bobbie, maybe I could contact her about living overseas. She and Khalil seemed to manage in Beirut. And Mo traveling everywhere with Stewart...oh, Mo only writes when she has a new address for herself or William. Living overseas? Oh yeah, I was cordially not invited, "No, not now."

She wanted to call Luis, to hear his voice, the deepness, the accent, if only she could hear him, no it would be worse. It would remind her all over again of where she was and where he was not. What was the saying, "You're there and I'm here, one of us is in the wrong place?" Whatever kind of life he lived in Colombia, he had no intention of making her a part of it. Besides she could not just leave and move to a foreign country, "No, not now." There were the obvious reasons, Lillian, Henry, Jack, and Luisa's stability. Yes Jill, learn to adjust to the transition. He said, "Not now." Did that mean yes, but later? A time frame? A calendar with her date on it?

When she left Southeastern, she called Sadie. Jill said her thoughts were making her crazy, and she needed to share them or

Sadie would have to take her to the state mental hospital in Logansport.

"My liquor cabinet is full. Always a cure for mental instability, Miss Sarah B."

Luisa had truly amazed her, ten days and not one slip about their friend, Señor Ochoa, Papa, nothing. "Mom and I" did this; "Mom and I" did that. Only one morning as Jill brushed her hair did she say, "I wonder if Mr. Ochoa will invite us to his house again?"

Henry sounded skeptical every time she had told him, "Yes, Dad, I had a great time."

"Why do you sound so sad when you say it, Princess?"

She answered by changing the subject. She did not want to have that conversation with him, "not now."

ᴚξᴚ

Claudine answered the door, looking like Claudine – dress stained, socks slouchy, hair tangled, and barrette hanging askew. Her dolls sat on the stair steps. She asked Luisa to play with her and the babies. Luisa shook her head and asked where Mike was. Claudine pointed toward the long hallway and said, "TV." Sadie's house smelled of baking bread. How did she have time to bake bread? Jill carried her bag of souvenirs and presents. She and Luisa walked into the kitchen. Sadie held baby Kate as if she were attached to her hip. She was almost a year old, Jill's birthday child. Kate had Sadie's dark eyes with long lashes, pale olive skin and straight dark hair. Jill knew when she got older Sadie would add the binta mark so they would look even more alike. Kate was Sadie in miniature. She was fat and looked like a mushroom growing out of Sadie's narrow trunk. Jill hugged them both, then tossed all of her things on the table. She pulled Kate from Sadie, "Where's Hilda?"

"Who knows? Cleaning upstairs somewhere. Master Fredericks' room could be a starting place. I'm ready to hire another person. I wish Sissy Zambrano was old enough to move in, but I'm sure there is something about child labor laws...Jill where's the island glow? I picked you up, you looked terrific, smiling, an island tan, a bunch of satisfied sex smirks, now you're back to a dolt farmer's wife. Oh, I know from coffee farmer to corn farmer, big change." She laughed.

271

"Sadie, it's been so hard," Jill sat at the table fingering the postcards and sorting through the pictures. "I have to learn how to do this better because he says I'll be vacationing with him whenever *he* gets ready."

"How do you handle that dictator attitude? You're a better woman than me. Okay, let me pour some of this frozen lime stuff I made. It tastes like popsicles."

Jill pulled postcards, pictures and bottles of perfume from her bag, scooting each thing to the center of the table to avoid Kate's quick grasp. Jill volunteered to change Kate while Sadie checked out the surprises and got Kate's dinner ready. Kate felt warm and squishy. Sadie with a fat baby and Luis, "no more," and Jack could not have any. She would have to use Sadie's babies when she could. She walked to the bathroom with Kate, biting her fat cheeks and fingers, but winced, no more babies. Kate held tightly onto Jill's bright bead necklace, from a shopping trip in Curaçao.

William had asked her about more children, but no, she admitted she did not really want anymore. At Sadie's with babies everywhere…her hormones…and a week with Luis, she wanted more of him, more pieces than he was willing to give. A baby would be another piece and he knew that and said, "No more, it is much too painful." Painful to give up pieces of who he is, who he was, the story of Mexico City was brief, not enough, too much pain in the retelling.

Jill bent over and kissed Kate's round belly and nibbled her tender neck buried underneath her fat jowls. Jill sprinkled powder on her tiny bottom, then pinned on her diaper. Sadie insisted on cloth diapers. Kate with her big thighs, Michael called her thunder thighs. The rolls of fat and curved calves were testament to Sadie's mothering. Sadie a mother of three? Jill shook her head, "Oh, Kate such a healthy girl. Your mama is….no, not yet. We'll talk when you get older. Oh, Katie, Katie, your mom is lucky to have such a pretty baby." Kate smiled at the mention of her name, her baby teeth showing with her smile.

"Mama, mama," she gurgled.

"No, no secrets about your mama." Jill leaned down and gave her a kiss on her neck. "No, no, no secrets about mama."

"Mama, mama."

While Jill snapped the crotch on her corduroy pants, she grabbed Jill's hair. Jill stood Kate on the bassinette hugging her tightly as she walked back to the kitchen.

"Sadie, I want another one, maybe I could just kidnap Katie for a day…"

"By all means take as many as you want for as long as you want. Michael got Mike a t-shirt that says, 'Rent-A-Kid, Make me an offer." Sadie laughed.

"Sadie, Dad said," Jill paused, lowering her voice to imitate Henry, "'Wistful, Princess, you look downright wistful. When we gonna talk?'"

"When are you, Princess?" Sadie mocked Henry's tone when he called Jill, Princess, "He reads you like the palm of his hand and you know he knows when there's a splinter no matter how many calluses he has."

"Wistful? Do you think it is about having another baby?"

"Take a look around here; no one gets wistful about this mess. No, it's your heart. San Francisco? No, you left your heart in Curaçao."

"Let's look at this stuff…" Jill said, grabbing the envelope of pictures.

"Hey, sweetie, you do look kind of 'wistful.' I thought you'd be dancing on the clouds after a week with your true love."

"I am," Jill said, rubbing the pictures of Luis's house.

"Yeah, just like the widow at her husband's funeral. Come, let's toast something, maybe in the details, if you tell me about the black nightgown. Ah, yes, there's a smile and the bedroom? His bed? Big enough for some shaking under the sheets? Oh, pink, Grandma Caitlin Galway pink, your face is saying it all."

"Sadie, he…it…it's so intense," Jill closed her eyes and shook her head, "Sadie, how do you make love with the man you love, then have sex with your husband? I don't know if I can do that for very long. I just want to sleep in another room and fantasize about Luis. I hate this, how I feel right now. Help me Sadie, say something."

"Have some more of this frozen daiquiri stuff. You have to do it. Be the actress you are Miss Sarah B."

"After a fight about this very thing, then this," she held up her bracelet that she had not taken off since he had given it to her.

"Oh, Jill, he is such a romantic. 'Remember Curaçao.'"

"Did you hear yourself? Dictator then romantic? All rolled into one like one of those rolled cigars he smokes."

Sadie touched the tiny octagon-shaped links. Jill explained the shape was the same as the Bolivar Museum on the island. "Connie made the greatest fish dishes and the tropical fruit. I ate my first papaya. Caz recommended it, telling me in Spanish, try it, try it."

Jill gave Sadie the Aigner purse and sandals she requested. She also gave her a French bikini.

"Jill, first you gush, then you stop. I think you need to get a grip on what is going on here. You're having a Disneyland relationship. And believe me I know what Disneyland is all about, lots of craziness, food, and fantasy. He is going to call and you're going to Disneyland. But really, sit in that front porch swing of yours and think about what you are saying. Divorce Jack, move your pitiful self to Colombia. What in god's name do you know about that?"

"But Sadie…"

"Don't 'but Sadie' me! I'm getting your emotional train on track. Okay, you leave me, all of us and live on some mountain while he goes and makes sure his coffee beans are being picked. No Sadie's house to run to for rum-lime popsicles. You just haven't gone through the steps. What you do need is to figure out how to keep Jack 'in love' with you. Seriously, you need to rise to the occasion Miss Sarah B. Make him happy and he will love it that you take off for three or four weeks a year.

"Rise to the occasion?"

"Yes, and we have to figure out how to make the trips possible. Michael can only win so many sales awards. Now let's drink to that as you tell me about these souvenirs."

"All this stuff," Jill said, "duty-free. What a great way to shop. But there was plenty of money. Money, oops, I don't have to tell you what it's like to have plenty to spend. Dad said you adapted to it like corn took to Kansas. I bought Jack a nice batik shirt."

"And who paid for that?"

"I did take my own money. I do have principles."

"Please. I thought maybe Luis was buying Jack a present for letting him use his wife for a week."

"Sadie, I ought to…" Jill laughed, reaching to recover her gifts, attempting to put them back in the bag.

Sadie took Kate from Jill's lap and put her in the high chair. Sadie gave her a spoon and chopped up spaghetti in one section of the divided baby plate. The plate was suctioned to stay put.

"Oh, Mrs. Jones, or is it Señora Ochoa? You can't take a taste of Henry sarcasm? He would be giving it to you if he knew."

"Señora Ochoa, what do you think? He introduced me like that."

"Señora Ochoa, will there be more baby Ochoas?"

Jill quickly shook her head and took a bite of her alcohol-laced popsicle.

"Uh-oh, did I say the wrong thing? I know you had to talk about this," Sadie said, "He doesn't seem like the type to wear the raincoat, you know?"

"He said 'no more.' And Sadie, Jack accepts a lot of things, but my getting pregnant on a vacation away from him is beyond, 'for better or worse.'"

"Okay Mrs. Jones, and you're back in Sadie's kitchen a long way from Curaçao. But I want details. You left out the best part. What happened when you left?"

"Nothing. He walked us to the gate at the airport. We said, 'Goodbye.' He leaned down and whispered in my ear, 'Hasta luego, Gringa.' It means he will see me soon. He asked Luisa to come and see him again. Of course, she said, 'Okay, Papa.'"

"I love it. And when do you see Papa again?"

"Sadie, he makes me sick."

"Yeah, if Love Potion #9 makes you sick. No, Mrs. Jones, you love Luis Ochoa. He just refuses to sit up or roll over when *you* tell him."

"Sadie, now you're making me sick." They both laughed. Sadie fixed them some more of the popsicle drink they ate it with spoons and straws.

"Okay, my best friend, you have had enough alcohol to loosen the inhibitions. I want to know his reaction to the silk gown."

"You are such a voyeur."

Jill told of her effort to try to pin him down about the reference to Papa, how he said moments change and words change. Sadie suggested he was one of those "my home is my castle" men, "And you could try choking him using Emma Sue's method, 'They have to sleep sometime.'"

Jill told her it might be impossible because he had a gun in his drawer. Jill sighed and paused, then explained the discovery and his reaction as if having a gun was normal.

"That's it?"

"Put my silk gown back on and meet him in the patio and he did say, 'generals have guns.' Then he looked at me like I had *no need* to know. It's as though a vault door closes and he doesn't open it up until he is ready. I wish he'd let me take a picture of that look. I wouldn't need the freezer to make ice cubes."

Sadie shook her head, putting spilled spaghetti back into Kate's bowl. "He can be so strange, but that really is what you like."

"It scares me. Who is he Sadie? He tells me some things, but just pieces like he told me of going to school and then to work in Mexico City."

"Mexico City?"

"And leaving Mexico City. I told him he was trying to find me, heading north. I said that teasing, you know? But he just galvanized. I thought, Oh god, now I've done it again. But he said that I was right. Sadie, he was so serious, *very* serious."

"Okay, maybe there is a clue in the Mexico City story."

"No, I don't think it is Mexico City although he did learn that impeccable English. It's his first love that gets all the emotion. You can understand that."

Jill repeated Luis's story of childhood love, and how he carefully uttered each word as if it were his last. Lourdes, the love of his life, the first love, the mother of his son at age fifteen.

"Look at this picture," Jill pointed to a print of Luisa and Connie sitting by Luis's pool. "Connie, the Dutch maid, except Luis calls her the Spanish version, Conchita. All she needed was the hat with the blinders to look like the cleanser can." Jill told Connie's story of being abandoned by a captain. "She's silent on Luis, though, talk my ear off about everything, but him, 'Master,' she calls him."

"Not master? Oh jeez, the man is a case for Dr. Freud." Sadie lifted Kate from her high chair, and handed her to Jill. "Here, hold her while I get a rag to wash that pretty face. As usual wearing it instead of eating it."

Jill held Kate on her lap with one arm sorting pictures, "When I took this picture of Luisa and Connie, Luis had flown to Colombia, on business. She wouldn't give me any clues about that trip. But as we talked she slipped, I think. I said the house was in such a splendid location, more lush than most of the desert-like outer island areas. The view of the ocean, well, you can see it in this picture, where dark blue meets light blue, gorgeous. The place is so private. Connie agreed, then she said, 'Sure, sure, Royal Dutch Shell owns all the best pieces and they give them to their executives for vacation retreats.' She went on to explain about the refinery and the problems from the labor riots the year before, then she said, 'Lordy, Lordy, does Master hate that odor.' I looked at her, but then she knew, well she acted like she knew she'd said something she shouldn't have, because she said, 'Oh Mrs. Jones, let me get you some more coffee.' And that was it, no more slips and no more mention of Royal Dutch Shell."

"I told you I think it's in the details. Did you ask about Royal Dutch Shell?"

"No, I thought he'd be suspicious of how I knew anything." She bounced Kate and gave her a bottle.

At six Jill called Jack and said Sadie had kidnapped her for dinner, but she would be home right after that. When she hung up, Michael walked in. He became the hit of the kid brigade, "Daddy, Daddy, Daddy."

He hugged Jill and Kate together. He patted Jill's head. "How did you like my prize Curaçao trip? International Harvester always has the best prizes." He laughed.

Michael was easy-going. He looked at the two friends drinking, "So what bank are you plotting to rob now?" He smiled with his elfish grin and got himself a beer. He was a rectangular shape, like a well cut 2' x 6' plank. He let his hair grow and wore a madras shirt under his yellow Izod golf sweater, and khaki pants. His blue eyes twinkled as he teased the women. His age was agreeing with him. In high school he had gotten an offer to play professional baseball, but the draft loomed for him so he joined the Army, and married Sadie. He picked up Kate from Jill's lap.

"No banks, Honey, except yours." Sadie said, then kissed him "And dinner will be served in about ten minutes. Do you think you could clean up your most wild boy?"

Michael headed toward the family room.

ﺭﻉﺭ

Jill bounced up the steps of her parents' porch. The lilacs bloomed in huge lavender bunches on all sides of the porch. Her old farmhouse had come with a complete hedge of lilacs, a selling point for her. The once a year blooms announced in their sweet distinct odor that summer was approaching. The lilacs shouted "summer" now, just as the locusts buzzed the summer season's farewell.

Jill paused on the sun washed porch, spring sunshine. She tore a bunch of dark purple flowers to keep the scent filling her face. Lillian had opened the big windows on the front porch, "to let the fresh air clean out winter," Jill could hear her annual phrase.

The screen door banged as she walked down the hallway. Lillian's large crystal vases were filled with bunches of lilacs in all shades of white, lavender and rich purple. Jill took a deep breath of her handpicked bouquet.

After the early birthday card, "Para mis muchachas de Mayo (to my girls of May)" and presents – emerald stud earrings for her and binoculars made to fit Luisa's small face, she decided to talk to Henry. The birthday card included a short note in bold strokes as if written with a calligraphy pen. He said he'd made a deposit to buy Luisa a present, "whatever she wants, within her mother's parameters." The last word had been underlined.

The pressure of concealing Luis would take Henry's help. Henry always accepted, well sort of accepted, her antics and the consequences of them. Corners, the ones she backed into, forced decisions, and her walls had now met at one Colombian corner. She knew Luis's position, whenever he was ready. It seemed too difficult now as she walked towards the kitchen. Henry could open up space for her, give her some breathing room.

She had been snapping at Jack for no reason. She snarled when he asked her simple questions, "Do you want me to get some canned peaches from the cellar?" She heard Sadie's voice saying, "Rise to the occasion." Jack who never noticed much of what she said, accepted her as being like that once a month, the cousin coming thing, she tried to tell him Mo's term, but he had commented that she was "not herself." She wanted to scream, "I'm not myself. I don't know who I am anymore!" But she bit her tongue. He called it "magic" in the bed, but "not herself," in the kitchen.

Jack told her of all his accomplishments in her absence, the remodeled laundry room; she had hated it from the moment they moved in. He and Henry had extended it while she was gone, actually Farren and Ferlin helped them. It was a major remodel, but she'd reacted with a polite, "It's nice." Jack looked hurt and the guilt overwhelmed her.

She now walked into Lillian's kitchen, stopping to pour herself a cup of coffee. She wished she could give Henry some of the L.O. Ltd., and show him how to make it from the green beans, just like Luis. Oh, Luis, that is why I am here in the first place. She paused to look out the kitchen window. Lillian took clothes from the line. Luisa followed behind her, dropping clothespins into the pin bag. Henry's truck was parked in the driveway. She opened Henry's office door without knocking. He sat at his desk writing checks. He peered over his glasses, and smiled.

"Ha! You might know you'd show up when I'm writing checks. Let's get this over with, tell me how much you want." Henry laughed.

"No money, Dad. I want to talk to you, well, I think I do."

He stared at her face, "Princess, you sound like you have a problem. Are you sure you don't want me to write the check?"

"Dad, this isn't a problem you can solve with money. It's one of those heart things, one of those messes I seem to always get into."

Luis, she saw him, smiling at her in her bikini lying by his pool when he came back from Colombia. She and Luisa had stayed at the house all afternoon relaxing, soaking up the sounds of seagulls and crashing waves. She had wanted to stop time in the warm sun.

She plopped down now in Henry's leather overstuffed chair and took off her shoes, curling her legs under her. Outside Henry's window the spring breeze made the glass wind chimes clink like ice cubes in a crystal goblet. She rubbed the arm of the chair.

"Do you want me to ask questions, Princess? I was right about wistful. Something happened on that vacation of yours, you fall in love with some tall dark stranger? Jack was so excited doing that job with me, he kept saying, 'Oh, Jill will be so happy.' Have you stopped harassing that poor man?"

"Why do you feel sorry for Jack?" she snapped at Henry.

He frowned. "He's too nice to you. I try to tell him that every time I can. He needs to treat you rougher. Try some sarcasm, it goes a long way...."

"He never will. He can't...and if he did you would be all over him, sending me the divorce papers."

"Another story? Is that what this talk is all about? Divorce?"

"No, no. Sadie encouraged me to have this talk with you..."

"Oh, yeah, now that's a real rational choice to talk to about problems of the heart. She solved hers the day Michael showed her his bank account book." Henry tapped his long ledger type check book.

"There is more to Sadie than money. Dad, this isn't funny. I have a problem."

She told him the story of Luis, his coming to the school, the tickets and telephone call six months later, and she ended with the week in Curaçao. He sat silently, listening, his face creating more frown lines with each revelation. By the time she said, "Luisa calls him Papa," he resembled a shar-pei dog.

"Your story is sounding like one of Shakespeare's tragedies - the loves of life filled with frustration, sadness and chuck holes."

"Luis is so worldly, Dad. I don't know very much about him. He wants to give me money for Luisa. He wants us to continue to meet him in faraway places. And I want to do that…"

"Yeah, I know you want to do *that*; you've been talking about going all over the world since you were yay-high." He held his hand about three feet from the ground.

"But Jack, Dad, what do I tell Jack?"

He leaned back in his chair, leaning on one elbow pinching his lips. "None of it, you're talking about an affair, that's adultery, and Jack, he's never done anything to have his wife go commit adultery. He's decent. The church says you are not to covet your neighbor's wife…But Princess, your primary responsibility is Luisa. You wanted her more than anything else. I tried to talk you out of it, but no, you didn't listen to the old man, you were going to be the *perfect* mother…"

"I didn't say perfect, did I? But even if I did, can't I have an affair? Why is it an affair if it's Luisa's father? I mean is that really adultery?"

"Okay, okay, what's a perfect mother then? What's an adulteress? All these damn gray areas, it's where God lets you make a choice."

"I know it doesn't work. I can hear all those church ladies, talking about 'that Jill Jones'…"

"Church ladies?! What about the good Lord himself, Princess?"

"But Luis is not going to let me out of his life…" she paused, thinking of Luis's look, then edict: "You will make a choice, Gringa, because I have made a choice, until death separates us, haste que la muerte nos separe."

"Dad, I'm asking you…I need you to help me do this. It is wrong from everything you ever taught me, but Luis," she sighed and buried her face in the purple lilacs, "Dad, he holds my heart like I'm holding these flowers. But that's it; I mean Luis isn't asking me to marry him. He even said my marriage to Jack was the right thing to do."

Henry shook his head, "Worldly, isn't that the word you used? I don't think I quite figured that one out, but of course, you aren't telling the old man everything. I do kinda like it that he wants to be a part of his *daughter's* life. Lord knows every father should have the headaches I've had with my daughter. And you are right, you seem to have ignored *everything* I ever taught you. What is my part in this soap opera?"

"The money."

"I knew it," he slapped the checkbook, "Tell me how much and I'll write the check."

"Dad, quit, I'm serious. I have to explain to Jack where it comes from? He'll want to know how I can go places on *my* salary."

"You want *me* to conspire against your husband? Jack's a decent man, Princess. He loves you…"

"Guilt? I do that enough to myself. Will you help me?"

He frowned, his bushy gray eyebrows like twisted bramble. He stared at her, then to the window, and back to her. "And people want to know why I have these Grand Canyon craters in my forehead? Why I look like an old man?"

"You are an old man," she could not resist.

Jill reached into her purse and pulled out the bank book from Merchant's. "Here, Dad. Look at this. Please come up with something. He wants Luisa and me to join him this summer at an unknown destination."

"And what will you tell your mother?"

"Nothing. I mean right now. I don't know what I could say that would make her understand. She doesn't know about the heart stuff…" She stopped and thought of Hawk, "Maybe she did and learned it is too painful. She loves Jack."

"Jack's a decent man, Jill."

"Dad, you've said that three times, but also boring, oh-so planted in those damn cornfields."

"I told you not to marry an old man, but as usual when I try to give you advice, you never listen. Now when you ask, I don't want to give you advice. Do you have any idea what you are doing? Oh hell, we know you think with your heart instead of that brain God gave you. Okay, okay, I'll work on something." He picked up the bank account book. He opened it and then whistled. "I guess you don't need anything from this." He tapped his leatherette check book.

She jumped from her chair and ran around his desk, kissing and hugging him.

"Yeah, yeah, this is the first time I helped you when it didn't cost me a chunk of my annual income. Thank you for that Luis, I think." He hugged her, patting her shoulder. "Oh, Princess, 'what a tangled web we weave when first we practice to deceive.'"

ᴙξᴙ

Henry eased his truck into the dirt parking lot of the lumber yard. He squeezed in next to Hal Scott's truck. Hal Scott Masonry, the best in the area, but very expensive. Henry used Hal when price was not an option to the home owner, but chose his other friend Tom McDaniel when he was in a hurry. Tom did quality work, no bragging, only asking, "When do you need to have it done? When can I start?" Homeowners never complained, but he didn't have the reputation of Hal. Some folks just insisted on employing a guy with a reputation.

Bud's station wagon was in its reserved space, the man he wanted to see. Bud's father founded the business. The vintage clapboard front bore the name, "Watson's Lumber – Est. 1933." Construction began on the old comfortable store and warehouse in 1933. Pop had always done his business with Bud's father. Henry and Bud did a lot business, but another lumberyard built a few years ago constantly solicited Henry's business. Caylor had grown in the years after WWII. The automobile industry helped Caylor, and made Henry a fairly wealthy man in his own community.

With the addition of more complete lines of building supplies and some masonry stock, the original Watson building expanded obliquely, the work of carpenters, it was why they needed architects. Henry liked only one or two architects. They saw things in strange lights and forms, then expected the contractor to just read the specs and build it. However, when the roof leaked and the door warped or no longer fit, the homeowner did not call the damn fancy-schmancy architect, no, the builder. "Hank, seems like there might be a problem by the overhang on those patio doors…" But here at the lumberyard, he found the peace of fellow doers who understood.

Henry needed to order a lumber delivery and some nails, but also he needed to talk to Bud. Summer was approaching and he needed to know what projects were coming, the pulse of his business. And, well, Jill now had him trying to figure out something. Damn daughter, always into something troublesome. He parked, then walked on the gravel to the newly paved asphalt sidewalk. The large show room smelled of new wood, varnish and paint as if it had just been built.

"Hey, Henry, how's it goin'?" Jipson called out. James Paul Johnson, but for as long as anyone could remember the raspy-voice, old-sage, oral historian had been called Jipson. He knew everyone's faults and pet projects. Lillian said he was a nosey old gossip like their neighbor Mrs. Minnix. Jipson had slightly hunched shoulders, always chewed on a broom straw and wore a sweat-stained baseball cap from his beloved Chicago Cubs. If anyone went to a game in Chicago, they bought Jipson a new cap, but the hat stayed used and dirty. Henry called him an odds-and-ends man because Jipson worked with all the contractors as an extra hand.

"Sick-a-bed," Henry now answered, "old man, and you?"

"Who you callin' an old man? I heard they lookin' for a new exhibit at the park – oldest livin' builder. Your name was at the top of the list." Jipson laughed at his own ribbing.

"Saw your Cubbies, lousy like always."

"The season's barely started. Put your money where your mouth is."

"Sure. I'll give you two bucks, if they are any place but the bottom on August 1. You give me five if they're kissin' last place."

"Deal."

"Where's Bud?" Henry asked.

"He's 'round back. He's tryin' to find out the right sidin' for Doc Eaton's new place. Miz Eaton is terrorizin' Frank Crawford. You're damn lucky you didn't get that bid. Nothin' but Excedrin written all over it." Jipson threw his head back and laughed, retrieving his broom straw.

"I'm too busy the way it is. Been fishin' yet?"

"'Course. Did I get anything worth keepin'? Now that's another story."

"Hey Hank, what can I do you out of?" Bud said, coming through the swinging doors that separated the store from the mill and its open stacks of lumber, siding and blocks. Bald-headed, Bud wore a

Perry Como v-necked, blue cardigan sweater, to match a dark blue work shirt. Bud was pigeon-toed and bow-legged. His peculiar gait bent him forward and made him appear humble. He talked quietly in the noisy atmosphere of sawing and loud-talking builders.

"I need some 4' x 6's," Henry answered, "and fifty sheets of plywood and I'll be ready for trusses…"

"Sure, sure, Hank we'll get the order written up, but I want you to come back to my office and see what I have been working on all day."

The blue prints were thrown everywhere, paper cups with cold coffee sat on the desk and shelves. The interminable dust from the sawmill covered everything. Henry sat down in a straight back stuffed chair which looked like an original piece from the senior Watson's first office. A spring hung down below the chair. A cushion used in cars to elevate the driver served as the bottom. If it hadn't been for the access to nails and glue, the chair would have been used as kindling for the wood burning stove. Bud stretched the blueprint across his desk on top of layers of other blueprints, and used a couple of bricks to keep it from rolling back into its tubular shape.

"Whew! What a place, Bud. Whose is it? I suppose they got the lot."

"One of Jill's old friends from school, a Fredericks, Billy, a cousin to…"

"Sadie, Jill's best friend, I bet."

"Are you interested in bidding on the place? Five thousand square feet."

"A place this size? Of course. When do they want to start? You know I won't be finished where I am for another month at least. I might have to get the old geezer to help." He nodded toward the front of the store.

"They have a lot near the McKinnsey farm. McKinnsey had a nice woods with a creek, but there is talk, actually someone came in the other day and said they've been to the council for zoning a golf course out there."

"I never did play, but Lillian has that group of ladies she plays with."

"Well, it is starting because Billy said they want all the bids in by June 1. Take the print with you tonight and look it over. You'll enjoy some of the specifications, but I think we can get the stuff. We'll just have to order some of it from Atlanta."

"More farm land going to housing, times are changing, these days."

"Our business has really changed, bigger houses, golf courses on cornfields. Any big piece of land anymore seems more profitable if they put houses on it than soy beans or corn in it."

"It will make my daughter happy, all she does is complain about the damn Indiana cornfields."

They both laughed.

Bud said, "And you know Don Kippenburg has been talking to an architect, so I'm sure you'll get a call from him soon. Another of Jill's classmates, Marcia, married to a Webster, they've already contracted with Crawford to build out there."

"I'll do it justice and see what I think."

Henry knew it was the way of Caylor to get married, build a house, raise a family, but his sons headed off to the coasts and now his daughter having an affair, gallivanting off to foreign countries with a migrant worker or whatever he was, damn big bank account for a migrant. Henry shook his head at the thought. Okay, Henry you are here for more than housing prospects, "You been fishing?"

"Talkin' to Jipson? Well, we opened the cabin last week, second weekend in May, Ginny's mother's day present. I take off and leave her alone all day to do what she wants – no cooking."

Ginny, Henry thought, was one of the sweetest women in the world. She was quiet like Bud and packed his lunch every day. She rarely came to the business. He and Lillian had them over for dinner a few times during the year. "Old-fashioned," he told Jill, "they don't make them like Ginny anymore."

Jill laughed and said, "Thank God."

Damn daughter. Ginny would never ask him to do some harebrained scheme like commit adultery. Bud continued, "I plan to put the pier in next weekend. You want to go up? I can't say the fish are biting, but you're welcome to try. I put the boat in on Mother's Day. Give me a call."

Henry walked back through the store. Jipson took the broom straw and pointed it at Henry, "Hey Hank, how's your wife?"

"Yeah, yeah. Better 'n nothin' How's your dog?"

"I already did."

Henry shook his head, the same old tired joke he and Jipson had exchanged for twenty years.

Henry signed the order slip and took two gallons of paint. Lillian had scolded him before he left, "Don't fool around gossiping and forget my porch paint."

ᚱᚴᚱ

The Tippecanoe River slowed in front of Bud's small cabin. The place was thirty miles from Caylor, but the wilderness setting resembled the centuries before settlers arrived. Deer, raccoon, opossum walked freely in the dense isolated woods along the river. Fishing at the cottage was not as rewarding as exploring the little pools formed behind the broken-limb dams.

In a small rear-mounted motor boat, Henry and Jack now sat quietly fishing. The chattering birds and talkative river communicated. The narrow shallow river was used for fishing by Bud's cabin. The early fishing season attracted only the professionals who insisted on preserving each other's peace. The boat-landing for non-residents was safely a mile downstream from Bud's.

Henry watched his bobber as it moved slightly with the river's current. The sunny afternoon was cool in the shade of the newly leaved trees. The sun rays peeking through the branches turned spots on the water to refractors, dancing, sparkling light, blinding if they shot just right. The gentle tug of the line was a test, a fisherman's feel. Was there something nibbling? Was it biting or sniffing? To pull or wait? Jack concentrated on the white ping-pong ball. There was a small movement, then he jerked gently on his line.

Jack was Henry's favorite fishing partner. He liked the quiet and didn't drink beer. Unlike Jipson, he never bragged about the ones that got away. He'd offer his opinion on water temperature gradations, depths of pools, and probabilities of fish locations.

Henry often brought up Jill, but Jack did not respond in kind. He usually answered Henry's disparaging remarks with a single sentence, "I love Jill." Henry knew that, but he also knew his daughter and relished the joy to torment her. He wanted to share a joke or two about Jill, but Jack only laughed perfunctorily. If the joke concerned Jill past fifteen years of age, Jack would not respond. Henry concluded perhaps Jack would loosen up in time and share some of Jill's antics at the farm. He knew there must be a treasure trove of all new material to tease his daughter.

Now Henry sat watching his son-in-law, his handsome, serious, stable, responsible, decent son-in-law. Jack studied the river bank. Two squirrels played around and through a hollowed log. Jack, for crissakes, Princess, he's a decent man. Why? This fellow has done such a super job being a father to your daughter, a wonderful son-in-law for me and Lil. We sleep at night knowing he's right next to you. Oh, like all too complete stories, there's a chapter missing. Princess, it is an elusive piece, a tickler that will drive you to places and feelings beyond your comprehension. And then you will be calling me, "Dad, please, I need your help." Daughters. Thank God I only had one. When she does the right thing, oh, yeah, when does she do the right thing? She seems to have this weak link in her thought pattern.

When he bellyached too much about his Princess, Lillian often reminded him, "Henry, you two, that's *your* daughter. I just provided the transportation for her arrival."

And here I sit, ensnared. If I just help her through this, maybe, just maybe she'll see her way more clearly, come around, be Mrs. Jones, the way she should be. Keep her from running off all together to the other side of the world. Let her fall down and learn. I did let go of her seat and let her take off on her bike, what? Two scuffed knees and one scratched hand? Okay, God, give me two scuffed knees and one scratched hand....

"Jack, I've always worried about Jill. She is my princess and I feel responsible for her actions." Jack looked up at Henry, but kept one eye on the water and the line. "I know," Henry said, "she is grown up, but I still worry about her."

Henry stopped and took a deep breath, reeling in his line. The hook came up without the worm. He grabbed the line reached into the small box of dirt that held the worms. He pulled a twisting wiggly one and wrapped it around the hook, then flung the line and bobber back where they had been, "Must be something down there; they ate my worm. You know Jack, I'm an old man..." Jack turned from his fishing line and faced Henry.

"No, no," Henry held his hand up, "I don't expect to live to four score and ten, so I've always kept that in mind. Jill came late in my life and will be here long after I've crossed the River Jordan and taken my seat on the heavenly choir. Her mother thinks I'm a pushover when it comes to her and she is right, but it is the language of the heart." Henry shook his head as if shivering. Could I ever cross the River Jordan and leave her? Who would take care of her heart? Not Jack.

"Henry, don't worry about Jill. She is well taken care of. I've made ample insurance provisions and there is Swayzee and the farms, all of our property. It is all taken care of..."

"I didn't mean this as an attack on you Jack. I'm pleased you are generous to Jill. You're a decent man, yes, a damned decent man, probably too decent for my wayward daughter." Conspire against your husband, Princess? That's what you want me to do? Henry looked skyward. The scrambled oak, maple and sycamore branches blocked much of the direct sunlight.

"I love her very much. She and Luisa mean everything to me."

Henry caught Jack's earnest eyes. A decent man, loves those two, Jill and Luisa, not even his daughter. "Well, me too, and I guess that's what I'm driving at. I am driving at something here. I don't want you to take offense at what I'm telling you, I just want you to understand. John Kenneth Galbraith said not to worry about the long run because none of us will be here in the long run. I have tried to live life enjoying the pieces as it goes along. Fortunately or unfortunately for you, I've instilled some of this spontaneity in Jill. I accept full responsibility, but I want you to understand that is just a basic part of who she is."

"Believe me, I know." Jack sighed. "I try to let her, well, wrong word, I give her her head. I accept Sadie and her as a pair of cohorts along with their brazenness."

"Exactly, exactly my point. I encouraged and discouraged that, but mostly enjoyed her happiness, which brings me to the essence of this little talk. For many years I have tucked away extra income, a personal savings account in Jill's name. I didn't know if anyone would marry her, let alone be responsible, but you are an answer to a troubled father's prayer."

"Thank you, Henry, but she is easy to love."

"Well, I wouldn't go that far." They laughed. "I thought," Henry continued, "about this money and decided to tell Jill about it. I know she likes to get on a plane and go places. I also know she has wanted to travel all over the world. We talked of it often in mission meetings at the church. I told her and I want to tell you, so there won't be any secret about this. I let her know, if she has places she wants to go on her vacations from teaching, and it might cost too much for your budget, I'd help her out."

"Henry, I can pay for anyplace she wants to go. I have the money in trust to be utilized for emergencies. My grandfather Jones left money for all of his grandsons. He owned half of Gable County at one time. And with Hawk's relinquishing his final claim…."

"No, Jack. I know Jill, and she will not accept that from you. She fussed at me when I talked to her, but not too vehemently which meant, 'Thanks, Dad.' We did this with a nod and wink at Lil, so please just keep this between us for awhile."

"Sure, Henry," he spoke, pulling the line closer to his chest as he watched the water, "but…"

"Nope, that's it. Now let's see if we can bring home something the women can fry. Maybe next time we can bring Luisa, she is the only one of the bunch that likes putting the worms on the hook. Speaking of which, hand me that carton of night crawlers…"

Henry knew this was the beginning and Jill and he would write the end, or maybe this was the beginning of the end. Damn daughter.

An excerpt from **Book 3**

They Came to Pick Tomatoes
Trilogy

The Rainbow

Chapter 1

    The morning sun shone in a crystal clear blue sky. Jill wore coverall's over her shorts and a tube top. She took a deep breath, smelling the freshly plowed dirt, "God's promise to the farmer," she repeated Luis's long ago summation. June 1, only the chickens rose earlier today than she did. She'd shared the early pink and yellow sunrise with the farmers' alarm clocks, cock-a-doodle-doo. The promise, always the promise of the new day, and this day, her promise was to get out the rotor-tiller and work on her garden. Her garden? First it had been Jack's garden, and slowly she helped. She started to direct, when she knew which vegetables and herbs she wanted for cooking. Yes, Hector, I like to grow and cook the vegetables not just wash them.

She pulled the rotor-tiller through each row in the small garden. Jack had been so helpful in getting a smaller model she could use. She liked the sinking squish of plowed soil under her boots, and the warm sun on her back.

School was over for another year. They had finished earlier than the city schools, as they still set their calendars to coordinate with farming. And here she was *farming*. The planting had to be done this week in order to have a full growing season. Maybe she could have started last week, but there was all the end of school stuff and help with the Senior Week graduation activities. Yes, she had volunteered to be their class sponsor when they were freshman and then stayed with them until the end, commencement. High School Commencement that was her summer, ten years ago, at the migrant camp, and Luis. But he had not called, not written since last month's birthday note to her and Luisa. Summer vacation - his invitation would come. Invitation? Their vacation plan, but for now, today, this early morning her garden beckoned.

She visualized the abundance of vegetables and fruit that would emerge from the dark rich soil. Jack purchased fertilizer, and she would mix that in with her next rotor-tiller pass. The uneven strain of the steel blades jerked her arms, easier though than the mules of the pioneer women. She sank each foot into the newly plowed dirt, and laughed at her visualization of Jill Caitlin ankle deep in Indiana. Had Mother Nature planted her in this Hoosier earth? The cornfields conspired as she slept? Sneaking in through the open windows and pollinating her brain? She fed her family and Sadie with the vegetables.

The seasons eased into one another around and around, a complete cycle. Another summer, but now, how different the summers would be…Dad had talked to Jack and she would be able to travel with abandon. Okay not freely, but easier. She could hear Sadie, "Oh, Miss Sarah B., just plant."

Her garden plot would yield a wide variety of fresh things and canable things. The weeds disappeared with each scoop of the rotor, but they would quickly reseed themselves faster than the lettuce and cucumbers, and then sprout before the musk melon and watermelon. The weeds would try to choke her vegetables; she heaved a sigh of despair. In one swoop she had gone from the bountiful harvest to fighting dastardly weeds. Hoeing? Yes that would be in July, next month, no longer this cool early June morning temperature. What did Henry say, "If all the days in Indiana were like this, we'd have to build a fence to keep people out.

Planting her garden reminded her of Sadie's one and only attempt, a fiasco by anyone's definition. After planting the seeds and fertilizing, Sadie had done nothing else, no hoeing, no maintenance, and no weed killer. It became a jungle growth of tangled watermelon vines, ragweed, milkweed, buckhorns, beets and giant sunflowers. The friends took pictures in case Sadie felt the guilt rise within her that she should "plant a garden." Smiling, holding up a large beet choked with weeds, Sadie had complained, "I don't even like beets, why did I plant them?"

The enlarged pictures hung in Sadie's kitchen. Michael shook his head that their acreage was farmed by someone else, "Not even a single tomato plant graces this backyard." And he pointed to the acre of their pine enclosed yard. "My grandfather is rolling over in his grave that we have no garden on this property."

Jill yanked the small tiller from the last row and turned off the engine. She'd turned the weeds into a twenty-five foot square of black-brown dirt in the center of green grass. Smiling at her morning's work, she walked the short distance from the plot to the tool shed. As she unzipped her coveralls she inspected flats of seedlings sprouting under the window. The small ones were ready to plant. The garden shed was neat like everything Jack touched - spades and trowels hung symmetrically, watering cans stored on wood shelves, clay pots sorted by size. She walked out, "Time for coffee. Luis could you be in my kitchen fixing some L.O. Limited? Stop dreaming, Jill"

She closed the shed door and walked to the porch step, where she used a small putty knife to scrape mud from her boots. The phone rang, 7:15, too early for Sadie, and too late for Lillian. Dad knows I'm alone, but he should be at work. She tugged off her boots, then ran through the screened porch, grabbing the receiver on the fourth ring.

"Jill?" Luis spoke.

"Yes." It had been two months since she'd heard his "Hasta luego," at the airport in Curaçao.

"Gringa, the Undersecretary of Commerce has invited me to Washington. My friend Jorge has only one more year in office, and then I can go back to doing other things. There will be a new director for the Agriculture Department. I need to be in the mountains right now, but...What are you doing for the next three days?"

"Hi Luis!"

"I'm not really interested in the Undersecretary, but you. You are the one Jankee I want to see."

"I'm fine. It's a beautiful day. Luisa's in Vacation Bible School. Jack is in Cleveland conducting a seminar." The early morning peace evaporated. Lightning strikes on a sunny day. Never in the same spot? Always in the same spot.

"Si. The conference begins tomorrow and lasts to Friday. The American flight from Indianapolis gets you into Washington at 2P.M. I'll be there at noon."

"Luis, I'm planting my garden. American Airlines? What are you asking?"

"I want to see you in D.C., your capital."

"Si, I know the place," she said.

"Gina has made the arrangements. Your flight number is 602. Write that down. We'll be staying in Arlington. The limousine is compliments of Señor Sam."

"Uncle Sam." She shook her head. Washington, D.C. But my garden...

"Gringa, I must go. Your United States, mañana. Adios."

She poured coffee from a Thermos. She'd filled the Thermos with the perked pot in order to keep it hot and save the flavor. She held the coffee mug and dialed Sadie's number, then plopped down at the kitchen table, "Sadie, he's so damned inconsiderate!"

"I'm asleep. What time is it? You know I don't keep your farmer hours!"

"Sadie, wake up! I read a magazine article by some psychologist and she said I'm having an anxiety attack."

"Let me understand this before I hang up on you. You have awakened me out of my most needed beauty sleep to tell me about a magazine article? You know I pay Hilda good money to keep my children quiet while I sleep..."

"It doesn't matter why I woke you up, just talk to me."

"What time are we doing drinks at the club, the pool is open."

"Not today. We don't have time to do that. I have to pack. You have to drive me to Indianapolis first thing in the morning. Luis makes me..."

"Stop right there. You won't get the adjective right. I haven't received a letter from your friends in Bogota, so what is going on?"

Jill told Sadie of his invitation actually a command, but Sadie reminded her, "That's him and you know it, get used to it. Don't call me at these hours for shit you know. Sorry, you have me cussing first thing in the morning."

Sadie laughed as Jill explained her morning planting then Sadie volunteered to come and plant the seeds. They both laughed at the shared memory. Sadie said, "A trip to Washington is exactly what a woman who is having an affair needs. And you can visit Arlington Cemetery like you've been threatening to do for seven years."

ϫϛϫ

The plane trip seemed quick. The ticket was just as he had said. She had shown the reservation desk her driver's license; they handed her the ticket, then directed her toward the gate. Sadie promised to be at the same place in three days. This slipping away had been easy, as Jack was in Cleveland at his semi-annual conference, but she decided that Luis needed to give her more warning. It could have been inconvenient almost impossible and how awful not to be with him for three days. Henry had only said, "This is how it begins?"

What did that mean? She kept asking herself from Indianapolis. But now as the plane descended into National Airport, she answered Henry's question, no dad, it began in the shed.

She disembarked. A young man dressed in a black jacket, white shirt and a black bowtie held up a sign that read "Jill Jones." They walked to a Lincoln Town car. As they drove towards Washington, D.C. each green and white sign by the highway named another place – the Capitol, Arlington Cemetery, Lincoln Memorial. She had spent hours discussing the nation's capital with her students, but this was her first visit. Sadie had asked her to come the few months when Michael was stationed at the Pentagon with the admonition to go to Hector's grave in Arlington. And Jill refused, "Not ready for that Sadie."

The hotel bellboy took her bags from the limousine driver who said, "Please take Mrs. Jones to Luis Ochoa's room, number 825." The bellboy nodded, and they crossed the lobby, pink and maroon with the many subtle shades in between. Dark green plants matched the dark swatches in the rug. The lobby was filled with conventioneers wearing name tags on their business suits. A culture of professionals in the heart of power, yes, way beyond the cornfields. She could almost feel the beat, the pulse, the country. And the man she was meeting hated it so much. She and the bellboy walked to the elevator, leaving the buzzing conversations to the hushed whisk of elevator cables. She looked in the mirrored wall, and saw that her Hoosier wasn't showing and no mud on her shoes. She smiled.

Luis, wearing the hotel's white terry robe, opened the door. The bellboy set her bag down and waited, asking if they needed anything. Staring at Luis in the afternoon, no, she did not need anything else. Luis tipped the man, and then locked the door behind him. Fresh flowers and champagne waited on a glass-topped table. Thin rayon sheers curtained the patio sliding-glass doors and filtered the room's light. Jill parted the drapes and looked out at the Potomac River. The scent of his cologne filled the room. He walked to where she stood, hugged her tightly and kissed her, the taste of cigar. Yes, she was out of the cornfields, but the taste of Luis took her back to and in the middle of tomato fields.

Luis poured champagne. "Gringa, I have my first meeting in one hour. May I propose a toast to your safe arrival?"

"I feel as if I'm in some time machine. I don't see you, don't hear your voice for two months and in twenty-four hours," she touched his hand, "from Indiana to…" she squeezed his fingers, pulling them to her lips, "you."

She kissed his fingertips, then tipped her glass to his and took a big drink. The alcohol would calm the jitters. She would be sleeping with Luis all night, sharing the same bed. How many times since Curaçao had she wanted to do this very thing? Get in the bed, stay in the bed and wake up during the night to touch him and then when the sun came up, to lie next to him. Señora Ochoa for a few days.

He put their glasses on the table and kissed her without allowing conversation. They moved from the table to the bed, not speaking. Him, this moment the same, in the shed, the green room, in Curaçao under the rhythmic wood slats. Luis's grip built the wall separating her from her farm life. His presence, touch, and taste surrounded their own special world like a brick fence.

As she eased from their love-making to a complete awareness of the room, the quiet music of the radio blended with her sense of satisfaction. When she walked in the hotel room, she had not remembered music. Now The Guess Who were singing, "American Woman..." the ceiling sparkled. She rubbed Luis's shoulder with her index finger. The creamy sheets were twisted in a roll at the foot of the king-size bed. Looking over her to the nightstand alarm clock, Luis jumped from the bed. He smiled slightly, then said, "The angel's mother an angel herself, keeping me from ..." He slapped her gently on the butt. "They are singing your song, Gringa, American Woman, listen what I say...the English is not perfect, but having you, listen..." he laughed.

"No, it is your song, they are talking about what do you call us, Damn Jankees? Just say that instead of American Woman... Damn Jankees stay away from me... I got more important things to do...I don't need your war machine. I hope they are playing this on the West Wing Muzak."

"Señor Nixon...I hope he keeps buying Colombian coffee for his war machine."

She watched as he stood in front of the mirror. His husky body was a totally different shape than Jack's. There was not a slim muscle in Luis's cut. The salt and pepper hair covered his round chest, the body that fit hers as if made for her. Could she grab his arm and pull him back into bed? He shook his head as if answering her question. "Si, you were...the tiger in this bed." He walked from the bathroom and refilled their glasses. He stood before her like the winning bullfighter, "To my Gringa."

"Welcome to America from *your* American woman."

"I must go. Do you want to go to the White House for a special reception? I brought the tuxedo."

"Luis, you are...with President Nixon who won't end the Viet Nam War? No, hell no! I don't want to be near the White House with him in it."

"My Gringa," he laughed, "we threw tomatoes when he came to visit as Vice President."

"I worked so hard to defeat him."

"Politics? Jankee politics? You know what I think. This is supposed to be a place for tourists. You can find something to do? I'll leave you money. Don't get lost. Don't answer the phone. Don't use the phone unless I'm here," he said.

She thought she should say, "Yes, sir." He separated them as quickly as he had drawn them together. The way of Luis Ochoa as Sadie said.

He dressed in business clothes, a look that she had not seen, but more like the people in the lobby. He adjusted his tie under the starched white collar; combed his hair and moustache; and slipped on dress loafers over his dark socks. The double-breasted jacket of his suit was a summer weight light-gray. The silk handkerchief matched the navy and red silk tie. He pulled the long shirt sleeves down, barely visible at the edge of the coat sleeve. It all fit his bull-shape perfectly. He smiled as he caught her eye in the mirror, "London, Savile Row, Anderson and Sheppard. We'll go one day."

She had straightened out the sheet and pulled it up to her neck as he dressed. She was not ready to dress, not ready to leave the room, only to sit where they had been and smell his cologne on the sheets. He buttoned his jacket and snapped the lid closed on his briefcase. Turning he walked to the bed, yanked the sheet from her, "This is why…"

"Why what, Luis?"

"You're beautiful, Gringa." He shook his head slowly.

"Gracias, Señor Ochoa."

He reached with the back of his hand rubbing her breast, catching her nipple between his fingers, pinching her gently. He shook his head again, then walked to the dresser removing folded bills from his money clip. He placed two twenty dollar bills on the table, and then replaced the clip. Opening his briefcase and removing a leather case, he picked through several plastic cards, pulling one from the bunch and placing it on the money. "Here, use this card to call Siddhartha from the *pay* telephone. You do want to call her and tell her about your Latin lover?" He laughed a low chuckle, walked to the bed, leaned over, kissed the tip of her nose. "We'll have dinner later. I'll send the driver to pick you up. Everyone wants to meet with the Colombian, take him to dinner, but I have the only Jankee I want to have dinner with." He winked.

"Luis, I do want to see you in your tux."

"Handsome, Gringa," He looked at her flashing a cock-of-the-walk smile, then he left.

She resisted the temptation to go through his luggage. Sadie would say yes, but she knew Luis was too private and she did not want to run into another gun or anything even close. She curled under the sheets and closed her eyes. She was a million miles from the rotor-tiller as she woke to a knock on the door. The sun was setting. The clock said, 7P.M. She wrapped Luis's robe around her. The knock was more insistent. She peered through the small hole in the door, the limousine driver. He knocked again. Then asked, "Mrs. Jones?"

She opened the door a crack, the width of the chain guard, "Yes?"

"Mr. Ochoa wants you to meet him at Henri's at 8P.M. I am to take you. I'll be downstairs waiting."

The restaurant was all white: white linen table cloths, white uniformed waiters, with white towels on their arms, white napkins folded like sails, each table with a combination of white flowers in frosted glass vases. The crystal glasses and chandeliers sparkled. Couples sat in curved white leather banquettes chatting. Sitting at a private table for two, she and Luis talked and laughed. His face glowed in the candlelight from their centerpiece. He impressed her with his knowledge of Washington, no buildings taller than the Washington Monument, no thirteenth floors. He said, "The White House has a Lincoln Room, but do you think President and Mrs. Nixon use their green room like we used Siddhartha's green room?"

They laughed at the thought of the Nixon's doing any sexual act. He talked of his afternoon at the U.S. Commerce Department, letting her know Columbia needed the money of U.S. investments, but not the strings that always wrapped the money.

"With strings attached," she said.

"Si, American idiom." He smiled.

He ordered the wine from a long list; she recognized the light white Rheine of Germany, but only offered that she liked white. He ordered grilled salmon, then paused to confirm her choice of salad dressing.

He reached for her hand, twisting his gift to her, the emerald ring, allowing the candlelight to refract the light on the diamonds. She rubbed his gold wedding ring. Their conversation was about Luisa, school, her grades, mathematics.

"Spanish?" he asked.

"It isn't taught in the fourth grade at her school."

"You could teach her. You are the maestra, si?"

"And why do I say she should learn this language?"

"Her father is Colombian and she needs to be able to speak to him." He smiled and winked at her. "When will the school teach her Spanish?"

"In high school."

"You have school pictures?"

"I have one in my billfold, but I have our pictures from Curaçao."

She pulled the packet of pictures from her purse. They drank coffee and discussed the scenes in the pictures. He laughed when she told of Sadie saying Connie looked like the Dutch maid on the cleanser can. He said he would keep all the pictures, and the school picture.

"I will," he said, "put them with her mother's school pictures."

"You still have those high school prom pictures?"

"Si, in a very special place."

"Where?"

"You'll see." He tapped her finger with his.

"Luisa has not mentioned you to anyone," Jill said. He nodded, pursing his lips. "And," Jill continued, "asked if we would go to Mr. Ochoa's again?"

Luis explained he had another place in mind for August.

He ordered, "Bananas Foster for my Gringa." When the waiter brought the bananas in brown sugar to the table, he poured the rum sauce over the ice cream then lit it. Luis told her to eat it quickly before it melted. She tried to follow his directions.

"I've always said hot fudge sundaes are my favorite, but this was delicious, Luis."

He snipped the end of his cigar, "Let's go. I want to walk and smoke."

The sultry night in Georgetown was illuminated with store fronts and street lights. The driver said he would return to the same spot in an hour. Shops and boutiques, old townhouses with stoops leading down to brick sidewalks, lined the streets. She wanted to hug Luis and turned to him, "Luis…"

"Gringa," he stopped her sentence, "This is my birthday."

"Feliz Cupleaños, shall I sing?"

"Si," he smiled.

She quietly made it through the complete song in Spanish.

"Gracias. I like your accent. Puerto Rican?"

She stopped by a men's store window, "If it were open, I'd buy you…"

He turned her around to face him, stopping. As other people walked past them, young students, the flower children with their long hair held by leather beaded headbands, boys and girls looking the same, one accidentally bumped into Luis. His hair hung in long dark curls tied back with a bandana. The curls lay on his neck and shoulders. His eyes were dark, but he flashed a smile at the abrupt stop, the smile, and dimples, long and deep. He raised two fingers, making a v-sign and said, "Peace, brother," then backed up and walked around them.

"Such sadness on your pretty face. Why Gringa?"

"In America we say, 'It's a long story.'" She shook her head.

"Si, I understand. There is much for you to tell, but you are reluctant, why?"

"Hey! It's your birthday. We are together in Washington, D.C. My long story is personal, remember you said the shadow of death?"

He reached for her hand, "Gringa, I have missed much of your life, too much, I think. This will change. I want to know why singing a Spanish birthday song, caused this sadness." She squeezed his hand. Hesitating, he continued, "But when you are ready to tell the 'long story.' Si?"

"Si," she said.

"What present do you want to buy me?"

"Presents? Is that a Colombian birthday tradition?"

"No, it's Colombian to celebrate your birthday with a gringa. It's why I called you."

She laughed. Someone handed them a pamphlet on the "true revolution" with a hammer and sickle picture.

"Crazy Jankees. One revolution was not enough?" He dropped the brochure into a big green can that said, "Keep America Beautiful."

"I appreciate your happiness, but what if I hadn't come? How would you have celebrated your birthday?"

"Gringas are easy, when you have money. They smell money like bloodhounds. How long do you think it would take, if you left, before one of your gringa sisters came up to me?" He nodded to the sidewalk in front of them. Young women with scraggly hair, and political buttons on Army fatigues, tie-dyed dresses, Indian batik, long skirts, embroidered fringed vests and leather chokers with brightly colored beads. Jill looked down; her sundress was fitted at the top and short, slightly above her knees, in mint green with a white lace Peter Pan collar. There were four buttons down the front with hand-painted flowers in green and yellow. Did she look like the farmer's wife among this colorful group, most of them braless in see-through gauzy cotton?

"No, not these gringas, too young, too lost, too righteous," Luis answered her silent question. "Your face, Gringa, you have expressions that are like book pages, easy to…"

"Yes, Luis, I know. I have a hard time hiding my feelings. You hide all of it so well. Who are you?"

"Let's see, I'm 5' 11", I weigh 88 kilos, m-m sometimes, I weigh 90 kilos. I was born June 2, 1930. I'm Colombian, a coffee farmer…Remember feel first, Gringa. Because it is my birthday, I will allow you to ask *one* question, anything you want. Be careful, ask only for that which you want an answer. Honesty can be brutal."

"Just one question?"

"Si. And that was it." He laughed as she slapped his arm. She laced her arm through his, "You're not going to leave me? I think that is my question."

They stopped at the crosswalk of Wisconsin and M streets, several people stood next to them, the young hippies and the older dressed-for-dinner folks. Luis put his arm around her, leading her across the street. In the center of the street, he paused and looked down at her, "Jill, will you marry me?"

She turned her head. He smiled. When they stepped on the curb, she said, "Don't ask questions you don't want to know the answer to."

"As the French would say, touché, but I thought I was answering *your* question."

"I would never marry someone I don't know."

"Who is Jack Jones?"

Jill spoke, as if from a script, "He is an electrical engineer who works for Johnson Electronics. He grew up on a farm near Swayzee, Indiana. He graduated from DePauw University and got his master's in engineering from Purdue University in Lafayette, Indiana. The farthest west he's been from Indiana is Kansas City. He loves Indiana, loves his farm, his house, his wife, *your* daughter, and peach pie. He plays tennis, listens to classical music and likes to fish. He hates surprises and knows where he will be buried when he dies. He's learned to accept Sadie, and he and my mother are cut from the same cloth."

"Is that a Hoosier expression?" He arched one eyebrow.

"What do you know about Hoosiers?"

"Gringa, it is you. Indiana natives, si?" He touched her cheek with the side of his hand.

She nodded, "It means they are so similar the same material was used to make them. How about two beans from the same coffee bush?"

He chuckled, then stopped to look at a jewelry store window as the jeweler picked up the tiny velvet boxes from the window and rearranged the twisting display of watches. Luis talked to her reflection in the window, "You married your mother?"

Lightning, right to the same spot. Was she atoning for the guilt of having this man's baby? But he was here and she was here and they were a couple in...love. "Your degree must be in psychology?"

"I know my enemy."

"Human relationships are your enemy?"

"You already asked your question, perhaps next year on my birthday. Write this on your calendar, so you will remember." Smiling, his eyes sparkled, he was relaxed. "Our hour is up. I am ready to get my gringa birthday present." He winked, then bent and kissed the skin in front of her ear.

ɤ§ɤ

She awoke to his low voice, talking rapidly in Spanish. He sounded irritated, but his Spanish was much too fast for her to keep up. Listening discreetly to his responses required deliberate effort and when she figured out "order" and "kilograms" of verde "green," and General Foods, ICA, and Brazil two or three times, vehemently, then back to ICA, he was three sentences further into the conversation. She understood the angry tone and the argumentative answers to the caller. The natural conversational Spanish sounded like East Harlem at Hector's. He slammed the phone down. She looked at him pretending to be awakened. He rubbed her neck and the side of her face with the back of his hand. Could she purr?

His face was furrowed.

"I guess your birthday is over and you realized your true age?"

"Gringa, you are making a joke, but I cannot play. The Vice-President of the Federation is flying in to take my place. Politics, Gringa. You know about politics. You know about political wars. I spend too much time fighting fires, unfortunately, people get killed." He had not really addressed her, ranting, so she did not respond. People get killed. Hector was killed in a political war. Yes, Luis, I know, she answered to herself. Sadie and she would have to discuss Luis's political war.

"I am returning as soon as I can get a flight out of here. Do you want to stay? Do you want me to call and make a reservation for you? Can Siddhartha pick you up?"

He walked to the closet and removed a suit from the rack, then laid it in the garment bag that already had three neatly folded shirts. He glanced at her as he picked up his shoes and placed them in felt bags, and then wedged the leather squares into the bottom of his smaller leather tote. Opening the chest drawers he removed his black silk shorts and socks, packing them on top of the shoes. He walked into the bathroom.

She wanted to slow his departure, twenty-four hours was not enough. He seemed to be reacting as if moving on a moment's notice was normal. The source of pleasure, the affable Luis window shopping in Georgetown, now broke into a different stride. What happened in Colombia that just whisked him so urgently on such brief notice? He returned from the bathroom and stacked his toiletries bag on top of the underwear. He zipped up the tote, then the long "U" shaped zipper of the garment bag. He set the tote by the door and laid the garment bag on top of it, only his briefcase remained opened. He came to the edge of the bed, standing in front of her. He held her chin in his palm, "I apologize for my abruptness. You don't understand. I...Who is Luis Ochoa? I'll tell you." He raised his voice on the last phrase, and then said, "Luis Ochoa is a busy man!"

He instantly turned half away from her, his hand dropped to his side. The color drained from his face, his expression frozen, paralyzed as if something inside him had stopped. And yet he breathed deeply, taking a few brief hesitant steps toward the desk chair, then slumped down on the hard seat. His hands trembled, his recent urgency vanished as he shook his head like a small child refusing cough syrup, and then he bowed in prayer. He propped his forehead on one hand and crossed himself with the other whispering in Spanish, "Padre, Padre, perdóname porque he pecado…" (Father, Father, forgive me for I have sinned)

She watched him recede to another place, his shadow of death? He sat still, in supplication, holding his head in both hands. He had separated from her as she sat motionless on the edge of the bed waiting for him to look, to say, to ask…he continued to pray in a breathy whisper, repeating the Spanish, "Padre, Padre," then with another crossing of his chest, silence, eyes closed, head bowed.

[To be continued in Book 3, The Rainbow]

About the Author

 Jacqueline Hendricks grew up in Indiana. She received a BS and MS from Indiana University, but learned about life in Kokomo, Indiana a small town. She now lives in Boulder, Colorado, but insists Indiana will always be "home." She taught English, Journalism and Social Studies. She's published a non-fiction memoir, *Dear Joe Biden: 97 Months, A woman's Story of Six Years in Federal Prison as told in Letters to Senator Joseph Biden. 1990-1996*

[available at Createspace.com, BarnesandNoble.com, Kindle.Amazon.com and Amazon.com]

www.ingramcontent.com/pod-product-compliance
Lightning Source LLC
Chambersburg PA
CBHW030027180626
46810CB00001B/247